Praise for *Servant of a Dark God*

"[An] engrossing debut . . . breakneck paced and action packed. Patient readers will be rewarded with a thoroughly enjoyable fantasy adventure."

—*Publishers Weekly*

"A classic heroic saga, dealing with the bedrock issues of good and evil and identity. These are classic themes because they *matter*, and Brown makes them matter both to his young protagonist and the reader. It promises to continue for quite a distance, and I hope it does."

—Kage Baker

"Brown's first novel, the opener in a new fantasy series, creates an elaborate new world, with a rich and deep spiritual and political background. . . . Reminiscent of L. E. Modesitt Jr.'s Recluce novels and David Drake's Lord of the Isles series and David Farland's Runelords books, this well-wrought tale of families in conflict against both politics and religion represents a welcome addition to large-scale fantasy."

—*Library Journal* (starred review)

"Akin to Steven Erikson's Malazan Book of the Fallen or R. Scott Bakker's The Prince of Nothing . . . There is the sense right from the start that *Servant of a Dark God* is a tale being told by a first-rate storyteller. It may be his first novel, but . . . John Brown knows how to grab a reader's attention and hold it all the way through the book. That's a talent that works well in any genre and bodes especially well for the next two volumes in what promises to be an engrossing fantasy trilogy."

—*New York Review of Science Fiction*

SERVANT
OF A
DARK
GOD

JOHN BROWN

TOR®
fantasy

A TOM DOHERTY ASSOCIATES BOOK • NEW YORK

This is a work of fiction. All of the characters, organizations, and events portrayed in this novel are either products of the author's imagination or are used fictitiously.

SERVANT OF A DARK GOD

Copyright © 2009 by John Brown

All rights reserved.

A Tor Book
Published by Tom Doherty Associates, LLC
175 Fifth Avenue
New York, NY 10010

www.tor-forge.com

Tor® is a registered trademark of Tom Doherty Associates, LLC.

ISBN 978-0-7653-6230-8

First Edition: October 2009
First Mass Market Edition: November 2010

Printed in the United States of America

0 9 8 7 6 5 4 3 2 1

For Nellie

The Goat King danced the crags by day,
At night he came to feed,
And dupe the foolish farmer's wives
To hold his monstrous breed.
The husbands sought to hunt him down
And take him as he lay,
But the wily King, with a wicked touch,
Stole their souls away.

CONTENTS

SERVANT
OF A
DARK
GOD

1.

THIEVES

Talen sat at the wooden table in nothing but his underwear because he had no pants. Somehow, during the middle of the night, they had walked off the peg where he'd hung them. And he'd searched high and low. The last of their cheese was missing as well.

The cheese he could explain: if you were hungry and a thief, then cheese would be a handy meal to take. But it was not the regular poverty-stricken thief who roamed miles off the main roads, risked entering a house, and passed up many other fine and more expensive goods to steal a pair of boy's dirty trousers hanging on a peg in the loft.

No, there wasn't a thief in the world who would do that. But there was an older brother and sister.

Talen had two pair of pants to his name. And he wasn't about to ruin his good pair by working in them. He needed his work pants. And to get those, he needed leverage. The good news was that he knew exactly which items would provide that leverage.

It only took a few moments to find and hide them. Then he went back to the house, cut three slices of dark bread, and put them on a plate in the middle of the table next to the salted lard.

River, his sister, came in first from outside carrying a massive armload of rose stems clustered with fat rose hips. Talen sighed. She already had fifteen bushels of the stuff in the back. Were they going to make rose hip syrup for the whole district? And he knew he'd be the one who would have to cut each and every hip and remove the seeds so her syrup didn't end up tasting like chalk. It was a thorny business, even if he did wear gloves.

River walked to the back room to deposit her load and returned. Blood spattered her apron. A thick spray ran from her cheek to throat.

"What happened to you?"

"Black Jun," she said. "The cow that was bred by that rogue bull, her water broke last night, but the calf was too big for a normal birth." She shook her head. "Jun's brother-in-law from Bain cut into the cow this morning and made a mess of it."

"Did she die?" asked Talen.

"Not yet," said River, "but such a wound, even with old Nan's poultice, would take a Divine's hand to keep it from corruption." River had been apprenticed to Nan, who had midwifed as many cattle as she had humans. That's where River learned how to take a calf that couldn't be pulled, by cutting in from the side. That's where she'd learned about the virtues of everything from pennyroyal to seeding by moonlight. She could have learned far more, but old Nan went out late in a rainstorm one night and tumbled down a steep slope to her death. Even so, as unfinished apprentice, if River said the wound was bad, it was bad.

"And the calf?" asked Talen.

"Saved," she said. "For now." She took off her bloody apron and hung it on a peg on the wall.

Under the apron, River was wearing her work pants, which would have been a much easier mark for a clothing thief since River's room was on the first floor of the house. Of course, she'd only point out that nobody would look for pants in a girl's room. Which was true for most women, but River wasn't most women. She wore pants to everything but the dances and festivals, and even then she threatened to do so. Skirts were a bother in the fields, she said. A bother on a horse, and a bother when hunting. And nobody was going to tell River otherwise.

Talen gave his bloody sister his most pleasant smile.

She looked at his bare chest and legs. "Where are your clothes?"

"That's a good question," said Talen.

River shook her head and went to the cupboard to get her pot of honey. She searched about and then turned around, looking as if she'd lost something.

Surprise, surprise.

There was nothing like her cinnamon honey. It was not the thick amber that most of the honey-crafters sold. This honey was thin and clear and tasted like moonlight. River got it from a lovesick dyer who lived on the far side of the settlements and liked her despite her pants. He said the honey came from bees that made their hives in the cliffs there. He had also said that his love for her flowed like the nectar of the pale green flowers that clung to the cliffs, that she was his flower and he her bee, and that their pollinations would be more wild and splendid than anything a pot could contain. All of which proved that the dyer knew nothing of women. At least, not River. She had smiled at the dyer's sentiments, but that didn't make the dyer any less of an idiot or his hands any less blue. River was not a girl won with declarations of wild and amorous pollinations or delicious gifts, even if the gift was spiced honey that cost three weeks' worth of labor.

Ke, Talen's older brother, walked in next with flecks of barley stalks caught in his tunic. Ke was built like a bull. In the summer he looked even more like one because he shaved his hair short. He did it, he said, to keep his head cool and make it easier to clean. But it also allowed others to see the thick muscles in his neck. He retrieved his bow

and archer's bag from his bedroom. The bow was made
with wood, horn, and sinew, and it was so powerful only
someone with his massive strength could draw it more
than half a dozen times. Da, because of his strength and
size, was sometimes called Horse. Ke, having inherited all
of Da's muscle, had picked up the name of Little Horse,
but he wasn't a horse. That was too noble a creature. Ke
was a bull, no doubt about it.

Talen, of course, inherited all the wit in the family, but
nobody seemed to value that. He was never referred to as
"the bright one" or "that great blaze of brains." Instead,
he got names like Twig and Hogan's Runt.

Ke sat at the table. His bow was blackened with charcoal and linseed oil and then covered with a good layer of
goose fat and beeswax to protect it from the wet. He'd
always been an excellent archer. Da had seen to that. But
Ke was now something more. He'd proven last year in the
battles with the Bone Faces that he was an efficient killer
as well. He pulled out his crock of goose fat to rub in yet
another layer, then looked back into the bag. "Hey," he
said, and opened the mouth of the sack wider to fish
about in its contents.

"Lose something?" Talen asked.

"Where are my new bowstrings?" Ke said.

"Strange," said Talen. "All sorts of things going missing
today." He tsked. "What a negligent bunch we must be."

It took River about two seconds to catch on. "I want my
honey," she said.

"I want my trousers," said Talen.

Ke looked up from his sack. "You took my strings?"

"You took my trousers."

"What would I want with those?" asked Ke.

"What would I want with your bowstrings? They don't
fit my bow."

River put her hands on her hips. "That honey has a special—"

"Oh, don't act like you're offended for the dyer," Talen said and began to work his way toward the door.

"Who said anything about him?" River asked. "That honey's imbued with vitality. Now, hand it over."

"Pants first," said Talen. He continued to move until he stood between them and the doorway.

Ke narrowed his eyes.

River cocked her head, threatening a fight. She tightened the yellow sash she used as a belt. This is what she did when she wanted to run. The two of them exchanged an evil glance, and Talen knew if he sat where he was a moment more, they'd have him.

"Trousers!" he demanded. Then he dashed out of the house in his bare feet and underwear and into the yard.

To his surprise, Talen found Nettle, his cousin, opening the door to the smokehouse to get something to eat. He was supposed to be on a patrol with his Father, but Talen didn't care what he was supposed to be doing. He was here now, and could even the odds in this fight.

Ke and River charged out of the house hard on Talen's heels. At this point Talen was most worried about River. He darted left, and thanked his instincts. A short length of firewood flew past him. River, in addition to being a healer, was a thrower, deadly with spoons, pots, and sticks at twenty yards. She could whip off a wooden garden clog and fling it with ferocious aim at your head before you'd even taken five steps. Talen knew: he had the bumps to prove it.

Talen ran past Nettle. "Trip them!" he said.

Nettle, the Mokaddian traitor, did no such thing. He cut a link from one of the hanging sausage chains, took a fat bite, and stood back to enjoy the show.

Talen raced toward the woods beyond, but River had the angle on him and sprinted to cut him off. Thank the Six she hadn't had time to pick up anything but a stick. Talen veered toward the garden.

"Pick up the pace," Nettle called out. "They're gaining on you."

"Coward!" Talen yelled back. He dashed around the garden fence, turned to avoid Ke, ran back toward the house, and found himself boxed in between the midden and the barn.

He had two choices. He could make a run at one of his dear siblings and hope to blow by, or he could go up the old walnut tree and hope they would stay at the bottom and do nothing more than shout insults and threats up at him.

He wouldn't get by Ke and his long arms. Talen had enough room to get by River, but she was daring him, grinning at him to just try.

He made his decision.

Da had fashioned a wooden slab bench and put it next to the trunk of the giant walnut tree. Talen ran for the bench. When he was close enough, he took one running step to the bench then another to an old knob sticking out about five feet up the trunk. He followed the momentum upward, grabbed a branch, pulled himself up, and stood on a fat arm of the tree well out of the reach of his brother and sister.

"That's about the dumbest place you could have chosen," said Ke.

Talen climbed a few branches higher and looked down at the two of them. "The joke's up."

"We don't have your hog-worn trousers," said Ke. "You're the one who loses things on a regular basis."

Talen did not lose things on a regular basis.

He saw Ke bend over and pick up a number of rocks. "You come out of that tree or I'll knock you out," said Ke.

"No," said Talen. "I think you need to give up your childish games."

But Ke threw a rock instead.

Talen ducked. The rock flew straight and true and would have made a pretty bruise, but a small branch stood in the way and sent the rock wide. Goh, he needed to put more branches between him and those rocks, so Talen climbed until the branches were no bigger than his thumb.

He couldn't see Ke or River from this height. Nettle stood over by the well, finishing his sausage, and using one hand to shade his eyes from the sun.

"You smelly bum," Talen called down to him. "Do something!"

"Jump!" shouted Nettle. "He's coming up."

Talen heard the leaves rustling below as someone ascended toward him.

Nettle was a fine one to stand there and call out instructions. Talen must have been at least forty feet up in the air. The barn roof would have been perfect had it not been thirty feet away. There was nothing else around him but hard ground below. He had nowhere to go. He could not simply jump out of the tree at this height.

Ke was right—running up this tree had been idotic.

He caught a glimpse of Ke climbing below him and to the left.

Maybe he could get around him. Talen did not want to be at his mercy in the tree. He climbed down toward Ke. He would get close, then move to the other side and away.

"I'm going to give you one last chance," said Ke. He looked up at Talen with that happy look that said Talen was a rabbit and he was a dog that had just found his next meal. He was maybe only six feet away.

Talen scuffed the branch and sent small particles of bark down into Ke's face.

Ke ducked, and Talen made his move. All he needed to

do was get to a branch four feet below him and to the right. It would be a quick climb from there to the ground.

He swung down, but Ke had been expecting the move, and suddenly he was grabbing at Talen's leg.

Talen moved out on his branch. Ke followed. Talen jumped for another branch. He grabbed it with both hands, pulled himself upward, but before he could get a leg up, the branch cracked and swung him to the side.

It was dead and rotted.

Talen looked for something else to grab, but he couldn't see anything close; then the branch popped again and broke entirely from the tree.

Talen reached out, grabbing for anything, but it was too late, and then he was falling headfirst. He yelled. He saw Ke's face then a wide-open space beyond with nothing between him and the ground but a branch that would most assuredly break his back.

2.

STAG HOME

If this fall lamed Talen, he'd be good for nothing but the war weaves. An image of him at the wizard's altar in Whitecliff flashed in his mind, the Divine draining his Fire away, the essence that fueled the days of his life, so it could be used by a better vessel—by a dreadman. The dreadman would give Talen homage for the gift, but Talen didn't want any homage.

He yelled, a long "*Nooooooo!*"

A stick poked Talen's eye. Then his ankle caught, and

Talen swung into the center of the tree and smacked his head.

Ke grunted. "Grab a branch," he said.

Talen looked up. It felt like a piece of bark the size of his thumbnail was stuck in his eye; he could barely see, but it was clear that his ankle was caught not in a fork of two branches, but in Ke's iron grip. Ke bent over a branch holding on to Talen's ankle, his face set in determination.

"You're slipping," he said.

Talen twisted around and finally found a branch. He grasped it with both hands. "I've got it. Let go."

But Ke did not let go. He repositioned his grip and said, "You'll hang here until you tell us where you've hidden our stuff."

Talen's eye ran like a river. "What about my trousers?"

"Goh," said Ke. "If I come across your trousers I'm going to burn them. Then you'll have something to yell about."

"Hoy! What's going on here?" It was Da, standing at the base of the tree.

"They've taken my work trousers," said Talen.

"Is that so?" Da asked Ke.

Talen still hung mostly upside down, the blood rushing to his head.

"It is not," said Ke.

"You three," Da said. "Today I come out of the barn to find one of you hanging naked in a tree. What am I going to find tomorrow? Get down. Both of you."

Ke looked down at Talen. "You're lucky." Then he flung Talen's legs away.

Talen clutched the branch. His body swung around like a festival acrobat's. His grip on the branch slid. Then he reached out with one foot and caught another branch to stand on.

Talen steadied himself. When he'd finally cleared his

eye enough to see, Ke stood next to him. "You should thank me for saving your neck."

"You're the one who put me here," Talen said.

"I'm the one who didn't murder you," he said, and then descended to the ground.

Murder indeed. Talen watched Ke go and realized the truth was he *had* been lucky. Lucky Ke had been that close. Lucky he'd tumbled just the right way for Ke to grab his ankle. And Ke had held him as if he were nothing more than a sack of potatoes. Why couldn't he have gotten at least half of Ke's strength?

He sighed. It was going to be annoyingly inconvenient to have to wear his fine pair of pants to work in. And at week's end, when he cleaned them and hung them out to dry, he'd have to sit around in his underclothes and bat the biting flies away.

Talen climbed out of the tree and stood before Da.

"Did you look for the pants in the barn?" Da asked.

Of course he'd looked in the barn. He'd looked everywhere. "I'm not going to ruin my good pair."

"Then work in a leaf skirt. I'm not buying any material for another pair. Nothing in heaven or earth will make me feed negligence."

"I wasn't negligent."

"It doesn't matter anyway," said Da. "Put on your good ones. Get the peppercorns. You're going to the village to get some hens from old Mol the fowler. I've had too many days without eggs."

"Last night you said you wanted to see us up and in the fields with the barley."

"Well, I'm saying right now that I want some hens. And you're going to get them."

"Shall I go along?" asked Nettle.

"No," said Da. "You're getting back on your horse to take a message to the Creek Widow."

Nettle smirked. "The one who told you not to come around?"

"What other one is there?" asked Da. He held out a sealed letter to Nettle. The Creek Widow was a Mokaddian woman with a tenancy of almost twenty acres. She had been a family friend for years. But this last summer she had ordered Da out of her house and off her land. And try as Talen might, he could not get Da to tell him why. Talen suspected it had something to do with her perennial efforts to marry Da off. Half the time Talen thought she wanted Da herself. But Da was stubborn. And Talen was happy about that. While she cooked food fit for a Divine, she was bossy and a bit odd, talking to vegetables and rocks and always smelling a little like a goat.

Was this letter an indication that Da was making up?

"Paper," said Nettle, a tease in his eye. "You must be serious." He held the letter up to the sun as if trying to read it.

"You break that seal," Da said, "and I'll have your hide."

"I wouldn't dare touch it," said Nettle.

"Then go," said Da. He shooed them both away. "Be gone. And hurry back. I don't want to lose any of that barley."

TALEN PUSHED THE cart and the empty chicken baskets through the three miles of the muggy woods to Stag Home. When he finally broke onto the broad valley, he was so refreshed by the sunlight and breeze, so soothed by the smooth, sun-warmed dirt of the road under his bare feet that he didn't immediately notice the fields and orchards.

Instead, he basked in the glory of the day and the fact that not only had he escaped being maimed this morning, but he'd also avoided a number of hours sweating in the barley. The peppercorns hung in a pouch around his neck. It had been two years since any merchant had sold peppercorns in the New Lands and the value of pepper had risen.

Talen looked forward to seeing if the alewife's daughter would be selling her vegetables again. She was a looker, that one, with her dark hair, jade eyes, and the fabulous lines of her long neck. During his last visit, he'd ended up returning to her table thrice, buying a bunch of carrots each time, just so he could fix her features in his mind. And it hadn't all been one-sided. She had glanced his way when he stood across the road eating some of her wares.

Talen's reverie of the alewife's daughter broke when he pushed the cart past an orchard of apple trees bent with clusters of red and yellow fruit. There should have been children climbing with baskets in the tops of those trees. Instead, the apple baskets lay scattered on the ground.

Across from the orchard a yearling calf bawled outside a field. The calf searched along the fence separating it from its mother and a dozen others who stood with their noses down among the ripe white oats mixed with peas. There should have been a harvest master there promising someone a proper beating for letting the cattle in, but there wasn't even a beggar to chase the greedy guts out.

How could that be? Talen searched the fence lines and long rock walls. He searched the fields—nothing but a small carpet of blackbirds picking through a swath of barley that had been harvested and left to lie where it fell. There wasn't a body to be seen. It was as if the villagers had fled the fields.

Alarm scuttled like a crab up his neck. This was the fat season for pillaging. Of course, the Bone Faces hadn't attacked Stag Home or any of the surrounding villages for years. But that's precisely why Stag Home would be a perfect target. The villagers would have grown overly secure, just as Talen had.

What's more, the Bone Faces took more than livestock and goods. They took men, women, and children. Lords, he thought, if one of those Bone Faces got him, he will have wished he had fallen out of that tree and broken his back. He scanned the fields again, this time looking for signs of a raiding party.

It was said that when the Bone Faces kidnapped you for their slave ships, they cut off the pinky finger of your right hand. Then, with some black and feral magic, they used your finger to bind you to them. And so perverting was the binding that you never once wanted to even pine after what you'd lost. All your thought was to serve your master every day that blood flowed in your veins.

One of the first things they'd ask you to do, which you would do with joy, was to trick your own kin into their traps. And so it was that whole families disappeared. Some were enslaved, others were sent to the fearsome altars of Ishgar as sacrifices, for the Bone Faces were a bloody people. But Talen figured those who went to the altars met with a better end, for if the rumors were true, the Bone Face bindings were strong enough to compel a slave beyond this life and into the world of the dead.

He imagined the fate of his pinky. The Bone Face slave masters hung the fingers of their most valued slaves about their necks. The rest they locked up in a special room. And when guests came to call, especially if the slave master was wealthy with dozens of formidable slaves listed among his assets, he would take his guests into the finger room and show off his collection of desiccated and rotting digits, just as a good Koramite wife might show off her collection of dishes or lace.

There was no sign of struggle in the fields. The clans sent patrols along the coastlines during the harvest season.

Last year there had been battles, but those had been far out on the Finger Islands, not on the mainland settlements. Nothing this year. But it had to be Bone Faces. What else would make the villagers flee the fields on such a fine day for work?

Goh, but how he wished Da and Ke were here with him. If he only had his bow; that would improve his odds. Da, a Koramite bow master, had taught his sons well. Talen could shoot eight arrows a minute, and not to simply fill the sky with a haphazard rain of death. No, Talen could fire at that speed and hit what he was aiming at.

But he didn't have his bow. All he had was his knife and a pile of chicken baskets, which meant he'd have to slice open his own neck if the blighters got to him, for he wasn't going to be turned into a villain, nor would he allow himself to be used as feed for their terrible gods.

Talen thought he might be able to lose any pursuers in the thickness of the woods. But who was to say they hadn't already circled behind him? Besides, the safety of the village with its embankment walls was much closer.

Smoke trailed into the sky from behind the walls of the village. But it was thin, not the thick smoke of burning homes. Upon the timber and earthen wall he saw the glint of three men wearing helmets and carrying spears. The gates stood closed, which only confirmed his assessment of the situation.

Talen looked back at the woods once more. He searched along the tree line following the river that snaked its way through the valley, but saw no shallow-bottomed ship's mast. Perhaps they had landed farther downriver. Perhaps the village had been forewarned and the raiders had yet to attack.

He quickened his pace. He did not want to be caught outside the gates. The cart and chicken baskets clattered along the dirt road as he went. He watched the shadows and trees. He kept an eye on the fields. He prepared himself, at the first sign, to run.

He passed two large wicker creels on the bank of the river. One had toppled over. Its lid hung loose, and a tangle of fat, brown eels wriggled their way back toward the water. The sight raised the hackles on the back of his neck, and Talen began to run.

Down the dirt road he went, and then it was over the bridge. On the far side of the bridge, one of the chicken baskets bounced off, but Talen paid it no mind and let it lie in the grass on the side of the road. He didn't stop until he stood outside the gates.

The Mokaddian guards up on the wall were not looking out—they were looking in. The beef-heads were not going to see any threat coming that way. "Hoy!" Talen called.

The three guards turned.

One was that maggot Roddick, the cartwright's son who had tormented Talen with rotten plums when he was a boy.

"Let me in," said Talen.

"You," said Roddick in disgust. "Stay right where you are!"

3.

CHASE

Technically a Mokaddian village couldn't refuse entrance to Talen just because he was a Koramite. Even though the Koramites had been conquered and paid tribute to their Mokaddian masters, they still maintained some rights, and refuge was one of them. But that didn't mean they would open to him. Roddick yelled down to those within.

This village had fallen once, before it had a wall. The Bone Faces had rowed two of their small galleys up the river to a bend at the edge of the fields. They attacked just before dawn, setting the homes ablaze, running many good men through with their curved swords, and stealing anything of value, including fifteen young girls. The next year, the village built the wall.

The wall had been made by digging a wide ditch and throwing up an embankment of earth about three times the height of a tall man. Timber spikes had been planted into that steep slope and at the bottom of the ditch. Grass and tall thistle now hid many of the spikes, but any host charging up that hill would find the spikes' power to impale undiminished. And if the host reached the top, they'd face a timber palisade and tower. The timbers had been new when Talen was a boy. Pale yellow lichen now clung to much of the wood, but it was sturdy nevertheless.

He expected they'd be happy to give him a bow and set him up on the wall with Roddick. But there were no raiders, no sign of any struggle whatsoever. So why had they closed the gates?

The crossbar that held the gates closed scraped. Then the gates swung open.

Out walked a dozen Mokaddian men holding their scythes, sickles, and forks like weapons. About half had shaved their heads and dyed their scalps with henna, bearing witness that they'd performed their harvest worship.

Talen glanced over his shoulder, fearing the Bone Faces had decided to attack, but there were no Bone Faces, only the river glistening in the sun and the fields of grain beyond, rolling with the breeze. When he turned back, one of the beef-heads on the wall was stringing his bow.

"It's one of Hogan's half-breeds," said farmer Tilth. He held his hay fork before him as if Talen were the Dark One himself. "What are you doing here, boy?" asked Tilth.

"I've come to trade with Mol," said Talen.

"He's spying!" Roddick called from above.

Spying?

"Cast your weapons from you," Roddick commanded. "Then lie down in the dirt."

"You bum brain!" Talen yelled up at Roddick. "Who would want to spy on you? And I don't have any weapons. Unless you think I might kill someone with these chicken baskets."

"Give yourself up," said Tilth.

Long Lark, the cooper's son, stood next to Tilth. He tied a cattle noose at the end of one rope.

Talen looked at the men. There were the Early brothers, the one-eyed tanner and his two sons, and the young hayward who had killed a wurm not two weeks ago and received the intricate tattoo around the wrist of his right hand that signified he was no longer a boy, but a man of the Shoka clan.

These people knew him.

The men began to fan out.

"I'm honored," said Talen, "but isn't this a bit much for a runt like me?"

"He's going to run," Roddick called.

"I'm not running," said Talen.

"Come on, son," Tilth said.

They approached him like one might a boar caught in a trap: careful and bent on injury.

A flash of orange caught Talen's eye, and he spotted a tall, bald man with an enormous black beard standing in the gateway. He was an official, wrapped in the blue and orange sash of the Mokaddian Fir-Noy Clan.

Fear shot through him, and Talen took a step back.

The Fir-Noy had shed plenty of Koramite blood over the years. That was not to say the Koramites hadn't defended themselves. But everyone knew that Koramite and Fir-Noy didn't mix. Lords, Fir-Noy didn't mix with half of the Mokaddian clans, especially not the Shoka of Stag Home.

But there stood that Fir-Noy official, acting like he owned the place, and here the Shoka village men had their tools pointed at him as if he were a rabid dog.

By law, if a Koramite heard a Mokaddian cry out for help and did not run to the Mokaddian's aid, the Koramite would be punished. Depending on the urgency of the situation, he might be whipped. The law, however, did not go both ways. Talen's cries to be rescued from these madmen would go unheeded.

"I'm here for chickens," he protested.

It was then that Long Lark broke from the pack and set himself to throw his noose.

Talen hesitated for a fraction of a second.

Long Lark adjusted his grip on the noose.

By the farting lord of pigs, Talen thought. *I've done nothing. Nothing at all.*

Koramites had been dragged behind horses before.

Not here, of course, in a Shoka village. Not yet. But these were Mokaddians, after all. Fir-Noy, Vargon, or Shoka—did it matter which clan they belonged to?

He looked into their eyes and saw it did not. Talen took a step backward.

Long Lark swung his noose.

In his mind's eye, Talen saw himself hanging from the village wall with that noose around his neck. The thought jolted him. And despite his earlier protestations, he turned tail and ran.

A shout rose up behind him so full of menace that it almost loosed his bowels.

He stretched his stride, expecting that noose to fall about his shoulders or to catch an arrow in his back. He ran like a thief, like a rabbit coursed by dogs. He ran with the speed only fear and bewilderment bring.

He sprinted back over the bridge and thought he saw the flash of an arrow out of the corner of his eye. He needed to make the woods, the only place where he might have a chance to lose these madmen. Back up the road he ran, the dirt hard under his bare feet.

Talen was not the fastest runner in the district, but he wasn't the slowest either. He knew he should measure his pace, but he'd seen that lazy-eyed Sabin among them, him and his shaved head and violent speed, and Talen sprinted for all he was worth.

He could hear the men behind him and pushed himself until his breath came in ragged gasps and his head felt dizzy. But it did not last. By the time he reached the oat field the rogue cows had broken into, his lungs and legs were burning, and he had to stop. He panted and turned.

Sabin, a look of murder in his eyes, was almost upon him.

Movement farther up the road drew his attention: a

rider galloping toward him on a horse. They were boxing him in.

Lords, but he had to make the woods.

Two more ragged breaths and he hopped the fence on his left and the field-stones piled up next to it and struggled up a fallow field of knee-high grass.

The tall grass pulled at his feet. The slope sapped his strength. But neither seemed to slow Sabin.

The woods stood only a few paces away.

Talen glanced back to see Sabin reach out with his long tattooed arm for Talen's hair.

River loved Talen's hair. Loved it long. And at that moment he wished he'd never listened to his sister and her stupid appraisals of men.

Sabin grabbed a handful of Talen's hair. He yanked, brought Talen up short, then backward to the ground.

Talen scrabbled to his knees, but Sabin kicked his side and knocked the breath right out of him.

He couldn't move, couldn't breathe. By the time his body finally remembered it had lungs, the rest of the men were rushing up the hill.

Sabin kicked at Talen's face, but Talen curled up and the blow glanced off the back of his head.

Someone struck him with a staff. Another kick caught him in the hip.

Talen tried to get up and lunge out of the circle, but before he could get his legs, one of the tanner's boys landed a blow to Talen's head that dazed him and knocked away all sense of balance. He turned, falling, and saw a sea of men.

Someone kicked him in the back and the pain made him gasp. Someone else went for his neck.

Talen brought his arms up to shield his face.

"Where's that rope?" one of them shouted.

Talen tried to roll over.

"Out of the way!" someone shouted.

"Now you'll get it, half-breed," a man said.

The blows lessened and then stopped. Talen glanced up.

Sabin stood above him, lifting what must have been a forty-pound fieldstone the color of fresh liver.

He raised it high, preparing to crack Talen's head like a nut.

4.

BOUNTY

Talen rolled away, trying to escape Sabin's stone.

"Hold!" someone shouted.

A horse snorted.

Talen tried to dart through the legs of the men surrounding him and was flung back to the ground. He froze, cringed, waiting for the crushing stone. But it did not fall.

"Twenty stripes, Sabin," a man said. "I swear it!"

Talen glanced up. The men were not looking at him. They were looking at the bailiff of Stag Home who sat upon his dappled gray horse, glaring at Sabin. It was he who had been the rider bearing down on Talen from the other direction.

Sabin hesitated, and then, almost in defiance, he dropped the stone perilously close to Talen's head.

"That," said the bailiff, pointing at Sabin, "has just made you my riding horse."

The bailiff was not a large man. But he was strong and

fearless in battle. His face was shaven close, which revealed three scars where a bear had tried to take off his jaw. But it was his eyes, as pale as the horse upon which he rode, that fixed Talen's gaze. Those eyes had scared Talen as a boy. He had thought the man was full of evil. His father had convinced Talen otherwise, but, faced with those eyes, Talen could never maintain his certainty.

The bailiff directed that hard gaze at the other men. "What is this here? Why are the fields empty?"

"There are Koramite Sleth about," someone said.

Sleth? Soul-eaters?

Sleth were those who had given themselves over to Regret, the one Creator of seven who, when he'd seen what he and the seven other Creators had wrought, recognized that it was flawed and despised the work of his hands. To the men, women, and children who came into his twisted power, he gave horrible gifts—unnatural strength and appetites, odd growths and manifestations of beasts, and the power, with a touch, to steal Fire and soul. The stories of Sleth and the hunts the righteous led against them were legion.

Had Talen heard that right?

"This one ran like a monster," one of the men said.

"Yes," said the bailiff. "But it appears you caught him anyway."

Talen looked up at the bailiff, but a wave of pain and nausea slammed into him, and he was forced to turn and vomit into the grass. He hurt everywhere.

"Get up," said the bailiff.

Talen gagged once more, spit. He took three breaths to steady himself. He was dizzy and shaking.

He got to one knee. Something was running out of his nose. He wiped his face with his sleeve expecting blood, but it was nothing more than snot. There was a ringing in his ears, and he didn't know if he could stand.

But he did know one thing: he would not show weakness. Not in front of these men.

Two more breaths. He could barely open one of his eyes.

Goh, these arrogant Mokaddian garlic-eaters. This would go to the Koramite Council. And the Council would take it to the Shoka lords. He was within his rights—every one of these men should pay! And that thought was enough to take the edge off the flood of tears pushing up within.

Talen stood. He almost toppled over, but then his dizziness seemed to recede.

Two other horsemen rode up from the village and joined the bailiff. One was the bald Fir-Noy he had seen at the gate. His black beard and eyebrows were even bushier than they had first appeared. His Mokaddian wrist tattoo with its boar's tusk had been extended up his forearm, showing not only his clan, but also the military order to which he belonged. The other Fir-Noy was a small man, a messenger. He rode a horse that was lathered and blowing from a long gallop.

The bearded Fir-Noy shifted on his saddle and the leather creaked under him. "We tried to find you, Zu," he said to the bailiff. "There's been a Sleth hunt, and it appears that things have taken a turn for the worse."

The bailiff turned. "A Sleth hunt?"

The messenger eyed Talen, then addressed the bailiff. "We identified the parents of the abomination pulled from the river. Yesterday, our forces closed in on Sparrow, the Koramite master smith of the village of Plum. But things did not go as planned. His two hatchlings escaped. And then some Sleth spawn came back and slaughtered a family in the village."

Except for the buzzing in Talen's head there was dead silence. Sleth, he thought. What are these men doing wasting their time chasing me? They should be out—

Then his brain processed that last statement. There were Sleth among the Koramites, among Talen's people.

"We have reports," the messenger continued, "that they were spotted in this district. A Koramite girl and her blind brother." He turned to the men. "There's a sizeable bounty for any who bring them in, dead or alive. A miller's annual wage."

The reports of Sleth that sailors brought this spring had given him nightmares. A Sleth wife taken in Mokad who had filed her teeth into sharp fangs—they'd all thought it was to make her more fearsome in battle. But the hunters discovered the true reason when they broke open her smokehouse and found the bodies of four men hanging, butchered and half cured.

And that was just this year. There were stories of Sleth stealing your soul away, then walking about in your body. Sleth growing horns, growing gills so they could swim in close and drag unsuspecting fishermen into the watery depths. Sleth were forever stealing sisters, wives, and husbands to use in unnumbered abominations.

If these men thought he was associated with Sleth . . .

Or was this simply another Fir-Noy scheme?

He realized it didn't matter at this point. If these men thought he associated with such evil, then his life floated like a piece of duff over a bonfire.

"What are you doing here?" asked the bailiff.

"Trading for chickens, Zu," said Talen. "That was my crime."

"Then why did you run?" asked the Fir-Noy.

What a stupid question. "It's hard to tell," said Talen. "I'm usually quite solid when facing a charge of Mokaddian villagers."

Of course, stupidity was bred into the Fir-Noy. Their clan was forever trying to stir all the others up to push the

Koramites into the sea. It was probably this man who started this whole thing.

Sabin clopped Talen on the head and sent him reeling to his knees. "Respect your betters."

Talen steadied himself and stood again. The right side of his rib cage pained him. He took in a large breath, expecting to feel the sharp pain of a broken bone. There was a twinge, but it didn't feel like it came from a break.

He looked at the bailiff. "I'm sorry, Zu. Let me restate."

"No," said the bailiff. "There's no need to restate." His face was full of a pent-up anger. "There soon won't be any chickens, Talen. There will be nothing for you Koramites. You squander opportunity after opportunity, your race. You can't keep yourselves clean, can you?"

"Zu," said Talen. "All I did was come for layers. And these men, without provocation, set upon me."

"You ought to press him," the Fir-Noy suggested. "Who knows how wide their network is? And think about it. I'm told this skinny thing is a half-breed. But not just any old mongrel. This one's connected to high places, given special treatment. I'm told Argoth is going to adopt him into his family and give him a chance to earn the wrist of a Shoka man." He spat at Talen's feet. "This one can walk about and spy without being given a second glance."

It was true Uncle Argoth and Da had recently talked about marrying Talen to a Mokaddian. It wasn't necessary for him to be adopted into a Mokaddian family to do so. But it would smooth the process. However, there were some Shoka who thought it a scandal. Even among the Shoka of Stag Home there were still a few who still wondered how Talen's mother, a Mokaddian of some station, could willingly debase herself and foul her offspring by marrying and mating Da, a full Koramite. There were those who saw her untimely death as a confirmation of that poor choice. Nevertheless, Uncle Argoth was determined to make him a full member of the clan, wrist tattoo and all.

"Are you spying?" asked the bailiff.

"Zu," said Talen, "I mean no disrespect, but what would the purpose of such spying be? I have no idea what this is about."

"Don't feign ignorance," the Fir-Noy growled.

"I am what you see," Talen said to the bailiff. "Nothing more."

"He's lying," said the Fir-Noy. "Take him and press the truth out."

The bailiff turned to the Fir-Noy. "This is Shoka land, not Fir-Noy. Your news has caused trouble enough. I won't let it bring murder to my fields."

"Killing a Koramite isn't murder."

"It is here," the bailiff said.

The Fir-Noy licked his fat lips and shook his head in disgust, but he made no reply.

Talen addressed the bailiff. "You know my family. Surely, you can't think I am one of them."

"I can think anything I want," said the bailiff. "I stake my reputation vouching for you and your people. But your actions have begun to stain me."

"No, Zu. Not mine. We carry no stain." The bailiff *knew* him. Da had given his boy a foundling wildcat. He'd taught the bailiff himself a better way of drawing his bow. And, in return, the bailiff had invited Da on many a hunt. Surely, the bailiff's vision would not be clouded with Fir-Noy rubbish.

The bailiff looked at Talen as if he were weighing him.

"I find no cause to accuse this boy," the bailiff finally said. "Not today."

Talen bowed in gratitude. "Zu, you are clear-sighted and wise."

"Then prove me right. Packs of bounty hunters will begin to stalk these woods. But if a Koramite were to bring the hatchlings in, that would say something, wouldn't it."

"Yes," said the Fir-Noy. "It will say that Koramites, like crows, feed on the carrion of their own kind. It proves nothing."

Anger flashed up in Talen. Fir-Noy did nothing but pick and feed on the work of others. He knew he should keep his mouth shut, but he couldn't help himself. The words were leaping out before he knew what he was saying.

"Well, Zu," said Talen, "at least we're willing to make something useful of our carrion; it appears the Fir-Noy simply let theirs parade about full of maggots and stink."

Anger flushed the Fir-Noy's face, and he kicked his horse forward to get at Talen.

Talen cringed, but the bailiff grabbed the Fir-Noy's reins and pulled the horse up short.

"He'll take that back!" said the Fir-Noy. "I won't stand for this, Shoka land or no."

The bailiff turned to Talen. "This is the last time you can expect protection from your own stupidity. Apologize!"

"Yes," said Talen. "Of course." He faced the Fir-Noy and stood as tall as he could muster. "Zu, I've been knocked half out of my mind. I apologize. Such untruths are only given voice by fools."

"Rot," said the Fir-Noy. Then he wrenched the reins away from the bailiff. "Your territory lord will hear about this."

"I have no doubt," said the bailiff.

The bailiff turned to Talen, his pale eyes sending a trembling up Talen's back. "There's going to come a time,

Talen, when there will be no one to hold such men back. And the Koramites will be purged. It might be already too late. Now, you tell your da I expect him to order the Koramites in my district. I expect assurances. And know this: we'll be picking over every rock and stone. And by the Goat King's hairy arse, we'll make no distinction between those who harbor hatchlings and those who practice the abominable arts. Now go."

Talen nodded. "Thank you, Zu." He began to walk back down the slope. "Excuse me," he said, trying to get past two of the men to go back to the bridge to fetch his cart.

"Where are you going?" the bailiff demanded.

"Zu?" asked Talen.

"I just gave you an order."

Talen paused. He could see no sympathy on the faces of the men. He wasn't stupid, but at the moment he felt very much like a dunce. Then he realized there would be no picking up his cart and baskets.

"Directly home," said Talen, changing his course. "That's where I'm going."

The bailiff only looked at him with those pale eyes.

Talen walked across the field toward the trail. He hurt all over. But he could walk. He could breathe. And that was something to be thankful for. He remembered the peppercorns and felt to make sure bag was still hanging from his neck. He hadn't lost those, yet another thing to be thankful for.

As he departed he heard the bailiff lecturing his men, but he was so rattled he couldn't focus on what the man was saying.

Talen crossed the fence and began to follow the trail. He looked at the wood in front of him. The hatchlings had been seen in this district. And where would hatchlings hide?

They wouldn't be here. Not right here. Of all the miles upon miles of woodland available, why would the Sleth hatchlings choose this little section of the district right here in front of him? The chances were so remote that it wasn't worth thinking about. But his heart wasn't listening to his mind. It was said Sleth needed to feed often on the Fire of other men. And a lone stripling walking in the cover of a thick wood was a perfect target.

Furthermore, Sleth never came alone. There was always a big nest of them. So it was likely there were more than this one family, which meant there were probably adults, full of the dark art, looking for those hatchlings as well.

And even if the Sleth didn't find him, then there were the bounty hunters the bailiff had mentioned. Only the fiercest of men took it upon themselves to hunt Sleth. And because these Sleth had been found among Koramites, the hunters would suspect every Koramite they came across, and he did not want to fall into their hands for questioning.

He looked back at the bailiff and the village men making their way toward the river.

Goh, he thought. Mobs and monsters. Being chased about by Ke and River now seemed a pretty thing.

He faced the woods again. He didn't have much choice. Besides, even if someone were waiting behind a bend in ambush, standing here like a coward wasn't going to improve his odds.

He searched the ground for a sturdy stick and a few good throwing stones, and then Talen entered the wood.

TALEN TRIED TO keep himself from running. But the farther he got into the dark, old wood, the more he felt like a fat worm sinking on a hook into the water.

A fat worm that had already been worked over. He catalogued his pains. There were two spots on his head that hurt to touch them. There was his eye that was now almost swollen shut. His ribs smarted. His kidneys, he was sure, had been abused. It hurt his back to walk. Lords, even his toes protested. He looked down, saw a smart bruise on his left foot and realized someone must have stomped it.

But these were physical pains. They would heal. At least, he hoped they would, especially the blows to his brain. The Sleth, on the other hand, were different. And he couldn't tell what would be worse: to be taken by the Bone Faces and forced into a nine-fingered enslavement or to be kept in storage like a living carcass, to be feasted upon or twisted into something unnatural. At least with the Bone Faces he'd die a man.

And how could he follow the bailiff's suggestion and bring in the hatchlings, the children of these Sleth? A proper Sleth hunt required one hundred men. It required a Divine. Was he expecting the Koramites to field groups of hunters? But the bailiff had been looking at him. It had been clear he was suggesting Talen join in the hunt. Except, what could one runt do?

If he had his bow, he might be able to do something. That is if the Sleth didn't know the arrow was coming. He'd heard once at an alehouse that Sleth could whisper to arrows. Even so, he didn't have his bow. He was defenseless. What were a few stones going to do against Sleth? The thing to do now was get back to Da and the others as quickly as he could and alert them.

The hatchlings were somewhere in these woods. He tried to act calm—the last thing prey should do is act like prey. But then the distinct thock of a branch breaking sounded off to his right followed by a squirrel screeching out a warning.

His heart leapt up into his throat. But he told himself it

was a falling branch, told himself to stand upright and walk like a man. He quickened his pace despite the twinge in his back.

Then came a grunt and high keening, something moving toward him, scuffling through the leaves on the forest floor.

You are not prey, he told himself, you are not prey, but try as he might, he could not be calm. Could not walk. Could do nothing but abandon all pretense, ignore his injuries, and run.

Not once did he look back. He dared not. Eyes to the front, he told himself. He couldn't afford to smack into a branch or step wrong, or, most especially, see the face of the thing that surely was behind him. He knew if he saw the beast, his courage was likely to completely desert him. At that point it would be impossible to do anything but cringe upon the ground like a cornered rabbit. So it was eyes in front, even when the woods broke before him and he saw the river below and the farm stretching away from him on the far side.

Talen ran down to the river, stumbled through the shallow water of the ford, and scrabbled up the other side. Only when he reached the smoke shed did he stop and turn, and, with much panting, search the woods.

Nothing. Nothing at all.

The Sleth children, if there had ever been any, must have been one-legged pigeons. No regular monsters would have let him escape alive.

Of course, there probably hadn't been a thing in those woods besides squirrels and mice. The sound he'd heard was most certainly somebody's renegade pig.

Coward, he told himself, and bent over, resting his hands on his knees. He was such a coward.

"Where's the handcart?"

Talen turned. Da sat in the shady side of the barn, sharpening his scythe. Seeing that great horse of a man brought immense relief.

"Back at the bridge," said Talen. He took a breath.

"Ah, that's what I like to see. A boy who races home to work and leaves the chickens to fend for themselves."

"Da," said Talen. "The bailiff wants you."

"We're mowing the fields now. The bailiff can wait."

Then he stopped and looked at Talen more closely. "Is that blood? What happened to your face?"

Talen poured out everything that had happened, including his run through the woods. As the story progressed, Da stroked the braids of his beard with increasing anger.

When Talen finished, Da set his scythe aside and stood.

"Are you going?"

"It appears I am," said Da.

"Should we bring our bows?" asked Talen. "Or would billhooks be better?"

"Billhooks?" asked Da.

"In case we're attacked."

Da grunted. "You're going out to glean. We've got a field that needs stacking."

"But the hatchlings," said Talen.

"The hatchlings," said Da. "Son, did you not learn anything from your adventure this morning? Even if the children were Sleth, the greater risk is being mistaken for a Soul-eater by an idiot with hunt fever. We're talking about two children, however ferocious they may be." Da shook his head. "You said a Fir-Noy rider brought the message? That's the problem right there."

"SHOULDN'T WE AT least give the warnings some credit until we find out otherwise?"

"Sparrow was a good man," said Da. He heaved a great sigh.

Talen had not known the smith very well. However, he'd always wondered about his name. He'd thought it funny such a mighty man would be named for such a little bird. Talen, Ke, and Nettle were named after noteworthy ancestors. His sister was named so she might be granted all the qualities—the strength, life, purpose—of a River. But Sparrow? Talen had found out that the smith's family had a long line of Sparrows, all named after an actual bird that had saved one of the family's progenitors from drowning. He'd always wanted to hear that tale, but now he wasn't so sure.

A great weariness seemed to descend upon Da. "You could search this whole land. You could search the whole Nine Clans, and not find Sparrow's better."

"But he was Sleth," said Talen.

Da shook his head. "If Sparrow was Sleth, then fish swim in the deep blue sky." He turned to Talen. "Do you still have the peppercorns?"

Talen nodded. He opened the small pouch hanging around his neck that served as his purse, poured out the corns, and handed them over.

Da took them with his large fingers and carefully placed them in his own pouch.

"Get out to the field and help with the stacking," said Da. "I'm going to fetch us some hens and go talk to the bailiff." Da turned and headed for the barn. "By the way, I found your pants wadded up under your bed," he called back. "They're lying on the table."

"I looked under my bed," said Talen.

Da shrugged. "They were there, plain as day."

That was impossible. Talen had moved his bed out. He would have seen them.

Talen turned and went in to the house to get his old pants. These were stained, thanks to the Stag Home idiots, with blood and grass and would take an hour of washing to get them clean. When he came back outside, Da had Iron Boy saddled.

Da's unstrung hunting bow stood in the leather bow bag strapped along Iron Boy's side. He should have been taking his war bow. "I'll be back before dark," Da said. He secured what he called the Hog behind the saddle.

The Hog was an axe with a handle about as thick as four fingers and a shaft as long as Talen's arm. The head was not broad like a timber axe, but short and narrow with a blade at one end and a pick at the other. But it was used for other things. An archer needed a weapon for close work. He needed something for when he exhausted his supply of arrows. The Hog could pierce armor when wielded by a man half Da's size, and Da had killed three Bone Faces last year with it. But he did not reverence it as many men would: most of the time he used it to break up the bee propolis in the hives or to chop kindling.

"If you find any Sleth," said Da, "be sure to tell them you're tough and gamey and not at all fit for dinner." A little bit of a smile softened his grim expression.

"Easy for you to say," said Talen.

"We're going to be fine, Talen," he said. "Don't worry about a thing." He picked up the reins and led Iron Boy away.

Talen watched him go. Then he looked at the woods and swallowed.

5.

THE HUNT

On the day before Talen took his beating, Barg, the harvest master and butcher of the village of Plum, stood in the crisp light of early morning with a number of men, waiting to murder the smith, his wife, and their two children.

Oh, none of them called it murder, but all knew that's where this would lead. And what choice did they have?

The villagers had been joined by others in the district and divided into groups positioned around the smith's. One group hid behind the miller's. Another, the one lead by Barg, kept itself behind Galson's barn. The third waited in a small grove on the outskirts of the village.

The men with Barg stood for an hour, checking the buckles of what armor they had, wrestling with the shock of the matter, and waiting for the signal in silence. At first, a handful of the outsiders had boasted of what they'd do. "Mark me," a Mokaddian wearing the turquoise of the Vargon clan said. His Vargon accent was plain, rolling his *r*'s much too long. "I will land one of the first five strokes."

Barg cut off a handful of his hair with a knife to show his mourning. "You'll be one of the first five he guts." He grasped another handful of hair and sawed through it.

"What do you know?" the Vargon said.

"I know that today I will help kill a man who saved my life." He cast another clump of shorn hair to the ground. "The smith is a roaring lion. You had best beware."

The Vargon said nothing in return, but what could he say? He was only trying to cover his fears. Sparrow the smith was a formidable warrior, and if the accusations against him were true, then it was certain some of those who had gathered today would die.

The approaching dawn silvered the fields and thatch roofs about the village and set the roosters to crowing. The cattle in the paddocks began to low, a stray dog outside the alewife's barked at a snake trying to get to the tall grass, and down in the south field a few straggling deer decided it was now time to leave the fields and find cover. The men knew their signal was only minutes away.

ON THE SIDE of the village closest to the forest and the Galson's homes, the smith's daughter, Sugar, stood in the barn feeding their two horses and heard the jingle of a trap bell in her garden. It was followed by the panicked cry of a hare.

Nothing ever got away from one of Sugar's traps. And from the sound of the scuffling and ringing, this creature was big. All that commotion was sure to bring Midnight and Sky, her family's dogs. She'd trained them to leave her game alone, but these two liked to bend the rules whenever they could. So Sugar put down the hay fork, and told Fancy, their mare, and Sot, their draft horse she'd return later. Then she picked up her smothering sack and stepped out of the barn and into the yard in her bare feet.

The village homes looked like fat ships floating amidst a sea of grain. But it was not a quiet sea. Da had flung both doors to the smithy open and stood at the forge hammering away at his work. Farmer Galson's cattle bellowed. They were the noisiest bunch of cattle in the whole district. Sugar saw them bunched up at the far end of their paddock, waiting for one of Galson's grandsons to open the gate so they could go to the watering pond. But that was odd . . . someone should have led them out long ago.

Beyond the paddock gate stood the thatch-roofed homes for Farmer Galson, his children, and his adult grandchildren. Almost a village all by itself. The soft yellow light of hearth fires still shone in many of the windows. Outside, one of the wives made her way back from the privy in a pale nightgown. She held a wailing babe on her hip.

The woman looked up, and Sugar waved across the field at her, but she did not wave back; instead, she dashed for her house. Maybe she hadn't seen Sugar. But then again, maybe she had. Some of the Galsons thought they rode a lord's high horse.

Sugar walked to the garden, opened the gate, and stepped under the arch of climbing rose. The lemony scent from its pink blooms lay heavy in the air. She walked along the shadowed rows of vegetables until she came to the peas and salad greens.

There she found a large hare, a black-tail that was going to make a fine breakfast.

It was easiest just to brain them with a stout stick, but she didn't want to chance ruining the fur about the throat, so she readied the smothering sack and approached the animal. This part of the garden was still wet with yesterday's watering and the soil stuck to the bottoms of her bare feet.

When she got close, the hare began to kick in earnest. It was a monster. Twelve pounds at least.

She threw the sack over it to protect her from its kicking and clawing and quickly held its hind- and forequarters in place. It cried out in distress, but she kneeled on its side, pressing the air out of its lungs. She pressed until she knew she'd start breaking its ribs, then waited for it to suffocate.

The giant hare struggled underneath her. It bucked once more then lay very still. Sugar removed the snare noose from its leg. The hare felt dead. But she'd been tricked before. A number of years ago, before her mooncycles had come upon her, she'd picked up a hare and

carried it into the house and laid it on the cutting stone.
The whole time it had lain in her hands like a limp rag,
but the second she began to cut, it jumped up and knocked
the knife right out of her hand. Then it flew off the table
and bolted out the open door. And so she continued to
press this hare.

Across the paddocks the Galsons' dogs began to bark.
They were joined by another group down by the miller's.

The dogs would often bark this way when travelers
passed through. Sugar looked up to see what was causing
the commotion and saw a wide line of men on the far side
of Galson's paddocks.

The Mokaddians marched in battle order with bows
and spears, their helmets gleaming in the early morning
light. Those with spears also carried shields painted with
a grotesque boar's head circled by a ring of orange. It was
the mark of the Fir-Noy clan.

It was not uncommon to see such things. All men, Mokaddian and Koramite, were required to regularly attend
their clan musters. But something about this was not right.

She turned and saw another line coming up from the
miller's.

Then she realized: these men were converging, but not
on the practice field. No, they seemed on a direct course
for her house.

6.

KING'S COLLAR

Fear ran up Sugar's back. Not only were these men converging, but none of them wore the armbands that distinguished friend from foe during the practice musters.

Sugar stood, trying to get a better view.

The hare that had lain beneath her bucked free of the smothering sack. It bolted down the row of peas, pushed through a hole she'd missed in their fence, and fled to the short hedgerow that grew along a portion of Galson's paddock.

The men marched toward the house. She could see the intricate Mokaddian tattoos around their wrists and forearms. She could see beards and naked chins under their helmets, but they were too far away for their eyes to be anything but dark pits.

She ran to the back door and flung it open.

Mother bent at the hearth building up a cooking fire. She startled when Sugar rushed in. "Goh, you do that just to set my heart leaping in my throat, don't you."

"There are men dressed for battle in Galson's field," said Sugar. "Others down by the miller's. Was there a muster today?"

Mother picked up the bowl the potter had thrown just for Cotton, Sugar's infant brother who had been stolen the previous season. "I'm sure I would have heard something."

At that moment Da opened the front door. As the days turned hotter, Da had taken to wearing as little as possible. He stood there bare-chested with the morning at his back.

"Purity," he said to Mother, "this beard is going to be

the death of me. I'm sick of the braids catching fire. I'm not going back to the smithy until it's shaved off."

Sugar saw that two of his braids were indeed singed.

"Ach," Mother said, undoing the shutter latch, "they're so handsome on you. Half the men in this village would give a finger for such a beard."

"I don't want their fingers," said Da. "They can have the beard for free." His massive back and arms glistened with the morning sweat. He smelled like charcoal smoke.

Mother walked to the back door and looked outside. "That's odd," she said.

Da spoke to Sugar. "I heard the hare trap. All this time I've been lusting after beef. Why can't you catch one of Galson's steers? I'd even settle for one of the old ones."

"There's the matter of Farmer Galson," said Sugar.

"Bah," said Da, dismissing the farmer. "Make a trap for Galson as well."

"Sparrow," said Mother, "did you forget today's muster?"

"None that I know of." He walked over to her, but instead of looking out the doorway, he reached out with one of his massive arms and grabbed her around the waist. He nuzzled into her side and began nibbling.

"Stop," she said and pushed at him. "Sparrow, what are those men doing?"

Da looked outside.

Midnight and Sky began barking out front. Sugar looked through the front door Da had left open. "There's another group coming down the lane."

As Koramites, Sugar's family had no legal clan. The Mokaddian and Koramite fatherlands were far across the sea. The Mokaddians had beat the Koramites there in a great war not long ago, and one of the Mokaddian prizes had been the Koramite settlements in the New Lands. Of the nine Mokaddian clans that came to claim the prize, the Fir-Noy seemed to hate their Koramite vassals the most. Not two months ago a group of Fir-Noy had beat a Koramite woman until they'd ruined one eye and half her teeth.

But Da had said that wouldn't happen here. Those were upland Fir-Noy that had beaten the woman. They didn't have sway in the village of Plum, and Da had the assurances of the territory lord on that.

"They're surrounding us," Sugar said. The men were close enough for Sugar to see the set of their mouths—bitter as garden rue.

When Sugar was a child, a gang of four village boys had tormented her until Da confronted the boy's parents. But that didn't end the issue. So Da took it to the village council. He demanded the boys come fight her one-on-one. Mother was furious, taking him to task for making Sugar fight his battles. But Da stood his ground.

Da himself was a fighter, and for one week he sparred with Sugar, preparing her as best he could. Then the boys had come, some grinning, some all business. They brought most of the village with them. And in the wedge field, surrounded by grandmothers, children, and dogs, Sugar had taken a beating. But the boys had not left unscathed either. There was a black eye, a bloody nose. She'd kicked one so hard in the gut that he'd vomited in the grass.

Afterwards, some of the villagers cheered for her. A few of the fathers of the boys who had started it all came and made peace. Da was satisfied. Mother was not. She would not speak to him for two weeks. But even with her heavy fury on him, Da did not give up on Sugar's lessons. "There are those who act," he said. "And those who are acted upon. I'm not ever going to leave you in a position again where you have no choice."

Two years later when her moon-cycles came, Mother convinced Da he was ruining her chances of a good marriage, for what boy wanted to bed a bruiser? So he stopped teaching her how to use her feet and hands as weapons, and began to teach her knives.

That was a number of years ago. She'd never had to use the knife Da forged for her protection and made her wear. Not to draw a man's blood. Although she had let a few of the boys she'd been introduced to at Koramtown know she wore it. But mostly she'd used the knife around the yard in her chores. Now, even though she knew it would be useless against a host of men, she was glad she had it.

Mother turned to her. "Get Fancy saddled."

Sugar moved to obey, but Da held his hand up. "No. Running will only raise their suspicions or prod them to act. This might be nothing. Leave it to me. I know how to handle these men."

"And then it will be too late," said Mother.

"Woman," said Da in warning. Then he walked out the front door.

When he was only a few paces into the yard, Mother turned to Sugar. "You get Fancy."

"Do you want saddlebags?" asked Sugar.

"All I want is a horse. The Fir-Noy are not what they once were."

Sugar dashed out the back door.

The troops in Farmer Galson's fields had fanned out and were now walking as a line toward the house.

Legs, her younger, blind brother, stood in front of the chicken house, his head cocked at an odd angle as if looking off into space, which was what he did when he paid fierce attention to every sound and smell. His wild hair stood up. In his arm he held a basket of onions and eggs.

"Legs!" she said. "Get in here."

"I can hear men," he said.

"Move!" she said.

Holding the eggs to the bottom of the basket, Legs

jogged for the back door. He needed no stick to navigate the house and yard. If he knew a place, he could walk about as if he were sighted. It was only when he was in a new place that he might stumble, or when things were lying out of place. And so they all had learned to be very tidy.

Sugar ran to the barn. Fancy nickered. Sot had already moved out to the watering trough. Sugar grabbed the harness, slipped it over Fancy's head, and fitted the bridle in her mouth. Then she led the horse out and tied her to the post by the back door.

The Fir-Noy stood with their hideous shields only a few paces beyond the chicken house. They'd formed up into a loose circle that ringed both the house and smithy. "Mark the horse," one of the soldiers said.

For a moment Sugar thought they were going to shoot Fancy right there. Perhaps shoot Sugar herself. She rushed into the house and shut the door behind her. She went to her mother who stood in the doorway to the front yard.

"Fancy's not going to be enough," she said.

Mother gaze was fixed on Da out in the yard, but she reached out and smoothed Sugar's hair. "You did just fine. Now, if anything happens, you and Legs need to be ready to ride. You'll have the most cover in the woods. So it's straight through Galson's fields, low on Fancy's neck. And if someone stands in your way, you ride them down."

Fear seized Sugar's heart. Had it really come to this? "What about you and Da?"

"You ride them down," said Mother. "You flee to Horse."

Mother had always told her that if the Mokaddians ever attacked, she was to flee into the Shoka lands and find the farmer many called Horse. His given name was Hogan. And that's how she addressed him out of respect. Sugar didn't know him well, but she had been to his farm a few times. Still, how would she ride through that ring of men? They'd fill her or Fancy full of arrows before she'd galloped a rod.

"Do you hear me?" asked Mother.

"Yes," Sugar said.

She looked past Da at the soldiers out front. They'd stopped a number of paces from Da. Those with bows had strung them, and that was something fearful. Because keeping a bow strung all the time only ruined the weapon. You never strung your bow unless you were going to use it.

Midnight and Sky barked at the men until Da whistled sharply and called them back to his side.

Two men on horseback faced Da. She recognized the leader and the orange and blue patterns painted onto his armor. It was the territory lord, a man everyone called the Crab for his ruddy complexion. Next to him sat the district lord. Behind them stood Barg, the butcher and village harvest master, holding his spear.

Da bowed to the Crab. "My Lord," he joked, "have you at last come to wrestle your humble servant?"

But the Crab did not smile. "Sparrow, smith of Plum," he said. "You have been accused of dark magic. We are here to take you and yours to prove that you are whole and without spot."

Dark magic? Sugar did not believe she'd heard him correctly.

"What?" said Da.

"If you're clean," said the Crab, "you need not fear the ordeal."

An ordeal was designed to flush out Sleth. Supposedly, when such a creature was on the point of death or overwhelming pain, through drowning or torture, it would multiply its strength with its dark magic to save itself and thus reveal its true nature.

But how anyone could think her family was among such was impossible to fathom.

The Crab reached into a pouch tied to the front of his saddle and pulled out a thin collar, almost a necklace.

"I have here a king's collar. I want you to put it on." He tossed it. The collar shimmered in the early morning light; it landed in the dust two-thirds of the way between the Crab and Da. "When it's about your neck, you will bind your wife and children in chains."

He motioned to a man behind him who brought up a number of leg and neck irons and tossed them toward where the collar lay.

A king's collar was a magical thing, wrought by a special order of Divines called Kains; it not only prevented a person from working magic, but it weakened them and made them easy to handle.

Sugar realized the men did not come closer and bind the family themselves because they feared some kind of evil trick.

"This is ridiculous," said Da.

The Crab's horse danced to the side a few steps.

Then the district lord tossed a large sack towards Da. It landed heavily on the ground. "The contents of that sack were found last evening on the bank of the Green by a group of mothers and children doing their laundry. Open it."

Da walked over to the sack, squatted down, and pulled the mouth open.

"Whose child is that in the sack, Master Sparrow?"

Sugar heard her mother take in a sharp breath.

Da hesitated for a moment then gently worked the body out. He knelt there for quite some time, not moving, not saying a word.

Then Sugar knew who was in that sack. She could feel

it from the crown of her head to her toes. Her fear fled and she raced out the door.

Da turned and motioned for her to stay. "Get back!"

But it was too late. Sugar saw the baby that Da had exposed.

It was Cotton, her little brother. She knew it. Little Cotton, stolen out of his crib earlier this spring. By woodikin or slavers or wild dogs, nobody knew. Yet here he was.

She came closer and saw that the body was bloated and partially decomposed. It had the lighter Koramite coloring and Cotton's curly hair.

Cotton, their bonny little honey man.

Then Da opened the sack wider and slid the body of a stork out.

From the uncommon kidney-shaped spot of dark feathers on its shoulder she knew it was Lanky, the young stork with a wounded wing that she and Legs had found. They'd wrapped him up in Legs's tunic and brought home, careful to avoid the sharp yellow beak. Mother had nursed him back to health. And when Cotton was born, it seemed to think he was its brother. Mother was always shooing it away from him for fear of that long beak. And the stork would go, but only to perch on a fence post or the limb of one of the trees. It pestered them for weeks.

Lanky had disappeared the same day Cotton did.

Sugar had thought the mad bird had finally departed because Cotton had gone. But this was awful. Somebody had taken both and killed them.

Da turned the bird over. Something was wrong with the carcass. She looked closer.

The bird had wings and feathers. But where the talons of the right leg should have been, a misshapen human foot curled. And where short feathers should have graced the beast's head, patches of long blond hair grew. And underneath that hair lay what surely was a small, twisted, but human-shaped ear.

Sugar's sickness turned to revulsion.

"Look closely at the foot of the child," said the Crab. "Notice the nails. Notice also the few patches on its back. That's not matted hair; it's the beginnings of chick down."

Da stood, horrified.

"And now," said the Crab, "you will put on the collar and chains."

"Sugar," Mother called.

But Sugar was rooted to the spot.

Da found his voice. "You think we are soul-eaters? You think we would spend our child's soul like this?"

"What I know," said the district lord, "is that someone buried these two. And when the recent floods came, the waters opened the grave, tasted its contents, and spat them out."

"My Cotton was stolen," said Mother.

"Yes, yes," said the Crab. "Snatched by one of the woodikin and taken to the swamps or into the wild wood over the mountains. It's a fine story, but here he is."

It was common enough for the Divines of the many glorydoms to draw the Fire that fueled the days of a man's life. But not the soul. Never the soul. Sleth, on the other hand, stole Fire *and* soul from men and beasts. The singular nature of the soul was what gave each type of living being its distinct attributes. Consuming bits of another's soul transferred random aspects of that soul, aspects that manifested themselves in mind and body, slowly twisting the one that had consumed it.

Sleth stole from humans, but because animals couldn't tell their secrets, Sleth stole most often from them. So if one had stolen Fire from his goat, then he would also have traces of that goat soul in the draw, and over time that soul would manifest itself. Such a thief might develop the nubs of horns on his head or a slit iris in his eyes. If one had stolen from fish, he might one day find patches of scales instead of skin. Someone who stole from his cattle might be inflamed with lust by a heifer in estrus. Someone who had stolen from a bird . . .

But this was all wrong. How could a babe steal soul?

"You cannot controvert the manifestations of Slethwork upon both bodies," said the Crab. "Nor can you claim the child is not yours. The other Koramite children who died last season have all been dug up and accounted for. And no other has gone missing."

The bowmen trained their arrows on Da's heart. Some pointed their arrows at her and Mother.

Barg spoke up. "You haven't been sick in many years. And the tale your wife tells is suspect. Your dogs were in the yard the day your child went missing. This she swears. Yet she also said they did not bark." He motioned at Midnight and Sky. "We all heard today how they react to strangers. There could have been some charm put upon them. But it could also be the one snag in an otherwise well-spun lie."

"Purity does not lie," said Da.

"Then you have nothing to fear from the ordeal," said the Crab.

"My Lord," said Da. "I respect your office. But you are no Divine. An ordeal—"

"Master Sparrow," said the Crab. "Would you rather I let a mob deal with the problem? This is what prudence demands. Now, pick up the collar."

"There's not one of you that can revive us if the ordeal turns fatal. Let us wait for a Divine."

"That is not an option."

Of course, it was. But they thought Da was Sleth, and everyone knew you did not bargain with Sleth. You never gave them any quarter. Sleth were both fearsome and wily and too quick to escape their bonds.

"You live with me all these years and suddenly conclude I'm one who could devour his own children?" Da pointed at Barg. "Who was it last autumn, after those bloody battles on the Fingers, that cast aside prudence and rowed back at night to an island crawling with Bone Faces to save three doomed friends?" It had been Da who had rowed back. Da who had saved, among others, Barg the butcher.

Sugar looked into the faces of the soldiers. There were a number she recognized. Some had laughed with Da in the yard. Others had eaten at their table. Many of the villagers of Plum had drunk ale and been entertained by Legs singing his ditties. All had accepted the water he drew and delivered to the villagers as they worked the fields, him leading his goat and cart, feeling the road as he went with his stick. But those smiling faces were gone. They were replaced by faces grim and fixed on their purpose.

Mother grabbed her arm and pulled her back toward the house.

"I've drunk and danced with you," said Da. "I've shoed your horses. I probably fashioned most of those spearheads. You've nothing to fear from me. My heart is as clean and fresh as well water and you all know it."

"What we know is that all the evidence points here," said the Crab. "And now we've come to the end of our discussion. If we were uplanders bent on murder, you would already be dead. I've done more than give you the benefit of the doubt. This is the last chance I'm giving you. Pick up the collar and irons."

"You will kill us and learn nothing."

"Zun," said Barg, using the title of honor meant for warriors who were equals. "Just pick up the cursed irons."

Da did not move.

"Bowmen," said the Crab. "Ready yourselves."

The bowmen drew their strings to their cheeks.

Sugar could not believe her eyes.

She and Mother now stood at the doorway to the house.

Da looked back at Mother. Some communication passed between them that Sugar could not decipher.

The Crab raised his arm to signal the bowmen. "Let all here witness that Sparrow, smith of the village of Plum, has refused an ordeal."

"Stop!" said Da. "I'll take your wretched collar and irons. But you know only Divines can conduct hunts. The only reason you haven't killed us already is so that you can avoid the fines levied on mobs like this. Let it be known that on this day the laws of the Glory of Mokad have been set aside. Your blatant disobedience will be made known. And your own Divines will come to collect the debt of blood."

The Divines would come. And they would punish these men, for the laws on this matter were clear and ruthlessly enforced: no man could take upon himself even the slightest part of the honor of a Divine. But the Divines would come too late.

Da walked forward and picked up the collar and irons.

They would almost surely use water for the ordeal. And Sugar's family would drown. She'd once touched the cold, bloated body of a boy who had drowned. She envisioned Legs as that boy, and panic ran through her.

Da examined the irons and said, "It looks like your smithing is as bad as your judgment. I'll need a hammer to assemble these pieces properly."

"Those pieces are just fine," said the district lord.

Mother turned to Legs and in a quiet voice said, "Get the shutters. Slowly now."

Da began walking toward Mother and the open doorway.

Legs closed the shutters on the front of the house then moved to the back.

The district lord called out, "Stop!"

Da stopped only a few paces from the front step and looked back.

"Put on the collar," said the district lord.

"Of course," said Da. He dropped the irons in the grass. And then he dashed toward the house.

At that moment Mother moved back from the door and pulled Sugar in with her.

A cry of alarm rose from the soldiers.

"Shoot him!" commanded the Crab. "Shoot!"

7.

THE COURAGE OF WOMEN

At the moment of the Crab's command, the bowmen released their arrows, and Sugar saw the arrows fly.

Da took three, four strides. He leapt to the porch. Then an arrow struck him in the back below the ribs. Another flew like an angry insect into the house above her head and struck the wall behind her.

"Sparrow!" Mother called.

Da's momentum carried him into the house, and Mother slammed the door shut.

More arrows struck the door. A man cried out, "I got him! I got him!"

Midnight and Sky had not followed Da. They barked viciously outside.

Mother pulled the crossbar on the door in place.

More bows thrummed outside and the dogs' barks turned to screams. Then the dogs fell silent.

Da winced and looked down at his side. The arrow had not gone into the thick of his back, only cut the flesh on the side. But the blood still spilled from him like water. He pressed his hand to the wound.

"Those cursed blackhearts," he said. He pulled his hand away wet with blood. "Get me a wrap," he said to Mother. "All these years, and then they treat me like some feral dog."

Mother took a knife to her dress and cut a long strip. "We should have ridden when I first suggested it. Why you can't listen to me I'll never know."

"Well, you won't have to fret about that much longer, will you?"

Mother was furious. She made the final cut, then came and tied it around Da to cover and hold the wound. When Da took his hand away it was dark red. Heavy drops of blood fell to the floor.

"Did you get your mother's horse?" Da asked Sugar.

"I did," she said, and the enormity of that almost overwhelmed her. One horse was not enough for all four of them. She cursed herself for not having thought to get Sot.

Da nodded. "It's enough."

From outside, they heard the Crab yelling at his men. "I want all here to witness that Sparrow has refused the proving. Fire the smithy and the house."

Moments later Sugar heard arrows snake into the thatch above their heads. Those would have their points wrapped and burning with pitch-soaked rags.

"Fetch me my armor," said Da.

"What are we going to do?" asked Sugar.

Da looked down into her eyes. "You, my dear, along with Mother and Legs, are going to ride Fancy out of here."

"You fool," said Mother. "It's too late for that."

Sugar thought Mother had said that in anger, but when Sugar looked up, she could see Mother was not angry—she was wracked with grief.

"I'm going to draw them away from the back," said Da. Then he took Mother's hand and kissed it. "It's not too late. Not for a fool to remedy his foolishness. You three will ride away, and not look back."

"I don't want to ride away," said Sugar. "Besides, where can we go that they won't find us?"

"Mother will know," said Da. "Now fetch me my tunic."

Sugar hesitated, but Mother nodded, so she ran and brought the quilted undertunic and helped Da tie it shut. Then Mother dressed him into the mail tunic that extended down to his thighs.

Da couldn't rout so many men. They were all going to die, yet Da made her cinch the buckles on his breastplate as if he were dressing for a parade.

Legs found his way over and grasped Da's wrist. His hair stuck out, and fear shone plainly on his face. Da took Legs's hand and kissed it. "Be brave, Shen, son of Sparrow, son of Sparrow, son of Shen." Shen was Legs's given name. He was an ancestor who had been a powerful man, and Da loved telling his stories. Da kissed Legs's hand a second time.

By the time they had the breastplate buckled about him, Sugar could hear the fire above their heads and smell the smoke coming in through the cracks of the shutters.

"Peer out the back and tell me what you can see," said Mother.

Sugar looked out a small hole in the shutter and surveyed their garden. Fancy neighed nervously and clopped about trying to pull free from the post. The soldiers stood away from the border of the yard.

"They've backed up," she said.

"Did you see their faces?" asked Da. "Half of them are petrified. Those are not children out there. I should be stuck like a pincushion with arrows. But their fear has affected their aim. Would that I were a soul-eater. Then this whole so-called hunt would be at risk. With average luck, I'd kill the lot of them and green our garden with their blood."

Mother came away from the window. "Perhaps we can make the break together," she said to Da. "You can take off this armor. The children and I will ride off first. And in the confusion of them chasing us, you can get on Sot."

Da fastened his helmet on. "It's too risky. We need to split them. I should have run to the smithy to draw them away from you, but none of the pieces there would have fit me well. There's no armor there but what's made for these short whoreson Mokaddians."

Heat began to press down upon them as if they were loaves in an oven. Smoke hung about the room in hazy streaks.

"It's time," he said. Then he took Legs's face in his hands and kissed his cheek, embraced him, then kissed him again. He did the same to Sugar, but she could not let him go.

She would not. Lords, she would rather die with him. She had her knife.

"You are a delight and solace," he said. "We named you perfectly. Take care of your brother." Then he gently forced Sugar away.

He stood and looked at Mother with a fierce light in his eyes. "I could never have found a better woman," he said. "Even in your arguing."

"Take off the armor," Mother said.

"We're not going to be able to make the break together," said Da. "It won't work."

Mother seemed oddly calm. "Sparrow, my heart. Haven't you learned yet that I'm always right?"

What was Mother thinking? Then Sugar realized she had given up. She'd always said that if her babies died, she wanted to go with them. Sugar saw this logic extended to Da as well. And perhaps that was right. They would all die together.

"No," said Da. "We'll not take that route. We'll not walk into their spears and arrows without a struggle. If they want my blood and the blood of my fine wife and children, then they will pay for it. You're feeling battle dread; hold your course until it passes. You have a chance, Purity. A slim one. Don't throw it away."

"I'm not talking of giving up," said Mother. "We do have a chance, but not in this way. They'll cut you down before those out back even know what's happening. You're a mighty man, Master Sparrow, but even you cannot stand against fifty spears."

Da's face was full of confusion. "What better plan is there?"

"*I* will face them."

Da's face softened. "That, love, is my task. Now ready yourself." He turned, but Mother grasped him by the shoulder and held him back.

She had gone mad with panic and grief.

Da tried to pull her hand away.

"I will face them," she said calmly.

"Purity," he said. "Love." He removed her hands and tried to stride to the door, but Mother grasped him again.

"No," he said and removed her hand. But she took him by the rim of his breastplate and, like a man heaving a sack of meal, threw him across the room. He stumbled over a chair and slammed into the far wall.

Many men came far and wide to wrestle Da. Few had thrown him. None had handled him with such force.

Da looked at Mother, his face full of shock. He shifted his mail tunic, then tried again to reach the door. But Mother planted herself in his path. He tried to push her out of the way, but could not budge her. He renewed his efforts, his arms and neck straining. But it was to no avail.

His expression turned from shock to angry determination.

He took a step back and then lunged at her, but Mother simply stepped out of his way and with one sweep of her foot took his legs out from underneath him.

Mother reached down to take his war maul. "I will face them," she said calmly. "Take off your armor so you can ride more easily."

Da grasped the head of the maul. "Purity," he said.

"I will draw them to me," she said. "And you will ride with the children. It will be best that way. They will not be orphaned or caught and sold as chattel. You can provide for and protect them as I never could."

"I don't understand," Da said.

"Yes, you do," she said, then she tugged the maul out of his grip. Sugar stood back, confused and alarmed.

Mother turned to her. "The way to the woods will be clear. Be ready to fly."

Then she walked to the front door and put her hand on the crossbar. She paused, taking them all in with her gaze. "I will be waiting for you in brightness."

She lifted the bar, and in one fluid motion she flung open the door and raced outside. Clouds of smoke billowed in. The roar of the fire above them surged. Out back, Fancy cried with wild panic.

Luckily, neither Sugar nor Legs were standing anywhere within the line of sight from the doorway, for moments later more than a dozen arrows hissed through the smoke, some sticking into the walls, others glancing off a table or chair. Da had only just gained his feet when two struck him. One glanced off his breastplate, the other hit him in the mail over his thigh. He grunted at the second, but it did not have an armor-piercing head, and the arrow fell away.

Da stood and raced after Mother, but halted at the door. He coughed at the smoke and squatted to get under it. "Goh," he said with a look of wonder on his face.

"Da," said Sugar and rushed to shut the door. But as she grabbed the door, she saw what Da was looking at.

Mother had already reached the soldiers. Two men lay on the grass. One was dead. The other screamed out at the wound that had nearly taken his leg.

She moved like a snake, like the wind. She was graceful and absolutely horrible.

She swung into another man's wooden shield and sent it flying. He cried out and stumbled backward, but before he could reach the ground, she smashed in the side of his head.

Sugar could not believe her eyes. She would not. Such speed and power was unnatural.

"Purity," said Da, and Sugar could see the horror and disbelief on his face.

The great bulk of the men were falling back, some stumbling over one another. In his retreat, one of the bowmen loosed an arrow, but it flew wide of Mother and struck one of his fellows. Another man charged her with a spear, but she swung the maul with blinding speed and cleaved the spear into two.

The Crab yelled for his men to stand and close ranks.

Mother was about to put the whole mob on the run, but two men yelled and rushed her from behind, their javelins held high.

"Mother!" Sugar yelled.

Mother turned just as they cast them. She dodged one, but the other caught her in the shoulder and knocked her back.

Da roared.

He had been in shock, but fury now burned in his eyes.

Mother removed the spear and defended herself from the sword blows of the man who had thrown it.

A dozen archers came running round the corner from the back of the house. They began to form a line. Mother would not be able to dodge their arrows.

The flames thundered overhead.

"Get to Fancy," Da commanded, "and ride."

Then he rose and stepped out onto the porch and put his helmet upon his head. Someone shouted out a warning, and the mob turned to look.

Da stood in his dark, shining armor, the fire raging above his head, smoke pouring off the roof.

The men in the yard froze.

"You've met the mistress," Da bellowed. "Now face the master!"

A man dropped his spear, panic shining in his wide eyes.

Da roared and and charged into the fray.

"Da!" Sugar called after him.

He had no weapon, and at first, Sugar thought that he too would fly into the soldiers as Mother had with that awful strength and speed. But Da did not show any sign of dark magic. He charged as a normal man would, an actor playing a role.

But the soldiers did not see through Da's bluff, and they began to scatter.

Just then the Crab yelled out and galloped across Sugar's view toward her parents, his sword held high and at the ready.

The house burned like a furnace. The heat began to scorch her lungs with each breath, and she dropped to the floor.

She watched Da run to one of the dead men and pick up his spear. Then he turned just in time to meet the Crab's charge. Da yelled and shoved the spear into the neck of the Crab's mount. The horse screamed, reared, and threw its rider.

"Sugar!" Legs called out.

She turned and saw him holding his hand to his chest. His hand was bleeding. She'd been wrong: one of the arrows *had* found a mark.

She could do nothing against soldiers. But she could help her brother.

"Open the door!" she shouted.

"I can't," he said.

He could, but was too frightened to do anything. The wisterwife charm he always kept about his neck had fallen out of his tunic. Sugar hoped the wisterwives were indeed looking out for them. But the wisterwives would be able to do nothing if they let the house burn down on top of them. Sugar tore herself from the battle that raged out front and crawled to her brother.

"What's happening?" he asked.

"We're going to the woods," said Sugar. "And then . . ." And then she didn't know where. No, they'd go to Horse.

She opened the door.

Fancy was gone. She looked out through the haze and billows of smoke to the edges of the yard and could see her nowhere. But neither could she see any soldiers. They all must have run to the front of the house to join the battle.

A log above them made a deafening burst.

"Take my hand," said Sugar. "We're going to run to the pond, and from there the river. Are you ready?"

There was an immense whoosh, and the heat at Sugar's back seemed to increase tenfold.

"Now," she said. And she and Legs bolted from the house. Down the path they went between the barn and the pheasant house.

When Legs knew a course, he only needed to know where he was at any moment and whether any new obstacles lay in the path. He did not count steps or need to feel about him.

They had taken the path to the new pond many times, for Legs loved the feel of the sun-heated water. And so Sugar only needed to call out his orientation points as they came to them. They ran past the garden and privy to Mother's pheasant house.

Three of the soldiers far to her right fled the battle. She looked back, hoping to see that Mother and Da had scattered the small army.

The whole roof of the house raged with fire; the immense flames wheezed and roared dozens of feet into the sky. Beyond the fire, Da and Mother stood side by side. With one hand Mother pressed her wound; in the other she held a sword. Da held an axe and shield.

It appeared they had put the soldiers to flight. But then the soldiers stopped and turned, forming a line. They weren't fleeing, they were making a space so that the bowmen could shoot without killing a number of their own.

Legs tugged on her.

Mother tried to charge the line, but Da stepped in front of her to stand between her and the soldiers.

The bowmen loosed their arrows. These did not fly wide this time, and despite Da shielding her from most of the shafts, Mother fell to the earth.

Da's battle cry sounded over the raging of the fire. He too charged. The arrows did not penetrate his armor, but a multitude of spears did.

A shout of triumph rose up from the mob.

"Sugar?" asked Legs.

The fire blazed into the sky. The heat, even at this distance, burned her face. She could not catch her breath.

The soldiers converged upon Da like a pack of wild dogs.

She watched their weapons rise and fall. Some began to run toward Mother, but the Crab shouted and brandished his sword to keep them away.

It was a nightmare, but Sugar could not tear her eyes from it.

A man raised a black sword high over Da. That was a Fire blade from the temple.

No, she thought. No.

Then the man swung the sword down like he was chopping a mighty block of wood and hacked Da's head from his body.

She could not move. Could barely breathe. The Crab waved the black-bladed man away from Mother. Then a soldier pointed at her and Legs.

"Sugar," said Legs. "Why are we stopped?"

She realized he had been asking her that over and over. His voice seemed to come from a great distance. It seemed she was watching the whole scene from a great distance.

"It's too hot," said Legs and tugged at her.

She took a step; Legs followed. She broke into a jog. "To the woods, straight through Galson's fields." That's what Mother had said.

She glanced back and saw a number of soldiers running toward them.

"Then to the pond," she said, her voice sounding strange to her ears. "Over the fence and to the pond."

Hand in hand, they ran across Galson's paddock. She felt the knife at her waist. The knife Da had given her. A voice in the back of her mind told her to fight. But the voice was small, so very small.

She saw Fancy lying in the grass, arrows sticking from her, but Sugar only noted it. Her mind was filled with the image of Mother and Da and that terrible black blade. Twice Legs stumbled because of her inattention.

When they reached the pond, Sugar looked back. Soldiers ran through Galson's paddocks toward them. On the far edge of a paddock the district lord rode atop his horse looking for a gate through. She snapped back to the task at hand.

Sugar knew the woods well. She'd played hide-and-seek here and foraged for acorns and firewood. She'd hidden here from the village boys before Da taught her how to fight. The wood was old and in many places did not allow enough light to the ground to support much more than mushrooms. But mushrooms would not hide them. And even if they had cover, the mob would bring dogs.

So Sugar decided they would take the forest creek for their path. She and Legs had a small craft there they sometimes floated on. They would ride the water downstream. And just before they reached the confluence with the main river, they would leave the craft and escape into the woods on the other side.

Sugar looked down at the wisterwife charm Legs wore about his neck. Wisterwives were servants of the seven Creators. It was said that even Regret, the Creator who wanted to destroy the world, was served by them, but neither Mother nor Da had ever seen the creature that had left this charm. "Let us hope the wisterwife is watching us," she said.

Sugar looked back one last time to where Da and Mother had fallen. One of the village women bent over Mother, probably stripping her. It flickered through Sugar's mind that this was hopeless. She should stand here and meet her fate. But she quickly pushed that idea aside and faced the woods.

"You've done this a hundred times, brother. It's over the bluff and to the river."

8.

PREY

Hunger lay under the towering, fat spruce that grew in his glade and felt some small thing, a very small thing, scratching about the grass on his chest. The Mother had said not to devour the men, but she'd never said anything about small things, so he cracked one eye and spied the creature.

It was a . . .

The name floated away.

He grunted.

The names always floated away. His thoughts continually ran from him. Everything fled before his appetite.

Hunger could smell the creature's Fire, its tasty little Fire. Not much, not enough for a meal. But enough to taste.

He watched the creature grasp a stalk of grass on his chest and bend the ragged head of seeds to its mouth.

Before it could take a bite, Hunger snatched the creature up.

The little thing struggled, but in moments Hunger separated it. The Mother had shown him how to do that down in her cave. Fire, soul, and flesh: these three made up all living things, even him with his body of earth and grass. The Mother had shown him what bound the parts all together, and then she'd taught him how to pick and pry until the binding unraveled in his hands. Of course, there were some things he had not yet been able to separate. But the little thing he had in his hands, he knew its secrets.

The tiny body he cast away. The Fire he bolted, increasing the hours of his life, but the soul—the soul he nibbled, oh, so slowly for it was sweet with thought and fear.

Above him a swarm of insects made their comforting click and buzz. Farther up, the tops of the ancient spruce trees moved with a gust of wind. He could smell the Fire in the trees. But their binding resisted him. It was very hard to steal from trees, and he thought that this must be because they had a hunger greater than his. Why else would they hold it so fiercely?

The wind gusted again, and the scent that it carried made him pause.

Could it be?

He opened his mouth to smell it better.

A stink?

He stretched wide his great maw and felt the scent fill him, felt it pool alongside his tongue and down his throat. He began to tremble in anticipation.

Magic. The stink of human magic.

Mother, he called. *Mother!*

He'd caught the scent before, but each time he followed it the trail had vanished before he could find the source. The Mother had told him that was to be expected. He was still young, still growing into his powers. She'd said she made him to smell and see for her, and so there was no doubt that's what he'd do. It was just a matter of time.

He called again. *It's strong this time, strong like a river.*

Soon words came into his mind: *Yes, and can you smell a human female in it?*

Hunger could.

You are ripening, the Mother said. *You are ready. Find the female who wields the powers. Bring her and her brood to me.*

Will you give me some? he asked.

No, she said.

I'll eat them then, he said. *I'll eat them all.*

You'll bring them to me, and I'll know if you take a bite.

I'll eat them, he said. But he knew he wouldn't.

Hunger wanted to taste their souls. He craved their thoughts. Even the thoughts of a little thing full of fear tasted good. So what must it be like to feed on a human?

But if he did, the Mother would know. And she would hurt him. She would send him to the others who had asked her if they might lick and nibble bits of him.

No, he wouldn't tempt himself. He would find the woman and her brood and carry them back whole.

Hunger stood, dirt falling from him to the ground, and lumbered out of his dark glade toward the source of the scent.

BARG DID NOT want to stand watch around the burning ruin of Sparrow's house. Not in the dark. Not on this night. The hunt had gutted Sparrow, his horses, pigs, fowl, and dogs: every living thing. All of the organs went into the raging fires of the smithy and home, followed shortly thereafter by the chopped parts of the various carcasses.

Normally, a criminal's flesh would be left to the vultures and foxes and beasts of the woods. And if no beast would touch it, there were always plenty of maggots. But the hunt dared not leave Sparrow to such a fate. No trace of him could remain. His bones, if any survived the fire, would be scattered on the sea.

They'd obtained a Fire sword from the temple in White-cliff and used it on Sparrow and his beasts. And that gave them some comfort because a Fire sword, forged by the Kains, severed more than flesh. But they had no Seeker, no Divine with the powers to hunt Sleth, to confirm that the soul had fled, and the soul of such a man would be full of wrath. It would linger about. It might even try to possess and ride some weakened man or beast in an effort to ex-act vengeance. No, Barg did not want to go out. But some things had to be done.

He got up off the floor in front of his hearth. The cups and stones of a game of transfer lay before him. His daughter had just taken her turn and ruined his next move.

Their censer of godsweed had stopped smoking. So he picked up the tongs and fetched a hot coal from the fire. He put the coal in the censer and blew until the weed be-gan to smoke again.

They'd burned godsweed until the air was thick with it. Burned it in every room as proof against the souls of the dead. Even so, Barg did not feel safe.

They'd done a wicked thing today, killing the smith. Everyone had said he'd fought with the strength of twenty men, but Barg had seen it. He'd been there with his spear, and he knew Sparrow. The smith was clean, may the Six bless him. And that was all the more reason for his soul to seek justice.

The smith's wife, however, she was something else. She'd probably trapped Sparrow, trapped him like a spider. And like a spider, one day she would have eaten him. The clan lord had demanded they keep her alive for questioning. For bait. They placed the king's collar they'd taken from the royal house around her neck, laid her in the back of a wagon, and had taken her away to the healers.

And it was a good thing, for those who were sent to chase the girl and boy had searched past the river; they'd scoured the woods all the way to the swamps. Lords, they'd even used dogs. But they found nothing. It was impossible—a girl and a blind boy! But the hunt had come back before dark, haggard and empty-handed. That right there was evidence the children knew her wicked ways.

No, Barg did not feel safe. But he wasn't a coward. He felt a great welling satisfaction, for when others had run today, he had stood his ground. The Crab had noted it. And he wasn't going to ruin that honor tonight.

Barg looked at his daughter. She grew brighter each day. He was actually trying to win this game and failing.

He turned to his oldest son. "You're going to have to take my place," he said.

"Why should you go?" asked his wife. "Nobody else will be there. Nobody would dare." She sat at the table braiding the youngest boy's hair for bed.

"They will," he said. "They're counting on me. But I'll be back soon enough. And I think I know a way to take this whole bloody mess off of your mind. We'll go fishing tomorrow."

She looked at him in disbelief. "Fishing?"

He leaned in close, then whispered in her ear so the children couldn't hear. "Happy plans will put the children at ease."

She looked down and said nothing.

Barg kissed her gently on the cheek. Then he considered his girl and two boys. The firelight sparkled in their dark eyes. To think they had played with that woman's hatchlings.

"I'll be back soon enough," he assured them. "We're taking quarter watches is all." Then he belted on his sword and picked up his spear. Foss, their hunting dog, rose to go with him, and Barg opened the door.

The smoke in the room curled out into the night. Barg pointed at the children. "You do your chores and get to bed and when you wake up in the morning, we'll be off."

"To the river or the beach?" asked his oldest.

They loved the beach. It would be a long day, but it would give them something to think about.

"The beach," he said. "We'll roast crabs."

Then he shut the door behind him. He took a long drink of water from the bucket at the well then set off down the path that led to the smith's ruin, Foss padding along at his side.

He could see the last flames of Sparrow's house burning at the other end of the field. The fires burned low, but they still cast enough light to silhouette the remains of Sparrow's barn and outbuildings. The smoke of the fires hung heavily in the air.

Barg glanced back at his house a few times as he walked. The shutters were latched and snug. His wife had barred the door. They would be fine.

As Barg got closer to the flames he could see that something was amiss—nobody was there. There were supposed to be ten men on each watch.

Perhaps they were all bunched up behind the barn.

He rounded the corner of the barn and looked across Sparrow's yard.

Nothing. His wife had been right. None of the others were here.

The house and smithy had burned down to coals and ashes. Here and there a few fires still burned, but they were small. Much smaller than it appeared from his house. Still, he could feel the heat of the coals. The whole mess still produced a blistering heat.

A small flame rose at the edge of a blackened log close to him only to disappear moments later.

All was silent except for the crackling and popping of the fire. The circle of light did not extend far into the swallowing darkness.

Cowards.

He'd roust them out of bed, every one.

Then he saw someone standing in the shadows at the edge of where the house had stood. The man moved aside a log, kicking up sparks. He reached into the hot coals and pulled something out.

"Ha," Barg called to him. "It's good to see there's more than one stout heart among us."

Foss stopped and began to growl.

Then the man straightened up and turned, and Barg got a look at him in the firelight.

He was taller than anyone Barg had ever seen, but his arms and legs were thicker than they should be. And his face—it was all wrong. He had a mouth that was dark, ragged, and huge. A mouth that seemed to crack his head in two.

This was no man.

A tuft of hair on the creature's arm caught fire. The flame sputtered, flashed, and receded into red and yellow sparks that fell to the ground. Then Barg realized it wasn't hair. It was grass. Patches all along its arm had burned, some of them still full of dull red sparks. A clump of smoldering grass fell from the creature's arm to the ground.

Barg saw what the creature held. It was Sparrow's scorched leg, reduced to bone.

The creature flung Sparrow's leg aside and began to walk toward Barg. The ashes and coals of the smithy stood between them, but the creature did not walk around them. It walked straight into the blistering coals, over a tangle of charcoal logs, and through one of the remaining fires. The long ragged grass about its legs began to burn and smoke, but the creature did not waver or cry out.

Gods, Barg thought. Keep your calm. Keep your calm.

The thing's mouth gaped like a cavern. Its eyes. Lords, where were its eyes? And then he saw them—two pits all askew.

Filthy rot. Filthy, twisted rot. Regret himself had sent this thing.

Barg set himself for a throw. Then he took two steps, yelled, and, with all his might, hurled the spear.

The creature did not flinch or step aside, and the spear buried itself in the creature's chest.

"To arms!" Barg shouted and unsheathed his sword. "We're attacked! To arms! To arms!"

There would be others here shortly. And together they would dispatch this monster. All Barg had to do was keep his courage. Keep it like he'd done this morning and not run away.

The creature strode on as if nothing had happened. It plucked the spear out of its chest like a man plucking staw from his tunic and flung it into the ashes.

Foss surged forward to the edge of the coals, but Barg took a step backward, turned, and fled.

Foss snarled and barked. Then he yelped.

Barg heard the dog's footfalls behind him. He turned and saw Foss, neck stretched out, galloping for his life. Foss caught Barg up and sped past.

And behind, the creature loped after them, a thin line of fire burning up one of its sides.

Barg realized he was running the wrong way, away from the the other houses and help. But to go back to the houses meant he would run back toward the beast.

Then he saw the door to his house open, the firelight behind, and his wife standing silhouetted in the door.

"No," he yelled. "Go back!" But it was too late and he knew it. The creature would have seen her. Even if he were to change his direction now, the monster might not follow him.

"Get the children!" he yelled as he ran into the yard.

"Barg?" his wife said in alarm. Then her face twisted in horror and she backed into the house.

Barg heard the creature chuff behind him.

He turned around, holding his sword at the ready.

It stood not ten paces away. The fire had risen and burned the creature's shoulder and head.

Courage. All he needed was a bit of courage.

He saw movement in the village. He heard men shouting. But they were running the wrong way, running to the smith's.

"To me!" he cried. "To me!"

The creature opened its mouth wide and drew in a hoarse breath. It turned its head toward the door of the house.

"No, you won't," said Barg. "You filthy abomination, you'll feel my steel first." He let out a yell and, for the second time today, charged, his blade held high.

The creature took a step toward him.

Barg brought his blade down in a cut that would have cleaved a man from collarbone to belly.

But the creature simply grabbed the blade in midswing, reached out with its free, rough hand, and took Barg by the face.

Barg struggled in its stony grasp. And then he was slipping, twisting, falling into another place entirely.

MILES AWAY, SUGAR crouched in the moon shadows at the edge of the forest and looked across a river at the farmstead of Hogan the Koramite. The man she knew as Horse.

"Is the water deep?" whispered Legs.

"I don't know," said Sugar.

"Do you think he will help?"

"This is where Mother sent us," said Sugar. But in her heart she knew the chances of him helping them were slim. If Horse harbored them, he put his whole family at risk. But if he delivered them to the hunt, he, even as a Koramite, would earn a fortune.

"I think I'm wicked," said Legs.

"You're not wicked," said Sugar.

"I should have listened to the wisterwife."

"What are you talking about?"

"Sometimes, when I held the charm, she would call to me like I was lost."

Sugar looked at her brother. She'd never heard of such a thing. "She called to you?"

"In my mind. I could see her. She was beautiful. And sometimes I could see something else with her. Something made of earth, dark and wild and . . ."

Sugar waited while Legs found the words.

"Something in her voice," he said, "it was horrible and wonderful. Every time I heard her, fear stabbed me because I didn't want someone to think I was like old Chance. I didn't want to be mad and taken to the altars for hearing voices in my head. And so I never answered. She said that the fullness of time had come. She promised to make me whole. Promised all sorts of things. Lunatic promises. But I was too scared. I think she wanted to help."

Sugar thought about the wisterwife charm. All this time they'd thought it was a blessing, a gift. It was an annual ritual for most people to fashion a Creator's wreath and hang it above their door to draw the blessings of the wisterwives. It was fashioned with rock and leaf, feathers and bones. Many set out a gift of food or cast it upon the waters. But Regret had his servants as well. So who knew what this charm really was? She thought of Mother and her horrible speed, her terrible secrets. That charm could be anything. "You think it was real?"

"I don't know what to think." No sound escaped him, but his eyes began to brim with tears, and he ducked his head the way he always did when he was in pain.

Sugar wanted to cry with him, wanted to feel overwhelming grief. But she was empty, as desolate as rock. And that pained her as much as anything else. What kind of daughter was it that had no tears for the butchering of her parents? What kind of daughter was it who ran? She had a knife. She knew how to use it.

"Da always said you were an uncanny judge of character," said Sugar. "If your heart tells you to be afraid, then let's trust it. Da always did."

Legs leaned into her, and she took him into an embrace, putting his face in her neck and stroking his hair.

Things to act and things to be acted upon. She had a knife. Lords, she'd had at least six, for there were a number in the kitchen. She could have done something. She could have sent Legs to the pheasant house, gone around back herself, and surprised that line of bowmen. She could have distracted a whole group of men. She might have tipped the battle.

Why? Why had she run?

And if she hadn't run, if, beyond hope, she'd tipped the battle, what then? She'd seen Mother. Seen her horrible power.

Legs gently pulled away. "Will we talk to Horse?"

They had no tools to survive in the wild. Besides, an army of hunters would be combing the outer woods, expecting them to run there. If Horse helped them, and that was a desperate if, then maybe they might be able to survive until all but the most patient hunters gave up dreams of a bounty and went back to their normal labors. If she and Legs survived that long, that's when they would escape.

"I don't know," said Sugar. "Let's just take this one step at a time. Right now we need to find where they ford this river."

9.

HATCHLING

Talen still ached from the beating he'd taken at Stag Home. He stood, took off his wide-brimmed straw hat, and wiped his brow. Then he gingerly felt his ribs and looked for Da. Nettle had returned from taking his message to the Creek Widow long ago. But there was still no sign of Da.

Nettle threw another pitchfork full of dried bracken onto the wagon bed. They still had three windrows of the stuff to haul off the hill. From the time Da left until now, Talen had eyed the woods every chance he got. But after hours of vigilance, and seeing nothing more exciting than three hogs rooting for acorns in the distance, he began to think less of the dangers and more on the promised bounty.

The reward was a miller's annual wage. Goh, he could buy a Kish bow for that.

And why couldn't a Koramite bring them in?

Why couldn't *he* bring them in?

Sleth were wily and dangerous. And maybe he'd need help. After all, it was said Sleth had animal strength and could twist your head off as easily as a housewife could twist the head off a chicken.

Nevertheless, they were, after all, only children. Not full Sleth.

He and Nettle piled the wagon high with another dozen forkfuls of bracken then took it to the last haystacking site. Prince Conroy, their red rooster, clambered up on top, surveying the world as the wagon moved along.

They put a thick layer of the long fronds at the base of this last site for the hay they'd use this winter to feed their horse, cattle, and small flock of sheep. A thick bracken base kept a dry layer between the hay and ground. They'd also cut enough for lining bundles of foodstuff, for the rats did not like chewing through it because it made their mouths sore.

When they'd finished the last stacking site, Nettle said, "I'm hungry."

"You're always hungry," said Talen. "You stinking Mokaddian garlic-eater."

"Koramite goat-lover," Nettle shot back.

Talen smiled. This name-calling had been their joke for some time now. And with the possibility of Talen being adopted into Argoth's clan as a member by privilege but not blood, it took on a new meaning. Of course, Talen had already been recognized by the Koramite Council and granted a man's braid to hang from his belt.

The Koramites didn't proclaim their clan or male-rights by elaborate tattoos. One small tattoo was sufficient. Your clan was in your blood. What more did you need? And your male-rights were things you earned or lost by your actions. Talen's braid, which was only to be worn at formal occasions, was kept in a box with those for Ke and Da. It was a simple leather braid with three silver beads. Other men with greater capacities extended their belts and added disks. Some were worn from a shoulder. But regardless of the rights granted, the braid was a privilege that could be taken away. Not a right to be painted on.

In the meadow, River and Ke turned the rows of cut grass with their hay forks so it could finish drying. A flock of blackbirds followed behind, picking through the grass for a meal.

"I'll start on that acre your da wants cleared for the oats next spring," said Nettle. "You get something to eat."

"I thought you were supposed to be riding with your da today anyway, not here eating up all our food."

"No, the captain wouldn't let me come on patrol." Nettle referred to his father this way when he was dissatisfied with him. "He made some excuse again."

Uncle Argoth was responsible for watching a stretch of coastline. "He's just trying to protect you," said Talen.

"I don't want protection. Half of the men resent me because they've been ordered, behind my back, to keep me safe. So instead of being a full member of the patrol, I'm a burden. To the other half I'm nothing but a joke. They might as well bring along an infant in arms."

"You don't know what they're thinking."

"I can read a man's eyes," said Nettle. "I've heard their whispers and seen their patronizing smiles." He shook his head in disgust.

Talen didn't know what to say so he just nodded. Of course, why court death when you didn't have to? He was happy he didn't have patrol duties and was about to say this when Nettle looked at him honestly.

"I envy you," said Nettle.

"Me?" asked Talen. Nettle had everything: looks, wealth, the right blood. He might not be a giant like Da or Ke, but he was larger than Talen. And he had a father who was a captain in the Shoka clan.

"Not you exactly," Nettle said and grinned. "But your da trusts you. You have your braid. He treats you like a man. You almost have your life taken and he simply dusts you off and sends you out to the fields to work."

"If it's damage you want," said Talen, "let me find a stick. I'd be happy to give you a good thrashing. Especially since you failed to come to my aid this morning."

"See," said Nettle, "my passivity is becoming habitual. I'm sick to death of being coddled. I want to do something real."

No he didn't, Talen thought. There is no joy in being on the receiving end of the stick. "The acre that needs to be cleared is real," said Talen. "And don't worry about stumps. We'll just plow around them. When they're good and rotted they'll come out just fine."

"Whatever," said Nettle, obviously frustrated with Talen's response.

Talen picked up the hoggin. He might as well fill it back up with water. But when he turned to walk back to the house, he got a chill. There were stories of one Sleth lord who had lain in wait for his victims in their cellars. Talen and the others had been working out in the fields since before noon. That was plenty of time for hatchlings to move about and hide in a cellar.

"What are you doing?" asked Nettle. "I thought you were going to get some food."

"Nothing," said Talen. But, of course, he was doing something—he was acting like a coward again. "Just thinking about what we're going to have for a snack." Then he strode toward the house as quickly as his injuries would let him, hoggin slung under his arm.

Prince Conroy jumped off the wagon and accompanied him back.

Conroy was fierce beyond all reckoning. To rodents, that was. Or cats. Or weasels. Lately he'd been giving the squirrels what for. But it was his violence with rats that had won him his name. The real Conroy was a prince of story who had scoured his city of a nasty infestation of rats. Talen's Prince Conroy loved nothing more than to drop like a stone upon a rodent, skewer it with his talons, and then peck it to a bloody pulp.

There were other roosters that would fly into an attack when they felt threatened or one of their hens screamed. And most chickens would snatch up a mouse and run off with the prize to eat it. But Conroy, it seemed, went looking for rats. He was, in his rat hunting, better than a dog. Of course, he wouldn't be much against Sleth.

Conroy darted ahead of Talen to chase a white and black butterfly, following it into the tall weeds.

The barn, old house, and smoke shed stretched away from Talen like a crooked arm on his left while the pigpen, garden, and privy stretched out on his right.

When he came to the barn, he heard a scuffle by the wood stack alongside the far wall.

His heart jumped. He realized he had no weapon but the hoggin.

It could have been a rat, he told himself.

"Conroy," he called. He made the trill and yip that always brought the rooster. When Conroy came running, Talen looked down at the bird. "It's time to earn your keep," he said and pointed to the side of the barn to where the wood was stacked. They'd gone rat hunting like this many times before. He made another trill and yip and Conroy dashed around the corner of the barn.

He waited and heard nothing.

This would go down well in the stories, he thought. The mighty hunter stays back and sends his rooster in to deal with the danger. Talen took a deep breath and marched around the barn so he could get a good look down the wall.

Conroy stood alone, eyeing the woodpile.

So, it *was* a rat. Talen walked down to the spot where he figured the sound had come from and kicked the wood. He waited for a scrabble of tiny claws. What he heard instead was someone running away from the back of the barn.

Talen's heart quickened. He took the last three steps to the back of the barn, giving the corner a wide berth just in case something was there.

Conroy lingered for a moment, eyeing the wood stack, and then trotted after Talen.

Talen saw nothing behind the barn, but then out of the corner of his eye he caught movement. He turned toward it and saw someone's back and one of their legs disappear behind the old house.

Lords, he was not imagining it.

"Sammesh?" he said.

Sammesh was the ale sot's son. Da had caught him once stealing meat from the smoke shed. But instead of putting some fear into the boy, Da told him if he wanted meat, he'd have to bring something to trade. So from that day on, Sammesh slinked in and out of their place with his trade. Sometimes it was fair; other times, it wasn't. He'd once taken a rope and left a small bowl of blueberries for it. The blueberries had been delicious but they were not worth half the value of that rope. Talen had told his da that he was only fostering dishonesty—Sammesh needed to be taught a lesson. But Da said Sammesh had received far too many of those kinds of lessons already. Talen wondered if that's where all the boy's bruises came from. Or was it simply because he was a thief?

Talen picked up a short cudgel from the woodpile and walked toward the old house.

"Sammesh! Come out, or I'll thrash the stumps with you."

There was no answer.

"An honest trader doesn't skulk."

Then he heard another sound behind the old house. He paused and listened, but all was quiet.

Something was there.

He had seen the back of a figure too small to be that of an adult. Too small for even Sammesh.

"Who are you?" said Talen. "Come out."

Of course, maybe he didn't want them to come out. Ke and River were too far away to be of any help; and if this were a hatchling . . . who knew what it might do? He wished he had his dogs. Then he realized he hadn't seen them at all out in the fields. And that was odd. Where were the dogs?

Talen called for them.

Moments later Blue appeared from behind the old house, exactly where the skulker had disappeared. Blue wagged his tail and gave a happy bark.

Conroy made a low sound and hopped a few paces away. Then, with a great deal of noisy flapping, he flew up to the roof of the smoke shed. Despite Talen's attempts to make them reconcile, the bird and the dog did not get along.

The dog's warren lay underneath the old house on the far side. Blue must have been there the whole time.

But he should have barked.

Talen took a few steps, again giving the corner a wide berth, and peered along the side of the old house.

He saw nothing but Queen wriggling her way out of the hole they'd dug underneath the house.

Talen raced back to see between the old house and the barn. Perhaps whoever it was had run around. But he saw nothing.

If it was Sammesh, he'd clobber him. This was no time to be running about stealing meat.

Talen yelled and ran about the old house itself; halfway around he reversed directions to trick whomever it was.

Blue thought it was some game and followed him the whole way with playful woofs.

Nobody was there. Yet Talen had seen someone. He wasn't imagining it.

He looked down at Blue. What good was a dog that didn't bark? "You're a fine fellow," said Talen.

Blue licked Talen's hand then wiggled his way between Talen's legs.

Talen groaned and shook his head. Overfed and under-worked, that's what that dog was. Talen pushed Blue away and gave him the eye. Then he walked over to the side of the old house where he'd seen the figure disappear. The line of the woods was a good thirty yards from here. It would have to have been an exceedingly lively creature to cover that distance between the time Talen had heard that last noise and seen Blue. And it would have had to run very quietly.

That ruled out Sammesh.

Goh. He gripped the cudgel tighter.

He thought of the sod roof. The edges were low enough for someone to climb. They could be up there getting ready to spring. Talen spun around and scampered back.

There was nothing on the roof. He circled the whole house again, scanning the ground for footprints.

Nothing.

He took a step back and out of the corner of his eye saw something in the grass: one of their painted wooden spoons lying at an odd angle. He bent over and picked it up. It had not been out here long because soft bits of barley porridge still clung to it. Whoever or whatever it was had been in the house and dropped it here.

Talen scanned the yard about him.

The Sleth hatchlings were here, in the woods, watching. Talen was sure of it.

He studied the woods and backed away.

For some reason the dogs hadn't barked, hadn't even smelled the intruder when it was only a few paces away.

It was said that Sleth had some power over beasts. He cast a wary glance at Blue and Queen. Could they have been subverted?

He studied the dogs, but could see nothing that might reveal the truth of it.

Talen retreated back to the well.

He could run or bluff, but running was not proving a good choice today.

Talen kept an eye about and drew the first bucket of water. He cleared his throat.

"One of these days, you beast-loving tanner's pot, we are going to catch you and let you join your mother in the cage."

He waited for a response.

"You've come to the wrong farm, you yeasty boil."

Talen poured the water into the hoggin then dropped the bucket back down into the well.

He scanned the tree line again. If the thing charged at him out of the woods, it would catch him before he got to the pigpen.

But then, if the hatchling were going to attack him, it could have done it earlier.

His heart raced, but you had to fight fear; had to fake courage sometimes until it came of its own accord. Children, Da had said. Only children.

"Sleth child," Talen called out, "as you can plainly see, I do not fear you. Nor do we fear your abominable depredations." He realized his talk *had* taken the edge off his fear. So he continued, "You want something to eat? Eh?

Come out and I'll feed you. How about a moldy crust of bread eaten and shat out by our pig for supper?"

No response, only the leaves of the trees swaying in the small breeze.

The villagers this morning, they'd come after him, not out of fear, but dreaming of a fat bounty. Dreaming of this very opportunity.

Had the bailiff not said that a Koramite should bring the hatchlings in?

Something shifted inside him. His fear deserted him, and he suddenly wasn't thinking about what the hatchlings might do to him. He was thinking of what *he* could do with them. What they could do for him.

If he were adopted into the Shoka, he would still be Koramite, still owe duties to his ancestors. Being a Shoka by priviledge did not change your blood. But Talen didn't know if the adoption would really change his prospects. He'd still be a halfbreed in most people's eyes. However, if he could catch these hatchlings, it might not only mitigate some of the ill will against his people, but it might also prove the quality of Da's line, prove the quality of Talen's breeding.

Those villagers could dream all they wanted. They weren't going to get the bounty. Oh, no. He thought of the tales of the heroes who had hunted Sleth. Not all of them were from the ranks of the high and mighty. Maybe a little Koramite would win a spot in the chronicles.

He could see himself purchasing that fine, Kishman's bow, made of wood, horn, and sinew, wrapped at the ends with yellow and scarlet thread. There wasn't a people who could make better bows than the Kish. But why settle for a bow? He'd get himself a horse.

Talen drew up a third bucket, emptied it into the hoggin, and replaced the lid.

He addressed the old sod house. "Every soul worth his salt will be hunting your clay-brained trail. You're going to end up a boiled çabbage no matter what you do." He paused. "You should have never begun with the dark art. But turn yourself in to me and you'll avoid a wicked beating. That's a promise you'll not get from any other quarter."

There was no answer, only the voices of Ke and Nettle in the distance.

He realized then if the hatchling were an angry thing, it would kill Talen and stop his mouth. But it was either stupid or scared, for it had thrown away a perfectly good chance. Or maybe it was waiting for its master, the one that slew the butcher's family in the village of Plum.

That thought sent chills up his spine. That was a creature no lone Koramite would take. But he wasn't going to let the fear of such things overcome him. It obviously wasn't here now. And standing at the well all day wasn't going to do him any good either, so he walked to the house with as much ease as he could muster and fetched the figs.

When he came back out he paused. "You're a fool to refuse my offer," Talen called. He hefted the hoggin onto his shoulder, gave the farm one last glance, and headed back out to the fields. This time Blue and Queen came with him, Conroy bringing up the rear.

On the way he began to think of ways to catch the hatchlings. He wasn't going to be able to corner them like normal animals. Oh, no. He was going to need something entirely different.

TALEN DISTRIBUTED THE figs and passed the water to Ke. Nettle sat on the trunk of tree Ke and River had just felled. Next to him leaned the two-man saw. A strand of Talen's hair had come out of the leather string Talen had tied it with. After Sabin's yank this morning, Talen was about ready to have Nettle hack it all off with his knife. But he undid the string, gathered his hair up, and said, "You said you wanted to do something real? Well, we've got ourselves a whale of an opportunity."

Nettle plopped a fig in his mouth. "What do you mean?"

Talen faced the three of them. "I spotted the trouser thief."

"Somebody actually stole your pants?" asked Nettle.

Ke rolled his eyes.

"Not somebody," said Talen. "The hatchling. And we are going to get the bounty."

Nettle blinked.

"What are you talking about?" asked Ke.

Talen related what had happened back at the house.

"We need to alert the bailiff or territory lord," said Nettle.

"No, no. That's exactly what we shouldn't do. We don't want some idiot Mokaddian getting the reward."

"Excuse me?" said Nettle. "I don't think Mokaddians were the problem this time."

"I'm not talking about you," said Talen. "You know that isn't what I mean. Think about what people will say when a Koramite brings them in."

"Except we're not full Koramite," said Ke.

"That isn't the point," said Talen. "We have an opportunity."

"Did you see their faces?" asked River.

"There was only one of them."

"But did you see more than a leg?"

"No."

"Then it could have been anybody. It could have been a beggar. Could have been some stranger passing through."

"Nobody can run that fast."

"Come on," said Ke. "We'd all love to catch us one.

But it takes fifty to a hundred men to conduct a proper hunt."

"Not to catch children," said Talen. "Besides, I've worked it out. All we need is a counterweight and a rope."

"Have you forgotten Da's last words?" asked River. "This is how innocent people get killed."

"*Somebody* was there," said Talen.

"Then we keep our wits about us," said River, "and our eyes open."

"And our knives at the ready," said Nettle. He looked up at Talen, the turning of his mind showing in his eyes. "This isn't one of your pig-brained jokes, is it?"

"No pigs," said Talen. "And I don't intend on getting close enough to use a knife. I'm perfectly happy to use my bow."

AT THE FAR end of the dog warren underneath the sod house Sugar lay still as stone, her back pressed into the dirt wall. She hugged Legs to her chest. Above her head a monstrous yellow spider scuttled along the underside of the floorboards.

"I think he's gone," said Legs. "I can only hear the breeze."

She was hungry and thirsty. Her hair was full of dirt and filth. She had taken great comfort in the dogs, but now realized how childish that was.

"We're not safe," she said. "This place is not safe."

10.

BATTLE

It was almost midday and Argoth kept himself hidden behind a screen made by an immense rock and a thick clump of blackberry briar. With him on this side of the steep ravine were fifteen of the best fighters the Shoka had. The same number had concealed themselves on the other side of the ravine. All lay in wait, their bows ready.

The mouth of the ravine opened up onto a wide meadow, deep with brown and dark green grasses. A stream ran through the meadow and out of sight behind a thick grove of river birch on the far end.

Argoth looked at the group with him, gauging them. There were a few young men here of Nettle's age. He wondered, should he have brought the boy? Nettle was eager. He was of age. And when he'd demanded to know why he couldn't come, Argoth had no answer. Nettle was skilled, but he just wasn't ready.

A fly landed on Argoth's lips and he shooed it away. Where was Varro? It was past time. He and his ridiculous, bleach-streaked beard should have ridden into view long ago, leading their quarry into the trap.

Argoth was just about ready to break position and organize a search when Varro burst from behind the grove of river birch, riding his spotted steed at a full gallop.

Moments later a dozen riders rounded the same corner, their horses stretched out, racing to catch him. Most of them wore helmets and shaped-leather cuirasses festooned with various furs. One man rode with a mail tunic, another was bare-chested. All had their faces painted white and black. All of them Bone Face rot.

Varro splashed across the stream, and then he cut through the deep meadow grass, making straight for the steep ravine where Argoth and the rest of the men waited.

Argoth gave the hand signal to get ready, and his men nocked their arrows. Each man clutched four others in the hand that held their bow.

Their goal was to kill most of these dung heaps but keep one or two for the Shoka warlord to question. A band of Bone Faces had been sallying forth from this quarter, and it was time to be rid of them and find out if they were on their own or scouts for a far larger raiding party.

This was going to be like shooting rabbits in a hutch.

Varro closed half the distance to the ravine, then his horse stumbled and rolled, throwing Varro wide into the tall brown and green meadow grass.

The horse screamed and struggled to its feet, but it couldn't stand straight. One of its forelegs was broken. Argoth winced; it must have stepped into the hole of a fox or ground squirrel.

The horse limped, but Varro was up, running, cutting his way through the tall grass.

His pursuers gained on him, but not by much. Varro was a dreadman, one of those upon whom the Divines had bestowed a weave of might. He ran with the speed of that weave, flying through the meadow with enormous, quick strides. He was fast to begin with, and his weave doubled, almost tripled, the liveliness with which he ran.

But then he slowed.

What was he doing? This wasn't a time for tricks. All he needed to do was run into the ravine.

He slowed even further until he ran with the speed of a normal man.

Varro glanced back over his shoulder, and when he turned back around, Argoth could see from Varro's expression that something was terribly wrong.

He wasn't going to make the ravine. He wasn't going to make it out of the meadow.

Argoth rose. "Mount up," he called. "Mount up!" It was possible the Bone Faces had a dreadman among them. But he wouldn't be one of those in heavy armor. Dreadmen only wore such when they were sure to be fighting their own kind. In most battles it was speed they desired. Brutal, blinding speed.

Argoth put away his doubts about sending Nettle to help Hogan with his harvest. This type of battle would have thrown the boy into a situation he was not prepared for. Exactly the type of situation into which he'd put his son, of a different wife and in a different land, so many years ago.

In one step he mounted his stallion. Then he gave him his heels and was flying down the narrow trail, hugging his steed's thick neck, dodging branches all the way to the bottom of the ravine.

By the time Argoth galloped out of the ravine, holding his bow and guiding his horse with his knees, the Bone Faces had surrounded Varro and beat him to the ground. He lay on his face with two men holding him down, but Argoth could not tell if he was still alive.

The bare-chested man knelt at Varro's feet, binding them with a rope. The man's face, from his forehead to the crack of his mouth, had been painted black; from his lower lip down was white.

Argoth let out his battle cry and guessed if they had a dreadman, it would be the bare-chested one. None of them wore insignia, but that one had the hard-cut look of one who used a weave.

The Bone Faces turned.

Argoth stood a little higher in his stirrups and released his first arrow. He immediately took the second from the clutch he held in his bow hand.

The first arrow would have skewered a normal man. But Bare Chest dodged to the side, and the arrow flew past into the lower leg of the rider behind him, pinning the rider's leg to his horse.

The horse reared and screamed.

A volley of arrows from the thirty behind him buzzed past. Two of the raiders fell to the ground and writhed. More horses screamed and bolted.

Argoth raised his fist and made the sign for a split attack. There were two ways to deal with dreadmen. Either you smashed their support, or you ignored the support and hoped you got to the dreadman before he could build his Fire. Argoth chose the second. He signaled ten of his men to attack the regular Bone Faces. And he hoped with all his might they were indeed all regulars. Then he broke off with his remaining twenty men.

The two who had been holding Varro grabbed the reins of their horses and tried to mount. One took an arrow in the back and fell. The other made his saddle.

The end of the rope which they'd used to bind Varro was tied to the pommel of that saddle. The rider put his heels to his horse and shot away. Varro yanked about and began to drag behind. But, thank the Creators, the man only dragged Varro a few yards before he cut him loose to gain speed.

Argoth focused on the dreadman. He had not attempted to mount his horse. That, and the fact that none had been able to catch Varro before, meant that his horse had not been multiplied.

Bare Chest ran through the grass with a wild speed toward the wood. They couldn't let that happen. With the cover of bush and branches, he'd effectively reduce the odds from one to twenty to one to two or three. And that would be suicide for Argoth's men.

Argoth raced his steed, gave him full rein, but he wasn't catching up to the man. He and his men sent forth another volley of arrows, but within two strides the dreadman stopped, turned, and the arrows flew long.

Then the dreadman rushed at them, sword drawn. It was a simple tactic, and Argoth saw it for what is was, but they didn't have time to adjust. Within seconds they were upon him, still holding their bows.

The dreadman entered their charge on the far side, away from Argoth.

Argoth saw a flash of steel. Two horses stumbled and cried out. The dreadman turned, pulled a third man from his saddle. Then the dreadman, running alongside, jumped onto the mount's back and guided it to strike at another of Argoth's men. A flash of steel. An arm fell to the ground. The dreadman turned to another, threw a knife into the rump of the man's mount. When the horse cried out and stumbled, the dreadman severed the man's head from his body.

By the time Argoth shoved his bow into the hooks behind his saddle and drew his sword, the dreadman had either killed, dismounted, or incapacitated four others.

The remaining riders separated so the dreadman would be forced to commit to one target, allowing the others to regroup.

At that moment the dreadman could have made his move toward the wood, but he didn't. He rode after the closest man.

Brash, foolish. This one was a risk-taker.

Argoth wheeled his horse toward Bare Chest and gathered the Fire of his Days. He didn't need a gift from the Divines to multiply his strength and speed, for Argoth knew the lore of the Divines. Or, at least, a part of it.

But none of his men would see it that way.

The Divines had proclaimed and enforced their lies for so long that none knew the truth when they saw it. According to the Divines, any power wielded outside their control was Slethery, and since the Divines held the power, who was to gainsay them? It was true many who had used the lore on their own became abominations and horrors, but even the Divines were not immune to that. Many Sleth stole life from others, but so did the Divines.

In fact, not only did the Divines steal Fire, they stole soul. That was the difference between the Order Argoth followed and that of the Divines. It was the Divines who were the Sleth.

But who knew that secret? Not even his men would believe him if he told it to them, which meant that if he was exposed, they would kill him. They'd be bound to, they'd be compelled to, for in their minds he would present the worst danger they could imagine.

And they would have been right seventeen years ago before he found the Order. But that was all behind him now. He was a changed man. The Order had opened his eyes.

It was going to be risky going up against this foe, for who would believe a regular soldier, even one as skilled as he was, could best a dreadman? Nevertheless, he gathered his Fire, that spark of life that animated a man. Once he had enough of it gathered, he could expend it all in a rush, multiplying his natural abilities. Of course, it wasn't without cost. A man only had so much Fire, and when it was gone, the soul and body quickly separated from each other. But Argoth had decided long ago that there were things for which he'd trade the limited days of his life. Those close to him, including the men of his company, were worth such a sacrifice. But it took time to gather enough Fire to make any difference, and he didn't have time.

The dreadman galloped hard at the hindquarters of another of Argoth's riders. He raised his sword and slashed the animal's rump. The horse faltered, and the dreadman pulled even with the rider.

The rider parried two blows from the dreadman, but the third took him square in the face, knocking him into the grass.

This couldn't continue: the dreadman would kill them all.

Argoth cried out a challenge.

The dreadman saw him and turned his horse.

Argoth was not fully multiplied. But he didn't care. This bare-chested piece of rot was going down. He was going to be strung up with his own guts.

The dreadman put his heels into his horse, and, within a few strides, he and Argoth rode full gallop at each other. Joy gleamed in the dreadman's eye, and he smiled. The diseased beast-lover smiled.

Well, Argoth had a trick or two of his own. He took his sword in his left hand and drew his bodkin. With all the strength he could muster he threw it.

The bodkin flashed in the sun. The dreadman saw it and tried to swerve, but the blade buried itself in the horse just below its shoulder.

The horse stumbled and cast the dreadman off balance. But he didn't have time to leap away.

As Argoth's horse closed the distance, he swung his sword in a backhanded arc and sliced the man in the side.

The dreadman cried out and fell.

It was not a mortal blow. But it was a start.

Argoth brought his horse around for another charge. He put his heels into the horse's flanks and shot forth, sword held ready to strike.

And that is when the dreadman made his second mistake. He should have run. Instead he turned to face Argoth. One of Argoth's men had kept his bow. And it only took a moment for him to draw, release, and speed the shaft deep into the dreadman's back.

The dreadman arched, twisted. A second arrow followed the first and struck him in the ribs. Then Argoth thundered down upon him. The dreadman turned, the joy replaced by hate. He raised his sword, but it was too late, and Argoth drove his own weapon deep into the man's chest and left it there.

He galloped a number of yards farther and turned his horse, waiting for the dreadman to fall. When he did, Argoth's remaining men converged.

Argoth whistled and signaled for a portion of those remaining to find and help the ten who had split off from the main group to chase the other Bone Faces down.

The men would hack the dreadman's head off to ensure he was dead. Then they would remove his weave, although none would dare touch it directly. It was impossible to know what traps might be worked into any given weave by looking at it. And even if the men knew the weave had no traps, they would still handle it with great care.

Weaves were endowments, created by a special order of Divines called Kains, and bestowed upon a man or woman for a special task. Sometimes the Divines bestowed a weave upon a group, a family or company of men, who shared its use. There were many types of weaves. Some were crowns, others armbands, others necklaces or piercings. There was even one made by the Mungo Divines that was a coat of grass. Some weaves were given for healing, some for sight, some to allow its bearer to speak to the dead.

Some needed a loremaster to use them. Others, called wildweaves, could be used by anyone. Varro had been given one of these—a ring that would magnify its bearer for war.

Whatever the purpose of the weave, only those included

in its covenant could wear it. And then only the specific weave given them by the Divine. To use a weave outside a specific covenant was high treason and punished by death. And none of these men would want to be accused of even the slightest infraction.

Argoth turned to ride back to Varro.

Just a little more than a year ago Varro had been recommended by the Shoka warlord to become a dreadman. It was a great honor to him and his family, but it was also a burden. Dreadmen wielded immense powers, but they were expected to fight more frequently and with greater valor. Placing oneself in so many battles exposed a man to enormous risk, even for a dreadman. And so it was that while a weave might claim a long genealogy of heroes, it also claimed many who had ended up maimed or dead.

Argoth hoped Varro had escaped that fate today. He was one of the best men Argoth had ever commanded, and that was well before he'd been called to the covenant.

A Bone Face with a wounded leg tried to crawl away through the grass. "Bind him for questioning," said Argoth. Then he went to Varro, dismounted, and knelt at his side.

Varro was more than just another fine asset, he was a friend. His hands and feet were bound and he bled from a deep slice in his gut. He obviously had not gone down without a fight.

Argoth looked for Varro's bodkin, but it was not in its sheath. So he used a stick to work loose Varro's knots.

Varro groaned and looked up at Argoth.

"Are you alive, man?" Argoth asked. It was a joke among his troops to ask this. For if the man were dead, it was said Argoth would reach through to the other side and punish the man for slacking. Not even death would hide his men from discipline and drilling.

"Skewered, Captain," said Varro. Then he winced.

"Only a scratch, mind you. I've got a jig"—another wince—"or two still in me."

Argoth smiled grimly. The cut into Varro's bowels might prove to be his death. Yet another life consumed by this weave.

"What were you doing, running like that?" Argoth demanded.

"The weave," said Varro. He took in a sharp breath. "It failed."

But that was impossible.

Argoth picked up Varro's hand and looked at his ring.

The ring was gold. Cursed gold. Not black with magic, not even gray. Grass, silver, or gold, it didn't matter what the weaves were made of; when the Kains drew Fire into them, the device turned as black as a crow. The more power that went into it, the blacker the weave. But this one was now nothing more than a ring.

Argoth finished untying Varro. It was possible to damage a weave so that it leaked Fire. Argoth asked Varro if he might remove it, and Varro consented. Argoth held it up in the light, acting as if he were inspecting it, and probed it with his own magic. There was no flaw. The Fire had simply been used up. The magic was gone.

There were only three other such weaves among the Nine Clans with any blackening at all. All the rest had run dry. And Argoth could not fill them. Not because he didn't know the secrets. He knew the forbidden lore and had secretly bled his Fire into a number of the weaves they had. No, he simply didn't have any more Fire to give. He'd already sacrificed enough Fire to reduce his life by tens of years. Measuring the Fire of a man's days was an inexact art; he feared if he gave any more, he would forfeit his life. And he couldn't gather the Fire publicly. The Clans would rise up and kill him for that.

·"There will be more," said Varro. "What are we going to do?"

He meant the Bone Faces, coming in the dead of night, with only a crust of moon in the sky, dozens of galleys scraping up on the beach. They would come, their dark faces painted as white as bone. They would come as they had for the last four years.

Except this time they would easily overpower the force of the Nine Clans because the Nine had no Divines. They didn't need those who were Kains or Skir Masters. They just needed one Fire Wizard, a Divine who could fill their weaves of might. But they had none, which meant they also had no dreadmen.

"Mokad will send a Divine," he told Varro. "Why would they abandon us? Now muster your strength. We'll get you back to the fort and have the surgeon look at you."

The Bone Faces had come last year with dozens of dreadmen in their armies. Only Argoth's seafire had saved the Nine Clans. But it would not save them this year. The Bone Faces knew about the fire that burned on water. They would not make the same mistake of letting their ships be caught on the sea.

But even if they did, with dreadmen at their oars they would easily outdistance the clan galleys. His ships might be able to spew fire, but they'd never catch their prey.

Argoth cursed. In his heart he cursed Lumen, their Divine, their only wizard, who'd disappeared last year. He cursed Mokad for not sending another.

Unless the boy Glory of Mokad, the overlord of the Mokaddian Divines, sent help, the Nine would stand un-multiplied before their enemies, and they would fall. The boy Glory had failed to subdue the islands of the Kartong, failed to heed advice and prepare for the famine that blasted Mokad a few years ago, failed to protect them against the Bone Faces. Weren't his failures proof enough that the Creators had nothing to do with the selection and raising of Glories and Divines?

Argoth called his men to make a litter. Gut wounds were evil and tended toward corruption. They could only wait and see if Varro would survive. Of course, if they'd had a Divine or a working healing weave, they might be able to better Varro's odds.

He turned to the three Bone Faces lying on the ground. He needed information, and he needed it now. He commanded that the two prisoners who seemed likely to survive their wounds be stripped and bound to a tree at the edge of the meadow. While the prisoners were being dragged off, he helped Varro onto the litter.

At that moment a company of men on horse thundered out of the ravine and into the meadow. Argoth turned. He immediately saw it was Shim, the warlord of the Shoka, Argoth's clan. When they came closer, he saw that Bosser, a captain from the Vargon Clan, rode with them.

Shim pulled his large chestnut horse up in front of Argoth. It was slicked with sweat and tossed its head. Shim was not a large man, but wiry, weathered like an old post, and cunning as a snake. His voice was as dry and raspy as weeds.

"Always in haste," Shim said. "Can you never wait for us?"

"I don't know if that's possible," said Argoth. "I believe it's in my lord's nature to be like a blister: always showing up when the work is done."

Shim grinned.

Bosser, who grew a short-haired mustache on both sides of his mouth down to his jaw, laughed.

But Argoth did not feel the humor of his own joke. "Varro's weave is as gold and shiny as a lady's ring."

Shim's face soured. He grunted. He motioned at the

Bone Face prisoners with his chin. "At least I'm not too late for that." He turned in his saddle and addressed his captain. "Bring my tools." Then he rode to the prisoners who were each tied up at a tree.

He took his tooth pliers from the bag his captain gave him and turned to the Bone Face who seemed to be holding out the best. One of Shim's men spoke the Bone Face language. Shim turned to him. "Tell him I want to know where their island base is. Tell him he's got one chance."

The translator relayed the message. When he finished, the Bone Face spat at Shim.

Shim narrowed his dark eyes. "So be it," he said. He turned to his captain. "Get the wedge."

The captain withdrew from the bag a brass wedge used to force a man's mouth. Argoth took the Bone Face by the hair to steady his head then worked the wedge into the man's mouth. Shim gripped one of the Bone Face's molars with his pliers.

The man groaned and bucked, but Shim was not a man to play games. The Bone Faces had slaughtered thousands for no other reason than that they could. Shim squeezed the pliers, and with a sharp yank, pulled the tooth out.

The Bone Face cried out. His head lolled down with the pain. Blood mixed with saliva and drooled out the corner of his mouth. He looked up, rage in his eyes.

Shim held the bloody tooth out for him to see. "I'm fully prepared to hold you prisoner for a future exchange. But it's going to cost you some information. I am not a man that will be delayed."

The translator relayed the message in that sour Bone Face tongue.

The Bone Face replied.

The translator arched an eyebrow. "He says only a woman would think of taking a tooth."

Shim simply shook his head. "Perhaps we should cut off something more important to him." He pointed at the man's groin. "Tell him we'll take one, and if he still doesn't talk, we'll take the other."

The translator relayed the message.

Argoth looked at the second man. Shim's performance was having its intended effect upon him.

"Where is your ship?" asked Argoth.

The translator spoke.

At that moment, a messenger rode into the meadow at full gallop. He called out to two soliders searching the saddlebags of a Bone Face horse for the location of the warlord. One pointed in Shim's direction. The messenger galloped through the tall grass to Shim.

"What is it now?" Shim asked.

The messenger looked down at the prisoners. "My Lord," he said. "May I suggest a more private place?"

Shim sighed. "Probably more council instructions. Very well." He turned to his captain. He pointed at the Bone Face who had lost a tooth. "Lay out all our tools for them to see. A little think should do them good."

"Forgive me, Lord," the messenger said. "But I was asked to give the message to Lord Bosser as well."

"Very well," said Shim. He turned to Bosser and Argoth. "Why don't you both come?"

They walked a number of yards away and stood in the grass.

"What is it then?" asked Shim. His voice was so dry it made Argoth thirsty.

"Sleth have attacked at the village of Plum," said the messenger.

Argoth tensed. That was where Purity lived. Had she been exposed? Lords, had she revealed the Order?

The messenger then related to the three of them the tale of Master Sparrow and Barg, the harvest master.

With every word, Argoth's heart sank.

When the messenger finished, Shim told him to take a message to the lords of the Fir-Noy and dismissed the man. When the messenger rode off, Shim whistled through his teeth.

Bosser grunted and stroked his mustache the way he did when he was in deep thought.

"What do you think?" asked Shim. "Yet another Fir-Noy scheme to purge the Nine Clans of the Koramites, or have the Bone Faces begun to move their wizards?"

Bosser shook his head. "I do not trust the Fir-Noy, but even they wouldn't make something like this up." He spoke in the common Mokaddian, but his Vargon accent was still thick, rolling his *r*'s and turning his *v*'s into *f*'s. He sighed. "Dreadmen with failing weaves, Koramite spies, Sleth. We're a kingdom of dust. Perhaps it's time to flee these shores."

Shim's anger rose. "Flee? By all that's holy, I will stand my ground. I've spilled my blood here, sired children on these hills. I will triumph or die trying. I will hear no talk of flight."

"There are young ones with full lives ahead of them," said Bosser.

Argoth knew Bosser was thinking of his own children. The Bone Faces would make them nine-fingered chattel. They would rape the women, force those they thought were pretty into being concubines. And when they finished, they would draw the Fire of the people to build their armies. They would levy taxes of Days until people began dropping like flies.

"Perhaps it isn't Bone Faces at all," said Bosser. "Maybe the ruins have produced this."

When the first settlers had arrived in this land, they found a number of ridges and cliffs riddled with the ruins of extensive warrens. The Teeth, a six-mile ridge of limestone hills that looked from a distance like the maw of some fearsome fanged animal, was the biggest. These weren't nasty holes in the ground, but long passages with many chambers. Over the years, many parts had eroded and fallen in. Pools of water stood in what once must have been grand halls. Bats littered the floors in many places with mounds of excrement. But what was left showed the mysterious race had carved with intelligence. For lack of any other name, the settlers called the vanished race stone-wights.

Nobody had seen a living stone-wight. The carvings and bones found in the warrens gave a good idea of what the creatures looked like. They walked upright, some with the long hair of a musk ox, but they were clearly not any breed of human. Their heads were too long for that, as were the short tusks found in a few of the skulls.

Some said the stone-wights were the same type of creature that inhabited the desolate solitudes in the lands of the Kish. The Kish called those creatures Ungar. But Argoth had tracked one many years ago, back in his dark days. He'd never caught the creature, but he had glimpsed it, and it looked nothing like what was carved in the walls of the stone-wight caves. Some saw evidence the stone-wights had worshipped Regret and claimed the other six Creators had obliterated them for their wickedness. This had led Koramite and Mokaddian parents to tell dreadful tales of stone-wights to their children to keep them obedient.

But if the stone-wights had been so wicked, so dedicated to undoing the creation, then why had they delighted in carving so many beautiful things of the world above their lairs? Argoth had seen a people vacate a land because of pestilence or drought. Perhaps this same thing happened to these ancient inhabitants. Argoth suspected the woodikin, who inhabited the wild lands beyond the Gap, knew the true tale, for woodikin were recorded in at least one of the carvings. But humans had not been able to extend their borders much into the wild lands. Even if they could learn how to survive those places, there was too much hate between human and woodikin.

It was true what looked to be records had been found in the stone-wight caves, but nobody could interpret the language. It was as foreign as the tongue of fishes. The stone-wights were a race whose history had been swallowed up by time.

Yet something did live in the caves. The warrens were uncanny places. Odd lights were seen in some of the windows. It was said some passageways whispered. But that did not deter the curious. A scattering of treasure was found along with the bones of odd beasts. But as the first settlers delved deeper, people began to enter and never return.

"Nothing has ever come out of the ruins but bats and snakes," said Shim.

"That's not true," said Bosser.

Shim waved off his objection. "If anything is in there, then it's had decades of opportunities to come out and feed. Someone would have seen it before. No, this is something else."

"Whatever it is," said Argoth, "it finds us in a precarious state of affairs. We can only hope for an embassy from Mokad."

"Mokad," said Shim in disgust. "Our lords in Mokad will send nothing. The war with Nilliam has them on their hind legs. Any new Divine they might have raised has been sent to fight. If they were going to help us, they would have sent a Divine months ago. No, we cannot count on them." He rubbed a weathered hand across the stubble on his jaw in frustration. Then he paused. "But that doesn't mean we're lost. Sometimes extreme situations demand extreme measures." He put his hand on Argoth's shoulder.

"What measures?" demanded Bosser. "What have we left undone?"

Shim looked meaningfully at Argoth. "There are ways to combat both dreadmen and wizards, aren't there, Captain? There are alliances that can be made."

"Alliances?" asked Bosser. "Mungo will not lend their wizards to help us."

"I'm not talking about that type of an alliance. If the events at the village of Plum were not the result of some Bone Face plot, then that means there are"—he paused to find the right words—"other powers abroad."

Shim had come perilously close to speaking treason. But then Shim was always one to take risks. Shim's eyes glittered in his leather face. Argoth knew that look. He'd seen it a hundred times as he and Shim had fought and drank and laughed together.

Neither Bosser nor Argoth spoke.

"Such things would require great delicacy," Shim continued.

Bosser was indignant. "Lords, man," he said, his *r* clipped short in anger. "I'd rather die, rather run every member of my house through with my own sword than ally myself with abomination."

"Our good captain here saved us last year with his seafire. Of course, the Bone Faces obviously have adjusted their tactics. Still, he might save us again. So I'm not talking about casting our lot with monsters," said Shim. He cocked an eyebrow at Argoth. "Or am I?"

A warning shot through Argoth. Shim knew.

But if he did know, what did it mean that he had not revealed Argoth's secret?

Bosser turned to Argoth with a look of disbelief and indignation on his face. "What is this?"

Argoth had done all he could to not reveal his lore, to make his fighting look like that of an unmultiplied man. He stroked his neck and felt the husk of the brilliant blue beetle one of his daughters had found and made into a pendant for him. She and her sisters, his son, his courageous wife—they would bear the brunt of the violence that would be directed against him. Even if some individuals in the Clans trusted him, many more would fear him. And they would exercise their fears upon his children.

"Lord Shim," said Argoth, "I do not know what you suggest."

"Don't you?" asked Shim.

Argoth looked at his lord, his friend. As much of a friend as one might have and still keep the kinds of secrets Argoth did. He bowed his head. "I am sorry, Lord. I truly wish I knew how to help."

11.

HUNTERS

Da returned in the early evening and whistled Talen and the others in from the fields. Talen was more than happy to oblige. Most of the injuries from the villagers had receded to a dull throb. But the one close to his kidney had not. It hurt every time he tried to stand straight.

They loaded the saws, axe, billhooks, hoggin, and bush

knives into a pushcart and began to walk back, Prince Conroy following behind. As they approached the yard, Conroy must have heard the new hens, for he let out a squawk, made an end run about the dogs, and raced to the yard.

Talen put away his tools and joined his father. Conroy stood on the handcart eying four golden hens in their baskets and vocalizing whatever thoughts roosters did to their new ladies.

"Only four?" asked Ke. "I thought we had enough for six. Has Mol raised his prices?"

"No," said Da. "Mol's in a bad way. So I advanced him a payment for a load of goose down and a few hat feathers."

"Did you see anything in the woods?" asked Talen.

"In fact, I did." Da paused, looked at each of them, taking on an air of one about to tell a harrowing story. "Trees. There were lots of trees."

Talen shook his head and sighed.

"Of course, there was that one hatchling swinging about on a vine. But he wasn't bothering anybody."

Da's joking in the face of danger had worked when Talen was younger, but this wasn't just humor. He was mocking Talen's concern and that was annoying.

"That's nothing," said Ke. He pointed at Talen. "Mighty hunter here saw one in the yard."

"Really?" asked Da.

"Yes," said Ke. "A fine view of its leg and bum."

His brother made it sound as if he were making it up. "And a spoon," said Talen, "wet with fresh porridge." Talen folded his arms.

"I wondered where that had fallen," said Da. "I got to the barn this morning with my bowl, but no spoon. And I know I'd put one in."

So much for the spoon. "I saw *somebody*," said Talen.

"I'm sure you did," said Da.

But Talen could see he was going to give him the same lecture River had. And so he decided not to push it. Maybe they were right. What he needed was more evidence. "Come on, Nettle," he said, "let's go get some fish."

Nettle handed his hay fork to Ke with a smile, then followed Talen down to the river. The river ran so low this time of year that the gravel bars stood high and dry. Frogs croaked back and forth to one another from the edges of the slower pools. Talen fetched eight pan-sized trout out of the weirs, then he and Nettle took the fish back to the house. They filleted them, throwing the bones and guts into a bucket for the garden.

Talen looked over the meadow where they kept their mule. That thing he'd seen today, if it was a hatchling, could be out there in the shadows of the forest line right now looking at him and he'd never know it. One thing was for sure, his dogs were not going to be any help.

If it was a hatchling, he couldn't cower. He'd have to be ready. Have to have his bow at hand and shoot first. There could be no hesitation.

He went in the house and laid the fish fillets on the table.

Ke sat in his chair mending a tear in his tunic. He looked up at the fish. "You've got to make it hard for me, don't you?"

Ke was beginning yet another fast to purify his heart. He'd started fasting after the battles last year where one of his best friends had fallen and been taken by the Bone Faces. The Bone Faces hadn't removed his finger and enthralled him. Nor had they fed him to their gods. Instead, they put out his eyes, shredded his ears, broke his feet so he'd be lame the rest of his life, and cut off his manhood. Then they left him by the side of the road to die or tell his tale.

Ke changed. You could see it in his eyes, a frightening purpose. He killed with a ferocious rage after that. Talen was so proud, and jealous, of him and the respect he won. And then Ke began to fast and ruined it. At first, his fasts consisted of passing up red meat. Now he would go without food or water for a day, sometimes two.

Talen didn't understand all the fuss. It was right and good to defend home and hearth. It was right to take pleasure in the death of an enemy.

When he'd brought this obvious fact up to Ke, his brother had said, "Yes, but what happens when you begin to relish it like a roasted apple? What happens when you cannot slake the hate?" And so Ke fasted.

But the fasting didn't appear to give Ke any new insight. The only thing it produced, as far as Talen could see, was a loud stomach and a short temper. Besides, Da had killed, and he didn't fast.

Talen jiggled the basket of fish a bit. "They're going to be tasty," he said. "Are you sure you can't wait? Given what's happened, I would feel more comfortable with you at full strength."

"You've got to get the weeds when they're small," said Ke.

Talen grunted. There were things about Ke he just couldn't understand. He went back out to the well to wash up. Da had picked up this Mokaddian washing habit from Mother. Talen wondered if Da demanded they clean themselves because he truly believed in cleanliness or because it was his way of remembering her. Either way, Talen wouldn't eat until he'd scrubbed with soap.

A large basin sat on a table next to the well. Da had lined the ground around the well with bricks. He'd also laid a brick path from the well to the house. Another was half built from the house to the privy, all to keep the boarded floor of their house clean.

Talen took his shirt off and scrubbed his arms, neck, and chest. He dumped a bucket of cold water over his head, and that's when he saw the footprint in the soft dirt at the edge of the bricks.

He walked to the edge of of the bricks and looked down. There were three prints heading away from the well toward the old sod house. The toes looked a little long. The prints weren't deep. In fact, you had to be standing just right to see them. But they were there.

"Nettle," he said.

Nettle was slick with soap.

Talen pointed at the footprint. "What do you make of these?"

Nettle walked over. He took a wet cloth, wiped his chest, and looked down.

"Hatchling or woodikin?" asked Talen. Either way it was trouble. When the first settlers arrived in these lands, they found a number of small, hairy creatures sitting in a wild apple tree eating fruit. The first settlers had considered the creatures pests. But over time things had turned deadly, for the woodikin were not simple and dumb brutes. There had been much bloodshed between the first people and the tribes of the woodikin.

After a moment, Nettle said, "It's not woodikin. This foot is too fat. And the toes aren't nearly long enough. They're human."

"The prints are too small for any of us," said Talen.

"So it could be the Sleth children or someone else. If it is Sleth, you know we're bound by law to report it to the authorities."

"And have them take all the glory and the reward?"

"I'm just saying we need to think this through."

"What's there to think? We get my da out here, we execute our plan. We're not talking about some ancient Sleth. We're talking about children."

"I know," said Nettle. "But I also know you don't give some things enough time. You jump to conclusions. Look at your father's spoon."

"Are you saying you don't want to help?"

"No," said Nettle. "I'm in. But we need to have a solid plan. Not some half-baked thing. This one-legged hatchling snare scheme of yours is about as good as your running up the tree to escape Ke and River. This is one print. One hatchling. How many others might there be? We have to take that into account."

Nettle had a point, but sometimes you didn't have time to reconnoiter and strategize. "If you'd been in my shoes this morning," said Talen, "River and Ke would have had you before the chase began because you'd still be deciding which way to run. Sometimes what's required is immediate action."

"Yes, just do the first thing that comes to mind. That will win wars and conquer nations."

Nettle heard a lot from his father and his men about battle. But just because his father was a man of battle tactics didn't elevate Nettle to the same level. "You only get a perfect plan after the fact, Nettle. A good plan, boldly executed now, is far better than a perfect one next week."

"If they're Sleth," said Nettle, "then a hasty plan will get us both killed. I just want to make sure we do this thing in a way that will show everyone what we're capable of. Not a way that backfires on us."

Nettle was right, but that didn't make his resistance any less annoying. "Fine. Then let's look for more spoor, or are you just going to stand there dripping on the bricks?"

TALEN AND NETTLE found two other sets of prints: one by the privy and the second in the mud by the pigpen. Nettle had just measured the one by the pigpen with his hand and concluded they had found prints that belonged to two different people, not one, when a man spoke from behind them.

"What have you got there, boys?"

Talen turned. A huge, armed man stood only a few paces away. His dark beard was long and unkempt like the fur of a shaggy dog. The tusk in his wrist tattoo marked him as Fir-Noy. But his tattoo had been extended. He'd seen that same design on the Fir-Noy that had set the Stag Home villagers on him. But even that tattoo had been extended. The man's belt and leather cuirass drew Talen's attention. A blue hand was painted on the right breast of the cuirass. Each of the Nine Clans had many orders; the blue hand was one of the smaller Fir-Noy orders, but it was not made up of common men. This was an armsman, a professional soldier. His military belt with its ornate buckle and honor disks confirmed it. Only an armsman was allowed to wear that belt and the leather apron straps signifying his seniority.

"Armsman?" Talen asked. "Zu?"

How had this man sneaked up behind them? The dogs began to bark, and the shock of this man standing here hit him. Talen stood in alarm and glanced to the fields and river, looking for others.

"We're all about, boy," the man said.

Talen had expected some reprisal from the Fir-Noy at Stag Home. But he thought it would come as a fine levied by the Shoka authorities. He didn't think the Fir-Noy would send his men, and certainly not so quickly.

The cords of the muscles on his arms and neck stood out. Most soliders were levied from the ranks of the common people for a battle or watch, but it was always temporary; they served, and then went back to their lives. Commoners practiced regularly, it was true, but that could not be compared to the armsmen who did nothing but practice war. And not only was he an armsman, but the dark feathers in the tubes on either side of his untied helmet marked him as someone who held authority. Not a leader of a hundred, but a Hammer, someone marked for his performance in battle, someone who had proved himself and was marked for others to follow. Talen suspected this one had probably killed many men.

"Nothing terrible needs to happen here today," said the man. "We just need your cooperation. You ought to start by calling your dogs before they get hurt."

Talen didn't believe a word of it. Somebody was going to get hurt. Something valuable was going to be taken.

The armsman had tied a piece of black cloth around his left upper arm. It signified he was a Sleth hunter.

"Call your dogs," the man said again.

Talen called out for the dogs, but they did not come.

"What are you doing here?" asked Nettle. "This is Shoka land."

It was rude for Nettle to address the armsman without the formal "Zu." Uncle Argoth as a captain for the Shoka was a rank above this man. But that didn't mean Nettle could address an armsman in that way.

Nettle stood there, looking this man straight in the eye. "I am Nettle, Argoth's son, captain of the Shoka. You have no authority here."

The man grinned a surprisingly rot-free smile. Then he stepped up to Nettle and backhanded him in the face, knocking him to the ground.

Talen turned to help Nettle up, but Nettle only pushed his hand away. When he gained his feet, his face was red, eyes tearing from the pain of the man's blow.

The armsman drew his sword and pointed it at Nettle. "If I were you, I'd watch what I said. None of daddy's men are here to keep you from stubbing your toe. Now.

You're going to round everyone up. I want them standing by the well."

Suddenly the dog's barking rose to a pitch and then a scream.

"You see," the armsman said, "I told you to call your dogs."

"Blue!" Talen yelled. "Queen!"

Talen ran toward the sound over by the old house. He soon saw there were about half a dozen others with this man. All but two of them were armsmen. They had positioned themselves in a ring around the farm and now closed the circle. Blue lay on the ground, yelping in pain: one of them had stabbed him in the hindquarters. Queen stood behind Blue, facing down another armsman.

The door to the house swung open. Da strode out carrying the Hog. "What's going on here?"

Ke and River followed him out.

"You'll put that down," said the big armsman, "and tie your dog up."

"Who are you?"

"I'm here in the name of the Council. You will stand and account."

Two men closed on Da, their swords in hand.

Da considered them and then dropped the Hog to the side.

This was going to end badly. Talen knew it.

Da looked at Talen and motioned to the dogs. "Go get them."

Talen turned and found Nettle behind him. "You get Queen," said Talen. Then he put his hands under Blue so he could carry him. Blue cried out and turned to nip at Talen, but Talen murmured gentle words and carried Blue to the barn and laid him on a pile of fresh straw. Nettle tied Queen up to the closest post.

"Fir-Noy rot," said Nettle.

Talen ignored him and smoothed Blue's head and neck. Blood matted Blue's fur. "You're going to have to hold his head while I try to stop the bleeding."

"Just let him lie. He'll only fight us and pump more blood."

"Blue," Talen said. "You stupid dog." He stroked him again. Blood ran from the wound. "We've got to compress this. It's not going to stop on its own."

One of the other armsmen appeared in the barn doorway. "You two. Get out here."

Blue whined, but these armsmen had violence in their eyes. Talen stroked Blue's head once more and then walked outside.

"Over there." The man pointed with his sword at the well.

"Zun," Da said. He faced the big armsman. "You come onto my land and threaten me?"

"Actually, Koramite," the armsman said, flinging that word at Da instead of returning the proper title, "it's not your land."

"You can't hunt here."

"The Council has opened up the restrictions. Hunters are allowed free rein."

Da paused. "Then I'll need to see your token."

The big man pointed to his armband. "Are you blind?"

"Any fool can put on a band," said Da, "that doesn't mean anything. You need a token, even when restrictions are eased. In these lands it's the bailiff that determines who will hunt. I've already spoken to him about it."

"Listen to this clever Koramite," said the man.

"It's Shoka business. Not yours. If you want to search us, you'll come back with the bailiff's token."

The man grinned and dropped his gaze as if Da had

made some joke. He glanced at the two armsmen that were closest to Da, Ke, and River. "Boys," he said, "is this woman begging me to plow her field?" He turned back to Da. "Are you?"

"Would you allow just any band of men who came along free access to your home? Especially when they demand it at sword point? You need to move on," said Da.

"No," said the man. He rolled his shoulders to loosen them. "Actually we don't. Now I've given you an opportunity, but it seems you insist . . ." He walked forward toward Da. "I know who you are, Zun." He used the title in obvious mockery. "You think you're something—a master archer. But you're nothing more than a high-and-mighty camp lady."

Among some soldiers, bowmen were considered lesser warriors, fighting only from a distance. It was true that sometimes boys and women were found in their ranks. The real warriors stood their ground and faced the men they would kill. Of course, others didn't share that opinion, and Da had proven himself many times in battle. But this armsman obviously wasn't among them.

The armsman stopped two paces from Da and raised his sword point to Da's chest. "A Koramite, commanding his handful of cowards. Except, oops, you forgot your bow." He paused. "You know, all this resistance just makes me wonder what you're hiding."

Da did not flinch. "This has nothing to do with hiding. It has everything to do with order. You come back with a token and you can pry into every cranny. That's the law. And you know it."

"Don't lecture me, Koramite. These are the facts. One of your own was practicing the dark arts. And one of you is harboring—"

"Ridiculous," said Da.

The man raised his sword to Da's neck. "Don't interrupt me again. We're going to search this place. Then maybe you'll make us some dinner. Afterward, if we feel like it, your tasty daughter there will entertain us."

"This is why hunts are regulated. Now, I want you to move on."

"*You* want?" Then the man's face changed and he jabbed his sword forward.

But Da moved. One moment he was standing heron still, the next he dodged to the side and delivered a blow to the man's sword hand with such violence that the sword leapt from the man's hand and fell to the dust a number of yards away.

The man gasped. He clutched his sword hand.

Da kicked the man's leg and sent him to one knee.

The two men by the house rushed forward, but Ke and River, fast as snakes, snatched up the Hog and fallen sword and faced the hunters.

The two hunters hesitated. But Talen saw the others draw their swords.

Da knocked off the man's helmet and held him by the hair with a knife at his throat. "Now," said Da. "You—"

A man Talen had forgotten was behind him took Talen by the neck and pressed a knife to his back.

"Two can play that," the man said. "Throw down, you buggered Koramite!" There was nervousness in the man's voice. "I'll poke him! I'll poke him! I'll poke him!" Each time he said it, the pitch of his voice rose, and Talen felt the knife point push a little harder into his back just where his ribs ended.

There was a deep thud like the sound of a stick hitting a melon, and the man suddenly slacked his grip and fell to the ground.

Talen turned. There stood Nettle holding a hunk of fire-wood.

Talen felt his back. When he pulled his hand away, blood stained his fingers.

"The sword!" Nettle said. "Get his sword!"

Talen bent over, fumbled at the man's scabbard, and soon held the sword. It was heavy and did not feel right in his hands.

"You call your men off," said Da to the big armsmen whose head he held by a fistful of hair. "You tell them to drop their weapons."

"You're dead, Koramite," the big armsman said. He tried to break Da's grip, but Da simply pushed the knife closer.

"Now," said Da.

"We can take them," one of the hunters said, and the remaining four men began to move forward. Talen would not be a match for any of them. Ke might be able to hold his own. But if they had to fight these armsmen, they would lose.

In a flash, Da stabbed the big armsman's shoulder and put the knife point back to his neck.

The big man cried out in pain.

"The next one goes right into your neck," said Da.

"Put them down!" the armsman called out.

The hunters hesitated.

"Drop them!" the leader bellowed.

The men reluctantly dropped their swords.

"Everything," said Da and he pushed the knife harder into the man's neck. "And kick them away."

"Do it," the leader said. His face was red and strained, a massive vein standing out on his forehead.

The men threw daggers after their swords.

"Get the bows, Nettle," said Da, then he stood the big man up. By the time he'd walked the man past the weapons, Ke, Talen, and River each had a bow, and had strung it.

Da shoved the big man forward. "I'm going to give you

ten seconds to get across that stream. Then I don't want to see you here ever again. You can make complaints to the Shoka warlord to get your weapons back."

The man looked at the arrows pointing at him. "You're going to pay for this, goat-lover."

Da took a step toward him. The man raised his arm in defense, but Da was too quick. One, two punches to the face, and the man's nose folded to the side. Blood ran down in a thick stream. Then a kick to the groin.

The man doubled over in pain and fell to the ground.

Da grabbed him by the hair and wrenched his head back.

"Am I going to see you again?" asked Da.

The man sucked in great breaths. "No, Zun," he managed at last. This time there was no mockery in the tone. "No."

"Because if I do," said Da, "I'm just going to assume you're one of those men who hasn't got the sense to know when to leave well enough alone. And there's only one way to deal with those types. Do you understand?"

"Yes," he said.

"Good," said Da. "You're a big man, a fine asset; I'm sure your Fir-Noy commanders would hate to lose one with your good sense. And just in case you change your mind, I'm going to alert the Shoka warlord that there's someone lost on his lands."

Then Da released him and looked at the other hunters. "I think I'll start counting at one."

These weren't cowards, but Talen could see they knew they'd been beaten.

The big man got to his feet, holding his nose, the blood matting his unkempt beard, but he didn't say a word. He limped off toward the stream. Two others helped the man Nettle had brained.

Talen and his family followed a comfortable distance

behind the men, stopping at the crest of the stream bank. Talen kept his bow up but did not dare to keep his arrow fully drawn lest he accidentally loose it and strike one of them. Da may have beaten the leader, but the presence of these men still frightened him. What would happen next frightened him even more. They'd been sent by the Fir-Noy at Stag Home. You couldn't shame part of an order and not expect the rest to rise up against you. Who knew what string of events this had initiatied?

The hunters splashed through the water. On the other side, one of them turned. It appeared he was going to say something, but before he'd fully turned, Ke's bow hummed and Talen watched an arrow miss the man by only a foot and bury itself in a tree behind him.

The man jumped back and cursed.

"Don't badger them," said Da.

But Ke had another arrow nocked. "I won't. I'll just maim a few."

"Ke," Da warned.

The hunters hurried to the woods. Just before they disappeared around a bend, one of them turned and gestured a curse at them. Then he too turned and slipped into the trees.

"Those men will be back," said Talen. "And they'll bring the rest of their cohort with them."

"There's no cohort," said Da. "This wasn't a military mission. If it had been, we would have seen many more. And it would have been led properly. These were opportunists."

"Someone ought to follow them anyway," said Ke. "Just to be sure."

Da nodded. "But you use that bow only as a last resort. We blew the fire out of them. I don't want you stoking it up again."

"They won't even know I'm there," said Ke. Then he loped after the men.

"River," said Da. "I need you to scout the hills around the farm. I don't want any more surprises."

"Yes," she said.

Da turned to Talen and Nettle. "And you two: go see to that dog."

12.

THE MOTHER

Hunger stood upon the cliff. Hundreds of feet below him a river surged. He knew its name—the Lion. He knew many names now, all of them taken from the villager named Barg. And more would grow in him over the next few days as he finished digesting the soul of this man. But he wanted no more.

At first, each name had been a delight and thrill. Each had added to a building ecstasy, but then it all changed horribly. The image of the girl he'd killed in the village of Plum—the sons, the pretty wife—they rose in him again. Those images swelled a tide of grief, and he floundered in it like one drowning because it was not *the* girl, *the* sons, *the* wife, but *his* girl, *his* sons, *his* lovely, precious wife.

Somehow, in some wicked way, he was the villager Barg, twisted beyond all reckoning.

It made no sense. But new words tumbled into him every hour. New ideas. In some inexplicable way he'd mixed with the villager like copper and tin mixed to make bronze. He was Hunger and Barg and all the small things he had eaten: a rat, two lazy dogs, a multitude of insects, a horse.

After devouring Barg, he had reached out and, with his own rough hands, wrenched the life from his daughter. He'd separated her, taking her Fire and soul and casting her body aside. He'd swallowed her whole, but he hadn't eaten her like he had Barg. He'd swallowed her into the place the Mother had told him to.

But he could have chosen not to. He could have run.

The image of his wife's back breaking, of her folding over like a stick of wood, took his vision away.

Lords, he could have spared her, his son, and little Rose. Oh, sweet little Rose. His grief stretched wide and he roared at the confusion and pain. But Hunger had no tears. No way to purge the pain. And he could not escape. The souls of his family struggled within him, imprisoned inside that place the Mother had made. They would not get out. Even he didn't know how to release them. That was the power of the Mother. So he could not open his stomach, but perhaps it was possible to break this body and, thereby, set them free.

He looked down at his legs and arms. Earth and grass . . . it was not right. It was not his body. He could feel worms burrowing through his limbs. This morning he'd pulled away chunks of the grass growing on his legs and stomach and dug in. He was nothing more than dirt and sticks and stone.

There was a name for what he was, but it floated away from him. But name or not, he knew he must die.

The river surged at the bottom of the gorge below him. If he broke himself upon the rocks below perhaps he could undo the horror. It would not bring him back as father or husband. But perhaps it would release their souls, and they could find a way to continue in the world of the dead.

The Lion was a treacherous river and had drowned

many men. He spotted a run of thick rapids and marked it as his target. He would break upon the rocks there and sink to the bottom. In time the rushing waters would carry his body out to sea.

Stop. It was the Mother, reaching out to him. *This will do you no good. Have you not learned yet to trust me? I told you not to eat the humans. But you disobeyed.*

He felt her pull. Felt the pain only she could give him. But maybe she could ease the grief. Maybe she could ease his yearning and emptiness. Hunger looked at the waters below and hesitated.

She would hurt him. She would be furious. *I only ate one. Only one. And he didn't have any stink. You said not to taste the ones with stink.*

That is what I said, you're right. And you did cease your frenzy when you'd consumed one. Come back to me.

Maybe she wouldn't punish him. *But even this one*, he said, *even this one hurts.*

Of course. Don't you see? she said. *It's the man you ate that's riding you, filling your mind with these thoughts. The filthy man. You've given him power over you.*

The man wasn't filthy. He was . . . Hunger. Himself.

I am an . . . he paused, then the word came to him, tumbled in with the weight of a massive stone. *I am an abomination*, he said. *Let me go.*

Come to me, she said. *I will give you rest. I will show you how to eat these men and not suffer.*

Her pull was not overwhelming here, not like in her cave, but he could feel the ease only she could give him. He almost turned then. Almost returned to her. But Hunger now knew the name for what he was, and that thing was not meant for this world.

No, he said. *You made me. Not the man. You are a river of darkness. But I choose one of light.*

Then he stepped back, and before he could change his

mind, before she could say another word, he charged the chasm and, with a mighty leap, flung himself into the yawning gorge.

A satisfaction washed over him, for at least this deed was right. He plummeted in silence. He knew he should feel a giddiness, a rising thrill or panic. A man would feel that. And that's what he had been. But all he felt was the black hunger of his heart.

Then the surging river rushed up at him and he crashed violently into the rocks. Part of his body slipped away. He thought it would continue: he'd dissolve and disperse like sediment.

But the water pushed him off the rocks, and he did not die.

He did not die!

The rushing current carried him along.

Dirt! Cursed, rotten dirt! He should have known—how could you kill dirt? He hadn't even felt the pain of impact.

He sunk into the river's depths, scraping, rolling, bumping along the bottom as the water ran its turbulent path.

Maybe the river would carry him out to sea. He might walk in the depths there, might even be eaten by a leviathan. Surely such a beast could kill him. Or maybe it would avoid him altogether, for what creature of the sea ate dirt?

The force of the water soon lessened and he found himself in a deep eddy, deposited in the shadow of an overhanging rock. He lay in a bed of sand at the bottom of this calm nook of the river. A school of large trout eyed him in the dark green and blue depths. Far above them, the sun shone like a pale dot. Maybe he could lie here forever, let the river cover him up with sand and mud.

Lie here. But his family would lie here with him, imprisoned in his gut.

He needed help. And of the seven Creators, there was only one he thought might answer.

Regret, he prayed in his mind. *Deliver me. Destroy this creation, dissolve me forever.*

But it was not Regret who answered him.

If you will not learn obedience through pleasure, said the Mother, *then you will learn it through pain.*

Hunger braced himself. He did not know what magical bond she held him with. But she could always find him. And she could deliver a white-hot flame that burned all thought from his mind.

Come to me, she said.

Then she did something. She pushed at him, and Hunger found himself rolling over to get his footing.

The trout darted out to the bright water then into shadows farther away. But he stopped himself. *No*, he said. *Never again.*

You can fight me, she said. *But in the end, you will obey. It is your nature.*

She pushed again, and Hunger found himself looking for a path up out of the riverbed. He took two steps and stopped.

She pushed again.

Another few steps.

It will cost you, Hunger said. *I will fight you every bit of the way.*

There was a pause and he felt the first trickle of the pain. A trickle that grew into a raging fire. It hurt. It seared. It rose in him and consumed him in a soundless scream.

WHEN HUNGER REGAINED his senses, he found himself still under the water, lying on a stretch of river stones. This was a different part of the river. It took all his might, but he pushed himself up.

Hu, he said. *Do you see? I can withstand your pain. Perhaps you will always beat me, but it will cost your attention and time. I will take that from you. I will force you to always think of me so you can think of nothing else.*

There was a pause.

He felt her push.

He took a step, and then another. He tried to fight her. But she flooded him with ease. He could trust her. She was good. And if he asked very carefully, with much obedience, she would release those he had so horribly imprisoned.

Hunger turned and climbed up the steep, slippery rocks of the bank of the riverbed, up out of the water and into the sunshine. When his strength returned, he began to run along the banks, leaping between massive boulders, back toward the Mother and her caves.

HUNGER COULD SMELL the Mother here in the darkness. The warrens were full of her. She smelled of rock and sweet, clean magic.

She was smaller than he was, but quick and strong. He'd felt her sharp teeth and powerful hands. He'd seen her. She rarely left the caves, but she'd ventured forth with him a time or two, walking abroad in the night. He'd also seen her in the smallest of light that found its way into the depths from the mouth of the cave. She was pale. Pale as a mushroom. Pale as the moon.

He didn't know what she was. She had two arms, two legs. A head. She had a muzzle, which the villagers did not. Her skin was covered with a fur. Smooth and soft as the small things he had eaten: the mice and squirrels, the rat.

His ease grew the deeper he went in the inky tunnels. Her powers were always stronger when he was close.

He felt along the walls as he walked, smelled the scent of rock and water, of the sulfur springs, and of the strange beasts that lived in the bowels of this mountain. When he came to the carving that marked the hole leading to the lower chambers, he climbed down. Then it was up a small slope, over the bridge that spanned the cold waters of the underground river.

He found her in the warm room, surrounded by her light. But now he considered that light as if for the first time. It wasn't just light. It was—the word was "ribbons"—it was ribbons of light, ribbons flowing around her, circling her limbs. Living ribbons of light wriggling like the snake he'd eaten. And then he saw that her appearance was changed.

She no longer had a muzzle. Nor was she covered in soft fur.

The Mother was human. And beautiful. So stunning it took his breath away.

He wondered and marveled at the change. He looked closer at her. She looked like . . .

She looked like his wife. He was confused. "Lovely?" he asked.

"Come here," she said.

The ribbons of light reached out to him and circled his arm, caressed his neck, wreathed his head. A continual shimmer.

"What do you want?" she asked.

He only wanted to be here with her. But no, that wasn't right. Deep in his mind he knew there was something else. And then the nightmare of his family struggled past the feel of her beauty and stared him in the face.

He was going to tell her to free the souls inside, but he knew she must not know they meant anything to him.

"Freedom," he said.

She laughed.

"You need a servant," he said. "But you don't need me. I will find you another, and you will give me this boon: you will dissolve this body and let me go."

"And the souls inside you?" she asked.

Her face flickered like smoke. Alarm shot through him. He took a step back, but she grabbed him by the arm, and such was the power of her ease that his panic lost its grip. He knew he should run, but could not.

She thrust her other hand into his sodden chest. She reached deep into him with that powerful hand and grasped the part of him that held his family.

He wanted to struggle, but could not.

With a yank she broke them free—his bright daughter, his handsome sons, his admirable wife—and withdrew his monster's heart.

Hunger fought her ease with all his might and managed to grasp her hand. He felt what she held. It was then he realized she hadn't grasped his heart, if he even had one.

No, what she'd taken from his chest was a stomach.

It was a weave of willows. He'd been there when she'd made them; he himself had fetched the thin flexible willow branches she used for such weaving. They smelled of her magic. His body was packed with stomachs. Empty stomachs waiting to be filled. But this one was not empty. In this one Hunger could feel the souls of his family caught like moths in a wicker web.

The Mother pushed at him and yanked her hand away. "You stupid thing," she said. "I will devour them."

"No," he begged. "Please."

"Then help me prepare for the harvest. Bring me the ones that stink, all those that could fight against me. Bring me the young male that would be their leader. This is your duty. And when you have fulfilled that duty you will receive the boon you seek."

The pull of her dazzling beauty and the desires for his family tugged against each other. He wanted to obey her. But he also knew she was lying. She would not keep her promise to free his loved ones.

Then something she'd just said sparked an idea in his mind. She had spoken of a harvest before, but he had not known then what the word meant. "What do you want to harvest? I am strong. I can serve you as the harvest master and you can let these go."

Her anger seemed to flow away at this offer and her countenance smiled upon him. "It has been too long since any in my family have handled humans. So facile."

This made no sense to Hunger and he could not tell if she had been talking to him or herself.

"You do not understand," she said. "This herd of humans is mine. Mine by right. It was my mother's mother's before me and will produce for my daughters. But humans rebel against the natural order of things. It has ever been so. And if they would rebel against me, then think what they'd do if one such as yourself was set to watch over and harvest them. No, humans do best when one of their own sits at their head. Your part is to cull the herd. Nothing more."

A part of Hunger recoiled at this information. Harvesting humans? Then he thought of how she taught him to unravel things, and he knew what she wanted to harvest.

A wave of her ease washed over him. What did it matter what she wanted. Or if she lied. She was so beautiful. So kind.

His alarm faded away.

"They are hidden, the ones that stink. Hidden so even the Mother who stole this herd from my ancestors could not find them. But you have been created to root them out."

Hunger thought. A word came to him for the ones that

stink—Sleth. That was their name. And he immediately knew where the men had taken one of them. He'd learned this not from following any scent trail, for the scent had ended in the fires. No, that knowledge had been one of the first things that had tumbled into him from Barg. Purity the Sleth was going to be held in a stone cage in Whitecliff. He could take her. Sleth would do anything to keep their secrets. They would go so far as to hunt and kill captured members of their nests, which meant if he did take her, he could then use her as bait to find the others.

"You will spare these?" he asked.

"Your kind is so weak. How you ever overpowered the Mothers I will never know."

"Will you spare them?"

"You have two nights," she said. She held up the stomach that contained his family. "If you fail, know that I and my daughters are hungry, and these firstlings will be prepared for our feast."

13.

SNARE

Blue wouldn't let Talen near the wound. The dog had licked until the bleeding stopped, but if corruption set in and spread, they would have to put him down. Talen could not believe what had just happened. And Da was wrong: those men would be back.

He and Nettle went back to the house and found Da standing at the hearth. Three large red onions sat roasting on a pile of embers there. A pot of porridge hung from a crane over a cooking fire. The fish they'd filleted earlier were sizzling in yet another pan. Da poked at them with a knife. The ends of his beard braids were tucked into the collar of his tunic to keep them from getting into the fire or falling into the food.

Ke sat at the table, propping himself up with his elbows. There was no bowl or plate before him.

"Shouldn't River be back by now?" asked Talen.

Da swung the crane, and the pot of barley that hung from it, out of the hearth. "Don't you worry about River. She'll be fine."

Da was probably right. River could take care of herself. She might not be as strong as Ke, but she knew woodcraft. She had her bow. And, if it came to it, he doubted any but a dreadman could run her down.

Da lifted the pot off the crane with a hook and brought it to the table. He took off the lid and dropped a large spoonful into each of their bowls, then he put a small chunk of butter onto the top. They rarely ate their porridge in the sweet Mungo style. "By the time you've eaten that, the fish and onions will be ready."

Talen turned to Ke. "What did you find?"

"I followed the armsmen to their mounts," said Ke. "Then I followed them to the edge of the forest. They're headed out to Fir-Noy lands."

That could mean the armsmen had given up or were going to make an official complaint. But Talen doubted that was the case. Da had just humiliated a Hammer; that surely wouldn't go unpunished. "They're probably circling round or going to gather a mob," said Talen. He turned to Da. "We're sitting here like a bunch of cattle."

"We'll watch," said Da. "And it's true somebody needs to go talk to the bailiff, but it's too late now. I don't want anyone out past dark with the country full of imbeciles like those who showed up today. There's nothing else we can do at the moment."

But that wasn't true. The armsmen weren't the real threat. Sleth were. Talen looked at Nettle, who was chewing a huge mouthful of the porridge. They'd discussed their plans, but he didn't want to blurt them out now. Da needed to first see the prints. Only then would he listen.

Da walked back to the hearth. He grabbed the small frying pan from the wall. He put a knife full of lard in it and stuck the pan next to the andiron above the coals. When the lard melted and began to sizzle, he produced a large brown egg from his pocket, cracked it, and dropped the contents into the pan.

"Where did you get that?" asked Ke.

"Mol," said Da. "I got half a dozen." He grinned. "And if you're polite and grovel like a proper son I might save you one for when you end your fast. But you must promise to help me. We're going to be treating our four new ladies like fat Mokaddian city wives for the next few weeks. We need to hand-feed them grasshoppers and a slice of squash every day."

"Da," said Talen. "There *is* something we can do right now. We can solve the root of the problem."

"You're not going to reconcile Koramites with Fir-Noy," said Da and turned back to his pan. "We're oil and water." He added a strip of fatback to his egg and let it all sizzle.

"I wasn't talking about that. I'm talking about the hatchlings."

Ke groaned. "Och, here he goes again about a monster running about the woods wanting his pants to cover up its naked bum—"

"They've got Sleth caged in Whitecliff," said Talen, "and you seem to think the world is as safe as a pie bake."

"Perhaps the woman in Whitecliff isn't as dangerous as you think," said Da. "What's needed now is calm heads."

"I agree," said Talen. "And I am calm. But what you need to know is that not only did I see one of them, in broad daylight, but we've got its footprints in the yard."

DA AND KE followed Talen out to the footprints. The sun had sunk low, but there was still enough light to see by. In fact, the angle of the light made the track clearer. He led them to the one by the old sod-roofed house and then finally brought them to the one by the pigpen.

"That's too small for Sammesh," said Talen. He put his foot next to it to make the point.

Ke stretched one of his massive arms to scratch a spot on his back. "Looks like we've got ourselves a killer."

"Oh, come on," said Talen. "Look at it."

A horsefly landed on Da's arm. He looked down at it and let it prepare to bite. "That print could be anybody's," said Da. "Could be one of the children that came with that tinker family. They were here just last week."

It could have been them. "But that doesn't explain the sighting and my missing pants."

Da smacked the horsefly with the flat of his hand. It fell to the dirt where Da ground it in with his foot. "Yes," said Da, "the missing pants that were under your bed."

"I saw something today," said Talen.

"I'm sure you did. But I'm also sure that your beating this morning has you rattled. Do you remember when you were a boy and saw the shadows of a number of Og in the yard?"

Talen remembered. Their wagon had cast a shadow in the light of a full moon. And he'd been sure the creatures were in the yard ready to tear them all to pieces. Of course, Da had taken him by the hand, kicking and screaming, and forced him to face the fact that it was only moon shadows.

"I saw a leg," said Talen. "Why won't you believe me? I don't understand why you're not concerned."

"Concerned?" said Da. "I'm mortally concerned. But not about hatchlings. Nobody knows that the woman they've caged is Sleth. There was no Seeker, no proving."

"What I heard," said Nettle, "was that she moved with unnatural speed."

"Things are perceived differently in battle. When your mind is tinged with fear, the foe's strength and speed and ferocity are always exaggerated. But let's assume the worst. Let's assume she did move with power. She might have been wearing a weave. Did you think of that?"

"That's treason right there," said Talen.

"Is it?" asked Da. "A weave bestowed by some Koramite Divine to her family a century ago?"

"It is if she didn't bring it forth."

"But that's different from Slethwork, isn't it? It's a legitimate weave, outlawed not because it's evil, but because it might pose a threat to the current oppressors."

Talen sighed. Da never had anything good to say about Divines. Talen remembered when he was a child and had learned "The Six Paths" from a friend's mother. The poem described the different orders of Divines. He came home excited to perform and began to recite the poem with the appropriate actions.

The Fire Wizards harvest.
The Kains forge and store.
The Skir Masters ride the powers with traps and
*   ancient lore.*

At this point in the poem, Da's face began to sour, but Talen had thought it was because he'd done something wrong. He continued trying his best to remember the hand movements.

> *The Guardians live like dragons.*
> *The Green Ones heal the dead.*
> *And the Glories rule o'r them all with centuries in*
> *their heads.*

Da had clapped in a perfunctory way. "You're a sharp one, for sure," he'd said. "And such a sharp mind needs to be kept that way." Then he'd made Talen learn a poem he'd never heard before. It was long and started with a traveler visiting a tavern.

> *The Host spreads his table then calls with honeyed*
> *charm:*
> *A steaming loaf of Ignorance to keep your belly*
> *warm,*
> *An unending keg of Fear to turn your wit to froth,*
> *And tender cuts of poisoned Pride to turn your gentle*
> *heart.*

The poem continued, describing two companions, one who takes the host's offer and another who refuses. The first one is treated with firmness but kindness and put out, like a steer to pasture, to enjoy the gardens, orchards, and plenitudes of the vale. The second faces privation and a multitude of dangers trying to get his friend to leave. In the end, he fails, and the first one, the one who trusted the smiling host, is brought forth for butchering. The second makes a brave attempt to rescue him from his captors, but fails, barely escaping with his life. Powerless, he watches from afar as the mighty inhabitants of that awful vale kill, roast, and then serve his friend up on platters for a community feast.

It was a long poem, but the story was so fascinating Talen memorized it in less than a day. At first, Talen thought Da made him memorize it because he'd wanted to challenge, and thereby increase, Talen's mental skills. But after he'd learned it, he began to consider the story and see it was a moral tale, teaching how a man could be self-reliant and wise. For a long time he thought that was Da's purpose in making him memorize it.

But as he grew older, Talen began to suspect Da had planted that poem in him for another reason altogether. There were six families in that vale that seemed to correspond to the six paths of the Divine. The butchering was performed during the annual Festival of Gifts, which is when the Divines asked for the annual sacrifices. The name of the host meant the same thing as the name of the first Glory of ancient times. As he grew, Talen found many more connections between the inhabitants of that vale and the six paths.

It was as if Da had planted that poem in him so that it might bring forth, in its due time, a suspicion of all things Divine. But why?

He'd once asked Da what it all meant and if it was indeed his purpose to bring forth such a fruit, but Da only shrugged and said it was only an old poem he'd learned as a child. Talen tried to detect prevarication in Da's answer, but found none. Nevertheless, he knew Da was hiding something.

Talen had known two Divines in his life. Lumen and the Green Beggar. Lumen looked down upon the Koramites. But the Green Beggar went around healing people and teaching them the paths to joy. He refused all authority. Refused pomp, choosing instead to live in a log hut he made himself. He leased land to farm, established a following, and had done nothing but bless goats and vegetable gardens. Three years ago he'd sailed away, waving good-bye to the throngs of his "fellows" standing on the docks. Many still wore the green shoulder patch that marked his followers.

"What about the Green Beggar?" asked Talen. "He would have spoken out against the Sleth woman's use of the weave."

"What about him?" asked Ke. "The Goat King, the Witch of Cathay, the Scarlet Tiger, they were all once Glories of great nations. Benefactors. Who can say what the Green Beggar's real purpose was?"

Talen knew all the stories about Glories who had gone mad and eaten the souls of those they ruled. Divines had all once been men. Men who were raised to wield the powers of life and become almost immortal. But those tales were of Divines who had succumbed to the whisperings of Regret, the Creator who when he had seen what he and the other six Creators had wrought, wanted to destroy it and begin anew. They were stories of Divines who lost the favor of the Six.

"What if Lumen himself ate souls?" asked Da. "Who would have known it? Nobody. Isn't that a greater horror than some farmer's wife who uses a little weave to bless her and her family?"

"But the power doesn't come from the same source," said Talen. "It's like comparing an ale brewed using pure water with another made using swamp scum. They may look the same from a distance, but in the mouth they're night and day."

Nettle eyed the woods. "Are we sure we want to talk about this out here?"

"I'll tell you what I think," said Da. "I don't think this has anything to do with magic. I think this is nothing more than a bunch of cowards worried about their cattle and land."

"You don't believe the reports?"

"I believe that men see what they want to see. And what they saw was a Koramite smith who was richer than any seven of them combined."

Talen had seen his father's judgment blinded before by his pride and anger. And even though it grated, the Mokaddians weren't always in the wrong. "Maybe all you choose to see is the wrongs done to our people. To admit that one of us was evil would spoil your arguments. Wouldn't it be better to cut out the corrupted part than let it ruin the rest of us?"

"This is why we need a Divine protecting our shores," said Nettle.

They all looked at him.

Nettle had brought his bowl outside. He stuffed a large spoonful of porridge in his mouth. "A mere human cannot hope to unravel such mysteries."

"That's true," said Ke. "But you don't need one to know there's no greater risk now than there was before. Let's say Talen is right. It is no more dangerous to walk about now than it was yesterday or the day before. If there are Sleth lurking about, they were there before."

"What kind of logic is that?" asked Talen. "If you find out there are wildcats in the woods, then you take precautions. You don't assume they pose no danger."

"Ah," said Ke, "but if the wildcats always kept to themselves, are they really a danger now? Perhaps a hunt will only corner them and make them fight."

"Yes," said Talen. "But wildcats don't murder whole families and devour their souls."

"Maybe Talen's right," said Da. "We should take precautions. But this all leaves a bad taste in my mouth. The Fir-Noy had no authority to organize a hunt in the village of Plum. That band of armsmen today had no authority to hunt here. So even if there are Sleth, there are far more Fir-Noy eager to run a Koramite through."

"We need to post a watch," said Talen.

"Aye," said Da. "There's bound to be more than one group of idiots in the woods."

THERE WERE MORE than idiots in the woods, and Talen knew it. He was going to catch whoever had been lurking about. Normally, you only masked your scent when trapping animals, but it was possible that the hatchlings had eaten the souls of some beast in an attempt to obtain its finer sense of smell. He did not have days to let the snare weather, nor did he have any urine or gall from the last deer he'd killed to mask his and Nettle's scent, so Talen led Nettle into the fading light, down to a swampy bend in the river. He found a spot where there was plenty of rotting vegetation and dug out a pail full of mud.

By the time they hiked back up the bank and to the run between the barn and the garden, it was dark. Da had shuttered up the windows against the evening insects, and so they only had starlight and a half-moon to guide them. Talen had wanted to wait until dark so the hatchlings wouldn't be able to see much of what they were doing. Now he wondered if he had enough light to set the snare properly.

First, they pushed the wheelbarrow and eight empty barley sacks out to the cross-post fence of the mule pasture. A long mound of stones, taken from the field, stretched along the base of the fence. They doubled the sacks and then filled them with enough stones to equal the weight of a large man. Then they pushed the sacks back and into the barn underneath the pulley that allowed them to lift loads up to the barn loft and bound all four sacks together.

Next, they pushed the empty wheelbarrow out to the run between the garden and the barn. They set it next to the side of the barn and angled it out into the path in such a way that it would direct someone walking here to step right into the trap.

They dug some beets and carrots, complaining loudly about having to work in the dark as punishment for fighting earlier with Ke and River. Then Talen announced that he would leave the vegetables just inside the garden gate and finish in the morning. Anyone listening in the woods would have heard and known a meal was waiting in the garden.

Then he and Nettle coated their hands, the noose, and trigger pegs with the mud.

Nettle disappeared into the barn. A few moments later, he opened the loft doors. Talen threw him the end of his rope and waited until Nettle had fed it through the outside pulley to the one that hung above the stones.

When Talen heard Nettle's soft whistle, he knew Nettle had fastened the end to the sack of stones, and he began to pull. Both he and Nettle had to work to lift the stones aloft. When they'd finally lifted them to the pulley crane inside the barn, Talen began his work. He set the noose and trigger line and pegs.

Talen had caught deer with counterweight snares before. It was possible that the noose would grab a leg, but it also might tighten up around the neck. If all worked well, they'd have a hatchling before dawn. Of course, a real deer might trip it as well. But Talen didn't think so. The dogs were usually very good at chasing most things off.

And that reminded him: the dogs would have to come in. This trap could very easily choke and kill one of them. He went to where Blue lay then picked him up and carried him back to the house.

A double-spout lamp burned on the table. Da held the wastebasket to the edge of the table and brushed wood shavings into it. He'd been working on a rose carved in cherrywood. A soft light from one lamp spilled from River's room. Ke sat at the edge of the light rubbing sheep's tallow into his boots.

Queen went to Da silently, wagging her tail and asking for attention.

Da looked up. "I don't want the dogs in here."

"I'll keep them in the loft with me," said Talen. "Blue won't rest if we keep them outside."

"Huh," Da grunted. He motioned at a harness of parade bells. "Ke's going to take first watch. He's going to string a line around the property. That line will be rigged to these bells. Anyone trips that line and we'll hear it."

"And where's Ke going to be?"

"Outside the door in the shadows of the house," said Ke.

"What were you doing out there?" asked Da.

"Nothing," said Talen.

"You were doing something."

Talen glanced at Nettle and back at Da. Talen knew he'd make them take down the snare. "We were just talking."

"Huh," Da grunted again. But he turned back to his carving.

Talen took Blue, and all four of them went upstairs.

Nettle suggested they string their bows. They wouldn't have much time to get downstairs and out into the yard. It wasn't good to leave a bow strung, but in this case Talen thought it was best. They leaned the bows and the quivers against the wall and lay down in their narrow beds. The dogs came over and licked Talen's face until he told them to settle down.

The light coming up the stairs diminished. Someone scraped open River's tin candlesave and closed it. She loved the smell of beeswax and herbs, even if it did cost more than oil or tallow. But the mice loved beeswax so the candles had to be put beyond their nibbling. Soon the light from downstairs disappeared altogether.

Talen heard Da go outside and draw up water from the well then come back in and retire to his room. The house quieted and Talen heard an owl hoot outside.

He lay on his bed unable to sleep. He waited for what seemed a long time, staring at the ceiling.

A jingle sounded from below.

"Nettle," Talen said.

"I heard it," said Nettle.

Another small jingle, then one big one.

Talen and Nettle fairly flew down the stairs in the dark. Nettle slipped on the narrow steps at the bottom and crashed into Talen. They would have both sprawled out onto the floor, but Talen held onto the railing and swung into the wall instead.

"Ho!" said Talen. "The alarm!"

There was laughter in the darkness. One small candle ignited at the table. There was Da, holding a glowing piece of tinder, shaking so hard he almost knocked the candle over. River sat next to him holding her sides.

Da grabbed the alarm, gave it a good shake, and laughed even harder.

"Just testing your speed, son. Just testing your speed."

Ke stood in the doorway of his room, grinning like an idiot.

Da! He was worse than River. "What are you looking at?" said Talen.

That only set all three of them to laughing again.

Nettle wore a half grin on his face.

"Come on," Talen said to him and marched back upstairs.

When he'd lain down again, there was another jingle.

"Hoy," he heard Da say from below. "Sleep well, son."

Da would find crickets in his boots this week. And next week, he'd sink to the ground while sleeping with loose bed ropes. And then it would be Talen's turn to laugh.

He heard three more jingles and laughter, then Da called up a good night.

Talen knew what Da was doing—he was trying to relax

them, just as he did his bowmen when they went into battle. All of which meant that Da was taking this very seriously indeed. Maybe Da was concerned about Sleth after all. Maybe all of his arguing against the Fir-Noy was just a way to help them keep cool heads. This comforted Talen, and he suddenly found he could close his eyes for sleep.

14.

FUGITIVES

Shouts jolted Talen out of bed.

"Hold," Ke said from below. "Identify yourself." There was no joking in his voice now.

Talen grabbed his bow in the darkness. This time when he and Nettle reached the bottom of the stairs, the door stood open and Ke had his own bow drawn, pointing it out at something in the moonlit yard.

"Zu," the soldier said. "We are part of the barbican watch. I bring Captain Argoth's summons."

The moon had risen and Talen could see one man wearing a helm and a chain mail shirt standing outside. Men and horses stood behind him.

Talen's first thought was of the armsmen they'd beaten earlier. But there were no Fir-Noy markings on the soldiers he could see. Only Shoka. This soldier's wrist also bore the tattoo weave of Shoka bull horns. But, then, it had been Shoka that had beaten him at the village. Talen nocked an arrow and looked to the shuttered window at the back of the main room.

"What's this about?" asked Da.

"You know the Sleth woman?" the soldier asked.

"You're referring to Purity, the smith's wife?"

The soldier said nothing.

"Yes, I know Purity."

"You are summoned to be in Whitecliff within the hour."

"For what cause?" asked Da.

"Captain Argoth wants help interrogating her. I can only suppose he thinks a Koramite might win her trust."

Ke pitched his voice low. "It's a trap," he said.

"Only a fool rides at night," said Da.

"We've got a moon," the soldier said. "And we will escort you back."

"That's not enough assurance."

"No," said the soldier. "But this should be." He withdrew a linen handkerchief from his waist pouch and held it out for Da to take.

Da took it. It had embroidery upon one of its corners—three trees and red circle underneath. It was Uncle Argoth's sign.

Da took in and held it to his nose. "Spearmint," he said.

Uncle Argoth loved spearmint, planted it around his house, carried it with him. Talen lowered his bow.

Da sighed. "Let me saddle my mule."

"We have a mount."

"Moon or no, I'll trust my own, thank you."

Da turned to Nettle. "Your father, it seems, can't wait until morning." Then he turned back to his room to dress. "Ke, get Iron Boy saddled up."

Ke pulled on his pants, lit a lamp, and walked outside. The saddle was in the barn, but Talen didn't think Ke would notice the trap. A minute later, he changed his mind and walked past the messenger to warn Ke.

But before he passed the well, he heard Ke call out. "What's this?"

"Ke!" called Talen. "Don't touch anything."

Moments later Talen heard a loud crash and the clank of the cowbell he'd attached to the snare.

"Idiot!" Ke cursed. He stormed around the side of the barn holding the cowbell in one hand, the lamp out in front of him with the other.

"What's that?" asked Da.

Talen turned.

Da stood there in his riding clothes and boots.

Ke motioned behind him in anger. "Around the side of the barn. You'll see. I'm going to fetch Iron Boy."

Two watchmen stood at the well drawing water. Another three stood by the door.

Da addressed them all. "There's fish hanging in the shed. Help yourself."

He motioned for Talen to follow then walked around the side of the barn and stopped. He looked up and saw the rope and noose hanging limply from the pulley. "You know, it's one thing to give a man a beating. It's quite another to kill him. Then you've got blood debt and revenge and families to deal with."

"It wasn't for the hunters," said Talen. "You weren't going to believe me until I had one of the hatchlings swinging in the yard."

"Right," said Da. He sighed. "What if River had come here in the morning to fetch a few potatoes, sleep still in her eyes?"

"I'd thought of that," said Talen.

"No," said Da. "You hadn't. But I give you credit. It's a good idea, poorly executed—you don't hide things like this from your fellow defenders—but a good idea nevertheless. Still, you're not going to reset this. Not tonight."

He waited for Talen's reply.

Talen *had* put the others in danger. "No," said Talen. "I will not."

TALEN WATCHED DA ride off into the darkness with the men. When they disappeared into the moon shadows of the forest, Talen wondered: Da was formidable, so what would they do now if the armsmen returned? Or the hatchling worked some evil?

They restrung the alarm line and went back into the house. Ke pointed at Talen. "Since you're so eager to catch something, I think I'll let you take the next watch. In fact, you and Nettle can have the next two." Then he yawned and retreated to his room.

River said, "The water's hot. I suggest you make a cup of night-watch tea."

Talen stood their strung bows against the wall and opened the shutter to the window. He scanned the yard. Nothing, just the buildings and deep moon shadows. Of course, the shadows could hide anything.

He turned and retrieved the kettle from the hot coals in the hearth and made a cup of tea for Nettle. His cousin would take the first part of the watch. Talen didn't think he would be able to fall back asleep, but unrolled his blanket on the floor by the table and lay down on it anyway.

While the tea cooled, Nettle rummaged through the cupboards. He soon found a thick heel of two-day-old bread upon which he spread salted lard. He said around his mouthful of old bread, "I don't know who to worry about more—hunters or hatchlings. I'm beginning to think we should have laid half a dozen snares."

"Queen's out there now. She and the warning line will have to do. Besides, we still have our bows," said Talen, although he didn't know how much good they'd do. Nettle placed himself to look out the window, and soon Talen felt himself drift to sleep.

Sometime in the dark morning, Nettle nudged him awake.

"Did you see anything?" asked Talen.

"A family of skunks," said Nettle. He yawned. "Came right up to the window, but they must have gotten a whiff of you, because they turned tail and ran."

"Funny," said Talen.

"But true," said Nettle.

Talen rose and put the kettle back over the coals. Before his tea had finished steeping, Nettle lay asleep.

Talen waited at the window into the small hours of the morning. Twice he heard something and brought his bow up to the ready. But nothing materialized. Nothing moved but the night shadows as the moon made its way to the western horizon.

He thought about the upcoming Festival of Gifts, where the people celebrated the end of the fall harvest and all the gifts of the Creators. There would be no Divine bestowing gifts of healing and Fire. But that would not stop the merchants and entertainments.

He had planned on going and buying a few sweets and being content to look at everything else. But now he sat listing out in his mind what a hero and his reward might buy. He was going to surprise everyone. Nobody seemed to think he would amount to much of anything. But what would they say when he hog-tied the hatchlings and carted them into Whitecliff?

He waited and watched and waited and began to tire of waiting. A pressure began to build in his bowels. He stood, tried various positions to hold it, but soon he realized that if he didn't get to the privy immediately, he was going to soil his pants.

Lords and lice, he thought. There was an old chamber

pot in the back room, but he couldn't imagine the ribbing he'd get from Ke when he found out he'd been scared to go out. Besides, there was nothing in the yard.

He nudged Nettle, but Nettle only rolled over to his other side. Talen didn't want to go outside. While the moon cast enough light to see, the woods were dark. But he could not wait. He opened the door, scanned the yard and shadows. Truly, nothing was there, so he slipped out the door with his bow and a clutch of arrows and ran to the privy.

As he went about his business, he began to think of the story of the Sleth woman cutting people up and curing them like hog meat.

The hackles rose on the back of Talen's neck. Here he was, foolish enough to go out in the middle of the night when everyone was sleeping. It was possible the hatchlings had seen him go in and were waiting in the dark shadow of the house to steal his Fire.

It was a stupid idea. But he couldn't shake it.

But he had his bow. Besides, they hadn't attacked him earlier. Of course, that was during the day. It might be that at such times their power was on the wane.

Talen finished his business but then decided to wait and listen and peer through a knothole about a foot from the bottom of the door. He spent what seemed at least half an hour at it. He held his breath and closed his eyes to hear better, but there was nothing there.

He could stay the whole night in the privy if he had to. But then he thought of Ke. He'd laugh until he cried, and that thought put Talen on his feet. He wasn't going to give Ke or Da that satisfaction.

Talen reached for the door and heard the creak of the well crank.

He paused, and held his breath. Surely, it was a floorboard underneath him.

But he heard it again. Talen crouched at the knothole again and saw two figures at the well. The larger one was cranking the bucket up ever so slowly. It was a girl or young woman about his size. He could see her braid. The smaller one was a boy. He just stood there holding what looked like a goat's bladder.

TALEN WATCHED THE girl bring up the bucket and fill the goat's bladder. When they had plugged up the mouth of it, the girl turned toward the privy and began walking. The boy followed her without a word. And then he reached out, flailed a bit, and grabbed the back of her tunic.

Blind. He was blind.

One part of him felt the satisfaction of being right. The other shrunk in dread. The hatchlings *were* here.

There was no way Talen could get to the house now. If he were a coward, he might lift some of the loose boards off the seat and jump down into the cesspit. But they would hear him prying the boards. They would know to look down there. After all, it wasn't so uncommon for people to string a rope from underneath the privy bench to hang their valuables above the cess below. He thought of how Nettle and the others would talk about how he'd died while crapping, his pants down, shivering on the stink throne with fright, and the image of it snapped him out of his fear.

What was he thinking? This was his opportunity. Talen wouldn't be able to trap the hatchlings and take them in alive. So what? He had his bow. He had four arrows. Da had taught him well.

He would take them now, despite the fact that he couldn't hear anything but his heart banging in his ears.

He didn't dare miss. He'd have one shot. If it flew wide

of the mark, they'd be on him. But if he made the first count, they'd hesitate just long enough to let him nock a second. A second arrow that he could send into one of their hearts.

That meant he had to wait until they were closer.

Talen bent and looked out the knothole again. It was definitely a girl and a boy. These *were* the hatchlings. He gauged the distance between them and the privy. He stood and slowly lifted away the bar that secured the door. Then he picked up his bow and nocked the first arrow. He reminded himself that he was an expert shot. He might not pull a bow as strong as Ke's, but what he did pull was deadly enough for a girl and a boy.

He did not have enough space to draw his bow in the privy. He didn't want to wait for them to open the door on him anyway. That would be far too close. So he'd have to kick the door open, then draw.

But he didn't need to deliver a mortal shot the first time. He only needed to wound and surprise. Once he'd done that, he could take a bit more time aiming the second arrow.

This was not going to be hard. He could do this.

Talen took one more breath. Now was the time. They should only be a few paces away.

He kicked the door with all his might, but it banged off of something and swung back at him.

Someone grunted.

Lords, he'd kicked it into one of them.

The shock of his miscalculation panicked him. He tried to draw his arrow and step back, but the privy bench got in the way and he fell onto the wall.

He expected the door to fly open and one of them to rush him with claw and fang. But the door just hung ajar.

He heard the padding of feet running away, and felt

relief. Then he realized they were *running*. They were getting away.

He kicked the door again, and this time it flew wide and banged against the outside of the privy.

The girl ran, holding the boy's hand. They ran like the wind toward the old house and the woods.

He took a step forward and drew the string to his chin. Calm, he had to be calm. The string was locked behind his thumb ring. He had practiced this thousands of times. There were days when Da had demanded he draw and release his bow five hundred times. He had used up eight bows over the years, drawing, then relaxing the position of his thumb ever so slightly so that the string might jump away.

The precise moment of the perfect release, he had learned, would always come as a small surprise.

The string hummed and Talen watched the arrow fly. It snicked away into the dark, a perfect shot. But the hatchlings darted left toward the old house just as the arrow flew from his hand, and Talen's first shot missed.

He strung the second arrow. "Ware!" Talen shouted. "Ware!" He yelled again, and saw Nettle throw open the door just about the same time the creatures disappeared behind the old house.

Talen ran to get a clear view of the open space between the old house and the woods. The Sleth would not escape this time. But when he got a view of the open space, he saw nothing.

Nettle came stumbling out with his bow in one hand and a half-lit torch in the other.

"They're here!" said Talen. "I've seen them with my own eyes. They're behind the old house."

He and Nettle cautiously approached the old house. It was the first place his father and mother had built. Talen had slept in it now and again until a snake had come wiggling through the ceiling one night to land on him. Such were the hazards of sod roofs. Now it was only used to store things and shelter the dogs who had dug their warren underneath the old floorboards.

Talen and Nettle split apart, giving the house a wide enough berth, positioning themselves so that each covered two of the house's four walls.

"Nothing," said Nettle.

Where could they have gone? Talen realized he'd given the creature the opportunity to slip in the front door of the house both this and the time before.

He swung his bow and pointed it at the door.

"Open it," said Talen to Nettle.

River called out from the house. "Talen? What's going on?"

"We've got them in the old house!" he yelled back.

Talen nodded at the door. "Go on. Here's something real. Open it."

Nettle looked at the door. "Right," he said. "Cover me." Then he grabbed the handle, whipped the door open, and stepped back.

Talen almost released his shaft. But he was happy he didn't waste the arrow, for nobody rushed out.

"There's no use hiding," said Nettle. "Come out where we can see you."

Nothing moved.

"Queen," Talen called, hoping that she hadn't already been killed by the creatures.

A few moments passed, then Queen emerged out of the dog warren.

All this time in the warren, Talen thought, and not one bark. Something was very wrong. It was as if the dogs were deaf and blind.

"Stu, girl!" Talen said to Queen and pointed at the open door. "Stu!"

Queen looked at the house and sniffed, but then she turned away and came to him, wagging her tail.

"Are you sure it went in here?" asked Nettle.

By this time both Ke and River had arrived, Ke with nothing but his underclothes on. "What are you hollering about?"

"We've got ourselves a hatchling," said Nettle.

"Two," said Talen.

"Where?"

Talen pointed at the open door, and, to his horror, Ke walked right in.

"There's nothing in here," said Ke. "Goh, you're an idiot."

But Talen *had* seen them. Right here. Where else could they be? Then he looked at the dog warren and everything made sense.

"They're underneath," he said to Nettle. "With the dogs!"

Talen ran to the hole where the side of the house met the ground and pointed his arrow into the blackness.

"Bring the torch."

"No," said Ke.

But Nettle paid him no mind. Talen took the torch and knelt to the side of the hole. He saw that the hole had been widened. He should have seen it before, but who would have thought they were down there? He stuck the torch down as far as he dared and quickly pulled it back out.

It was enough. What he saw with the brief illumination was a leg that quickly drew itself back into the shadow. Talen dropped the torch and scrambled back.

"They're down there," he said. "They've subverted the dogs." He drew his bow and pointed it at the mouth of the hole.

"Put that down," said Ke.

"You can't doubt me now," said Talen.

"River," said Ke and motioned at the mouth of the dog warren with his head.

River calmly walked to the side of the house and knelt by the dog warren.

"Stop!" Talen warned. "Get away!"

Ke's hands closed around the bow. "Give me the bow, and shut up."

"Didn't you see the leg?"

Ke yanked the bow from his hands.

"What are you doing?"

"Get them," Ke said.

Talen watched in horror as River's head and torso disappeared into the blackness of the hole. He expected to hear her cry out or be pulled entirely in. But after a few moments, she backed out and extended her hand to help a girl and then a smaller boy out. The girl had long black hair and a scar on her cheek. She appeared to be about Talen's age, maybe a bit older. The boy stared off at nothing.

The girl looked at him with no fear. She looked at him like a bird might a bug. Talen noticed she was wearing River's trousers all rolled up on the leg.

"Douse that torch," said Ke. And when Nettle didn't move, Ke snatched it and ground its flame out in the dirt.

"What is this?" asked Talen.

"Will you shut up," hissed Ke. He studied the woods.

And then Talen heard the voices of men in the distance. Or at least he thought he had.

"Get inside," whispered Ke. "Now!"

Talen looked at his brother and sister. They were harboring Sleth. They were risking the anger of the Nine Clans and putting all of their lives in danger.

When Talen didn't move, Ke handed the bow to River. He grabbed Talen by the nape of the neck with one hand

and the back of his trousers by the other. Talen struggled, but Ke's grip was like iron, and he marched Talen back into the house.

Talen watched in dismay as the girl hatchling led her brother to the hearth. When they were all in, River quietly barred the door and shuttered the window. She faced Ke. "I told Da it would never work."

Someone called out in the woods.

River motioned for everyone to be still.

Ke turned to Talen. "If you've brought a pack of idiot hunters down on us," he whispered, "I'm going to kill you."

"Kill me?" said Talen. "Kill me? You two and Da, it appears, have already seen to that."

"Shush," said River.

They waited and listened. Queen barked twice and then fell still. Talen strained to hear what was going on outside, but heard nothing. Of course, that didn't mean a pack of hunters were not moving now to surround the yard or running off to alert the bailiff.

After what seemed like hours, River opened the shutters enough to peer out. A few moments later she closed them again. "Queen's right in front of the door. She would have barked if someone were out there. I think we're safe."

"She didn't bark at these two," said Talen. "The dog's gone traitor."

River left the window and moved to the girl's side. She stroked the girl's hair like one might a niece or sister. "Talen, this is Sugar."

She put a hand on the boy's shoulder. His hair shot up like a wildman's. "And this is her blind brother, Legs."

15.

PURITY

Argoth did not want one of the guards on the walls of the Shoka fortress, jittery from the attacks at the village of Plum, to mistake Hogan for the enemy and kill him. The guards had their orders, but it was night and the moon was only half full. And Hogan was Koramite. So Argoth waited atop the barbican, watching the roads for his friend.

He brought a sprig of spearmint to his nose. Serenity, his youngest daughter, had tied it to a string and made yet another necklace for him. He could never say no to wearing her gifts. In his pockets he carried at least a dozen tokens of affection—a small black stone with a slash of red in it, a finely woven lock of hair, dessicated bits of flowers, the pit of a plum. He inhaled the fine, strong scent of the mint.

Behind him rose the first of two rings of defense. More than seventy years ago, the early colonists had wisely located the fortress here on a wide outcropping of rock that capped one of the three hills of Whitecliff. One side of the hill sloped to the town. The backside of the hill, consisting of cliffs and precarious ravines, dropped straight to the sea.

The first structure built had been a simple timber tower and palisade. That had been torn down thirty years ago. In its place the Clans had erected two walls. The outer wall stood twenty feet high. The inner wall, placed almost twenty yards back from the outer wall, stood double that height.

Tonight, at the base of the outer wall, guards with dogs

patrolled the dry moat, expecting some Sleth attack. They stood out against the whitewashed walls of the fortress. The Shoka had learned that trick from an old Mungo slave who had won his freedom: whitewash the bottom half of the walls to make it easier for defenders to see below at night, but leave the top unwashed, allowing the defenders to use the cover of darkness.

They used the idea on the ramparts as well, painting the walkways to allow the men to navigate without torches. As long as the moon shone there would be no torches on the wall. Not a lamp. Not a whisper of light that might ruin a guard's night vision except in the one tower where men were eating.

The distant sound of laughter carried down from the tower. Then a guard somewhere up on the outer wall called out, having spotted movement in the town.

Argoth looked out toward the town. In the distance he could see the dark, squat towers of the town wall. Closer in and off to the left stood the temple of the Glory of Mokad on its hill. It was too dark to see, but within the round, domed structure stood the altar of sacrifice where the Divines drew Fire. Directly behind the altar stood the raised seat of the Glory. And behind the seat stood the statues of the seven Creators in a semicircle, looking down upon the altar.

During the Festival of Gifts, seven fifteen-foot statues would be made of wood and erected around the temple. They would then be paraded in a long procession to the fortress and then to the sea. Seven statues to represent the seven Creators.

Each was festooned with the creations for which He or She was responsible. The first and greatest was smeared over with rocks and clay. The second was in the form of a tree, woven with garlands of seaweed, flowers, and sheaves of grain; the third had the horns and hides of animals and eyes made of butterfly wings; the fourth wore the skins of sharks and whales; the fifth bore great wings upon its back and was clad in feathers; the sixth was in the form of a man with a face of gold. These were the six, dangerous as they may be, who brought life. The seventh was misshapen and black. Upon its head sat a crown of thorns and about its chest was woven a breastplate made from the bones of a thousand animals.

Who really served Regret? There were rumors of men and women who bound themselves to him. Was the creature that killed the harvest master in the village of Plum one such? Or did Regret work in more subtle ways, coming to you smiling and with an open hand so that you served him and never once thought you were doing anything but standing in the light? Argoth thought of his past before he found the Order. He had been a servant of Regret, even though he didn't know it at the time. Bless the Six, the Order had found him.

At the base of Temple Hill a light moved along a dark street. It passed behind a number of dark homes. Then it reappeared on the fortress road. Whoever held the torch rode a horse and was accompanied by other men.

A half minute more and Hogan rode into the torchlight at the base of the gate road. Beside Hogan sat one of the barbican watchmen. The man called out his name and rank. "We have delivered Hogan, Bowmaster of the Koramites."

"He's mine," Argoth called down. "Dismount, Bowmaster. Then proceed."

Argoth descended the stairs from the top of the barbican. Before he reached the bottom, he overheard the guards below.

"What's the warlord doing letting that thing among us? Who can tell which of them is part of the Sleth nest?"

"Good lord, man, it's Captain Argoth's brother-in-law."

"I don't care; this isn't right—"

Then someone must have heard him because the conversation fell silent. Argoth walked into the main passageway and then out to the front of the barbican to stand with the five guards standing posted there. Hogan's escort had departed back to the city barracks, so Hogan walked the ramp alone.

Argoth could have ignored the guard's earlier comments, but he chose not to. "Do you know what I love about that Koramite?"

"Zu?" said the most senior of the guards.

"Not his might, nor the many Bone Face kills to his name, but his loyalty."

"Yes, Captain," said the guard.

"Mark him," said Argoth. "I would rather have that one loyal Koramite at my side than a whole company of backbiters."

"Yes, Captain," said the guard. "Of course."

ARGOTH WALKED WITH Hogan out of the barbican and onto a wooden drawbridge that led over the dry moat and to the first gate of the fortress. The gate stood open before them like the dark maw of a giant beast, the raised portcullis a sharp row of teeth.

A set of guards with mastiffs stood just inside that mouth out of sight, waiting and watching for an enemy who might be able to slip by all the outer defenses.

On the drawbridge, away from the guards, Hogan ran his fingers through his beard braids and said, "I will hate to lose this tree."

The Order patterned itself after an aspen tree. Aspens sent runners under the ground that would shoot up saplings, which in turn would grow and send out runners of their own. A grove of aspens could cover acres and acres, and yet, they were not separate trees. They were all connected to one another at the root. And so it was with the Order. Each area where the Order was established had a Root, a trio of leadership, that governed the tree and branches that might grow in that area. Hogan was the chief Root here, Argoth the second. Matiga, the Creek Widow, was the third.

Of course, the guards wouldn't call the grove an "order." To them all combinations of people such as Argoth and Hogan were nests, tangles, or murders. For some combinations those were appropriate terms. But not for those of the Order. Nevertheless, the guards would be horrified to know that a Root of the Grove of Hismayas was about to walk right past them.

A tree might be felled by Seekers, but unless they pulled up the whole grove, the Roots would grow another tree somewhere else, and another and another, until the Order filled the earth. Of course, some trees had to be culled to protect the grove.

"Did you contact Matiga?"

"I did," said Hogan. "She is prepared."

In each conflict, the Order took great precautions to make sure the full trio of leaders could never be found together at the same time. If two fell, the third would have a better chance to bear the rest of the grove off to safety and start again somewhere else. Or to mount a counterattack.

"I told her to take the victor's crown," said Hogan. The crown of a victor was a special weave. An ancient device used by the old gods that bestowed great might upon its wearer.

"Do you think it will come to that?" asked Argoth.

"This situation is odd. It's not right."

Argoth nodded. "So be it. Although I do wish she were

here. How can we make a decision to cull this tree without her?"

Matiga was strong-willed. Sometimes to the point of being obstinant. She was currently many months into a grudge against Hogan. She had found an excellent woman for him. The widow of a Koramite boat builder. She'd prepared the woman and asked Hogan and Argoth to consider her for admittance to the Grove. Of course, the woman knew nothing of the Order. She could not. They had tested her in many ways for almost a year. Argoth and Matiga had been satisfied. But Hogan found her wanting. The trio had to act in perfect unison on such matters. And so the woman was rejected. Matiga had been furious. In this case, Argoth thought she had grounds. Matiga might be strong-willed, but she was also perceptive in her odd way. The woman would have been an asset.

Purity was an asset. Matiga's clear vision was needed here. It was a terrible decision before them. Purity had been a friend for so long. But the Grove couldn't risk putting all three roots together in this situation. And even if they could, he doubted he would have been able to convince the lords of the Shoka to let him bring in yet another person to see the prisoner.

"If this tree can be saved," said Hogan, "we will do it. But if it cannot, are you prepared?"

"I am prepared," Argoth said, his heart heavy. He had brought the required poison with him.

They said nothing more. Argoth led Hogan past the guards and mastiffs, and into the first bailey. They turned left and walked to the second gate and another set of guards.

The whole design of the castle was to create a series of killing fields, areas where attackers would be forced to expose themselves to fire from many directions. The path from the first to the second gate was just such a killing field. The moat, the fortress road, and the spaces before the gates and barbican were killing fields as well.

Something small, probably a rat, scurried out of the gate tunnel before them and into the inner courtyard.

The courtyard itself lay in darkness. An armsman on a horse trotting to the gate nearly collided with Hogan. He jerked his horse to the side and headed for the gate, the clopping of the horse's hooves on the cobblestones echoing in the tunnel.

Across the deep courtyard, the sea tower rose into the sky, moonlight gleaming dully off its ramparts. From the top of that tower a watchman could see miles out to sea. On a clear day he could see the outer islands.

In most fortresses, prisoners held for ransom were kept in the tops of towers. To escape they would have to make their way through all the defenses below. Besides, it was more comfortable living at ground level, and the lower rooms would be taken by those with authority. But Sleth were a different matter. They could descend heights and break timber floors that other men could not. Experience had shown that they needed to be held behind tons of rock. The cleansing room, the only place in all of the New Lands capable of holding Sleth, was built in the cellar of that tower.

Argoth led Hogan across the courtyard to the tower. They passed a group of soldiers drawing water from the well. A number of yards farther they arrived at the first gate of the sea tower and stopped. The gate was a low wall a dozen paces from the door of the tower. Half a dozen guards stood along the wall with two more mastiffs in their midst.

"Hold," one of them said.

"Captain Argoth, here at the warlord's request. We've come to question the woman."

"Aye," said the man, then he walked back to the tower

door and knocked. The door of the tower was set deeply between two wings much like a fortress gate, but in a smaller dimension. There were dark arrow loops in those wings that would allow archers to cover the door with crossfire.

Moments later, a small block of wood set behind bars opened at eye level revealing lamplight within. Part of a face filled the opening.

"Your visitors have arrived," the man said.

The face disappeared and the block closed. A moment later the crossbar on the other side scraped, then the door opened. A giant of a man with a bushy beard held the door with one hand and a lamp with the other. His name was Droz. Many straps hung from his armsman's apron—for not only was he experienced, but he was also a dreadman of immense ferocity. Argoth had seen him chop men in two. Both his right and left forearms were covered with warrior tattoos.

"Ah, Captain," Droz said. "We've been waiting for you." He motioned for Argoth and Hogan to enter.

Argoth led Hogan through the opening in the wall and to the door. When they entered the dimly lit room, Droz shut the door behind them and swung down the crossbar.

The room was windowless, wide, and bare, with only a plain hearth burning to one side. There were no wooden tables or benches. Not a chair or cupboard. Nothing a Sleth might use as a weapon. The only seats or shelves were those carved in the stone. It was purposely large enough for half a dozen men to wield spears and bows freely. A few guards slept on the floor. Three stood behind Droz holding their weapons. One stood at the far end of the room next to an iron lever set in the wall.

The giant motioned at Hogan with his lamp. "I expect you want irons for him?"

"No," said Argoth. "He's working with me."

"But he's not working with me," said Droz, "now, is he?"

"Actually, Droz," said Argoth, "he is."

Droz stood a head taller than either Argoth or Hogan. He folded his massive arms across his chest and looked down at them. The three men behind Droz shifted ever so slightly into a stance that would allow them to quickly spring into action.

"Search him," said Argoth. "In fact, if you're worried about it, order him to strip. Send him to the cleansing room naked."

"Now, now," said Droz. "We're not in the business of sending pretty men to the witch. This isn't a brothel, Captain."

The other men smiled, but they did not laugh.

"Well, there's your problem," said Argoth. "Not all prisoners can be cracked directly. Sometimes you've got to build a little trust. And Zun Hogan here will do that. So perform your search. It's late and I want some answers."

"You're not going to get any," said Droz.

"Is that so?"

"We've been pressing her. Quiet as a fish, she is. Oh, she'll struggle and cry out as loudly as the next one, but she won't talk."

Argoth truly hoped that, if nothing else, Purity had been able to keep their names hidden. "We'll see if different methods produce different results."

Droz motioned for one of the other men to search Hogan. "How many of us do you need?"

"It will be just me and the bowmaster this time."

Hogan took a wide stance. Then the guard began to pat him down.

Droz grunted. "Just the two of you? Are you sure that's safe?"

"She wears a king's collar, doesn't she? So she's nothing more than a woman. And an injured one at that."

Droz nodded. He pointed at Hogan. "He's her lover then?"

"She had one love," said Hogan. "And he wasn't a man even you would want to cuckold."

Then the guard checking Hogan stood back, looked to Droz, and nodded.

Droz considered Hogan. "So, Zu, why are you here?" He used a polite title, but not the one deserved by a bowmaster.

"I'm a friend," said Hogan.

Droz looked at Argoth then, and what was going on in that mind Argoth couldn't tell. Droz was a cunning man. And a man with such a mind just might suspect everything here was not as it seemed.

A beat passed, then Droz said, "Before you go down, you should know: Anything happens, anything at all, and Pony there"—he pointed to a man standing by the doorway to the back chamber—"will pull that lever. That will bring down two portcullises that five dreadmen together cannot lift. One will seal off the cleansing room. But, just in case someone makes it out of the cleansing room and to the stairs, the second will seal that back chamber. Should you be caught behind them with the witch, do not expect us to even think about saving you. You're on your own."

"I wouldn't worry about her getting out," said Argoth. "I'd be worried about her kind getting in."

"Nothing's getting in here," said Droz.

"Of course not," said Argoth, hoping he might provoke Droz into revealing more of the defenses. "Who would dare?"

"We've got archers in the wings of the entrance," said Droz. "Men on the wall above. Nobody is getting in."

"And have you set a crossfire up in here?"

"You don't need to worry, Captain," said Droz. "We're tight as a drum."

Argoth nodded. They'd planned for everything but a traitor in their midst.

Droz led them to the back of the chamber and through an arched opening. Argoth glanced up as they walked through the short passage. The heavy portcullis hung there. It would not be made solid. No, they'd want holes in it so they might shoot arrows at whoever was caught behind it.

Another lever was set into the wall of this chamber. Argoth supposed it would release only the lower portcullis. There was a stench in this rear chamber. "What is that?" asked Argoth.

"Bones," said Droz. "The man has the noxious flatulence of the Dark One himself. I think the designers of this tower wanted to suffocate their prisoners. There's no second window and, therefore, no cross breeze. So what do we do? The best I could come up with was to order the man to release his poisonous vapors back here. They still waft out to torment us, but at least their potency has diminished by a degree."

Argoth wrinkled his nose. "I tell you what: forget the crossfire. Just put Bones at the door."

"I'd put him out " said Droz, "if the man wasn't such a good swordsman." He motioned at the numerous squares on the floor with handles in them. "Mind the covers."

"Murder holes?" asked Hogan.

"Exactly."

Droz lit and handed both Argoth and Hogan an oil lamp, then held his aloft to reveal the stairs.

"Here's another thing," Droz said. "They spent a fortune making this small fortress; you'd think they'd make it safe for the guards. But no, the fifth stair will try to kill you. Just mind its slope as you go by."

They descended the stairs. Argoth stepped over the fifth one. The stairs followed the curve of the tower wall to what looked like an empty cellar that lay directly below

Bones's stink chamber. This chamber too had murder holes in the floor.

It also had an iron grate door set into the floor on one side. Droz lifted the bar on the door and took them down another staircase. This stair opened onto a flat area about ten feet deep. At the end there was yet another grated door. Two massive iron bars held it shut.

Droz unbarred the door and opened it outwards toward himself.

There was a whistling somewhere above. Argoth suspected it was a window. He glanced back up the stairs and saw nothing but darkness. There was an odor on the air. Old urine and excrement and something else he could not identify. So it wasn't as tight as Droz wanted them to believe.

The light of their three lamps was only strong enough for Argoth to see the grated doors of the first few cells.

"The woman's down at the end," said Droz. "I'll wait here."

"Actually," said Argoth, "I think we'll accomplish more alone."

"I don't like it," said Droz.

"If you want to rouse the warlord to discuss our methods with him, go ahead. Or maybe we can wait until he wakes. Of course, she doesn't have many hours left in her. If she dies tonight . . ."

Droz grunted. "You like to push it, don't you?"

"No, Droz. We just need some answers."

"Fine," said Droz, "But that means I lock you in."

"Thank you," said Argoth. "We'll ring the bell when we're ready." Argoth dropped his voice to barely a whisper. "I expect you'll want to watch. But, please, don't uncover one of the murder holes directly above her cell. If she is Sleth, she'll know you're there. In fact, I'd recommend against opening any of them. Your stink will come through, and she'll not say a word."

Droz looked at him, and Argoth couldn't tell if it was suspicion or curiosity behind those eyes. But then he nodded, locked the grated door behind himself as he left, and retreated back up the stairs.

Hogan stepped forward toward Purity, but Argoth restrained him, and motioned at the murder holes in the ceiling. They waited for the time it would have taken Droz to walk back up the stairs, but they heard no murder hole being uncovered. Nevertheless, Argoth walked about the room, holding his lamp so he could inspect every one. When he was sure nobody was listening, he motioned Hogan to Purity's cell.

Purity lay in a blanket at the bars of her cell on a bed of straw. Underneath the blanket she was naked except for her bandages. Her head had been shaven. The silver king's collar ringed her neck. Hogan knelt close to the bars and held his lamp up. Her wounds from the arrows were stitched in tidy rows. Even so, the wounds were red, angry, and corrupting. She would not last long in this room, but she might survive long enough to do the Grove damage.

"Purity," said Hogan.

She spoke, but did not sit up. "I hope you brought wolfsbane roots," she said. "If I'm to be poisoned, let it be quick. Not an insufficient dose of hemlock and honey or some two-day mushroom."

"Calm yourself," said Hogan. "It hasn't come to that yet. First, we need to know what has happened."

She coughed and her breath rattled in her lungs. "I'm sure the Fir-Noy gave you the full report," she said.

"I don't care about the battle," said Hogan. "I want to know about the stork and your child. And what happened to the harvest master's family afterwards."

"I thought maybe someone else in the Grove decided to take justice in their own hands," said Argoth, "but it wasn't anyone in the Grove. Nobody I know could have drained the bodies like that. Not even a Divine can do that. I inspected the bodies, and they were dry. Completely wrung out."

Argoth referred to the Fire in the bodies of the family. Death was the separation of Fire, soul, and body. Some said the soul took the Fire with it. Others claimed the Fire poured forth like smoke or steam. However it separated from the body, there was always some that remained and leached away only very slowly. Fire could be found in bones a hundred years old, yet the bodies of Barg's family had been empty husks.

Argoth continued, "There were the markings of an immense draw of Fire, a blackening of the skin. It looked almost as if some monstrous hand had grasped hold of each victim's face."

Purity was silent for a long moment. And then, "I know nothing of what happened to the harvest master's family."

Hogan squatted down next to the cell. He reached in and gently stroked Purity's shaved head. "Whatever you're hiding, you need to let us know so we know how to set it right."

Purity looked at them then. Large cuts and bruises covered her face. Her left eye was almost swollen shut. Her lip was split.

"Give me the poison," she said. "You cannot free me. I have broken our trust. I am willing to abide by the covenant; cut me down and preserve the rest."

Not a tear fell. And how could she weep? She was broken. Argoth's heart ached for her.

Hogan continued to softly stroke her hair. "We decide

if the covenant is broken. Besides, not all is lost. Your children yet live."

Argoth had not known that.

Purity looked at Hogan, and now the tears began to well in her damaged eyes. "I have done horrible things."

They waited for her to continue.

Purity was a handsome woman, but her grief had shattered her. And now her face twisted with what she was about to tell. "In the early autumn of last year the children brought in a young stork with an injured wing. It could not join the others in their flight south, so we decided to nurse it back to health. Sugar and Legs made a pen for it next to the chicken coop and brought it frogs and fish to eat. They loved the excitement of that long, dangerous beak.

"It was a smart bird, and a temptation came to me, a forbidden and foolish thing. I wanted to reach out and touch its soul, to see what the mind of this great bird might be like. I'd done it before with other animals and knew how to be careful. Every few generations someone in my family manifests this gift. I'd been taught by my great-grandmother. But I had never done this while pregnant. I was only a few weeks from delivering Cotton."

Argoth suspected he knew where the story would end. This poor woman . . . and yet, that's why the codes were so strict.

Purity continued, "Something in me slipped. I felt it leave. I knew it was soul and broke the connection. I was horrified, but nothing happened. I lay awake at nights worrying what might happen to me. I inspected myself and the bird every day. But there was nothing. Nothing. Then Cotton was born. He was jaundiced, but that's common enough and the yellowing quickly faded in the sun.

All seemed right. And I thought I had perhaps imagined the slipping.

"The bird healed, but would not fly with its kind. It always stayed close by, as if it were one of the family. We stopped feeding it, but it would not leave. And whenever Cotton was outside, it would come down and eye the babe. At first we thought it saw the babe as a tasty morsel, but it never tried to nip. It would only turn its head to eye him and then settle down somewhere close. This went on for weeks, and we just accepted that the bird thought we were his flock.

"Then one frosty morning I went out to the garden to dig onions. Cotton lay wrapped in the bassinet. This bird rose from its perch on the roof and flapped down to join us. But this time I noticed something . . . a sore on its head. Of course, I thought it had been in a fight with some animal, but when I inspected, I saw the bud of an ear. And then hair where feathers should have been."

Purity stopped her tale and stared off into space. Moments later she continued. "Cotton's foot had been roughening despite the butters and salves I rubbed onto it. And it was very clear what had happened; my soul hadn't slipped—Cotton's had. I probed, hoping to untangle them, but the two of them had mixed. My honey child"—a dry sob wracked her—"and that bird. I killed the bird, thinking only a small portion slipped and might return to my boy. But Cotton did not heal. He worsened, then died not many days later, lying in the bassinet on our kitchen table. I could not bring myself to burn them."

She did not continue, but Argoth could guess. In despair, she'd buried them together, because her son had been in both bodies. She concocted her kidnapping story. And it would have worked had the floods not come this year.

Hogan looked up at Argoth, but they didn't need to say anything. Argoth drew back his coat and showed Hogan the poison. By the Order's law, she should die.

"Why didn't you tell us?" asked Hogan.

"How could I?" she asked.

"Then what about this family that was slain? Is there some dark grove we know nothing about?"

"No," said Purity. "No. I would never."

"You were not supposed to touch souls either," said Argoth.

Purity didn't answer. She didn't sob, beg, or plead.

Hogan shook his head. "There's no way to redeem you from the Order's law," he said.

"What about my children?" asked Purity.

"They're safe for the moment," said Hogan, his pain showed plainly on his face. "My dear Purity. This can't be a quick death; we don't want them to link it to our visit."

Purity nodded. "Tell them I'm sorry. Tell my children . . ." but she couldn't finish her sentence.

Argoth reached for the tin and then stopped. She wasn't someone who flouted the covenants of the Order. And if they could get her away from this place, if they could give her another chance, he knew great good would come of it. To be sure, there were many covenant-breakers who needed to be put to death. But the good to be achieved by this woman's death was so little compared to what could be achieved by devising a way to help her live.

"She must die," said Argoth. "But I don't believe there is any part of the covenant that determines how soon that must be. In fact, is there not precedence for delaying execution?"

"For a day or two. A week," said Hogan. "But it was expedient in those cases."

"What if I said we could get her out of here?"

Hogan waited for Argoth to continue.

"We could use the sally port," he said. "Tomorrow night. The sally port and then down the cliffs to the sea."

"You can get her past Droz?" asked Hogan.

"That's the one sticking point in every plan I've devised."

"It's too risky," said Purity. She held her hand out. "Give it to me now."

It was all fine to have strict rules requiring the death of renegade members, but rules could never have prepared him for this. Lords, but this woman had advised him on how to repair the seemingly dead relationship with his own wife. Her strong purpose and wry humor had been invaluable. He couldn't do it.

Hogan's face was grim.

"I have a plan," said Argoth. "Tomorrow night I drug the guards and free you. You dress in the garb of one of the men. I take the drug so they don't suspect me. Then you walk out of here on your own with a report from Droz to the warlord. I will hide another set of clothes. You change into them and as a servant escape through the sally port."

"Except I can't walk on my own," said Purity. "I am one tree. I am not the Grove."

"Then we'll think of something else."

"Please," said Purity. "You risk everything. You risk the lives of my children. If you want to save me, save my children."

Hogan put a hand on Argoth's shoulder. "Brother," he said. "I shall never forgive myself." Then he reached down and twisted off the lid to the tin. And Argoth couldn't tell if Hogan was saying he would not be able to forgive himself for killing Purity or if he could not forgive himself if he put the rest of the Grove at risk.

Purity reached out, but her wounds prevented her from extending her arm far enough.

Argoth hesitated, looking at the few inches between the tin and her damaged fingers. And then, as if it were someone else's hand holding the tin, he moved it close enough for her to take a pinch of rough powder.

"How much?" she asked.

"Two," he said, his voice miles away. "Two should be more than enough."

Purity took a pinch then put her fingers to her mouth. She grimaced at the bitterness, sucked her fingers, then reached out and took another pinch.

Hogan's face fell. He stroked her shaved head again. "My dear," he said. "My dear, dear—"

Something scraped above them. Argoth motioned for Hogan and Purity to be silent and looked up.

Argoth took another tone of voice, as if they had been interrogating her. "There are many more things you must tell us," he said. He stood as if to stretch his legs. "To-night is the beginning. And your children will reap the reward. But it all depends on what you do tomorrow when we return. It is your choice." He continued in that line as if he were a reasonable interrogator, all the while furtively searching the ceiling. And then he found one of the holes in the ceiling that did not reflect his lamplight back.

It appeared Droz had not been able to contain his curiosity. He was only amazed Droz had waited this long. He made a small motion, letting Hogan know they should leave.

"You've been helpful," said Hogan. "Every Koramite will thank you in their hearts." It was a good touch. Argoth only hoped it was enough to fool Droz.

Purity said nothing in reply, only sucked on her two fingers.

He led Hogan back to the grate door. A chain hung from the ceiling. It connected to a bell in the upper level.

Argoth gave it three good tugs and waited. A few minutes later, Droz opened the massive door and let them out.

On the stairs, Droz broke the silence. "So did you get our fish to speak?"

Argoth looked at Droz. "We know that the murder of the butcher's family was independent of this woman," he said.

"Goh," exclaimed Droz. "There are two groups?"

"At the very least," said Argoth. "Of course, we'll have to verify what she said. But if it's true, then it raises many troubling questions."

"What else did you find?"

"I've already thrown you a bone," said Argoth. "The rest is for Lord Shim."

ARGOTH AND HOGAN found a place in the middle of the fortress courtyard where they could speak. They didn't want to be up against one of the walls where their words might echo. And even if their words didn't echo, they couldn't know who might be close enough to hear: there were too many crannies and windows and deep shadows. No, it was best to talk in a spot where they could see everything that was to be seen.

Hogan held the reins of his mule. A smattering of clouds had blown in and obscured part of the night sky, but there was still enough light to see most of the court-yard.

"My heart is ash," said Hogan.

Argoth could say nothing.

"We will make a sacrifice," said Hogan, "so that her ancestors may be strong."

A sacrifice of Fire would help her in the world of the dead. But he knew it wouldn't lighten the pain he felt in his chest.

After a few moments of silence, Hogan said, "So, what emptied those bones? Wizards?"

It had always been a wizard's dream to collect the bones of slaughtered animals and deceased humans, to harvest Fire without cost. The soul has departed; so there shouldn't be any power there to resist a harvest of what remained in the bones. Battlefields, slaughter pens, dinner plates heaped with the remains of a meal—they should all be rich with easy Fire. But they weren't. The bones resisted them. "Either someone has finally discovered how to persuade bones to release their treasure," said Argoth, "or there's a new power abroad."

"Or an old one," said Hogan. "Perhaps that is what killed Lumen."

The ancient stories told of gods inhabiting many places. In the beginning, the old gods were servants of the Creators. There were gods for fish and beasts and trees, each chosen from its own kind. Each taught the lore by the Creators themselves so that they might guide and bless a certain small territory: a vale, a wood, or a group of hamlets.

But these old ones had proved unstable. One never knew if a god would end up being a curse or a blessing. And so the legends say the six Creators withdrew their presence from them. Regret, of course, did not. In time, a new order arose, an order of human Divines who sought to battle the old ones and rule huge territories. Some said the new order began with a group of gods seeking the ways of the first parents; others said it had nothing to do with the old ones, but had been established by the Creators directly.

Whatever the origin, the new order began to hunt the old gods. There were many tales of the ancient battles. In the end, the Divines triumphed. They claimed total extermination, yet there were always rumors of old ones that had slipped through the cracks. Could this be one of the old gods who had survived?

"This changes everything," said Hogan.

"It does," said Argoth. "Of course, why Barg? That part makes no sense. He was the key to . . . nothing."

"A mere butcher, a harvest master," Hogan said. He shook his head and looked up at the stars.

"Hogan," said Argoth, "Lord Shim has been making suggestions again. Perhaps this is the opportunity we've been looking for. We do have the Book and Crown. Perhaps our time has come."

"And who can read it?" asked Hogan. "No. We won't risk that."

Hogan was overly conservative. The Book and Crown of Hismayas held many things now lost to the world. It was said that Hismayas, the founder of their order, knew things not even the Glories of this world knew, things given him by the Creators themselves.

"We've discussed this before," said Hogan. "Rushing to harvest only ruins the crop. The Order is not yet ripe."

What would happen if they declared their powers openly? Some would join. Perhaps many. They might defeat the Bone Faces. But many might also prefer to submit themselves to that rot rather than ally themselves with Sleth. Bosser was one of those. He would fight against Argoth, and sooner or later, Mokad would find out; they would send an army to obliterate anyone having anything to do with the Order. The Nine Clans would join with them. Hogan was right: it could only end in chaos and ruin, but that did not make this cold logic any easier to bear.

A guard yelled back at the tower door, a mastiff snarled and was cut off. There were grunts, the sound of something metal clanging violently into the wall.

Argoth turned and looked at the gate, but the shadows obscured everything.

Something dark flashed in the corner of his vision and dropped from the sky. It thudded to the ground not two paces from where Argoth stood. At first Argoth thought it was a pile of rags, and then he realized it was one of the mastiffs that had been guarding the tower door.

It lay in a broken heap.

16.

BREACH

A thundering crack sounded from the base of the tower. A dim light briefly shone where the door should be. Argoth thought he heard Droz's roar, but almost as soon as it started, all fell silent again and the light vanished.

There was no moaning that would suggest someone had been injured. No movement. Nothing but moon shadows and the monstrous dog at his feet.

Argoth drew his sword and began to increase the flow of his Fire.

Hogan walked over to the dog and pushed at it with one toe. "She said she wasn't part of a dark grove."

"That is what she said."

Purity had a past with the lore before she came to the Order, just as Argoth did. He had broken all ties with his former masters. Was it possible she had not? "Be ready for anything," Argoth said.

A guard called down from the battlements. "Ho? What's about?"

They ignored the guard.

Hogan took off his mantle and laid it over his saddle. Then he removed the Hog from its bindings. The blade of the weapon shone with a dull gleam in the moonlight.

They moved forward, but could take no more than a few steps before Argoth stumbled across three bodies, all of them broken and lying in a heap like the dog. He found a dead guard a few paces farther, and another. When he reached the small wall, he saw the tower door hung ajar.

Someone or some thing with immense power had come through here. Oh, Purity, he thought. Secrets within secrets.

"A breach!" Argoth yelled up. "Breach!"

The guard on the battlements took up the alarm.

Hogan pushed the door open with the business end of his Hog.

Inside two lamps had fallen and spilled their oil onto the floor. Two pools burned. The dim light revealed guards lying in broken heaps. Droz was among them. There was no blood, but the gruesome angle at which he lay told them all they needed to know.

Shouts rose in the courtyard. But Argoth couldn't wait for those men. Besides, they would probably meet the same fate as their comrades. A dreadman of a high level might have been able to cause such carnage. But how fast must the man have been moving to dispatch all these men with hardly a sound?

"Let's try to take this one alive," said Hogan. He picked up a lamp. "I'll go first."

They approached the pitch-black chamber that led to the stair. Nothing.

Something crashed below, then silence.

"Hurry," said Hogan and began his descent, Argoth

close on his heels. They could not move as fast as he'd like because the movement would extinguish the lamps.

They took the second set of steps three and four at a time, their flames guttering with the movement. Hogan's lamp blew out. Argoth didn't expect that to be a problem because whoever had forced his way in would have a light. But he was mistaken. They soon found themselves facing the open doorway to the cleansing room, and all inside was as dark as ink.

They heard Purity's frightened voice from inside. "What do you want?" she said in terror.

It wasn't her words that stopped him. It was the fact that the intruder hadn't brought a light. Who would have come down without a lamp?

Hogan turned and relit his lamp with Argoth's flame, then stepped through the doorway. Argoth followed.

Hogan held his lamp aloft. There on the floor lay the door to Purity's cell. It had been wrenched completely out of its fittings. Argoth looked at the cell itself and saw someone large hunkered over her. Purity struggled in his grasp.

The man seemed not to have heard Argoth and Hogan approach. Hogan changed his grip on the Hog. But it was too dark to see clearly. They needed light. Argoth spotted a small pile of straw used for the cells lying in a heap to one side. He kicked a portion of it away then lit it with his lamp. When it ignited, he threw his lamp down into the middle of it, cracking the lamp and spilling the oil about.

The fire flared, illuminating the room and the back of the rough figure.

By this time, Hogan had approached the cell. He stood, lamp in one hand, axe held high with the other. "Put her down," he commanded.

The man supported Purity with one arm and with the other fingered the king's collar around her neck. Her blanket had fallen to the floor to expose her injured and bandaged body. Purity struck at the man, but she was so weak her blows had no power.

The huge man wore an odd cloak of grass. But then he turned, and Argoth saw it was not a man. It was nothing like anything Argoth had ever seen. The grass he'd thought was a cloak was part of the creature, some patches whole, some burned. Then it opened its too-wide mouth and took in a ragged breath.

"Purity," demanded Hogan. "You said there was no dark grove."

A terrible fear lit her eyes. "Run," she said. "It's full of souls."

HUNGER HAD TRIED to devour Purity like he had all the others, but the thing at her neck fought him. It stunk of the men's magic. As he tried to feel along its weave to untangle it, the word for what it was came to him; it surfaced from the murky waters of his mind like a giant fish. It was a king's collar, something forged in the secret fires of the Kains that could prevent even a Divine from using magic. He marveled for a moment—how could Barg, a common butcher, know such things? He couldn't, shouldn't know such things. Unless Barg wasn't the only man he'd eaten.

He looked more closely at the collar. If such a thing could harness a Divine, it might be able to harness a Mother.

That thought made him hold very still. The Mother had been sleeping and shut him out. She could not know about this. He could not wake her. Hunger kept his thoughts quiet.

The Mother was going to eat his family. He knew that.

No matter what he did, she would eat them. Perhaps in the end, she would eat him as well. But this collar, this might bind her up tight. After all, humans had beaten the Mothers before. She said so herself.

Humans with magic.

Hunger looked at the Sleth woman. He'd need to plan very carefully. The Mother was strong. But perhaps this time the prey, with this slip of magic, might turn the tables and catch the predator.

Someone called out from behind him. He turned and saw two men—a Mokaddian with a sword and a Koramite with an axe. Stink rolled off both of them in waves. There was the Mother's magic, but hers was always fresh and clean. This, this was something else.

Hunger recognized the Mokaddian but couldn't put a name to him.

Then the Koramite struck him with his axe.

The force of that blow knocked Hunger back a step. Such power surprised him. But it didn't matter. Hunger was a man of dirt, and he caught the Koramite by the throat and held him up. He could snap him like he had the other men above.

But there would be secrets in these two men. Plenty of secrets. Some of which might show him how to defeat the Mother. He should eat them. They weren't human. They were Sleth. In fact, by all laws he should kill them. Eating them would not make him any more abominable than he already was. And it just might prevent the Mother from working her evil further.

Hunger tried to shuck the man, but he could not find a crack. It was like trying to use a spoon to peel the bark from a maple: all he could do was chip off small chunks.

He searched over the man's body and snagged on the tiniest of gaps. He could feel the man's fear. He could taste him.

Something flashed and Hunger lost his grip. The Koramite fell to the floor.

Hunger turned. The Mokaddian had joined the fray. The flash had been his blade, cutting clean through the wrist of the arm Hunger had been holding the Koramite with. The Mokaddian swung his blade again at Hunger's neck, but the Mother had built him solidly there, and the blade simply lodged in the rock she'd used for his bones.

Hunger drew back the stump of his arm and swatted the Mokaddian to the other side of the room. He looked down at his hand on the floor and then at his stump. The dirt in his forearm had already begun to shift and form itself into a new ragged thing that looked not so much like a hand as it did the wild growth from a coppiced tree.

These two knew how to resist him. This meant he was going to have to kill them before he unraveled them. That was trickier than just taking them live. Trickier, but he could do it.

The Koramite backed up by the burning pile of straw. He held his useless axe ready. The Mokaddian knelt at the far wall, looking as if he were trying to regain his senses.

Hunger would take the Koramite first.

Then he felt the Mother stirring and all his attention turned to the collar. He had to hide it, had to busy himself with some other task. Otherwise, she would know.

She would know, she would know. She would command him to bring these men to her, and he would have to obey. Eventually, he would have to obey. But if she didn't know, she couldn't command.

Hunger turned and rushed back to Purity. He threw her over his shoulder like a sack of grain, then ran for the exit. The Koramite tried to stop him, but Hunger flung the man aside. Then it was up the stairs and into the dark, back the way he'd come. He'd get out, then he'd remove the collar before the Mother fully wakened. He'd cover it and all thought of the men. And when she fell asleep again, he'd come back for them all.

ARGOTH SAW HOGAN bury the Hog deep in the creature's leg, but it had no visible effect. The creature knocked Hogan aside as it had done to him, tossed him like he was so much straw. Then the creature rushed out of the cleansing room with Purity clutched to its chest and the Hog still buried in its leg.

Hogan struggled to his knees. He grimaced and held his arm close as if it were broken. He winced. "That just might have cracked my collarbone."

"I've never—" said Argoth in amazement. The power of that creature. What was it?

"I felt someone there," said Hogan. "Inside the beast."

"Who?"

Hogan shook his head. "I don't know."

Men yelled above. There was a crash, something heavy tumbling down the upper stairway.

"They're not going to be able stop it," said Argoth.

Hogan's face twisted in surprise. "Lumen," he said.

"What?"

"Lumen's soul."

Lumen, the Divine who had overseen the Nine Clans. The Divine who had gone missing last year. Is this how he had disappeared, in some experiment gone awry? Or had the Bone Faces taken him and put him into this rough creature?

Another crash sounded from above.

Argoth raced out of the room to the stairs. He saw the Hog lying on the steps where it must have fallen from the creature's leg and called back to Hogan to pick it up. Smoke from the straw fire below rolled up along the ceiling. It choked him, so he kept his head low and ran up into the darkness. He burst into the first cellar and heard the clamor of many men above.

On his way up the next flight of stairs he jumped over two guards. One was dead, splayed out in a horrible pose. The other lay on his back, moaning.

Argoth reached the main level and saw that the battle had moved outside. Men with torches and pikes stood outside the door and shouted. They surged to one side as if hit by a large wave.

He'd been able to hack off the thing's hand. Of course, it had done as much good as chopping a worm in two. But he'd much rather face that thing in pieces. And if all they could do was dismember it, then that's what they must do.

He charged outside. A number of the men shouted and pointed at something on the wall.

Argoth turned. The thing climbed the wall like a dark, three-legged spider, shielding Purity against its chest like a mother might her newborn babe.

Men threw spears. The half-moon made silhouettes of a number of guards on the wall who were in the process of stringing their bows or taking aim.

Those would do nothing to the creature, but they could kill Purity. And if this was her monster, that might dissolve its bindings.

"The ballista!" he shouted. "Turn the ballista!" At various points upon the wall stood seven ballistae. Argoth shouted up the orders a third time, and the guards manning the one closest to the creature began to turn it.

Hogan appeared at Argoth's side. "How can this be?" The Hog was in his hands.

"I don't know," answered Argoth.

"It's hers, isn't it?"

"We'll soon find out," said Argoth.

The creature moved with such speed he knew the ballista men were only going to get one shot.

"Take it when it crests the top!" Argoth shouted.

More archers arrived and the thrumming of their bows made a chorus. He could hear the ballista men on the wall cranking their engine back. One five-foot, iron-headed dart from these machines could transfix several armored men. The only weapon more powerful would be one of the warwolves, casting a massive stone. But those would be ineffective against such a small, mobile target.

The creature neared the top.

"Lead it!" a man shouted.

The moon suddenly shone through a gap in the ragged clouds and lit up the wall. It was hideous how the thing moved, like an insect. Then it reached the top and raised itself up, its back bristling with arrows.

Now, they should fire now! Argoth heard the loud thwonk of the ballista. The creature took one massive step upon the wall, a dark, hulking figure, Purity's naked form like a small, pale flower held at its chest, then, in the next moment, both were swept away.

"Lords," said Hogan.

"Quickly," Argoth shouted, "to the bailey!"

By now most of the fortress guard had awakened and had come to the call to arms. Torches were lit. A quarter of a cohort, almost a hundred and fifty men, rushed to the gate of the inner wall, Argoth and Hogan following behind. When they reached the bailey between the two fortress walls, they rushed to the spot where the creature should have fallen.

Argoth expected at any moment to hear the men in front call out that they'd found the creature. But no such shout arose. Then one soldier lifted the massive ballista dart into the air.

"Scan the walls!" someone shouted. Men stood back to examine the moonlit walls. A group of soldiers charged forward, beyond the location where the ballista dart was found.

Argoth grabbed a torch from a soldier and stepped up to examine the tip of the dart. It was clean. Not a drop of blood. Not a speck of dirt.

He looked at the ground where the dart had fallen. Nothing heavy had landed here. He looked up at the wall. He knew the soldiers searching the rest of the bailey would not find the creature. It was gone, vanished into the night just as it had come.

"Purity," he said. "What have you wrought?"

17.

SOUL MEAT

The dart from the ballista might have passed through Hunger like a stick through a pile of sand, but the Mother had created him with more than dirt. He had a skeleton of wood and stone. Of course, it was not just wood. Not simple stone. Whatever power the Mother controlled had bound him. He wasn't just a piece of carpentry, for then the ballista dart would have shattered his chest. But it didn't. The dart stuck in his ribs and the force of the impact threw him backward.

But it did not throw him directly away from the wall and into the bailey. Instead, it cast him off the rampart and into the bottom wall of the hoardings used to sweep attackers off the slopes and cliffs on the back side of the fortress. And that saved the Sleth woman, for Hunger was able to grasp one of the hoarding timbers and swing up underneath.

Hundreds of feet below him the sea sparkled in the moonlight. The waves surged and crashed upon the rocks, spraying forth great gouts of pale foam. Hunger would have survived the long drop to the sea, but the Sleth woman would have broken on impact.

He heard the men yelling, and he felt . . . pain? It was not sharp, but there was an echo of hurt. And then he realized it was not him, but the Sleth woman. He could feel the emotions roiling inside her body, feel them like one might feel a puppy thrashing in a sack. He realized he'd always been able to feel the souls of his victims. He wanted to devour her, but he ignored his appetite.

He didn't have much time, and he didn't dare climb down the cliff, for the men would see him, and then she would die. So Hunger skittered like a spider along the belly of the hoardings until he was on the other side of the fortress, far away from the shouting.

He lay the Sleth woman onto the rock and sparse grass that grew here. He had probed the collar down in the cellar of the tower, but could not find its clasp. It was said only a Divine could remove a king's collar, only they knew the lore of unbinding. But did he not have magic also? He examined the collar again. There was no break, the collar seemed to have been woven around the woman's neck. But nothing was that perfect. He could find the part if he searched slowly.

It seemed he had only just begun when the Mother stirred again. Hunger bent his concentration, moving faster and faster along the loops and whirls. Nothing. Nothing. Nothing.

She was coming, he could feel it. Feel her fingers reaching out to his mind.

Panic rose in him. She couldn't have it. She mustn't have it. Then he found a spot that seemed different from the rest, but he couldn't tell for sure if it was the spot of joining. It wasn't a break; it was just a spot.

Hunger?

He tried to unravel the collar at that point, but he could not. It resisted him. Then he mustered all his strength, he pulled, and, when he thought he'd failed, the collar snapped.

Fire and stink billowed up around him and into the sky.

What is that? the Mother asked.

He could not resist her question. *Fire*, he said. *Fire, from the pretty collar about the Sleth woman's neck.*

She pushed into his mind, and he feared she would discover his secret, but she didn't care about the collar, only the Sleth woman.

This is the one? asked the Mother.

Yes.

She's weak.

The men beat her. They do not like ones that stink.

Fool, she said. *They worship them.*

Not this one, said Hunger.

The Mother directed her attention at the collar, and Hunger held very still.

A king's collar, she said.

Yes, said Hunger. *I broke it.*

You did indeed, she said. And then she laughed.

HUNGER RAN THOUGH the woods like a dark wind, carrying the Sleth woman to the Mother. He held her like he had held his bonny girl when she was only a pint. He ran through the dark, piney forest, keeping the branches from the Sleth woman, and the memories of his littlest, Rose, for that *was* her name—the memories of her dark eyes came to him. Dark, little, shining eyes, and him dancing with her held to his chest, her squealing like a piglet for joy. Around and around he had gone with her, dancing his jig on the banks of the stream in a piney forest, his fine wife singing her ballad for the fifth time, the boys clapping the beat, impatiently waiting their turn to whirl in the arms of their da. Around and around until his head spun and he fell into the grass. And little Rose climbing up on his chest to look down at him with those dark, sparkling eyes, the blue sky at her back.

A man of dirt does not weep. He cannot sob. Hunger knew this all too well. But in his deepest parts he felt a longing, an emptiness, a something so vast and lonely and bleak that he stumbled with the Sleth woman and fell to one knee.

The Green Beggar had taught him that if a soul escaped the creatures that waited to devour them; if it managed the long trail in the world of the dead with all its perils; if it were wise, it would find that great Brightness that awaited even the most plain and rude of creatures. The everlasting burnings of joy prepared by the Creators for those who sought the wisdom of the heart.

He, obviously, had not had much wisdom, for the Mother had caught him and devoured great portions of his soul almost as he was born into the other world. And he, in turn, had devoured others. Surely, the Six would destroy him should he ever win his freedom. But Rose, the boys, his good wife. They had done nothing.

The Mother called. She wanted this woman so strongly that her compulsion made him stand.

He held the broken collar in one hand and looked at it.

The Mother had laughed at him. At that moment he'd seen that it was indeed broken. Dead. His hope was nothing more than a scrap of metal, its stink carried away by the wind. But he had the woman. And the Mother had promised to release his family.

No, she hadn't said that exactly, had she? She'd never promised to release them.

The Mother called again, and he could not resist her. He ran across a meadow and down to the rocks where one of the mouths of the Mother's caves lay.

This kidney-shaped entrance to the warrens sat hidden in the folds of the ravines and cliffs along the sea. He climbed up to it and eased himself in. It was almost too small for him by himself, so he held the woman close to his chest and belly with one arm and scrabbled along.

Again, he met the Mother in the warm room, the one that smelled of what he now knew was sulfur.

"Here," said Hunger. "This is the one that will lead us to the others."

"Yes," said the Mother. And she took her from him and laid her on a soft bed of grass and furs. "We will need to keep her for a number of days. That will be your task."

"She'll die down here," he said. "They need light."

"Then you fetch it. If you want those pitiful souls, you keep her alive."

"Yes," he said. She would need food. She would need someone else to be with her. But someone who would not run away.

He did not want to ask her the question, but he had to. He had to know. "Will you release one of the souls to me now?"

"Perhaps," she said.

"You said—"

"Quiet!" she commanded.

She wouldn't do it. She was a liar. But a thought had been forming. All was not lost. No, he had an idea buried deep down. If the collar could be made, then it could be remade. He didn't know how. But those men . . . he turned to leave.

The Mother stopped him. "I want the others as well," she said.

She'd heard his thoughts, knew who she spoke of. And his inability to hide from her filled him with dismay. "What others?" he asked.

"You'll bring them here, those two men, and keep them as well."

"Even you don't have the appetite for three," said Hunger.

"I'm not going to eat them," she said. Then she sighed. "It is unfortunate that, when I found you, your soul was bound to the Mother of Mokad. I could only recover pieces." She shook her head. "Understand, the human wizards, those that stink, must swear allegiance to me. All of them."

A memory rose in Hunger's mind. Before, when he was not in this body, he had been searching for something in her caves. Something dangerous. He had been under orders from a different master then who had yet another master. And the Mother had stolen him away from them. "I had a name," he said.

"That name doesn't matter," she said. "You are no longer that creature."

It came to him. "Lumen," he said, and knew it was true. "That was my name." He himself had been a master.

And a thrall. The realization of this crashed upon him—the Divines, the Glories, the rulers of men were nothing more than servants to creatures like her.

But that wasn't right. He was Barg. He was many names. Confusion clouded his mind.

"You are mine now," said the Mother.

That also was true, but it didn't mean he was hers willingly. "The Sleth will fight you. They will not serve you."

"They will all serve me, one way or the other. I will

find my human to lead the harvest. And those who rebel will be put to another purpose."

"They will die here in the dark."

"Not before we use them to quicken the children."

"Children?"

Hunger tried to probe her mind to find out what she was talking about, for there were no children here.

"Come," she said and led him down a passageway he did not know to a large room.

The Mother sang and suddenly the ribbons of light that wove their way about her ranged out into the room and illuminated it. Half a dozen bodies lay slumbering in the dirt. They were not human or animal. And they were not small, not the bodies of children. They were bodies like his, made of earth, but they weren't exact matches—one had multiple arms, another had a vicious snout and head, another was tall and thin. One had a head shaped like an onion.

"These," said the Mother, "are your brethren."

Hunger knew she'd formed these bodies just as she'd formed his. And he knew when they were ready, she'd call them forth just as she had called him.

"There will be more. We shall quicken them, you and I. And the master of the harvest shall lead them."

"You're going to make war on us?"

"War?" she said. "You weren't listening."

But then what were these for?

"War is the last thing I want. This land and people have been neglected. Koram is ours. It always has been, even far-flung fields like this one. We could not stop the Mother of Mokad from taking them before, but we have recovered some of the old ways. The Mother of Mokad is failing. Soon all her human herds will be mine, and I shall make them fruitful. They will become the envy of the earth and yield a rich harvest for many, many years to come. And these," she gestured at the children, "will be the first of those that will protect them."

Hunger stared at the Mother. Memories tumbled in, stories of a time when there were many minor beings with power. The old gods—this one ruling a valley, that one a small village, this one living on her own in the woods, that one farming with his people. Some protected and blessed. Some, like the Goat King, did not. "You're one of the old gods," he said, "aren't you?"

The Mother shook her head. "What you call the old gods were humans and, sometimes, other creatures who knew the lore. They were like wild animals. They fought us, but in the end, we tamed them and put them to the use intended by the Creators."

Hunger looked at the children. He knew the powers the Mother had taught him: how to separate Fire from body, how to shuck a soul. He knew what she ate. But he'd never seen the implications, probably because until he'd eaten Barg he'd never had the mind of a man to grasp them.

He was stunned. Horrified.

The Mother smiled. "You need not worry about facing the wrath of the Creators," she said. "Did they not make us? And is it not the nature of creation for one thing to master and devour another? Humans feed on cattle, cattle on grass, grass on the earth. It is only natural that something should feed on humans."

It was natural, Hunger realized. And there were creatures that did so—bears, lions, sharks. But something about her logic was wrong. It took him a moment. "It's natural to devour a body maybe. But not a soul."

"That's not true," she said. "There are all manner of creatures that feed on the soul."

"I don't believe you," said Hunger. But he knew about the perilous journey after this life. She spoke the truth.

"There may be predators," he said, "but the prey sometimes turns and fights."

"Your cattle and chickens do not fight you, do they?
They do not flee, but come to you, depend on you. And
that's what humans have been doing for ages—they've
been depending on us. And just as it's easier for you to
manage your cattle, it's easier to manage humans when
they don't know they're mastered."

Hunger thought of his family. Were humans delicacies
or the staples of her diet? It didn't matter: she would eat
his family. She had never planned on doing anything different.

"I've made you a promise," she said, "and I keep my
promises. An obedient servant deserves a reward. That is
the best way. Do you not sometimes pass over a favorite
cow or goat when it's time for slaughter and instead let it
die from old age? This is no different. Fulfill your duty. I
will let them free, and you, not your family, will be the
first fruits of the harvest."

18.

A COLD KISS

Sugar was not safe here, not with men in the woods,
and that idiot Talen making a scene. Goh, that one,
that stinking load of scours, scaring the life out of her.
He'd nearly broken her nose throwing that door in her
face. He'd nearly killed her and Legs both.

But then . . . what would she have done in his position?
These folks were risking their lives. Obviously, he hadn't

been asked if he were willing to do that. Wouldn't she want to be asked to risk her life for a stranger?

Nevertheless, she could not sleep. Yes, it was vastly more comfortable in the cellar under the kitchen floor than out in that hole. Hogan's family hadn't filled the cellar yet with their winter stores, and so it was both wide and deep. She didn't have to contend with mosquitoes, and she had not found any of the monstrous black and yellow spiders that seemed unable to stay out of the dog warren. But the cellar was also the first place anyone would look.

Legs slept on the narrow bed River had placed down here, next to old cabbage leaves and the scattered old potatoes with their multitudes of long, pale stems, looking like a nest of ghostly, spindly legged crabs. He'd fallen asleep brushing her hair with his fingers, picking out the knots and debris.

He was putting a brave front on as Da had always taught him to do. And Da had taught him so much. He had spent hours, days demanding Legs learn do hard things despite his blindness—chores around the yard, holding pieces on the anvil while Da hammered them, working the bellows, learning every foot of the village and the surrounding fields so he could take water in his goat cart to those that toiled there.

Da had seemed a force of nature. And now he was gone.

What would he do here? He'd tell her to stop worrying over things she couldn't change. He'd tell her she was bred to do hard things, it was in her blood.

She began to organize the potatoes and cabbages, putting them into tidy rows and stacks. It comforted her. Calmed her. Tidiness helped a person think.

They *weren't* safe here. This was why she couldn't sleep. Sooner or later these folks would find out that

Mother really was Sleth. It was hard to admit. But that was the truth. The Questioners in Whitecliff would pry things out of Mother. And then these good folks would turn both her and Legs in. No, it wasn't safe. She and Legs needed to leave. They would do so tonight under the cover of darkness. But that left a whole day of danger. What would she do if they turned on her today?

She pulled the spindly legs off of a potato and placed it on the pile she was making.

And if they didn't find out about Mother, they still had to deal with the hunters in the woods. It was likely another group would come. She needed to plan should that occur. Because, sooner or later, here at Hogan's or in some other bolt-hole, they would come. They would find her, and she'd better have a cover.

Ke had suggested a cover to Zu Hogan when she'd first come. "She could be a girl from Koramtown," Ke'd said, "visiting."

"Visiting who?" Zu Hogan had asked.

"Have your pick," said Ke. "Both Talen and I are of marriageable age. Or maybe she's visiting River as a friend."

"Maybe," said Zu Hogan. "Maybe." But he'd never come back to tell her what he'd decided. Sugar had visited friends regularly in Koramtown. They were some of the happiest moments of her life. There was such an ease being among your equals. She knew what friends did when they visited. And while Ke was of marriageable age, all the neighbors around this farmstead would already know who he was courting and what his prospects were. Her tale would be news to them. And she didn't want to be news. She wanted to be nothing. Talen would probably not be making such arrangements. So he was an option. But she couldn't be sure. It would be easier if Sugar was River's friend visiting from Koramtown. Someone come to help with the harvest.

"Sugar?" Legs asked in a quiet voice.

She said nothing, and stacked another potato. He hadn't slept all last night and needed rest.

"You're not sleeping," he said.

"Oh?" she said.

"You breathe different when you sleep," he said. "It's something like this." He began to make small grunting noises like a pig.

"I don't either."

"Yes," he said. "You do. But then so did Mother."

A momentary silence fell upon them both. Sugar should have felt something in that silence, but she was empty still. How was it that she could not feel?

"Does," Sugar corrected. "She's not dead. You heard those soldiers. And not only that, but it's possible she will be freed."

Those had been Zu Hogan's words when he'd shown them the dog warren: "Have hope; if your mother survives her wounds and is taken to Whitecliff, then there is a chance I can free her."

"But how can that be true?" Legs asked. "He's just a Koramite."

And Mother was just a smith's wife. Sugar had not yet told Legs what she had witnessed of the battle and Mother's horrible speed.

Sugar put down the leggy potato in her hands and moved back next to him. She reached out and began to smooth his hair, tracing the whorls of his wild cowlicks.

"I don't know," she said. "Zu Hogan has a powerful brother-in-law. A captain of the Shoka. Perhaps he will save her."

But he wouldn't. Not even a Mokaddian territory lord would save a Sleth.

The lines of her world were shifting, and where they'd stop she did not know. It was like the one time she'd seen a perfect rock to rest upon, but as she neared it the lines and shadows shifted and she realized the rough stem she'd thought was a weed at the base of the rock was really a brown viper, coiled in the dry grass and ready to strike.

"This isn't a good place to hide," he said.

"I know," said Sugar.

"We should make a cubby," he said. "Like we did in the woods to escape the miller's son."

There weren't enough cabbages and potatoes to make a pile big enough to hide both of them. But if she used the bushel basket there might be enough for Legs.

"You're right," she said and began to move the piles she'd already made.

Before they'd finished, Sugar heard someone walk on the floor above her. Alarm shot through her. They weren't ready with the cubby. Then she heard River singing the fisherman's lullaby, the all-clear signal, and relaxed.

But Sugar did not join River above. It was safer down here in the dark and they needed to finish what they'd begun. After some time, someone came to the cellar door and stopped. She heard them grab the hook and then the door opened, spilling in the dim light of early morning.

River looked down at her. "Did you not hear me?"

"Yes," Sugar said. "We did."

"I see," said River. "Well, come on up; eat while you can. The boys are all out in the yard doing chores."

"Do you have a chamber pot?" asked Legs.

River smiled. "Somewhere," she said. "We refused to carry out each other's stink years ago. And who wants to carry their own when you can trot out to the privy? But I don't think we threw it away. Besides, I know someone who would benefit from playing the good host. Come up. You can eat and take care of your business like people instead of grubs."

Sugar and Legs climbed out of the cellar. A hard loaf of bread sat on the table. Fat slices of dark sausage sizzled in a pan over the fire. And a thick broth, for softening the bread, bubbled in a pot.

River led Legs to the back room. When she returned, she sawed off a sizeable piece of bread and gave Sugar a bowl of the broth.

The three boys came in shortly after that, taking off their muddy boots and setting them alongside the wall next to the door. When Talen saw Sugar, he stopped short.

"What is she doing up here?" he asked.

"It looks like she's eating," said Ke and shoved Talen along.

Talen gave her an angry glance, then he handed Nettle the fish.

Nettle walked over to River, eyeing Sugar the whole way, opened the creel he was carrying and pulled out an enormous catfish that had been cleaned, gutted, and skinned. "Here's our afternoon soup."

"Put it in there," River said, motioning with her chin toward an empty pot on the floor.

Nettle slid the fish in the pot.

Talen still stood on the other side of the room, brooding.

"What are you doing?" River asked him. "Go sit down."

"I'm not getting anywhere close to that," Talen said and pointed at Sugar.

Just then Legs appeared in the doorway of the back room holding the covered chamber pot.

"Sugar," River corrected. "And you are going to be the gracious host. In fact, it appears you have a little business in the back room that needs to be dealt with."

"A little business?" asked Talen in amazement. He turned and saw Legs standing there. "No." He shook his head. "I will not."

"You will empty the chamber pot for him, and then you will empty it for Sugar."

"No," said Sugar. "Please." They'd already put this family in grave danger. She didn't want them to do one thing more.

"You can't go outside," said River. "That would be foolhardy. Besides, we wouldn't have this problem except for Talen. So he can take responsibility for the messes he makes."

"I'm not doing it," said Talen. He looked at Nettle.

Nettle held up both hands. "This is your house, not mine."

Ke shifted his enormous frame in his seat to face Talen squarely. "You're going to be the little chamber pot man," said Ke. "And you're going to be happy about it."

The threat was obvious, but Talen didn't move. The tension built for a moment, but then Ke stood and took a step toward Talen.

"Fine," said Talen. "Tell him to put it down and step out of the doorway."

"Legs," said Sugar. "Come. We'll go back down."

Legs set the pot on the floor, then felt his way to Sugar's position. Only then did Talen brush past. He picked up the pot with great distaste and went outside.

"Please stay here," River said to Sugar. "Talen will be all right. You just sit down and enjoy your meal."

It felt so good to stand straight and see sunlight. Perhaps she could stay up here for just a little while.

"I can understand his reluctance," said Sugar.

"He's not the only one that's reluctant," said Nettle.

THEY ATE IN relative silence, River asking Sugar questions that would make any normal guest feel comfortable. But these were not normal circumstances, and they only made the meal more strained.

Toward the end, River turned to Talen and said, "Because of last night, Ke and I now must find Sugar and Legs another place. So we'll be hunting one up today. That means you're going to stay here to finish the chores and to keep an eye out. Sugar and Legs are your charges until we return."

Talen just looked into his bowl.

"Look at me, Talen. Do you think Da and I are stupid people? I know Ke, of course, is suspect." She grinned.

It was a good effort to break the tension, but Talen did not accept it. "Yes, given the facts, I do think you're stupid. But then I know you're not stupid, so that means you're hiding some of the facts."

River glanced at Ke, then back to Talen.

"And you've been hiding them for quite some time," said Talen.

"It wasn't supposed to happen this way," she said. "Da knows these people. They're good, Talen. And there's more to this than you realize. So much more. But now's not the time or place to explain. All you have to do is finish the chores and keep an eye out. I want you to give Sugar and Legs some time up here. And that means you'll have to stay in the house. Because you won't be able to warn them or cover their retreat if you're outside."

"Then how do I do the chores?"

Both River and Ke looked at Nettle.

"Right," said Nettle. "I'll be out in the fields."

"Oh, no you don't," said Talen. "You're not leaving me alone with these two."

"Chores have got to be done," said Ke. "It will look odd, a fine day like today and nobody working. Besides, a man shoulders his own burdens."

"Sure," said Talen. "And when these two eat me, I guess you'll be the one cleaning up what's left."

"Look at them, Talen," River said. "They are not dangerous."

"Just the presence of them," Talen said, "is enough to put a noose around every one of our necks."

WHILE RIVER HAD been there, Sugar, for the first time since the awful events, felt a lightening in her mood. There were some people that possessed such great quantities of openness and hope that it spilled over to others. River was one of these people.

Of course, when River closed the door behind her, Sugar and Legs were left with Talen.

He threw the bar on the door then turned to her. He shook his head as if he still couldn't believe his predicament, then he picked up his bow and withdrew two arrows from one of the three tall baskets that hung on the wall. Each basket held arrows that were ringed with a different color just below the fletching. She assumed the colors distinguished a different spine strength and weight, matched to the strength of the bow. He nocked one of the arrows marked with an ochre ring. The other he kept in the hand that held the bow. Both had gray goose feathers. Both were plain, but they had clearly been heated and straightened and would fly true to deliver the iron tips that shone with grease to keep the rust off.

"Here's the first thing we're going to get straight," said Talen. "Me and my immortal parts are off-limits. You see that smudge on the lintel of the doorway to the loft?"

Sugar turned to look where he pointed. But before she had fully turned her head, she heard the bow hum. The second shaft flew almost as the first hit a dark coloration on the pale whitewashed lintel.

She turned back to him. He held another two more of the ochre-ringed arrows, one nocked just as before.

Legs sat at the table eating the last scraps of his food. He put down his spoon and held very still.

"I've been thinking all morning," Talen said. "I don't know what game my father is playing, but I do know this: you cross me, I won't hesitate. In fact, by all rights, I should shoot you down now."

Sugar knew the look in his eyes. She knew he was considering it. Her father had taught her to never show fear in a fight. Never show pain. Never give an opponent any reason for courage unless you wanted to lure them into a trap. What kind of a fighter was Talen? Was he one that only respected force? Or was he one that was more interested in avoiding a fight?

"Why does my father harbor a hatchling?" he asked.

"I'm not a hatchling," she said.

"Whatever you call it."

"I practice no dark art," she said.

"No, you wouldn't think it dark, would you?"

"I don't know *any* lore," she said.

"But your parents do."

She had no response to that.

"Right," he said. "So what's been done to my father? Or is some threat being hung over us?"

"Nothing has been done," she said. "There are no threats."

He was agitated. Angry. Scared. She could read it all in his face. And she would have the same reaction in his situation, was having the same reaction to what her mother had done.

"How do I know River and Ke aren't already under the spell of some foul master?" he asked. "How do I know they'll even return?"

He raised his bow to the verge of drawing it. "Nettle said to wait. But I can't see how that will help."

He was serious: he did want to slay her. He truly believed she was Sleth, and prevarication would only confirm that assessment. She and Legs would not survive the afternoon with him in this state. That much was clear. "I will not lie to you," she said. "My mother did things that—"

She didn't want to say it. Legs sat as motionless as a heron at the table, his wild hair sticking up. She didn't want for him to hear it this way. But that wasn't the reason she'd stopped. She didn't want to name Mother aloud. There were other explanations for what she'd seen. Maybe what she saw her mother do had been distorted by her fears. Maybe Cotton had indeed been stolen and magicked by woodikin. Maybe a dark soul rode in the body of the stork they'd found. There were a dozen maybes.

But the easiest explanation would not go away. She had to face the truth. There was no salvation in lies. "I saw my mother charge an army. I saw her cleave a man's head in two. I saw her move with a dark grace that horrified me. And I saw the Sleth signs on the dead body of my little brother."

The words dropped from her lips like heavy stones.

"I know you have no reason to believe me," she said. "But I found out about this only a day before you."

He had not raised his bow, but he hadn't lowered it either.

"I am not associated with any murder of Sleth. I have nothing to do with any art, unless my mother has done something to me like she did to my brother. But I don't know what that would be. I'm as confused as you are, Talen.

"Think on this as well," she added. "If we were so wicked, wouldn't we have risen from the cellar early this morning and worked our mischief on you when you were all asleep?"

"I didn't sleep," he said.

"Even so," she said. "If that's what we were, it would have been the perfect time, would it not?"

He said nothing, but she could see the wheels of his mind turning, see him weighing her, weighing the situation.

At last, he said, "That's the line," and pointed at the edge of the table where Legs sat. "Come across, and my arrows fly."

She exhaled and realized she'd been holding her breath. But his decision didn't mean they were safe. She needed to have another plan to neutralize that bow. He might be quick with it. But a bow was a hard weapon to wield in close spaces. A knife was much better in this situation.

She turned so the knife sheathed at her waist was hidden from his view. She ran one hand through her hair and with the other she removed the loop that held the knife in the sheath. She and Legs were going to get out of here. Her mother had told her to take Legs and ride. She should have disobeyed her mother before and fought. But now she'd make up for that. She'd take Legs and stow him in a safe place. And then what? How could she, of all people, rescue Mother?

But that wasn't important right now. Right now she had to figure out how to deal with this boy. And what if hunters came? It would not do to have them find him sitting there guarding her and Legs. That was not how you treated a visitor. She began to clean up the breakfast dishes. Began to tidy and let her mind work. The first thing she noticed was that he'd placed himself in the wrong part of the house.

"You cannot look out of the windows from where you're sitting." When he didn't respond, she said, "You can't watch for hunters from that side of the room."

"You look out the windows and watch for hunters. I'm watching you."

She nodded in acquiescence. That meant she wouldn't retreat to the cellar. She didn't want to do that anyway. If Talen should change his mind, she didn't want to be caught like a fish in a barrel.

Legs stepped toward Sugar with his hands out. When he found her, he felt for her hand. "Should I go down?" he asked.

It would probably be best. That way she wouldn't have to worry about him should the situation change. But she didn't want him to sit down there alone thinking about what she'd just revealed. He needed to know she was strong. That things would be all right. At least that's what she told herself.

"Stand with me," she said, "and smell the morning coming in through the windows. We'll visit the potatoes soon enough."

The shutters by the dining table looked out over the farm. She pulled them completely open then walked to the the back of the house and opened the shutters on the window there so she had a view of the river.

After a few moments Legs began to hum one of the songs he'd often sang to entertain the men and women of Plum village in the evenings as they sat drinking their ale. It was the one about a stupid boy trying to outsmart a gang of crows. She smiled. Perhaps it was she who needed him.

Legs sang another few songs, then he stopped, and Sugar could see he was thinking. A few minutes later he began again. A half an hour must have passed that way, Legs humming or singing, stopping to think, singing again, all while Sugar tidied up, first breakfast, then the floor, always keeping an eye on the windows. And across from them, Talen sat with his bow at the ready.

Sugar ran through a number of scenarios. She knew if Talen changed he mind and decided to use his bow, that she would pick up a chair as a shield and charge him.

He'd only get off one shot that way. It would pierce her body or it wouldn't. And if it didn't, then she'd be in close with her knife. However, that wouldn't solve any issues should hunters show up. They needed to seem friends, and that would never happen with him holding the bow.

She finished the floor, cleaned the ashes from the hearth and put them in the tin ash bucket, then took a good long look out the window. Nettle worked in the distance.

Talen spoke. "What kind of a name is Legs anyway? It's not like he's tall for his age. I can't imagine he's quick either."

"No, Zu," said Legs. "It's rather hard to be speedy when you can't see where you're going."

Talen looked surprised that Legs had talked. Sugar herself was a bit surprised, but she knew the tone in his voice. He'd made up his mind about something. This was him wanting to make a point.

"Legs," said Sugar in warning.

"So that means it would be a bit difficult for me to catch and eat you."

Talen raised his eyebrows. "What's he going on about?"

"I'm just pointing out the obvious," said Legs. "And you can talk to me directly if you want. I'm not deaf."

Talen stood. "Maybe I don't like the way your eyes slide around."

"Sorry, Zu," said Legs. His eyes had been sliding and he closed his lids. "I know all the stories about Sleth. I've sung all the songs. I've been thinking about them. And you'd expect if my mother had the powers she's accused of, she would have given me my sight. Why wouldn't she have done that?"

"What do I know about your mother's Slethy ways? Ask her yourself when they put you in the tower."

"It's because she's not," said Legs.

Sugar wished she had Legs's confidence. But she didn't

want him to provoke Talen further. "Legs," she said. "We didn't answer his question." She turned to Talen. "It's his nickname. He was born legs first."

Sugar didn't tell him that the midwife had said when Legs's feet first appeared, he'd pulled them back from the cool air in the room and refused to come out. The first time she'd heard that as a girl, she'd laughed and laughed. She had made her mother tell it again and again. The memory of that happy time seemed so far away, so un-real, as if it weren't true at all, but only a story.

"I think I want to go down now," said Legs.

"Yes," she said. "I think that's a good idea." And who knew what he'd say next? Lords forbid, but he'd probably try to tweak Talen with some comment about him taking care of Legs's business earlier.

Legs walked to her, hand in front feeling the way. She took his hand and led him to the cellar door.

When the door was up, Legs turned to her. "I don't care," he said under his breath. And she knew he meant he didn't care even if Mother were Sleth.

"Neither do I," she agreed, but that was a lie. She did care.

Legs descended the stairs into the darkness with the potatoes. She found leaving the cellar door open put her on edge. Not everyone had such a cellar built into the floor. Many were outside the kitchen. She could see how having it in the kitchen would be handy, and it was not in the way, but she was not used to working so close to such a hole, so she shut the door.

She turned back to the window and knew she couldn't stand there doing nothing while Talen watched her. "You can hardly make a lunch over there," she said. "I will make us something to go with that fish. Can you tell me if your sister keeps any savory?"

Talen hesitated. She expected him to say something about poisoning the food, but he didn't. He pointed at a cupboard. "It's in there."

"Thank you," said Sugar and began washing and cutting vegetables.

When she finished with the vegetables, she found what she needed to make flat cakes. She had her hands in the flour when she glanced out the back window and saw half a dozen Mokaddians wearing leather cuirasses and helms crouching at the top of the riverbank.

Her heart jumped.

A handful of them broke off and approached the house, crouching low as they walked.

These were not Fir-Noy. At least they did not wear the Fir-Noy colors. She couldn't tell from this distance, but it appeared their wrist tattoos were those of the Shoka. But it didn't matter—Shoka or Fir-Noy, they were still Mokaddians, still sneaking up on the house.

She drew back from the window so they wouldn't see her.

From her angle of view she saw the first man run up to the house and take his position at the corner.

She couldn't catch her breath. The moment she'd been dreading had come and found her making flat cakes. All her mother and father had suffered to give them a chance to escape would now go to waste.

But that couldn't happen. She wouldn't let it happen. She didn't have time to open the door to the cellar, descend, and close it up again.

She looked out the front window and saw nothing but Nettle working the field in the distance.

She whirled round and faced Talen. "Hunters," she whispered.

Talen had been leaning against the wall in his chair,

balancing it on two of its legs. He came away from the wall and brought all four legs to the ground.

She motioned with her head towards the river. He needed to put that bow down. If he had truly been guarding against something in the woods, then he would have been outside. Both of them would be. They needed to appear to be friends. No, they needed to appear to be more than friends. It would have been better if Ke had been sitting there, but Talen would have to do. She only prayed he wasn't a fool.

She could not speak, not if she didn't want to alert the man outside, so she hastened across the floor toward Talen. He must have seen the alarm in her face because he stood and looked with worry to the windows.

One, two, four steps, and she crossed the line he'd drawn. He began to raise the bow, but either his fear had paralyzed him or he wasn't a fool after all because he allowed her to come right up to him, grab the wrist of the hand that held the bow, and whisper into his ear.

"They're outside," she said.

"Fir-Noy?"

"I'm going to sit on your lap," she said. "Like a lover." Then she pushed him back into his chair.

Talen's eyes were round with alarm. He clenched the bow.

She pushed the bow away and settled on him. "Put the bow down," she whispered. "Put your arm around me."

He was frozen.

"I am your girl from Koramtown," she whispered. "I'm visiting."

Something rustled along the outside of the house. He turned his head toward the sound. He reached back and leaned the bow against the wall, but he didn't let go.

She raised his free hand to her ribs.

"I'm Lily," she said.

"What?"

"Lily," she repeated. "The daughter of Ham, a farmer, living just the other side—"

She could hear a man at the door, and from the corner of her eye she saw the shadow of someone take position by the open shutter. She immediately dipped her mouth to meet Talen's. She'd kissed boys before. None of the Mokaddians in her village. Her mother had made sure they traveled to Koramtown regularly, more often this last year since Sugar was soon to be of age for marriage negotiations. She closed her eyes and cupped his head with her free, flour-dusted hand.

Talen sat as stiff as a piece of furniture. She opened her eyes and found him staring at her, his eyeballs big as her face. It was like finding a large caterpillar on the end of your nose.

More men gathered outside the door.

"The bow," she said midkiss, "drop the bow." His mouth was parted in shock, frozen open like the stone of a statue. She had stolen her share of kisses from Koramtown boys, and this one wouldn't fool anybody. She flickered the tip of her tongue inside his mouth. Maybe that would bring him around.

The bow and arrows clattered to the floor. And to Talen's credit he tried to move his lips. They were dry, and the whole thing smelled of the morning's sausage, but he acted. Of course, she didn't think either of their performances would be enough.

Then someone tried to force the door.

"You there," said a man, looking in at them from the window. "Open that door!"

Talen shot up like a flushed animal and dumped Sugar to the floor. She was still getting up when he swung the door wide.

Three men pushed in, weapons bristling: a young one

in front with half of his teeth missing and two older men behind. Before Sugar could move, the young one stuck the point of his sword inches from Talen's neck. "You," he said. "Where's your father?"

"He was summoned to Whitecliff," said Talen.

"We should have known your family would cause problems," he said.

A man with eyes like ice appeared behind the three that stood in the doorway. "Put the sword down," he said.

Sugar did not know him, but from his clothing, she suspected he was the bailiff. "Talen," he said. "I told your da to order the Koramites in the district. I wanted them calm. Instead, I get reports of all sorts of things happening here last night."

Sugar froze. Had someone seen Talen rousting them out from underneath the old house? They'd heard voices in the night, but they'd been in the distance. And what if Talen decided to turn on her and Legs? He was half convinced she was Sleth already.

It had been a mistake to stay. She should have taken Legs and run. They could have hidden in the woods somewhere until dark fell. Now it was too late.

"Why did you have to provoke the Fir-Noy?" asked the bailiff.

Talen said nothing. He stood there like a scarecrow.

The bailiff looked from Talen to Sugar and back again. "Who's this?"

"Nobody," said Talen.

"Nobody?" asked the bailiff.

"Zu," said Sugar, "I'm Lily from Koramtown."

"And why did you bar the door in the middle of the morning?"

Talen said nothing, just stood there with his mouth open.

"We . . ." said Sugar and looked down. That's what she supposed someone caught in a forbidden embrace would do. She hoped she hadn't hung her head too quickly.

"Speak up!" said the bailiff.

"We were," Talen said. He looked as if he'd swallowed a chicken whole. "Sporting."

"While the father is away," said the bailiff. He shook his head and looked around the room. "You and your altercations with those Fir-Noy armsmen have caused me a bit of work. I've been ordered by the Shoka lords to conduct a personal search of every Koramite homestead in my district."

"I am sorry, Zu," said Talen.

"Look at me," said the bailiff. "What are you hiding?"

Talen's eyes were wide with fear. If anyone was going to give them away, it would be him. "Nothing, Zu. Nothing."

The bailiff shook his head. "Of course not." He signaled to his men to search the house. "I need something to drink."

"We have no beer," said Talen.

"Then fetch me a draught of sweet water from your well," said the bailiff.

Talen complied without hesitation, leaving Sugar alone with the men. One of the bailiff's men stood on the far side of the room opening cupboards. She could hear the second upstairs and the third in the back room and still others out in the yard. The bailiff himself paced about the room and then noticed the cellar door.

"Girl," he said. "Open this up." Then he drew his sword and stepped back.

"You do not need to worry, Zu," she said, indicating his sword. "I will gladly open the door, but nothing is down there. Only a few cabbages and potatoes. I saw them myself this morning."

"Oh, is that the trysting spot for Koramite youth?" The bailiff shook his head. "I thought Talen was being prepared for a Mokaddian marriage. I expected more of Hogan."

Sugar looked down. They would consider it filthy for him to sport with a Koramite. Was that why he'd been so stiff? She walked over to the door. She hoped Legs had heard the men and had hidden in the small cubby they'd made last night.

"Get a light," he said.

"Yes, Zu," she said, and then moved to the other side of the room to fetch a lamp.

The man searching this end of the main room was poking his sword deep into barrels of beans and barley. What he expected to find there she could not guess.

Sugar found one of Zu Hogan's lamps and the oil jar. She poured a bit into the lamp. Then she took it to the fire, retrieved an ember with some small tongs, held it close and began to blow.

"I don't understand why a girl from Koramtown would risk hunters, alone it seems, to come all the way up here."

Sugar blew once more and the wick caught fire. "I came early yesterday," she said. "News of the Sleth had not yet arrived." Then she pulled up the cellar door.

He pointed at the stair with his sword, indicating she should go first.

Sugar nodded and began to descend the stairs a few steps. As she did her light illuminated the room below and the fact that while Legs had crawled into the cubby, he had not hidden his foot. It, along with the end of his trousers, was plain to see.

The bailiff positioned himself above to get a clearer view of the cellar.

Sugar switched the lamp to her other hand, moving it so that it cast a shadow over Legs.

"Lift it higher," said the bailiff, "I can't see."

"Yes, Zu." Her mind raced. What could she do? What lie could she tell him?

None came to her mind.

She shifted the lamp.

"Ho," boomed Zu Hogan from the doorway. "What is this?"

The bailiff turned, and Sugar saw her chance. She quickly descended the remaining steps and hurried to stand in front of Leg's foot. She held her lamp out as if she were trying to give the room its best possible illumination.

"What kind of a lunatic challenges Fir-Noy armsmen?" asked the bailiff.

Zu Hogan put his hands on his hips. "The same kind that challenges Bone-Faced rot."

"That's all good and fine," said the bailiff. "But you've put me in a position. Do you know how lucky you are? Any other Koramite and you'd lose your head. I would have to take it myself."

"We have far greater things than Fir-Noy honor to worry about," said Zu Hogan. "The woman held in White-cliff, she's gone."

"Gone?"

"Stolen out of the tower by a creature that cast Droz and his whole guard about like puppets."

The bailiff stood stunned. "Goh," he finally said. "Her creation, then, come to free her? Or that of her hatchlings?"

"We don't know where it came from or whence it bore her. The dogs can't track it."

Sugar sat down. There was no doubt about Mother now. She wondered what kind of creature it was that had rescued her. But she couldn't imagine it. She couldn't picture her mother as Sleth any more than she could picture her as a dog.

What would Zu Hogan do? He wouldn't turn her in, would he? Not after hiding and lying for them.

"She's probably all safely tucked away now in some wicked bolt hole." The bailiff cursed. There was a brief pause in their conversation then the bailiff said, "This does not bode well for your people."

"It does not bode well for any of us," said Zu Hogan. "Because when you do find them, even if you take one hundred men, it won't be enough. The creature was shot through with arrows and stabbed with spears. Captain Argoth delivered a blow that would have beheaded a horse. Nothing. The ballista men shot a dart and smote the beast squarely in the chest, and it still managed somehow to vanish. It cannot be harmed by normal means."

The bailiff looked down at Sugar.

"What's more," said Hogan, "if it's taken her, then I suspect it most certainly has the two hatchlings that escaped."

The bailiff nodded. "We're done here."

He called his men off, and as suddenly as they'd come, they left.

Sugar whispered to Legs to stay put then she walked back up the stairs.

Hogan, Talen, and Nettle stood out in the yard. She joined them to watch the bailiff and his men walk back to the woods where they'd tied their horses.

"Do you think he suspects?" asked Nettle.

"No," said Zu Hogan. "Although I do wonder how he missed marking Sugar."

"We created a ruse," said Talen.

"Oh?"

"We were . . ."

"Yes?"

"Sporting," finished Sugar.

Nettle raised an eyebrow, but Zu Hogan looked down at her with a sad smile. "Purity's daughter indeed," he said.

What that meant, she could not tell. But she could guess what he was thinking. Her mother was a monster. So what did you do with the child of a monster? Sugar knew the answer to that question.

She also knew her mother. There would be an explanation if she could talk to her. There had to be.

ABOUT A QUARTER mile down the road from Hogan's place, the bailiff halted the men. Prunes reined in his horse with the rest of them.

"I've been commanded to post a watch on Hogan," said the bailiff. "So two of you are going to stay behind. Prunes, you and Gid will have the first day. I'll send someone to relieve you in the morning."

That was just Prunes's luck. He gets an opportunity to sleep, but he has to do it with that garlic-eater at his side. Still, some rest was better than none at all. Prunes simply nodded then peeled his horse from the column, Gid following behind.

They hobbled their horses in a small glen on the far side of the hill and began hiking to find the right position to watch the Koramite.

A few steps up the slope and Gid began to sing under his breath. "A lady green with lips so wide, I could not help but kiss her. But when I'd had my fill of tongue, I put her in the roaster."

"Will you shut up," said Prunes.

"They're not going to hear us."

"I don't care if they do hear us. We're not going to find anything here."

"How do you mean?"

"This is Captain Argoth's brother-in-law. We're not going to find anything here but some rest. And that's what I intend to take. And that is also why you're going to be quiet as a mouse."

"You don't know what loyalties flow in that Koramite's veins," said Gid. "In fact, for a Koramite on the run, this might be the very best place to hide."

"See," said Prunes, "that's what comes of eating too much garlic. You get brain vapors."

"It's got nothing to do with what I eat."

"Stinking vapors of the mind," said Prunes.

Gid made a rude gesture, but Prunes ignored it.

Soon they found an outcropping of rock that gave a clear view of the farm, then positioned themselves just behind the brush line.

As soon as they sat down, Gid took out a whetstone and began sharpening his knife.

Stupid eager—that's what he was. If Sleth did indeed pay the Koramite a visit, then they'd need more than knives. Goh, the Koramite's reports of that creature in Whitecliff gave Prunes the shivers. And if that thing showed up, the best thing to do would be to run. Run or hide in some hole. Then Prunes realized he'd sat in the wrong place. "You need to sit over here," said Prunes.

"Why?"

"Because that places me upwind of your stinking carcass."

But Gid gave him a look that said he wasn't moving. After a few moments, Prunes sighed in irritation. The man was an affliction, but it wasn't worth a battle. He picked himself up and found a better spot. "You've got first watch," said Prunes. "If I catch you sleeping, you're going to dance to a hard pipe."

Gid grunted. "And who do you think will be my partner?"

But Prunes had already laid back and closed his eyes and wasn't even going to consider giving Gid an answer.

19.

SUMMONS

Talen stood in the house, facing his father who had just related the events at the Whitecliff fortress the night before. Da's face was bruised from when the creature had knocked him aside. His throat was worse. It looked like he wore a blue-and-purple collar. The creature had throttled him and damaged his voice. When he finished his tale, none of the others spoke.

Talen didn't care that the boy and the girl were standing right here with them. "The evidence, it appears, is overwhelming," he said. "The Fir-Noy were not making this rot up."

Earlier, he hadn't known what to do. He and Nettle had not been able to sleep. They had discussed the situation from the moment the girl and boy had gone down into the cellar last night until the sun rose. They could give the girl and boy the benefit of the doubt, as it seemed Da, River, and Ke were willing to do, and assume huge risks. They could distract the two until Nettle could call the authorities to come collect them. Or they could kill them. But the questioners would want them alive. The laws of the hunt would demand punishment. Furthermore, if they were Sleth and there was a nest of them, then anyone who killed the boy and girl could expect the same retribution that was visited upon the village of Plum.

But to leave them alive in the house? And then the girl had confessed. All his talk of bold action, and he had been able to do nothing. Then the bailiff had shown up. But he hadn't known it was the bailiff. He'd thought they were the Fir-Noy armsmen come back. He couldn't tell *them* the boy and girl were the hatchlings. Those armsmen would automatically assume Talen's family had been harboring them.

He should have never let her sit in his lap. Never let her kiss him. Lords, her tongue . . .

He kept expecting something to happen, to feel a shift of some kind. He could detect no change in himself, but that didn't mean she hadn't worked some kind of magic upon him with her touch. How could you kiss a Sleth child and not be changed?

It was obvious they had only two options—kill them or bring a hunt. And he preferred someone else face the ire of the nest. "It's time to give them up," said Talen.

"No," said Da in his rough voice. "That will never happen."

And yet there Da stood with that massive bruise on his face. Perhaps he was trying to tell Talen it was foolish to talk about such things in front of the boy and girl.

"River and Ke will be back soon enough. We're going to keep them safe, Talen."

Da wasn't acting. He was serious. "With that woman's beast looking for them?"

"We don't know what that thing was," said Da.

"Who cares what it was? It rescued her. That's all we need to know."

"That's not all we need to know."

It was obvious from the events at Whitecliff that there

were powerful masters ruling this nest of Sleth. Had they gotten to Da? Had they themselves delivered the boy and girl here?

It was terrible to contemplate, but he wanted to know the situation. "You can tell me," said Talen.

"No, I can't. Not right now."

"Have you been threatened by other members of this nest?"

"Son," said Da. "Trust me."

"Trust *me*," Talen said. "If the masters of this nest have something hanging over us, I want to know. I want to help."

"There are no masters," said Da. "No threats. This is very simple. Sugar and Legs are innocent of any offense."

"You're kidding me?"

"No," said Da.

Talen glanced over at Nettle for some help, but Nettle looked as concerned as he was. He turned back to his father. "I'm sorry," he said. "But I don't think you're in your right mind. If they're innocent, then let the questioners absolve them."

"Talen," Da said more forcefully. "You don't know of what you speak. So keep your mouth shut."

Shut? When they had armsmen seeking their lives, a Sleth on the loose, and the children of that Sleth standing right there?

"Why don't you enlighten me? I can clearly see the troubles these two have cost us. And it doesn't require a lord's councilor to multiply such troubles across all the rest of our people. You were a fool not to turn them in."

The girl stood to the side of Da, cold calculation in her eyes. The boy was looking off into space, his head shaking oddly. It unnerved Talen. That right there was probably the result of some Sleth abomination.

Da's eyes narrowed. "You'll put a bung in that mouth of yours."

"Somebody is going to die because of these two. And that's not going to be me. I'd also like to avoid any torture that might be involved."

"We'll find them another place." Da's mouth was tight with anger.

Talen wondered if all this speaking hurt his throat, but someone needed to talk sense.

"Some wicked servant came to fetch their mother, and you want to harbor them?"

Da's anger broke. He lifted up one side of the table and slammed it back down again. A leg gave way and the table slid over to one side. "I'm about to lose my temper!" If his voice had been normal, it would have come out as a bellow. But this voice, as if he were sick, was worse to hear.

Talen was going to say, don't worry you've already done that, but Da's eyes were as round as eggs. His face was red.

Years ago Da had let Ke and even River feel the open face of his hand. Ke had many a story; he also harbored much resentment that Talen didn't receive the same good instruction. But Mother had made Da give it up before she died.

Da violently scratched the side of his head. He said, "I can forgive you your ignorance. But I won't stand your disobedience. Do you truly think I'm such a drooling idiot that I would invite monsters into our house?"

"No," said Talen, "but you might blind yourself so you couldn't see the danger. All this time it's been about Koramite oppression, jealous Mokaddians. Well, the facts are staring us in the face, but you won't look at them."

"*You* are the one that won't look at them," said Da. "What do you think the questioners will do with them? What do you think the Fir-Noy will demand?"

They'd demand the children be locked up as bait. They would torture them until they produced answers. Or they'd kill them.

"Only a coward lets the innocent be punished when it's within his power to stop it," said Da.

This was crazy. These weren't two children accused of stealing apples from their neighbor's orchard. "It's not cowardice," said Talen. "We're talking about Sleth, Da. Sleth."

"Sleth," said Da. He sighed. "Fine. I suppose River's right. It's time. Although I do not believe you're ready." He turned to Nettle. "That would go as well for you. Of course, this should be your father's office, shouldn't it? But we can take care of that. You two are coming with me today, we're—"

Talen didn't understand half of what Da had just said. But it didn't matter. "What about them?" he asked, pointing at the girl and boy.

"What about them? River and Ke will return soon enough. And it doesn't appear you enjoy their company much."

"You're just going to leave them here unattended?" And then he understood what Da was doing. "You're going to give them a chance to run, aren't you? And that way if someone asks, you can truthfully say you have no idea where they are."

Da shook his head. "Them running is the last thing I want, Talen. Because then they'll surely be caught. You might want to think about that. Even if you haven't a nit's teaspoon of compassion, you'll want to consider what will happen when the questioners begin their work. How long will it take before the boy is tortured into revealing who hid him for so long?"

That was easy to calculate. As were the consequences.

Da had placed them all on a crumbling precipice and asked them to dance. "I don't understand why you're doing this," said Talen.

"Nettle," Da said, "tell me. Does your da tell you everything that goes on in his councils? You're his son. If you were to ask him, would he tell you all his battle plans?"

"He tells me a lot."

"Everything?"

"No."

"Why is that? He trusts you, doesn't he?"

"Well," said Nettle, then he fell into silence and shrugged. "I guess he thinks I've got a butter jaw."

Da laughed. "Hardly. It's because some truths, if shared, would hurt those who do not deserve it. And it is at such times that you cannot simply pass the responsibility of the secrets you hold to someone else. You either carry the burden of the secret or release the whirlwind."

"Secrets?" This did not sound right. This did not make him feel comfortable. What secrets did Da keep that concerned the girl and the boy?

"There's more to this than the flimsy logic you've tried to fob me off with today, isn't there?"

"There's more to everything, son. Even when all the words have been spoken. But right now I have an appointment to meet the Clan Council. I was overtaken by a messenger earlier. I've been summoned back to White-cliff to testify about what happened in the tower. I can understand your frustration, but I can't trust you here alone. So you're going with me. Now get the wagon hitched."

TALEN BUCKLED THE second loin strap about Iron Boy, their mule. Nettle was gathering food because, despite the current turmoils, Da said there were families needing supplies. And now, according to Da, was just as good a time to deliver what they needed as any other. Talen suspected it was only to cover something else, but he could not guess what that was. He didn't understand his father.

Talen stroked Iron Boy's neck. He almost wished he could trade places with the mule.

"I'm not oblivious to all the dangers about us," said Da.

Talen turned. Da had walked up to the wagon. He secured the Hog under the seat. When he finished there, he came to stand before Talen, an unusually dark braid of godsweed in his hand. Despite Da's protestations, River had wrapped his neck with a poultice. "I want you to wear this for protection."

Godsweed was used to ward off things not wholly of this world. Its smoke was potent. But even having it upon you was supposed to have an effect. "Why are you giving me that? This isn't about malevolent souls."

"Oh, but it is," said Da. "Did you not listen to what I said about the creature at the fortress? It was full of the dead. Now, hold out your arm."

Talen pulled back the sleeve of his tunic and let Da tie the braid about his upper arm. The braid was thicker than most, woven in an odd pattern. But he'd never seen Da or River braid it.

"Where did you get this?"

Da said nothing. When he finished tying the braid, he pulled the sleeve of Talen's tunic back down over it, nodded, then reached out, cupped the back of Talen's neck with his large hand, and looked deep into his eyes. "Courage, son."

This was Da's habit since Talen was a boy. He'd look him in the eyes and make him focus on a word.

Talen felt stupid. Annoyed. He wasn't a little boy anymore. He tried to shrug out of his father's grasp, but Da's grip was even stronger than Ke's. Da waited for Talen's response.

"Courage," said Talen.

Da smiled. "See, you feel better already."

"All I felt was your hand, cold as the tomb." Talen hated that little ritual, and he swore at that moment he would never subject his sons to anything like it.

Da nodded. "We're almost done here. I just need a bit of barley."

Nettle returned shortly with what looked like most of what had been hanging in the smoke shed, including the salmon Talen had caught just last week. Nettle placed it next to a basket of cabbages and another of carrots resting in the wagon bed. Then Da came out of the house rolling a medium-sized barrel of barley.

"Goh," said Talen. "How many are we to visit?"

"Not enough," said Da.

Every two weeks Da went to Whitecliff and delivered supplies to struggling families along the way. Most were widows whose Koramite husbands had died or been maimed in the battles with the Bone Faces. One of the families had lost both mother and father, and the oldest son had sold himself to one of the clans to pay their debts.

Talen didn't know how Da knew who to visit. He supposed they discussed such things in the Koramite council Da attended. All the Koramites in the area were supposed to donate their surplus to help the affected families. But it seemed a large portion of what Talen delivered came from his family's own larder and garden. This time was no different.

Da drove the wagon and made Talen and Nettle walk alongside to spare Iron Boy. They traveled in silence for a time. Then Da tied the reins to the wooden hook under the seat and began undoing the thin, black leather strips holding his beard braids and combing the the hair out with an old bone comb. Iron Boy plodded along. When Da began to retie the first braid, Talen figured he'd had enough time for his temper to die down. He looked up at his father on the wagon seat and said, "So have you got some godsweed for Nettle?"

"Not today," said Da. He held the braid with one hand and brought up the leather tie. "That's his father's office."

"That's the second time you've said that."

"I'm glad you can count," said Da.

"It never does any good to hold on to your anger," said Talen.

"You're absolutely right," said Da.

Talen walked in silence for a few more yards waiting for more. When Da didn't respond, he decided to take another tack. "So what are all these facts you were going to bestow on me?"

"What?" asked Da in mock amazement. "An idiot like myself attempt to explain anything to you? I wouldn't presume."

"Oh, come," said Talen.

"You'll get your facts," said Da. "Both of you. Just a little patience is all you need."

"WE SHALL BIND her first," said the Mother. Hunger approached the woman with a weave the Mother had directed him to make, but the woman scrambled back, and before he could reach her, she rose and, with what only could have been multiplied might and speed, ran headlong at the wall of the chamber, crashing into a rock.

The woman fell to the floor.

"You careless fool," the Mother said. She delivered a blow of pain that sent Hunger to his knees.

The Mother turned back to the woman. She bent to her and began singing the odd music of hers, pressing herself into the world of men. Soon the scent of her clean magic filled the room. But the woman did not move.

"She's dead," said Hunger.

"Quiet," commanded the Mother.

He didn't deserve the reproach. He hadn't been careless. It was the woman, the wily woman. How could Hunger know she would try to break her head like a squash? He did not know how the woman could survive such a blow. But then she spoke.

"No," she said.

"It is time," said the Mother.

"Nightmare," said the woman, "depart." She was still unsteady from her injury and slurred her words.

"Your son," said the Mother. "Where has he gone?"

"Dead," she said.

"No," said the Mother. "I can feel him through the weave. He is not dead."

"He is dead," said the woman. "My son is mingled with a stork."

The Mother paused, agitated. "Do not try to deceive me." Then she did something and the woman groaned. "Where is the one with the weave?"

"Why do you torment my dreams?" asked the woman.

"The weave."

The woman was silent again. But again the Mother did something that pained the woman.

"With horse," she said.

"Where did he go with the horse?"

"You can't have him. You will not sacrifice him for his Fire."

"I would never do such a thing," said the Mother. "He is precious to me."

The woman hesitated. "They're looking for him."

"I will protect him. Where is he?"

The woman paused, and the Mother asked again.

"To horse," said the woman weakly.

It made no sense. The woman was babbling. She was

not going to live. Not here in the dark, not with that injury.

"Who is horse?" asked the Mother, but the woman closed her eyes. The Mother tried to bring her back with pain, but the woman fell limp in her hands.

"She's dead," said Hunger.

"Her heart is still beating," said the Mother. "But what's this?" She sniffed. The Mother put a finger to the woman's bloody head and licked the blood off. "Sickness." She savored the blood. "And something else. She'd been eating something. But I've tasted worse. I can fix this one. She's going to live and lead us to others."

HUNGER HAD WANTED to watch the Mother as she attempted to heal the woman, but he'd caught a whiff of magic and she'd sent him out into the night to track it. It was odd how often he'd smelled the magic of late. Perhaps the woman was bringing the Sleth out of hiding, drawing the nest to her. Or perhaps he was simply maturing in his powers. One thing was for sure, he could smell a male in this magic.

Hunger thought of the two men who had attacked him in the tower only a few hours ago. He knew the Mokaddian. It was Argoth, a captain of the Shoka. Perhaps this was his stink.

He followed the scent for miles, up onto the plains, to a farmstead past all settled parts. He paused in the woods on the edge of a field.

A bat darted above him and flittered out over fields of ripe grain shining pale and blue in the moonlight. On the far side of the fields stood a simple cabin with light shining from its small windows.

Hunger took in a great breath of the scent. He knew he shouldn't do that because it only enflamed his appetite.

And the Mother had wanted this human live. But he couldn't help himself.

He walked along the tree line toward it and noticed a number of new stumps. Somebody had been busy this year clearing the land. When Hunger finally approached the cabin, he could hear the soft sounds of a man humming over the thrum of the night insects. He circled the cabin until he found a window. The scent of magic was pouring from the cracks around the window frame. Hunger looked in.

But he did not see Argoth. A burly man stood naked in a large round tub set close to the hearth. He was washing himself. A pot of water steamed over the cheery fire. The man took a cake of soap and lathered his hairy chest. Hunger did not recognize him. He was not the Koramite that had attacked him in the tower. Yet he stank.

Hunger considered the Mother's promise. It had raised his hopes at first, but the more he pondered it, the more it unraveled. What cattleman did his cattle favors? When did one spare a healthy animal from slaughter? You might keep a bull or cow a number of years; the slaughter might be delayed, but when they ceased to be productive, they, with all the rest, were harvested. It was that simple. The Mother thought he was stupid. And maybe he was. But he could see through her lie.

The Mother had forbidden him to eat the ones that stink. Why was that? They couldn't be trusted to serve her. She was going to cull them. So why not order him to do it for her?

He knew why: she didn't want him eating their secrets. Because if he knew their secrets, maybe he could challenge her. Surely they would know how to remake the collar. And if they knew that, they might hold other secrets far more powerful. Secrets strong enough to overpower the Mother.

Hunger walked up to the door. The man sang a few words then continued to hum his tune. Something about the tune pricked Hunger's mind, and he paused, listening. The music filled him with longing as wide as the sky, but no thoughts. Nothing to hang the longing upon.

He felt a revulsion at the thought of eating this man. He realized he'd felt this revulsion before, but it had always been lost in the raging fire of his appetite. But the revulsion didn't matter. It didn't matter that what he was doing was abomination. What mattered was that he had an opportunity to stop the Mother. What mattered was that he could free his family.

The humming swelled.

He would eat this man and satisfy his appetite.

Hunger thrust open the door.

The man did not look at him in horror, only surprise that turned to intelligence. Then the man lunged out of his tub toward the window.

Hunger followed.

The man took two steps and dove at the window. He burst through the shutters.

He was quick and would have escaped, but Hunger was quicker and caught him by the leg just before it disappeared through the window. The man kicked like a horse, but Hunger dragged him back in.

The man did not cry out. He simply turned and delivered a blow to Hunger's throat that would have killed a bull. But the Mother's handiwork wasn't so easily defeated. Instead of felling Hunger, all the man succeeded in doing was breaking his own hand. He drew it back, pain wracking his face.

The Mother didn't know he was here. She was crooning to her children, deep in the caves, and watching over the Sleth woman. Nevertheless, he expected to fight her compulsion.

Then he realized she hadn't said not to eat this one. No, she hadn't said that.

The man used his good hand to pick up a chair. He hammered at Hunger's grip. But Hunger did not let him go. Hunger would not bend to the Mother's wishes like some idiot cow whose only thought was of grass. He was, underneath all this dirt, a man. And even though this Sleth didn't realize it, he was going to help save Hunger's family. He was going to be put to good use. And who knew: if Hunger learned the secrets and defeated the Mother completely, then this Sleth would be the means of saving every mother and daughter and son of the Nine Clans.

Hunger felt along the fiber of this Sleth's being. Soon enough he found an edge. It took only a few moments and Hunger shucked his soul. He was sweet and beautiful and Hunger could not help but bolt great portions of him.

Then the Mother stirred and Hunger froze. He immediately released the man's soul. The remnants flew to the wind as Hunger waited. He stood quietly for some time bracing himself for her ire. But the Mother didn't search him. She didn't walk into his mind. She was too busy. Much too busy.

The man was gone.

Hunger hated himself and yet delighted in the savor of the man. He only hoped he'd eaten enough.

He stepped to the table and fingered the comb. He knew the tune the man was humming. He played it in his mind, waiting for the memories to digest. Waiting for the secrets.

But Hunger did not receive secrets. All he felt was the growing of an unaccountable sorrow. And then the picture of a tall, plain woman with laughing eyes.

He should not have let the man go, but it was too late now. The rest of his secrets were gone. Hunger stood at the man's table for a long time, handling the things there—a seashell brush, a polished mirror, and a length of green cloth—all woman things. He could not say why, but he threw all these in the fire. Then he watched them burn to ash.

I am a ruin, he thought. He picked up one of the red, dying coals and held it in his hand. But if he had to become a ruin, if he had to become ash, then so be it. He knew the location of another Sleth. He knew where he could find the Shoka's hammer, where he could find Argoth.

HUNGER ARRIVED IN the dark of the early morning and walked up to the door to Argoth's house. He slid a tendril from one of his fingers between the back door and its frame and silently lifted the bar.

The dogs surprised him, but he quickly twisted their necks, gulping down their Fire and soul. Hunger stood in the kitchen with the dead dogs at his feet, but when nobody came to investigate, he proceeded to search the house. He found four rooms. There was nothing in them but beds filled with sleeping children and servants. He creaked down the hallway and found Argoth's wife asleep. Argoth was not with her.

Hunger retreated to a dark corner of the room and waited for Argoth, watching his wife toss and turn and finally kick the bedcovers to the floor. But when he smelled the beginnings of the morning winds, Hunger exited as quietly as he had come.

He took the bodies of the dogs with him and waited in the tree line by a fat chestnut. He would catch Argoth when he returned.

The night turned to morning. Argoth's daughters came out to hang clothes on a line to dry. The wife stood in the back doorway and whistled for the dogs that lay at his feet. Meanwhile, a group of servants walked out to the vineyard with baskets and cutting knives and began to pick grapes.

When he was a man, he would have salivated at the thought of the red table grapes, the skin colored with a blue dust, and all of it bursting with a tangy sweetness. But grapes held no appeal to him now. It was only a memory of a desire that ghosted by.

He supposed Argoth would be conducting a search for him. But could they track a man of dirt? He did not think so. Morning grew toward noon, and then the breeze brought him a whiff of magic. The scent was barely detectable, almost a lie, but it was there.

Hunger prepared himself, but the scent disappeared and did not return. It hadn't come from the direction of Whitecliff. The breeze was blowing from a different direction.

What did this mean?

It meant Argoth had simply crossed the wind's path and had moved on. Argoth wasn't coming home.

Or maybe it wasn't Argoth at all. Maybe it was someone else entirely.

That idea burned in his mind. Someone he might use to remake that collar. Someone different. Someone he would not have to fight the Mother's compulsion to eat.

He had been stupid with the other man. He would not be stupid with this one.

Hunger jolted upright and ran in the direction of the breeze. He kept to the wood line, not because he feared attack but because he did not want to raise an alarm and scare off whomever it was.

For a few minutes he lost the scent. But he ran perpendicular to the general direction of the breeze, and then there the stink was again, more powerful than before.

He traced the scent, moving like a dark animal through

the woods, avoiding clearings and meadows as best he could, and when he couldn't, running with utmost speed through the grass.

The scent grew and grew. He realized it was taking him toward Whitecliff, but Hunger ran out of woods before he caught up to the source of the stink.

He stood in the tree line at the foot of a hill and looked over the acres of fields that lay between him and the walls of Whitecliff and the shining sea beyond.

Leagues to his left rose the ridge of white cliffs for which the city was named. The forbidden cliffs, riddled with crumbling warrens and wondrous carvings wrought by creatures that had vanished long before the first settlers arrived. Below him ran the Soap Stone River. A toll bridge spanned it.

Hunger looked along the road to the bridge and then beyond. It was crowded with people. The Festival of Gifts was not too far away, and then the whole land would be celebrating the blessings of the Creators given this year. There would be games and dances. Sacrifices. And the Divine would grant boons to even the most humble petitioner.

A bearded man on a wagon rode out from behind the bridge house. Beside him walked two boys. Hunger recognized the man. It was the Koramite who had been with Argoth.

A mighty stink rolled toward him in great waves. It was more potent than anything Hunger had encountered so far. More potent than anything he'd experienced from the Mother. He must have incredible power, that Koramite.

But, no, it wasn't the man.

Hunger could see it clearly now. Small fingers of brightness rose from the boy like steam rose from wet clothes in the winter. They were fingers of Fire, fingers of his life spilling out into the wide world.

It was the boy making the overpowering stink.

Hunger looked closer. Was this the young male the Mother spoke of? The band around the boy's arm wasn't a normal godsweed band. It was a weave, smoking with power. He wondered if that weave was the cause of this reckless waste.

He opened his mouth and took in a great breath of the stink. None of the Mother's magic was in it, which meant this was not the male they sought. Another memory tumbled into him. The second boy, the Mokaddian, was Argoth's son. Suddenly Hunger knew who the man was. Argoth had a Koramite brother-in-law. That's who this man was; he was sure of it.

But why release Fire like this? Why waste it? Fire, spilled like this, would draw frights just as a dead carcass would draw crows. Frights were creatures not completely from the world of flesh. Most were small and very difficult to see because they only gained substance in this world as they fed. They were leeches, but not of blood. There were three parts to all living things. Frights fed on Fire. They did not have the power to separate a living thing like he did. But sometimes, if someone was mortally sick or wounded, their Fire might bleed out. And this gave the frights an opening into which they could burrow and feed.

Hunger did not know the full powers of such creatures, but it didn't matter; he would deal with them. And he would be careful of the boy. Who knew, perhaps the boy was not being used to bait frights, but Hunger himself. To throw off a stink he could not resist. Perhaps these Sleth thought to trap him.

But what trap could hold him? He could see none here. He should take them, the Koramite and his son. He should chase them down now. And while the Mother had commanded him to bring the Koramite to her, she hadn't said anything about the boy. Surely he knew some secrets.

Hunger identified the the line of pursuit that would cut them off, then stopped himself. The Koramite and his boy were Sleth; they would simply multiply themselves and run away, and then, when they were safely surrounded by the thousands in the city, they could cease their magic. The stink would die, and Hunger would lose them. They'd disappear, leaving Hunger exposed. The trap, if there was one, was in the city.

Hunger sat down where he was next to a tangle of red-flowered trumpet vine.

The Koramite lived on this side of the river. He and his burning son would surely return from the city before long. And Hunger would be there along an empty stretch of road to greet them.

TALEN HAD NEVER received so many hard glances in his life. He doubted they would have been allowed to cross the bridge had Da not been wearing the token of the Council—a sash that was sewn with the patterned cloth of all Nine Clans and draped over one shoulder.

Almost everyone they passed or overtook on this over-crowded road to Whitecliff looked at him like he himself had committed horrors. And the one man that hadn't given him the eye had shouted and waved his goose stick, rushing his gaggle of geese off the road so quickly you would have thought Da, he, and Nettle were a pack of wolves just come out of the wood. It was obvious the events of Plum Village had only turned the ridiculous rantings of the Fir-Noy against Koramites into truth.

The road ran almost straight to the Farmer's Gate in the outer wall of the city, taking them through fields that stood half harvested and on to the gaming fields.

Every fortnight two or three of the Clans would send

their best to compete here. Their best horses, runners, archers, slingers, and swordsmen. Along with the competition there were jugglers and singers, storytellers and alewives. When the weaves had been full, the dreadmen would compete, sometimes against each other, sometimes against an animal. Only recently had Koramites been allowed to compete in the games. But Talen was sure the events of the last week would reverse that privilege.

Between the gaming fields and the city moat stood plots with timber houses on them. At one a woman sat outside her door delivering well-spaced blows to the bottom of a kicking boy she held across her lap. At another a girl with long black hair stood feeding old vegetables to a number of piglets. At yet another, two brown-and-white goats stood on the low-hanging branch of a tree chewing what leaves they could find. A third attempted to clamber up the woodpile next to the house to get to the grass growing on the sod roof, but she only succeeded in slipping off and bringing pieces of wood down with her.

Beyond the plots rose the outer wall of the city. Four men, tiny in the distance, worked on the red roof of one of the newer stone towers set in the wall.

The city of Whitecliff had three rings of defense: an outer wall, a fortress wall, then the fortress inner wall. The fortress walls were made of stone. But the city wall was made of a steep embankment and timber palisades, like the many walled villages. A few years ago the clans had begun to replace that outer wall with stone, but it was far from finished. More than half of the seventeen towers were still made of timber.

As they approached the Farmer's Gate, a guard motioned Da to pull the wagon into a separate line from the Mokaddians.

At least a dozen guards stood on the rampart with

strung bows. From their colors, he could see they were a mixture of Fir-Noy and Burund. Down at the base and off to the side of the gate, a guard held a dead rabbit up by its hind legs, baiting the two mastiffs chained to the wall. He told the handful of guards standing with him to watch, then he tossed the rabbit between the two dogs. The result was a violent scuffle, but in moments the smaller dog had most of the rabbit and gulped it down, leaving only a tuft of fur and one leg that had flown off into the weeds when they'd pulled it apart.

"See," said the guard. "That's the one to watch. And now I'll take your coppers."

"They've posted double the men," said Nettle.

"It won't do them any good," said Da. "Not against that creature of grass and stone."

Two guards motioned Da to come down off the wagon. One told Da and Talen to strip completely.

"Do you not see the token of the Council?" asked Da. "I've been summoned."

"Then we'll have to be double sure, won't we?"

"They're not going to strip," said Nettle. "I vouch for these men."

"You little piss," the second man said and reached out to strike Nettle, but the first grabbed his arm and stopped him.

"That one is Captain Argoth's."

The second man wrested his arm from the other man's grasp. "Well, well. The Koramite lover's boy," he said. "All alone out here while daddy is in the fortress. Where's your wet nurse?" He pointed at Nettle's belt. "I see they're letting you dress up like a man, are they? Good for you."

Nettle clenched his jaw, but he didn't say anything.

So Talen spoke up. "He's man enough to knock one of your armsmen about."

"Quiet!" said Da.

The second guard licked his bottom lip. "Our orders," the first guard said, "are to search every Koramite. Now strip."

"And you," the second said to Nettle. "You may move along. Wouldn't want you to get a boo-boo."

"Don't listen to them," said Nettle.

Da held up his hand. "Talen and I will satisfy the requirement." Then he began to pull off his tunic.

Dozens of Mokaddians in the other line stood and watched. One wife stood with her arms folded and a scowl across her face as if this were his just desserts. Talen turned his back on her and gave her the bum. Soon the two of them were naked except for the poultice around Da's neck, standing in the sun, their legs spread and arms held wide, while the guards and flies came to investigate.

When the guards found no Sleth-sign, they allowed Da and Talen to pull their clothes back on and bring the wagon round. But another guard stopped them there.

"It's four coppers to enter," he said. One of his ears looked to have been chewed off.

Da shook his head. "Every man who works on the wall has rights to enter."

"Every clansman," said the guard.

"No," said Da, "every man." He pointed at the Sea Gate in the distance. "I helped build that tower."

The guard looked over the contents of the wagon. "Four coppers, and I want that small sack of barley."

Da did not raise his voice in anger, instead he enunciated every word. "I am here at the Council's request."

The man put his hand to his sword. "There are many who think we should just beat you on principle. I'm doing you a favor."

"You're robbing me."

The guard shrugged. "Everything has its price."

Da clenched his jaw.

The guard flipped open the basket with the smoked meat. "Ah," he said. "This looks good." He pulled out a strip of salmon and took a bite. Then he grabbed another handful and tossed it to the other guards. "See," the man said. "I've got to let you in, but I don't have to let your wagon through."

"I'll pay you four coppers," said Da.

"No," said Talen.

"Be quiet," said Da.

"Very good advice," said the guard.

Da reached into his purse and withdrew the coins. "The Council's going to hear about this."

"Give them my regards."

Da picked up the reins and flicked Iron Boy on.

Smoke from a multitude of chimneys trailed into the sky, the wind blowing it like a sooty smear toward the sea.

Talen hated the Fir-Noy. But he was beginning to hate some of the members of his own race. The smith and his wife. They had tainted all the rest of them. Brought down a load of grief. He was happy the smith died. He deserved it. His wickedness was treachery, a stab in everyone's back. He thought about what Da was doing with the hatchlings. That was treachery too. Couldn't Da see that?

The farther they traveled, the houses became taller and more closely placed. More and more were made of brick and stone. Yet, between roofs, Talen caught glimpses of the temple on its hill and the seven statues for the coming Festival of Gifts. At the end of the festival, the community would pull down the statue for Regret, tie it to a boat, and send it out to sea. And while it burned upon the water, thousands would sing the hymn of defiance along the shorelines. This same ritual would be repeated by the other clans in their cities, but none would match the festival held here in Whitecliff.

Of course, this year it would not be the same. Usually, the reigning Divine would bestow gifts during the festival, including healings for man and beast. The festival was one of the regular times for people to offer the days of their life up for the good of all by letting the Divine draw quantities of their Fire. It was also during the festival that common men were raised to the ranks of the dreadmen. But none of that would happen this year.

Talen took his eyes from the temple and looked up the road. They were almost upon the lodgers field. Not all of the merchants could afford to raise a booth or tent in the central square. Those slots went to many of the permanent families who held homes in the city itself. But there were three other spots in the city where merchants paid to set up their business. This was the largest of those, a ten-acre field filled with tents of all colors—blue-and-white trimmed with yellow, scarlet-and-black, green-and-blue—each with pennants above them declaring who they were and what they sold.

"Look," Nettle said and pointed. "The Kish."

Talen looked and saw the black-and-white tent of the Kish bowmaster. He was surprised that merchant was here. In the last four years of Bone Face raids, many merchants had become wary of sending ships to the New Lands. And now with the Sleth, it was a wonder those who did come would stay. Kish bows were the finest made. They were small and powerful, made of wood, sinew, and bone. He could have the finest bow for sale along with a few dozen bundles of arrows; all he had to do was turn those hatchlings in.

Talen watched a merchant's guard chase two boys away from a wagon, and then, with a jolt of the wagon, the road turned from a humped dirt affair with weeds growing in the middle to a flat cobblestone street.

What a fine arrangement for the rich to be able to step out of their houses in the middle of a rain and not muddy their boots.

Up ahead, people thronged the way. In front of them a man led an ass laden with bundles of dried hemp. To the side a young woman wearing a yellow hat pointed to a clay prayer disk laying on a holy man's table. Each disk was engraved with some type of boon—the holy man would write your name on the disk in ink, then you could hang it on the wooden statue in front of the temple and let the fires carry your request to the ears of the Creators.

A young boy carrying a yoke of water across his shoulders cut in front of the wagon, followed by a girl in a pale blue dress selling candles that hung from a pole fitted with a double cross.

Da halted Iron Boy. When the two had passed, he flicked the reins again. A few minutes later, Da turned off the busy street, following the lane that led to Master Farkin's. Farkin's house stood three stories high and had half a dozen smoking chimneys. Talen wondered how it would be to have a hearth in almost every room. A lot of work or money in firewood, that's what it would be. Perhaps that woodsman was on his way here.

A servant stood outside the door. Da went inside to see what price he could get for the pelts they had brought.

While Talen waited on the back of the wagon, two carriages rolled by, their curtains drawn. When Da came back out, he had Talen and Nettle help him carry the pelts down an alley into a yard in the back of the house.

Master Farkin was, according to Da, one of the few merchants who bargained a fair price with every man, regardless of clan.

While they were making the exchange, Master Farkin said, "Have you heard the news about the Envoy?"

"Mokad has sent an Envoy?"

"Not only an Envoy, but a Skir Master. The message just came today. We're saved."

"Is he here to stay?" asked Da.

"Nobody knows. There was no word of his coming until the birds arrived today. But it bodes well. We can, at the very least, hope for a hunt."

"Creators be blessed," Da said, smooth as cream. But Talen knew he didn't mean a word of that.

"And look at this one," Master Farkin said of Talen. "I would suspect that the girls would find much to admire there."

"If they do," said Talen, "they have a funny way of showing it."

"Oh?"

"They tend to run away," said Nettle.

Master Farkin chuckled. He asked after Captain Argoth, told them he needed more mink, suggested they avoid the Dog Street tailors, then bid them goodbye.

Da asked Talen and Nettle to join him up on the seat. When they'd pulled out into the road, Da said, "Kindness, boys. It's irresistible. Don't you think?"

"Some people are immune to it," said Nettle.

"I don't know," said Da. "Sometimes kindness can even renew the hate-salted field of a man's heart."

"But people won't see kindness if they don't trust you," said Talen. He was thinking of the lies they'd told the bailiff. The small lie Da had just told Master Farkin. What if Master Farkin discovered Da's treachery? And that's what it was, legally. How much kindness would he show then?

Da ignored his comment and asked, "How does your arm feel?"

The question annoyed Talen. "It feels fine," he said. Then he realized it felt more than fine. His whole body felt rested and fresh, like he'd just woken up from a long and lovely sleep.

"Good," said Da. "A little more patience, son. And we'll have our chat. You're almost ready."

"You talk as if you're waiting for a loaf of dough to rise before you put it in the oven."

"That's not a bad analogy."

What in the Six was he talking about? "I don't know that I want to be a loaf of bread."

"I don't know that I want to wait for my father," said Nettle. "I'd like to get it straight from you, Uncle."

"We'll see," said Da. "But Master Farkin's news has changed things a bit. I don't want you to wait for me. You must not. Deliver the goods we have left and take a message back to River. Tell her the news of the Envoy. Then tell her to prepare the garden for a frost."

"But we're weeks away from a turn in the seasons."

"You want to be trusted?" asked Da. "Then do this thing."

The way Da said that made Talen think there was more to the message than he supposed. "I'll take it."

"Tell her not to delay," said Da. They threaded their way through the street up to the fortress. At one point, Talen heard a woman singing to the sound of a lyre and found the sound was coming from an open window one level up on the other side of the street. He was at such an angle that he could see in the window. It wasn't a woman at all, but a girl. A tall Mokaddian girl who watched him as she sang.

When they came to the intersection that ended the street they'd been traveling and started the one to the fortress, Da stopped the wagon. He reached under the seat and retrieved the Hog, then opened his purse and gave Talen a number of coins.

"Do not wait for me. They might keep me for an hour

or seven. So get the supplies and make the visit to the widow Lees. Now tell me the list."

Talen recited all the things they needed. When he finished, Da said, "Don't pay the smith one grain more than fifteen measures for the maul."

Talen didn't know how they'd fare without one of them wearing the token of the Council. "Are you sure you don't want us to wait?"

"You'll be all right," said Da. "You've got Nettle with you." Then he handed Talen five more coppers. "Purchase some honey; we'll let your sister eat her own poison."

"I'm just thinking that it's not safe for you to travel back through the wood at night," said Talen.

"I'll be fine," said Da. "Finish your business and go directly home. Remember, not everyone here is like the guard at the gate." Then he put the Hog over one shoulder and walked up the road to the fortress.

Talen took the reins. That was all fine for Da to say, him and his Hog and the Council's sash about his chest. But Talen had nothing more than a whittling knife. Then Talen realized that maybe Da was trying to tell him that he trusted him. In fact, the more he thought about it, the more sure he was of Da's intentions. Talen appreciated the thought, but Da could have chosen a better time to make his point.

Talen looked up at the sun. It was past noon. He would have to hurry to make it home before nightfall. And if he didn't?

Well, he would. So he didn't need the answer to that question.

20.

SNAKE GAMES

As Talen drove the wagon, watching the faces of those they passed, he became sure of this fact: sooner or later some overvigilant Mokaddian would see Talen and decide he didn't belong in this city. Someone would decide he needed to be taught a lesson. It was common for such lessons to be delivered in the form of a thrown object—rotten food, dog turds, the ever-handy rock. But Talen didn't think he'd get off so easy this time. So he watched where he drove the wagon, but he kept his attention on the corners of streets, on odd windows, and sudden intersections.

Having Nettle along should dissuade some from molesting him. But while there were many even-headed Mokaddians like Master Farkin, there were others who were not.

He stopped at two houses to purchase harness rings and forty feet of tight hemp rope, keeping an eye out the whole time, but the owners of neither house would let him in. Nor would they allow Nettle in his stead. At the third house Talen sat back at the wagon like a servant and sent Nettle to the door as his master. Only then were they able to obtain the goods.

When Nettle came back, he asked, "What have I got to do to get something to eat?"

"I've got people giving me the eye and all you can think about is your stomach?"

"What?" asked Nettle. "I can't get hungry?"

Talen shook his head. But after stopping at the honey-crafter's, Nettle walked over to a new baker's house to buy a small meal.

Talen waited again in the wagon. A group of men only a few yards down the road talked among themselves and kept looking up the lane at him.

He didn't dare look at them directly, but it didn't matter. They reached some conclusion and all turned to face his direction.

At that moment Nettle exited the baker's, holding something folded up in the bottom of his tunic.

Talen was only too happy to release the brake and flick the reins and start Iron Boy. Nettle shouted, but Talen didn't pull back.

Nettle caught up to the wagon, holding his tunic with one hand, then jumped in and sat beside Talen on the wagon seat.

"What are you doing?" asked Nettle.

Talen glanced back, knowing the men would be following, but they hadn't. They stood watching him and Nettle go.

"One of these days," said Talen, "your stomach is going to get me killed."

Nettle followed Talen's gaze. "Goh, those dogs weren't about to do anything but bark. Besides, look what I got." Nettle let his tunic down.

In it lay a disgusting half loaf of bread pudding and a dozen ginger cookies. "Am I good to you or what?" asked Nettle.

The cookies were one of Talen's favorites, but now wasn't a time to think of food. He glanced back once more. The men had not dispersed nor turned back to talking among themselves.

"Lords and lice," Talen said.

Nettle took a fat, moist bite of his pudding. "I don't think they like you."

"Really," Talen said. "What gave you that idea? We've got to get out of here."

"Act natural," said Nettle. "Here, have a bite." He held up his pudding. It had currants and cashews mixed in with a good helping of something green and shaggy. The whole thing was held together by a wiggling gelatin that reminded Talen of animal birthings.

"I think I'd like to focus on the matter at hand."

"What you want to do is distract yourself because if you spook, those men will spook. Now take a bite."

Nettle had a point. Talen waved off the bread pudding mess, took one of the ginger cookies, and bit into it. It was baked with sugar, and while it crunched on the outside, the inside was soft and just about melted in his mouth. Any other situation and he'd swear he'd visited the gardens of the righteous.

Talen glanced over at Nettle, who promptly showed him the contents of his mouth.

"I hope you gag," said Talen. "And when folks ask how you died, I'll tell them you did it eating pig food."

Nettle laughed. "No, you won't. You'll remember I used it to save your life. And then you'll eat it the rest of your days."

"Being sickened by animal birthings is hardly a rescue," said Talen.

"It's a distraction," said Nettle. "And it worked, didn't it?"

It had, but Talen wasn't going to give him the satisfaction.

They crossed a small bridge spanning a muddy canal and then turned onto Fuller's Lane.

Down the lane two young men circled a large black rat snake. It was as long as Talen's leg and as thick as his wrist.

Talen tensed. He didn't have to see their faces to know who they were. It was Fabbis and that lazy-eyed Sabin with his head shaved and dyed with temple henna.

So much for disgusting mouthfuls of bread pudding. Suddenly Talen's cookies didn't taste so good anymore. He took a drink of water from a goat's bladder to wash them down.

"Fancy pants," Nettle said.

Fabbis wore a pair of finely woven scarlet-and-yellow trousers. The worth of the fabric covering that moron's sweaty bum alone was more than everything Talen had put together.

Talen turned his head, not wanting to make eye contact with Fabbis.

"They're going about it all wrong," said Nettle. "Look at them."

Sabin held a stick and kept heading the snake off. Every time he did, the snake coiled up and tried to strike him. If they wanted to catch it, they needed to let it slither and then snatch up the tail.

"Let's just get to the fuller's," said Talen.

Sabin reached in to snatch the snake, but it struck at him.

As they rode closer, Talen could overheard their conversation.

"You've got to be faster than that," said Fabbis.

"Okay, lord of the basket," said Sabin, "you try."

Fabbis snatched the stick from Sabin then flung the beast a few feet. When the snake landed, it tried to slither to the safety of some weeds, but Fabbis chased after it. He grabbed its tail and held it away from him. At that moment he glanced toward Nettle and Talen.

Talen purposely ignored Fabbis. He simply pulled up to the fuller's and set the wagon brake, hoping Fabbis would decide, for once, not to torment him. Of course, Fabbis, being a horned bunion, was unlikely to do that.

Talen steeled himself and turned, knowing they must be close, but to his surpise the two pisspots disappeared behind a cluster of trees, Fabbis holding the snake out before him.

He let out a sigh of relief. Maybe his luck would hold out. "Quick."

"I'm going," said Nettle. "Be calm."

"Fine for you to say with your Mokaddian wrist tattoo. But you weren't beaten by a pack of village idiots a day ago. Or forced to strip at the gates."

"This lane is full of people friendly to the Koramites," said Nettle. "You'll be fine."

Talen waved him away. "Try to avoid offending the household this time."

"Bah," said Nettle.

Talen stepped from the wagon and tied the reins to the hitching post. Nettle walked to the porch and knocked at the fuller's door.

The young foreign woman from Urz who Nettle had offended the last time they were there opened the door. She was beautiful, copper-skinned with eyes as blue and bright as the silks she sold. But she only narrowed those eyes in irritation at Nettle. Nettle had flirted with her, but he'd said something that by the customs of her people indicated Nettle wanted to hire her as a prostitute. By the time word reached Uncle Argoth of the incident it had been blown into a tale of unwanted pregnancy. Two families who had expressed interest in Nettle as a potential marriage candidate for their daughters had concerns. Nettle had been made to apologize to all of the parties involved.

On any other occasion Talen would have relished the exchange playing out on the doorstep, but Fabbis and Sabin made him nervous. He eyed the clump of trees Fabbis had disappeared behind and hoped Nettle would have enough brains to know that the quicker they finished their business here the better.

Talen suspected Fabbis had caught the snake for a game of Fool's Basket. The rules were very simple. You put a snake into a basket, irritated it until it was ready to strike, then you tried to catch it without being bit. You could use a short stick to draw the snake's attention, but the only thing that could touch the snake was your hand.

Talen had played three times before with a small garden snake and had been bitten every time. He'd seen five dreadmen play it once. Their speed was shocking. They would catch the snake at the base of the head before it had time to strike. Futhermore, they had been playing with a lance of fire, not a simple rat snake. One bite would have killed them.

He hoped that Fabbis was slow and the snake's fangs were long and bit deep.

Nettle began to explain to the copper-skinned beauty what they'd come for. When she let Nettle in to fetch the cloth River had ordered, someone in the clump of trees into which Fabbis had disappeared screamed like a river gut held him in its maw.

Talen glanced at Nettle, but he was already in the house, shutting the door behind him.

Whoever it was cried out again. The fear and pain in that scream could not be ignored.

"Please!" someone cried.

That wasn't Fabbis or Sabin. Nettle was never around when he needed him! Talen glanced once more at the fuller's.

"Stop! Help!"

If a Koramite sat around while a Mokaddian called for help, the Koramite would be punished for not lending a hand. Even if it was someone like Fabbis who deserved every misfortune that came to him.

Another scream. Surely someone in one of the houses heard that one and would shortly appear.

Talen waited, but nobody came.

He could just sit here. Nobody else seemed to have heard. But he wondered. That was Fabbis down there. The voice had been high-pitched like a girl's.

Talen cursed. Then he left the wagon and ran to down the lane to the source of the commotion.

He didn't need to get involved. He could just assess what was going on, and, if needed, run to one of the houses and raise the hue and cry.

Talen skirted rounded the clump of trees and immediately saw the situation. There on his hands and knees was a boy. Talen didn't recognize him. He was scrawny and dressed in filthy rags. Obviously, out of place here on Fuller's Lane.

The boy attempted to scrabble away from Fabbis and Sabin. When he tried to rise, Sabin kicked the boy's legs out from underneath him. But that wasn't what made this beggar boy cry out.

Fabbis still held the rat snake by the tail. He was laughing so hard he was almost doubled over. Talen thought that maybe they were simply threatening the boy with the snake. But Fabbis regained his composure enough to swing the snake's head up against the boy's buttocks. The snake's head bumped the boy, once, twice. On the third bounce it opened its mouth wide and bit deeply.

The boy cried out again with his high-pitched squeal, terror written on his face. He tried to run off again, but Sabin kicked him in the gut so hard it knocked the boy over.

"Pull up his tunic," said Fabbis. "We'll see if Zu Snake wants a taste of walnuts and sausage."

Leave it to Fabbis to think something like this up. Rat snakes carried no venom, but that didn't lessen the pain of their bite. Fabbis and Sabin had both gotten their clan wrists, which only proved those tattoos meant nothing. These two weren't men.

Talen turned to see if Nettle had followed, if anyone had come, but he was alone.

Talen did not know this boy; he could quietly step back around the trees and wait for Nettle. Step back and let the Mokaddians do what they pleased. That would be the smart thing, but this would only get worse. Besides, hadn't he been that boy only yesterday?

"Surely," said Talen, "you could get at the vital parts a bit better by making him stand."

Fabbis looked back over his shoulder. When he saw Talen, his face broke into a wicked grin. "I was just saying to Sabin here, wouldn't it be nice if Turd Soup joined us? Where's the Koramite lover you came with?"

"At the fuller's."

"Well, we don't need to wait for him. Come on over here, half-breed. You can help."

At one of the musters last year Talen had momentarily left his lamb soup to fetch a load of arrows for Da from the wagon. When he returned, he took a spoonful and found someone had slipped rabbit turds into the bowl. When he looked around, he'd seen Fabbis and Sabin watching him, grinning with delight.

Talen knew exactly what kind of help Fabbis meant. Usually Fabbis also had Cat with him, a boy who kept his dark hair oiled and shining and painted his eyes with kohl as many of the sons of the clan lords had begun to do. Talen looked about, but it appeared Fabbis and Sabin were alone. "Actually," said Talen, "you've done me a great service. The fuller asked that I find his stable boy. And there he is. I'm sure the fuller would be interested to know how you've corrected him." Talen held his hand out. "Now, come along, boy."

The boy's eyes were red. His face covered with dirt and tears.

Sabin began to let go his grip, but Fabbis put a hand out to stop him.

"This, a fuller's boy?" Fabbis shook his head. "I don't think so. Besides, the thief was sneaking into that house when we came along. We only thought to wring a confession from him. Maybe identify the members of his cabal. There's never just one, you know."

"I wasn't stealing," said the boy.

"Shut up," said Sabin and clopped the boy on the head.

Talen knew what that felt like as well. He was positive the boy hadn't been doing anything close to breaking and entering. He'd probably been walking along, minding his own business, and Fabbis had spied him and seen an opportunity for yet another small-minded torture. "I'm sure the street boss would commend your vigilance," said Talen. "Not to mention the fuller. Think what it would cost him were his servant to be caught stealing. Let's take him to the fuller; I'm sure he'll reward you just to keep your mouth shut."

Talen glanced about. Nobody had come to investigate the cries. His best bet was to leave now and get some help.

Fabbis looked at Sabin. "Maybe he's right. What were we thinking? Deliver the boy to Master Half-breed."

Sabin approached, malevolence in his lazy eye. But Talen knew exactly what he was going to do, and he wasn't going to let Sabin within a dozen feet. "Just let him go," said Talen, taking a step back. "I'm sure he's seen the error of his ways."

"Of course," said Sabin, but just then Talen heard something behind him. He turned and saw Cat, painted eyes and shining hair, with a rope. Talen dodged out of the way, but he wasn't fast enough and the rope fell about his shoulders.

Talen grabbed at the rope, but Cat gave it a yank, and the rope tightened about his neck. Cat yanked again and Talen stumbled to his knees, the rope choking him.

Talen pulled at the noose with one hand and grabbed the rope with the other.

"It looks like we've rolled double pleasure with today's dice," said Fabbis. He kicked Talen in the side. "Get his feet."

Panic rose in him, and Talen yanked at the rope with all his might. He didn't expect to wrest it free from Cat so easily. But Cat could not keep his grip. He yelled and opened his hands as if they'd been burned. Talen loosened the noose and rolled to his feet.

Fabbis pulled back the snake to swing it into him. But Fabbis hadn't taken a good stance, and Talen delivered a sweeping kick that knocked Fabbis's feet from underneath him.

He fell, arms wheeling, the snake flying wide.

Talen saw his chance. He snatched the snake as it flew. And before it could coil about his arm and bite him, he grasped it by the base of the head.

Fabbis landed with a thump, and Talen fell upon him, driving his knee into Fabbis's gut.

Fabbis grunted. He tried to roll, but Talen stuck the serpent in his face.

"Should we see if Zu Snake wants a taste of walnuts and sausage?" asked Talen. "No? How about a kiss?" Talen shoved the mouth of the snake against Fabbis's cheek.

Fabbis turned his head away.

"No kiss?"

Fabbis tried to struggle away, but Talen found he could hold him.

He couldn't explain it. This shouldn't be happening. Da forced Talen to wrestle Fabbis in the musters. He said the best practice for fighting someone bent on your death was to fight someone bent on your death. And since they didn't have a large supply of young Bone Faces about, he found the next best thing—a Fir-Noy. Fabbis always beat him. Once he'd broken Talen's nose just to spite him. But perhaps Talen had finally begun to get his speed and size. He glanced over at Sabin to make sure he didn't get blind-sided, but Sabin just stood there with his mouth hanging slack like some great fish.

Cat had not moved. He still stood in the same spot, his hands held out in front of him.

Then Talen noticed Nettle just beyond Cat, a look of surprise on his face.

"Oh, now you show up," said Talen. "Grab the boy."

The beggar boy looked at Talen with fright on his face. He pulled away from Sabin and ran down the lane.

"How sad," said Talen to Fabbis. "Your bounty has just floated down the river." He got up, making sure to push down extra hard on Fabbis's gut with his knee.

The snake tried to coil itself around Talen's arm, but Talen simply changed his grip, grabbed the tail, and let it hang loose.

Fabbis scrabbled to his feet and backed away, weeds clinging to his clothes and hair. He had a strange look in his eyes. "Nobody moves like that," he said.

"I just did," said Talen. Then he swung the snake at Fabbis. "Don't be scared."

Sabin and Cat backed away as well.

"Oh, come," said Talen to Sabin. "You were willing enough to tangle with me yesterday."

"Stay away," said Fabbis. He backed up, Sabin and Cat not a pace behind him.

Talen couldn't believe it. "Cowards," he said. Da had

always told him that the meanest bullies were always the biggest cowards. He had never believed that. But maybe it was true.

Fabbis pointed at him. "You're a dead man."

"Ya!" Talen shouted and lunged at them.

The three of them startled, turned, and ran.

Except Talen knew Fabbis: he wasn't running away. Fabbis wasn't one of those who could be satisfied knowing he'd been beaten. He'd be back, and he'd bring others with him.

Talen gently let the snake to the ground, and the creature slithered away toward the cover of the trees.

"That was," said Nettle in amazement, "unexpected."

"You were right," said Talen. "I didn't need to spook."

"No," said Nettle. "I meant you."

What was his cousin talking about?

"You plucked the snake right out of the air."

"So?"

"So," said Nettle, "I came around the corner and saw Cat holding the rope and Fabbis coming at you. But before I took another step you were on him. It was . . . too fast."

"Too fast?"

Had he always been so slow? "Maybe, at last, my speed has come upon me."

"Yeah," said Nettle, but Talen could see he wasn't convinced.

"Is it impossible that Hogan's runt suddenly got some of his old man's growth?"

"No," said Nettle. "But I can tell you this: Fabbis won't see it that way."

"What do you mean?"

"That was dreadman quick, Talen."

"I just grabbed the snake," he said. He'd just been lucky. Lively with alarm and fear.

Nettle said nothing, that look of astonishment still on his face, but he was right. Fabbis would twist what had happened. He *would* be back. About that there was no doubt. And if Fabbis ran into that group of men by the baker's, it would be only a matter of minutes before he returned.

"We need to get out of here," Talen said.

"Act normal," said Nettle.

"Will you stop with the normal," said Talen. "Get in the wagon."

21.

THE DIVINE

The severed hand of the creature lay upon a table in the center of the Mokaddian Council chamber. Almost two dozen Council members crowded about Argoth as he probed the hand. They had heard almost two hours of testimony about the hunt at the village of Plum, the taking of Barg's family, and the battle at the fortress. It was now Argoth's turn to relate his tale. He wondered where Hogan was. He should have been here an hour ago.

One of the fingers broke off, and Argoth flaked away small pieces of dirt and grass with his knife. "You can see," said Argoth, "what appears to have been bone and sinew. But look." He scraped at the finger innards with his knife.

The men crowded in. A nearsighted lord of the Harkon clan leaned over close.

Shim stood next to Argoth, his bright eyes shining in

his leathern face. "It crumbles like common dirt," Shim said. "As if it were nothing more than a child's mud doll."

One of the men cursed. "Who can fight dirt?"

None spoke. All knew the answer to that question. But Argoth wondered. Matiga kept the weaves of their Grove. She had the ancient crown that gave its wearer incredible might. The powers it bestowed were not just those of the flesh as were given to dreadmen. It was power from the very earth itself. Victors is what the wearers of such crowns had been called. And, though the records were sparse, it appears these victors had put armies to flight. They had toppled fortress walls. Surely, such a one could overcome this beast.

Of course, much had been lost. They knew how to quicken the crown. But could they wield it like those of old? Abilities ran in bloodlines. Some men could multiply themselves. Others who couldn't might be able to do other things. Hogan and Ke could control some of the crown's power. But they had been waiting to see what Talen might do. He had not yet been awakened, and so whatever gifts he might have still lay dormant. But he was full of peculiarities. Full of possibility. There was always much anticipation seeing what a new member of the Grove was capable of.

The Crab caught Argoth's gaze. He was not looking at the hand like the other men. He was looking directly at Argoth. What was he hiding? Did he have reason to suspect Argoth as Shim had?

Finally the warlord for the Mithrosh spoke up. "And what of its bones? Are those dirt as well?"

A clamor arose outside the chamber. The men crowding around the table turned and the doors opened. In walked three dreadmen, the only three with any power left in their weaves. Between them they escorted Hogan as if he were a criminal. About his neck was a king's collar.

Argoth's heart dropped like a stone. Did they know about the Order? He met Hogan's gaze, but he could read nothing there.

Shim turned to the dreadmen. "What is the meaning of this?" He did not raise his dry voice, but every face turned to look at him.

The Crab, the red-faced Fir-Noy territory lord, raised his hand in a placating gesture. "It is what prudence demands. If he's innocent, we'll find that out. If he's not, it will have prevented us from having to hunt him down. Because, once alerted, I am sure we would not have gotten a second chance."

Argoth looked at the Council, wondering who was in on this. The Council was made up of a primary and secondary body. The Primary, those who spoke for each clan, consisted of the territory lord and warlord for each clan. It also included the bailiff of the Koramites. Their faces revealed nothing. Argoth looked at Shim.

Had Shim revealed his secret? Had he been trying to trap him before at the fort?

Shim did not look like a man playing cat and mouse. Argoth knew his lined face. The expression he wore now was the same he wore when preparing for battle.

"You cannot simply collar a man without cause," Shim said to the Crab. "Unless, of course, this is some ploy to goad us into doing the same to some troublesome relative of your own."

Some in the room smiled at his joke. But the Crab did not.

"We do have cause," said the Crab.

Shim folded his arms and waited.

If the Crab and his allies knew Arogth's secrets and

had devised a trap, this would be a good time to spring it. He glanced at the dreadmen to see if they were positioning themselves to overcome him, but they remained by Hogan. Nevertheless, Argoth began to build his Fire.

"The Koramite was there when the creature broke into the tower," said the Crab. "You yourself say that you were only there for a short time. What are the odds that this beast would show up exactly at that moment?"

"Nonsense," said Shim. "I charged Captain Argoth with that very task. And the Koramite himself fought the beast. Look at him. The bruising on his neck and face belies your charges."

"Almost," said the Crab. "But when Captain Argoth was cast aside and only the Koramite stood in its way, it suddenly ran away. Isn't that odd?"

"That is not what happened," said Argoth.

The Crab turned on him. "Your devotion to the man's deceased wife might be clouding your vision."

Argoth had borne all the backbiting when his sister had first decided to marry Hogan. He had told everyone that Hogan had indeed enchanted her—with his wit, his handsome strength, and his good-hearted laugh. He thought that had all been put to rest, but he saw that there would always be people like the Crab who thought it their duty to keep such doubts and rumors alive.

"My vision is crystal clear," said Argoth. "I was there. You were not. We were outside when it broke into the tower."

The Crab turned back to the Council. "It had no eyes. The Koramite might have been acting as a guide."

Argoth had seen something that looked like eyes on the monster, pits they were. But all askew and in such an unnatural position. "You assume it needed to see," said Argoth. "But, if you remember, we found it in the dark. It navigated well enough to elude the cohorts of the fortress. If it could do that, I do not think it needed a guide."

"We only want to be sure," said the Crab. "Nobody can speak with any authority about this creature. But even if we could, you are right, the timing of the creature's appearance is certainly not enough to accuse a man. But there's more, a pattern, if you will. The Koramite refused a legal search."

"Legal?" asked Shim. He looked to a bailiff with the ice-cold eyes. "Did those armsmen apply to you for a token?"

"No," said the bailiff. "Nevertheless, I myself conducted a search."

"And?"

"We found nothing but two youngsters sporting behind a closed door."

"They were alerted by the first attempt at a search," said the Crab. "They had a night to remove anything that might compromise them."

"Oh, come," said Shim. "Your zeal has exceeded all bounds."

"And here is the third part of the pattern," said the Crab. "We just received word that the Koramite's own son has been seen in the city performing feats only dreadmen can." He turned to the whole Primary then. "And this witnessed by at least five Mokaddians. What's more telling is that Captain Argoth's son was with him."

A murmur arose in the chamber.

What had happened in the city? Argoth hadn't even known Talen and Nettle were here.

Shim waved his hand, calling for quiet. "Anyone can make up a story. Where is the corroboration?"

"One or two stories," said the Crab. "I agree, we could discount them. But too many swirl about this man. He was a friend to Sparrow the smith."

Argoth looked at Hogan, still wearing the token of the Council, obviously a ploy to get him to come in. The Crab and his allies here had maneuvered Shim.

"On that basis then you yourself should wear this collar," said Shim. "Didn't you visit Sparrow's smithy many times? And did you not visit the tower on the night it was struck? A pattern, is it not?"

Argoth could see that Shim's comments struck a chord with some of the Council members.

"We will proceed with the correct protocol," said Shim. "Let those who accuse Hogan's son come forth and swear to take upon them the punishments prescribed by law should they be found to bear false witness. If they swear, then we shall proceed. And I will oversee every questioning session."

"But we have already applied to a Divine to oversee the questioning," said the Crab.

A Divine? There was no Divine here.

A murmur arose. A lord of the Vargon spoke. "Mokad has finally sent us aid?"

"No," said the Crab. "Not just aid. The Glory of Mokad has sent us Rubaloth, Lord of the Winds." Many of the lords stood straighter. Surprise shone on their faces, then it turned to hope.

There were only a few dozen Divines in the whole realm of Mokad. Unless, of course, the Glory had raised others since Lumen disappeared. Rubaloth, the Skir Master, was the most ancient of them all. He was powerful. Some said as powerful as the Glory himself.

"When did he arrive? We heard no report," said Shim.

The Crab smiled. "His ship came in the harbor just after the Council convened."

"By Glory," a bailiff from one of the outlying vales said, "why did you keep this good news? Word must be sent. He must come here and see this creature."

"Word has already been sent," said the Crab.

Smiles broke out on many faces. On the outside Argoth mimicked those who welcomed the Skir Master, but on the inside he cursed. There was nothing he could do should the Divine agree to seek Hogan. Of course, members of the Grove practiced avoiding a seeking, one of them playing the role of the Seeker, the other the subject. But none of them in the Grove here were masters at it.

"Gather your witnesses," said Shim. "Even Divines are bound by protocol. And when the Divine comes up empty-handed, you, since it seems you are his primary accuser, you will proclaim his innocence and act as his footstool. That, perhaps, will be worth it all."

The Crab's face revealed the smugness of a man who had just won a battle. He inclined his head, accepting Shim's burden. But he couldn't do otherwise. The laws governing the hunting of Sleth were very strict. Heavy consequences were put upon those making accusations to prevent any from bringing casual charges.

Both Argoth's and Hogan's life now approached a precipice. If the Divine searched Hogan and uncovered his secrets, they would collar Argoth. The Grove would be exposed. His family would be tortured and killed.

Argoth knew his duty. His duty was to eliminate yet another friend, then run and take the Grove with him.

Hogan looked at him and Argoth knew he was thinking the same thing.

Argoth did not want this burden. Even if he could save many lives. One thing was for sure: he wouldn't be able to kill Hogan here. He'd have to contrive his death. More poison or some torture gone awry. Perhaps he'd kill him on the way to the Divine. And then he'd have to face Ke and River and tell them he'd just sacrificed their father for the good of all.

Yes, that's what he was supposed to do.

Argoth looked at Shim. "I will escort Hogan to tower." Then he turned to Hogan. "Come, brother."

Hogan gave him a look, and it was as if Argoth could read his mind. Hogan was a man of duty. But Argoth would not kill him. Not yet. There had to be another way.

Suddenly, the trumpeters outside the building blew a fanfare and a crier announced the arrival of the Divine.

Hogan stiffened. Alarm ran through Argoth.

It was all moving too fast. But he and Hogan could fight their way out. He had surprise on his side. Yet when the doors opened, he saw fighting would not be an option.

A crier proceeded the Divine's company. He stood forth and proclaimed Rubaloth, Divine Skir Master, Holy Defender of the Glory of Mokad. All in the chamber stood and bowed.

A dozen guards followed the crier into the chamber. Upon their sparkling brass cuirasses was the white lion of Mokad. All of them were dreadmen. Argoth could see it in their walk. He could read it in the tattoos on their forearms and around their lips.

Another dozen dreadmen stood in the hallway. So many—enough to form what the Mokaddians called a terror. Enough to route three cohorts given the right terrain. More than enough to subdue him and Hogan.

The guards took up positions around the square room, facing all the Council members while the Skir Master and his guide walked to the Divine's throne.

The Skir Master was ancient, and, some said, failing. But he did not look it. He stood upright and alert in his finely cut clothes. His skin was as weathered as that of a middle-aged man. His hair was cut short, only his beard and eyebrows that shot out like gray growths of wild grass betrayed his real age. He too wore the Mokaddian clan tattoos, but they were from another time—simple, small, and elegant, as were the tattoos of his raising.

The Skir Master surveyed the room. Argoth had seen Skir Masters before in Mokad, before he'd made the journey to these lands, but it didn't help. The Divine's eyes unnerved him—glass black and glittering with the light from the windows. The path of magic Skir Masters followed did that to them; it blinded them to the world of the flesh.

Except the Skir Master did not walk with the caution of a blind man. At his side stood a massive man. Another dreadman. But he didn't wear armor as the rest did. This one moved with the languid power of a great cat. He was speed and power waiting to be unleashed. Odd tattoos flared out from his eyes. This was the Skir Master's guide, even if he did not hold the Divine's arm to lead or steady him.

All in the room bowed more deeply. Argoth did as well. He knew this Skir Master was just a man, holding on fiercely to secrets that should belong to everyone. A thief and liar, that's what he was.

But Argoth's heart quailed nevertheless. If the reports were true, this Skir Master had once summoned a being that had laid waste to an entire city. He was more than two hundred years old. He'd had a century more than Argoth to learn and grow in the lore. Argoth glanced up at those glittering black eyes and wondered how the Order could ever think to challenge such a man.

He waited for the Skir Master to tell them they could stand upright again. But the Divine did not give the command. Instead, he slowly swept the room with his black, snake eyes. Then that black, empty gaze settled on Argoth.

Argoth lowered his eyes. He held that pose, but the silence stretched too long. When he glanced back up, the Skir Master held his glance and then looked away. Or had he been looking at Hogan? And why was he looking at them anyway? What could he see with those eyes?

The Skir Master turned and addressed the Council. "Lords of the Nine Clans, the Glory of Mokad bid me come to announce your burden, for you have sat in your ease, withholding resources from your brethren in the heartland. You've been hoarding water, while those about you scorch in the sun and faint. You have stood by and watched as the wolves devoured your neighbor's flocks. You have joined the enemies of the realm. You have but this one chance to repent and turn back to your heart. Refuse and by my hand on the morrow the Glory of Mokad, the Morning Sun, the Guardian of the Righteous shall rise up and utterly destroy you, starting at the head. And these lands will be given to those who do not turn their backs on the slaughter of their brethren."

The room stood in stunned silence.

What evil had they committed? It was Mokad that had neglected them, refusing to send a replacement Divine.

"Great One, how have we sinned?" The question came from the Prime Councilor, the one who presided over the Council's deliberations in a Divine's absence. "Teach us, we beg, the error of our ways."

"We received reports last year of a weapon that put your enemies to flight. Yet you did not send it to your brethren who were dying every day by the hands of Nilliam. Twice we sent a command to aid us. Twice we were denied."

This was about the seafire? Argoth had unlocked the secret to a fire that burned on water. He'd seen it used before in battles with the Rajan of the east. They cast it in pots like many other armies cast pots of living snakes or scorpions. In the end the pots of fire were not enough to hold back his army. But they had caused havoc, and Argoth had captured one who knew the lore of its making.

Before the captor died, Argoth learned part of it was firewater distilled from the substance that came out of black springs. But he didn't know what else had been mixed with it to make it into a semiliquid. He'd experimented with various mixtures until he mixed it with pitch from pines and terebinth trees and sulfur. He did not re-create their fire pots, he went beyond it, for his substance burned and would not be extinguished except by vinegar, urine, or earth.

But that wasn't what had turned the clan galleys into fire ships. Fire pots of various kinds were used by all armies. No, Argoth had dreamed one night of a brass tube that hissed and spat fire on the ships of the Bone Faces.

Argoth's smiths had forged four brass tubes the length of a man. On one end of each tube was a nozzle fashioned to look like the head of an animal or person with its mouth open wide. Argoth's favorite was of the beautiful woman looking like she was about to kiss her lover. The other end of the tube was connected to a flexible leather hose, which led to a barrel of seafire. Midway from the tube to the barrel was a pump. A five-man team operating the tube, pump, and barrel could spray a thick stream of the fiery liquid almost sixty yards. More if the wind was at their backs. One tube was placed on each of four ships.

The violent sound and large quantities of brown and yellow smoke was enough to shock any man. But when the Bone Faces saw that it burned on water, clung like tar, and could not be extinguished, they surely must have prayed to their bloody gods for deliverance.

Being able to force the fire out in a stream turned fire into a weapon that, instead of merely harrying an enemy, could turn the course of a battle.

His men had sent five of the raider's ships to the depths that way, spearing those that survived the flames in the water like so many carp. Then they'd burned the Bone Face secret island port.

His fire, Argoth's Fire, had saved the Nine Clans last year.

The Prime inclined his head in respect. "Great One, we did not deny your request, but sent, asking the Glory to provide a ship of dreadmen so that we might convey the fire lances. We dared not send them forth only to be lost into the hands of the enemy."

"You should have supplied your own dreadmen."

"But we had only a handful, Great One."

"You had enough for the battles last year."

"But the winter storms were too severe; besides, sending them would have left us defenseless. We—"

"Do you argue with the Glory's envoy?"

"No, Great One. I merely explain that we delayed not from indifference or traitorous alliance, but from the greatest concern that this weapon would fall into the hands of those who would use them against you."

"And when you fell, when your weaves failed, and the enemy overran you, what then?"

But their weaves shouldn't have failed. Mokad should have sent a replacement.

"We were foolish, Great One," said the Prime. He prostrated himself on the floor. "Please show us how we may repent."

"Who cast the lances? Who devised the liquid?"

"The lances were cast by a smith of the Fir-Noy, Great One. As for the liquid," the Prime pointed at Argoth, "the Glory's servant who created it stands there."

Argoth deepened his bow, but he saw that the Skir Master did not turn.

"A Shoka," the Skir Master said, still facing the Prime. "Hard to believe a Shoka could devise this. Besides, wasn't it a Shoka who spied for the old widow of Cath so many years ago?"

Decades ago there had been one family of Shoka who

had spied for the widow Glory of Cathay. But their perfidy had been discovered and the family destroyed decades ago. The Skir Master had a long memory, but that isn't what bothered Argoth—how was it that the Skir Master knew the Prime had pointed at him?

"A blight upon our name, Great One," said Shim. "But those elements were culled from the clan. Our loyalty has been tested. Was it not a Shoka who saved the Glory's blessed father from the avalanche?"

The Skir Master turned and smiled. "Indeed. And now, it seems, the Shoka have yet another opportunity to do a great deed or a greater evil. What will it be?"

An anger began building in Argoth. But Shim dropped to one knee and Argoth followed his lead.

"The Shoka serve the Glory of Mokad," said Shim.

"Does anyone else know the secrets of your firewater?" asked the Skir Master.

"No, Great One," said Argoth. "A handful know parts and help with preparation. But only I know how it all combines at the last." Actually, that was a lie. Hogan knew all the steps. And Hogan had sent the secrets along so that the Order might have this weapon.

"Then you shall be the savior to lift the burden from this people's neck," said the Skir Master. "You now have your ship of dreadmen. You will gather up every fire lance—every part, from the cannon to the fittings on the ships. You will collect every drop of the firewater and all the tools and substances used to create it. You will have them loaded on my ship by morning. And you," he turned to Shim, "you will deliver all those who help prepare it. Do this and the Glory of Mokad will forgive this people its cruel inattention."

Argoth was stunned. Did the Divine not know he was taking their last defense? With those words he'd just ordered the deaths of all the fine warriors of each clan.

He'd ordered the rape of their women. With those words he had put the collar of slavery upon every child born for as many generations as it took to rise up against the the invaders and finally throw off their chains. With those words he had cut the hearts out of hundreds to be burned upon the barbaric altars of the Bone Face priests.

"Do you waver?" asked the Skir Master.

"No," said Argoth. "I—"

"Great One," said the Prime. "Does this mean that the Glory has blessed us with your wise leadership?"

The Skir Master shook his head. "All of the arms of Mokad must now defend the heart. I too will sail in the morning."

Again, the room fell silent. Argoth could not believe he was hearing this. And then he realized he did not believe this. The Skir Master was deliberately provoking them, testing them.

Why would he do that?

"Deliver your burden," said the Skir Master, "and I will reward you immediately with a replenishment of three weaves."

Three? Three would never be enough to protect this land.

"Great One," the Crab said. "Did you have time to consider our request for a seeking?"

"A proper seeking takes many hours," said the Skir Master. "I cannot draw for your weaves and perform a seeking by morning. And I will not delay my departure. No, take your prisoner and put him to the question yourself. You can break through a man's defenses with a proper questioning almost as easily as you can with a seeking." He gestured in a way that took in the whole Council. "Or is this seeking the boon you desire?"

"Weaves," said the Prime. "Bring our weaves to life."

The Skir Master signaled for his guide, but before he

left, he gazed at Argoth again. "Lest something happen to such a valuable resource as yourself, ten of my dreadmen will accompany you. Losing you is a risk I will not bear."

"Very wise, Great One," said Shim. "Very wise."

Argoth looked into the Skir Master's eyes—did he know Argoth's secret? Argoth glanced at Shim. Had he revealed his suspicions about Argoth?

Argoth bowed. Ten dreadmen to guard him, but only three for the whole of the New Lands?

"Do not disappoint me," the Skir Master said to the whole Council. "Now, I have heard of your baths. Lumen wrote incessantly of them and the delights of your blueberries, and I mean to enjoy them both before I leave."

THE COUNCIL ERUPTED after the Skir Master left. But the Crab, ever fixed upon his purpose, came to take Hogan.

"It appears we'll have to find another to oversee the questioning," he said.

"It will be one of the Shoka," said Shim. "And it will be done in the fortress of Whitecliff."

The Crab hesitated and Argoth wondered if he was going to try to forcibly take Hogan from him, but he only made a gesture of surrender with his hands. "As you wish."

Shim caught Argoth's eyes, as did the Shoka territory lord, but Argoth ignored them. He took Hogan, pushed through the Council's chaos and rushed him outside. The ten dreadmen assigned by the Skir Master followed behind.

Before they had exited the building, a messenger entered and set off another round of alarm—Larther the hunter had been found dead on the upper plains with the same blackening about his face as was found on Barg's family.

Hogan looked at Argoth.

Larther was one of the Grove. At one time he had thought River would marry Larther, but that had never come to pass. Instead, Larther had cleared numerous acres of Argoth's land up on the plains that he might satisfy Gil the carpenter. The carpenter had demanded that his daughter, who was smart and clever and had waited so very long for a man to notice her, would not spend her life in a dirty hut. Three years Larther had cut and cleared. They were to be married this season.

Hogan passed his hand over his face. Then he spoke with his eyes closed. This was his habit when trying to catch and pull together the threads of many elusive thoughts. "It is not a coincidence."

The dreadmen were too close for Hogan to speak loudly. So Argoth put his friend's arm in his and began walking out of the hall and left into the street, toward the fortress. The dreadmen followed a few paces behind.

Hogan did not speak for some time. They walked down the cobbled lane, the great houses towering like walls on either side. They passed a man pushing a vegetable cart loaded with enormous radishes, two boys chasing after a yellow cat, and a serving woman in blue and white, cleaning a doorstep.

Hogan pitched his voice low so the dreadmen couldn't hear. "Purity, Larther," he said, "and suddenly a Divine appears who doesn't care to do a seeking. Doesn't even mention the fact that some creature of legend stalks our land. I can't see it yet, but he's tightening some noose." Hogan licked his dry lips. "And here's another thing: what if the creature was his to begin with?"

If that were the case, then the Skir Master had already peformed a seeking on Purity. He might already have their names and the names of contacts in other Groves.

"The Grove must flee," said Hogan.

"Who? You and me? Guarded by ten dreadmen? And if we do the noble thing and kill ourselves, it won't help the others."

"Matiga is ready. She's strong. Her knowledge runs deeper than either of ours. She will bear the Grove off to join with Harnock."

"But what if that's precisely what this Skir Master is hoping for. The Order always flees. He's expecting it, expecting us to send out warnings. And what if he already knows about Harnock and is waiting for us to lead his men to him?"

Hogan said nothing.

Harnock, rarely seen, was a ghost of man and beast. It was he, in his secret mountain valley, who kept the *seed*, the hope that would start the One Grove. It was he who kept the Book and Crown of Hismayas, the ancient god who had founded the Order. Into these two objects Hismayas was said to have put all his knowledge and power. The problem was, none had yet found the way to unlock them. Nevertheless, if those two objects fell into the enemy's hands, the Order might never recover.

"I have a better plan," said Argoth. One that just might save the Grove here and all the unknowing wives, sons, and daughters who would not be able to flee with the power of the lore. One that would not only discover what exactly the Skir Master knew, but also ensure that any secrets he had extracted would never reach the other side of the sea. One that would allow Argoth to put the tools he had before he came to the Order to a righteous purpose.

"No," said Hogan.

"Yes," said Argoth. "I'm going to run right into his teeth."

22.

RIDERS

Talen suspected the Mokaddians would be watching for him at Farmer's Gate. For that matter, they'd be watching for him at all the lesser gates on that side of the city. So he decided to use a gate on the far side.

Gallow's Gate was manned not by the city guard but by commoners performing their required three-day service. A city guardsman oversaw them. But the bulk of the dozen men here were commoners, mustered for this purpose. One man eating slices of raw fish with his fingers, saw Nettle, knew him, and waved them through with a "give the Lord the Lani family's compliments."

Nettle nodded, and they passed through the gate. They rolled through the dry moat, over a slight rise, and continued on toward the river. They'd made it out!

Talen felt a surge of relief and something he didn't expect—sympathy for the hatchlings. Perhaps it *was* as Da said: perhaps what was wrong was that the world was full of Fabbises.

With every rod they traveled it seemed that Talen felt better and better. A great sense of energy and well-being washed over him. He felt like a spring day, one where the mud had dried and the leaves had begun to break their buds and color the world with a light green. It was odd. It was as if the earth itself had touched him and given him an extra portion of life. Perhaps he'd been more scared than he thought and so felt a greater relief.

The wagon bumped along and kicked up a haze of powdery dust. Not far down the road, along a bend of the river, rose a fat grove of cottonwoods.

A number of naked bodies hung on ropes from the massive limbs of the trees. They were criminals. Of course, Sleth would never hang here. Sleth were dealt with in an entirely different manner.

"I want to ask you something," said Nettle. "And I want a straight answer."

Talen looked at his cousin.

"When that hatchling girl kissed you, did you feel anything odd?"

"Besides being panicked out of my mind?"

"I've heard the lovemaking of Sleth is feral."

"Goh," said Talen. "We weren't lovemaking. You need to get out more. Forget your parents' ban. Slip out and kiss a girl now and again. You have enough who are willing."

"Are you joking? My father would skin me. Especially after the incident with the fuller's maid. You'd think I've got a life of cake and pie. But my parents have got me so hemmed in and roped down I'm going crazy."

"The bailiff was right outside," said Talen. "You think we had time for sport?"

"But you said she put her tongue in your mouth. That's going a bit far for playacting, isn't it? And I'm not interested so much about the lovemaking anyway. What I'm wondering is if she did something to you."

She'd done nothing to him. Nothing he could feel. But Nettle wanted a story and it was clear he wouldn't be put off. Talen gave him an earnest look. "You won't tell anybody?"

Nettle's face lit with curiosity. He raised his hand in oath. "Silent as a mole."

Talen took a deep breath. "I was helpless."

"Helpless?"

"Yes, she took my arms and pressed them down so I couldn't do a thing. You wouldn't think a slip of a girl could do that. I wanted to tell her to get back, but the words wouldn't form. I was helpless before her. You cannot imagine what it felt like when she pressed in close to me."

Talen paused for effect and waited. He could almost feel the silence drawing Nettle's curiosity like a bow.

"So she pressed in?"

"Oh, snug as a glove. It wasn't proper. And that's the troubling thing. Despite all logic, despite my fears, I cannot deny the desire that rose in me."

"I see."

They were almost upon Gallow's Grove, and the stench of those twisting in the breeze made Talen bring his tunic up over his nose.

These trees could hold a prodigious number of bodies. After last year's battles with the Bone Faces, a horde of prisoners had been executed. They'd hung along these limbs thick as candles on dipping rods. But those had been cut down. These here were criminals. The rumors of their deeds and hangings had spread quickly. Such news was always part of the talk in the houses of the alewives.

Talen motioned at the bloated and decayed bodies. "Look at that one. I bet he's that cattle thief from the Sinks." The man in question had obviously been dragged behind a horse. His flesh was torn and open. He had no eyes. He had no hands for that matter. Those had been cut off. Wasps mixed with the flies in a cloud, all of them buzzing in to get their tiny bites.

Nettle pulled his tunic over his nose.

Some of the bodies here had been hanging for weeks. The first was withered, but it was clear he'd been emasculated. When they rode close to the second, a hawk that had been tugging at the flesh of the man's face rose and flapped away, revealing a half-eaten, gruesome smile.

They passed another. Talen stopped the wagon by the fourth and fifth, a man and a woman. The man was hung with a thick rope punched through the skin and threaded through his ribs. The woman's dark hair hung over her ruined face. She tilted slightly, twisting gently in the evening breeze, one arm sticking out as if she were reaching for them. Both had been in the trees long enough for the maggots to hatch.

"Killed her mother-in-law," said Talen. "They said she struggled and bucked for the better part of an hour."

"I don't need a history," said Nettle. "Move it along."

But Talen didn't want to move it along. He looked up at the bodies hanging about him. If anyone found out about the girl and boy at his house, this is where his life would end.

Why would Da risk something like that?

Talen started Iron Boy again. When he put enough distance between them and the grove to erase the stink, he pulled his tunic from his nose.

Nettle did the same.

They were both quiet for a time, then Nettle produced another half loaf of bread pudding. Where he'd been hiding it, Talen had no idea.

Nettle took a big bite. When he'd gulped it down, he said, "So?"

"So what?"

"So, what did she do after she slid in?"

Good old Nettle, Talen thought. Not even death hanging about in the trees could sway him from girls or his gut.

"I was fearing for my soul," said Talen. "But not minding it either. The hunters were outside, and yet I could not think of them. Only the creature on my lap." Talen shook his head. "She took my hand and pressed it to her."

"Her side?"

"Oh, no," said Talen. And he gave Nettle a look that said she'd done nothing as innocent as that.

Nettle's eyebrows rose and Talen fought to suppress his smile.

"You mean?" said Nettle.

Talen nodded. "I tell you, I was paralyzed; my brain was cider muzzy. Her with a wicked gleam in her eyes, and me thinking to myself that she's done this before, these are experienced hands. I am only thankful she exposed herself when arms-men were about. Who knows what she would have forced me to do. As it is, I fear I've been touched."

"It is said that they make sounds."

"Sounds?"

"The beast in their natures takes over."

"There was no sound," said Talen. "But she did indeed bite."

Nettle narrowed his eyes. Talen could see he'd pushed the tale a bit too far.

"You're such a bad liar," said Nettle.

Talen pulled his collar down to show Nettle his neck. "Look for yourself."

"I don't see anything. Why I ever listen to you, I'll never know."

"Look," Talen said and pointed.

Nettle leaned in close. "There's nothing here."

Talen clopped him on the side of the head. "Of course, there isn't. No glamour, no petting, no grunts, or lustful moans. No wicked babies conceived. I told you. It was like kissing the wall." Except that wasn't entirely true.

"Look," said Talen. "If she's there when we get back, you can have a go. Tell her to not forget the tongue."

"She wasn't that bad-looking," said Nettle, as if considering the idea. "Better than most."

"Who cares?" said Talen. "She's a hatchling."

"You yourself said nothing happened."

Nettle *was* considering it. "You can't be serious," said Talen.

"Gotcha," said Nettle and grinned.

Talen pointed at him. "You can't fool me. You were actually thinking of kissing her."

"If if makes you happy to think that, go right ahead and think it."

Talen refused to rise to his bait, instead he fetched one of the last of his ginger cookies and plopped it in his mouth.

They had just entered the trees on the hill that lay beyond Gallow's Grove, and Talen wanted to see if there was any sign of pursuit. He stopped the wagon, hopped out, and went back to the tree line. Nettle followed.

About a mile back, well before Gallow's Grove, a group of mounted men followed the road. He watched them disappear behind a small hill. Talen groaned "You think they're looking for us?"

"I think we'd better act as if they are," said Nettle.

They scrambled back to the road and got into the wagon. Talen urged Iron Boy on, knowing there was no way two boys in a wagon could outrun mounted men.

23.

SCENT

Hunger lost the scent of the Koramite and his son. At first, it didn't bother him. He watched the people and animals come and go. But toward late afternoon it occurred to him that the Koramite and his son might not have gone to the city at all. They might have simply ridden on by.

This gave him pause. What if they weren't coming

back this way? What if they weren't coming back at all? Argoth might hold lands in that other direction. They might be gone visiting; they might be gone for a week-long hunt for all he knew.

He shouldn't have let them go. No, he'd made a miscalculation. He should have given them chase.

But then he calmed himself. They were either in the city or they were beyond it. The wind was blowing in from the sea. All he needed to do was walk the edge of the forest in a line running toward the city.

If the Koramite and his boy were in the city or going to travel back, he'd pick up their scent. And if they weren't, well, then they had quite a start on him.

But Hunger would find them. Of that he had no doubt. He'd been a great hunter in his time. At least, one of those he'd eaten had been.

Hunger stood and began making his way down the hill. Below him on the road, three boys in red hats herded a large flock of sheep. Their long-haired, black and white dogs barked to keep the sheep from straying too far from the road.

Hunger stepped out of the brush into the middle of the flock and sent the sheep running. The second boy, walking perhaps only a dozen feet ahead, looked back. His expression of curiosity turned to horror.

Hunger could catch the shepherd and eat him. He paused. He could smell him, taste him on the wind. He could eat them all.

No, he told himself. He would not. If he did, he wouldn't be able to stop himself the next time.

One of the dogs began barking.

Something drifted to him on the breeze. He opened his mouth.

The burning boy. The scent was faint but unmistakable.

This time, Hunger thought, you won't get away. He turned from the shepherd and his sheep.

The dog followed him to the brush on the far side of the road, snarling. The young man found his voice and yelled a warning. But another three steps and Hunger was well into the wood, the sounds of the shepherds and their dogs receeding behind him.

24.

TREES

Talen peered out from the wagon bed. The men following them had begun to trot their horses.

"I'm jumping out around that next bend," said Talen. Nettle could continue with the wagon while Talen tried to escape on foot.

"They've already seen you," said Nettle.

"You don't know that."

"You don't know that they haven't."

"It's the only way."

"Just act normal," said Nettle.

"Will you shut up with your normal nonsense."

"I'm Captain Argoth's son. It will count for something."

"Yeah," said Talen. "That's why I was standing around this morning at the city gate batting horseflies from my naked body."

"As soon as they realize you're gone, they'll know. They'll send one back for help. The rest will watch the area. And the woods here don't run unbroken. They'll see you."

"No," said Talen. "They won't." But he knew they would. By the stinking lord of pigs, they would.

Unless he hid so well, so quietly, like a mouse in a tuft of grass, that they'd have to be standing right on him to know he was there.

"Just get me to the bend in the road," said Talen. They didn't have dogs, and it would be dark before they could bring them. That was the only thing he had in his favor.

Talen caught another glimpse of the men, perhaps a half-dozen rods behind. There were eight of them, all Shoka.

The wagon bumped along, making it difficult for Talen to keep himself flat and out of sight in the wagon bed. At this pace they weren't going to make the bend. "Speed it up," hissed Talen.

"We'll say you're sick."

"It won't work," said Talen.

Behind them, the men urged their horses into a canter.

"Faster," said Talen.

Nettle flipped the reins and Iron Boy began to trot. The wagon bounced off a rut.

Talen readied himself.

It was odd, but the sensation of energy and well-being he'd noticed passing through the city gate had not vanished. If anything, it had built. He felt as if he could keep pace with a horse, maybe outrun one.

Of course, that was stupid. Still, with every jolt of the wagon his strength grew. He could feel it, like a crazy itch seeping through him. He wondered about the ginger cookies. This would not be the first baker to mix a come-back into his breads. Come-backs were something to make a body depend on his bread, something besides taste to make a person come back and continue to buy. Of course, such herbs were outlawed in the New Lands, but it had been a Whitecliff baker. He probably didn't think such rules applied to him.

"We're almost to the bend," said Nettle.

The men were closing fast. One of them yelled out.

The wagon passed into the shade of trees and out of the the men's sight.

Nettle reined in Iron Boy to slow the wagon.

Talen rose to his feet.

"You're not going to have time to find cover."

Not if he ran into the woods. The forest floor was covered with leaves that would crackle underfoot. If they didn't see his tracks, then they'd be sure to hear any step he took.

Talen looked up. The trees here were massive giants. All the lower limbs had been cut by clan road gangs, and the closest branch towered more than a dozen feet overhead.

It was an impossible height for him. Except, he knew he could reach them. His limbs ached to jump. What did he have to lose?

Talen stood on the wagon seat and eyed the limb of a towering elm in front of them. The branch was as thick as his leg and hung almost twenty feet above the trail.

The tree limb was too high. He knew it. But he couldn't help himself. His legs cried out for a sudden burst of power. He had never imagined his growth would come upon him in this fashion.

He stood on the wagon seat and held his hands out to the side for balance. He would jump a bit to the side just in case he missed.

"You'll never make it," said Nettle.

"Maybe my legs are as quick as my hands."

"That wasn't quickness back there with Fabbis," said Nettle. "That was you grabbing a snake that was just about dead."

No, Talen thought. It had been as live and wriggling as any serpent he'd ever held. Not to mention that he'd moved quickly enough to take both Fabbis and Cat off guard. Talen steadied himself; he was still a bit light-headed, but the itch inside him had built. He could feel the power.

The sound of the horse hooves beating the ground sped from a canter to a full gallop.

"They're on us!" hissed Nettle. "Sit down!"

Talen focused on the branch. "Tell them I struck out on foot after leaving the gate."

He was almost there.

The galloping sounded as if it were right behind them.

The wagon passed underneath the branch, and Talen leapt.

He soared.

He must have got a bounce from the seat, because the branch was suddenly within reach.

He grabbed it with one hand, and the wagon passed below him.

Talen reached up with his other hand and swung over.

It was impossible that he'd made the jump. He looked down. The distance between him and the ground yawned below. Lords, a fall at this height would break his leg.

He wanted to whoop. Such a leap.

Nettle turned in the wagon seat and stared up at him, his mouth hanging open. Then Nettle's attention snapped to the bend in the road.

Talen got to his feet, and in one, two, three balancing strides, worked himself to the far side of the trunk and flattened himself against it. Nettle was now on the other side of the tree.

The first rider rounded the bend.

With a thunder, the others followed. By this time Nettle

had pulled the wagon to the side of the road, as if giving faster travelers the right of way as courtesy demanded.

Please, thought Talen. Let them ride on by. Let them ride on by.

But the horsemen did not. They pulled their horses to a stop and commanded Nettle to hold.

Talen dared not move, dared not even attempt a glance below him. He tried to meld into the trunk. He couldn't see what was going on, but he could hear.

"Where's the Koramite?" one of the men asked.

"And who are you?" asked Nettle. "I haven't seen you before."

"You've seen *me*," another man said, the anger clear in his voice. "Now where is he?"

"I don't need to answer your questions," said Nettle. "You can address your concerns to my father."

"It appears," the second man said, "that your father has made the wrong friends. And he's not here to protect you."

"What do you mean?"

Metal scraped against metal—a sword being drawn!

"Where is the Koramite?" the man demanded.

"Don't threaten me," said Nettle.

A pause. A scuffle.

"Stop," said Nettle, his voice distressed. "He left on foot the first chance after we passed through the gate."

Talen wished he could see what was happening. All he could see was the bark before him and the rumps of three horses.

"We saw two sitting on this wagon seat."

"That's what we meant for you to see," said Nettle.

"You lie."

Nettle cried out in pain.

Talen almost leaned out to get a better view. What if they had found the hatchlings back at the farmstead? If they had, Nettle was in terrible danger.

"Fool," said Nettle. "I rode with that barrel and sack of potatoes next to me, all covered with cloth. He's gone, flown!"

"You're lying," the second man said. He raised his voice. "Search the woods."

25.

A SHORTNESS OF BREATH

Talen could hear the men fanning out in the trees below him, their boots crunching to the leaves. One man called out to the others, telling them to look for spoor in the leaves. Another told Talen to reveal himself or face harsher consequences.

He pressed himself further into the rough bark of the elm. He could not see any of them at first. Then one man with a black-and-gold-checkered scarf tied at the back of his bald head walked into view in front and below him.

The man held a short sword out in front of him. If he turned around and looked up, he'd see Talen as clearly as a pig at a party. And there was nowhere Talen could go. If he moved, if he scuffed one bit of bark to fall below, someone was sure to see.

Lords, this was a bad idea. Talen thought of his experience with Ke in the tree back home just the day before. You couldn't escape someone in a tree. Why had he jumped up here?

The man with the gold-checkered scarf turned around, scanning the brush around him.

If they saw him, what would he do? Not climb higher. He'd tried that with Ke. He'd have to go lower. Or, like a squirrel, he could run along the limb of one tree to another until he had put enough distance between him and his pursuers to drop to the ground and run like a madman.

The man in the checkered scarf examined the ground. He turned his back on Talen, squatted and examined the forest floor more closely. Then he looked up at the trees in front of him.

He began to turn about, to scan the trees.

Talen couldn't spring to another limb of this tree. It would rustle the leaves.

He looked about for any escape. To his left he saw a small stub sticking out from the trunk. It was barely enough to stand on.

The man continued to turn.

If he could use that, if it didn't break under his weight . . .

Talen quickly stepped to the stub.

It held, and he gripped the rough elm bark to steady himself.

The move hadn't taken him totally from the man's view. But Talen couldn't go around to the other side of the tree because that was in full view of the road. He looked up. The next branch was too fat to grab easily, and far too high above him anyway.

Despite Talen's fear, his limbs felt miraculously full of energy. His legs—it felt as if they carried nothing, as if his entire body weighed no more than a feather.

He could make that leap to the next branch above him. He could leap and hang there if he had to. His arms felt that strong.

Talen could almost see the profile of the man's face. One more turn and he'd spot Talen.

Standing on the branch stub, Talen coiled himself as best he could.

The man began to turn.

Talen sprang.

The power in his legs was immense, but it wasn't enough.

Perhaps the perch had been too small. Or perhaps it had twisted just a bit at the last moment. Whatever the cause, he didn't make the branch. Didn't come close.

He reached out for the trunk of the giant old elm, his fingers spread wide, reaching out with toes and knees, reached out and grasped it in a bear hug. He clung to the rough bark with all his strength.

He expected to fall, to dash his worthless brains on the ground below. But he didn't. His fingers, like his arms and legs, were full of life, and he clung to the trunk like some great, four-legged insect.

It was odd. He had to breathe like he was straining under a great weight, but it did not feel like a great weight. It felt easy and natural.

He looked down. While he hadn't made the branch, he was high enough to be covered by a large block of leaves.

Light-headedness washed over him. He was panting. Hyperventilating. But he couldn't stop. He felt dizzy. The world below began to spin. He was going to lose his grip.

Talen closed his eyes. The fat branch above was not so far away. If he could shinny up to it and rest, he was sure the light-headedness would pass.

He reached up, his arms and legs wide, moved his foot, reached up again. Climbing the trunk was as easy as climbing a ladder. In moments, with barely a scrape of sound, he reached the branch. He dared not open his eyes because he knew the dizziness would take him. With a final move, he pulled himself on top of the branch and straddled it. He would have lain on his stomach, but he was panting, straining, laboring for breath. He was suffocating.

The edges of his vision began to blur.

Talen struggled for another breath, but it wasn't enough. He'd never felt panic like this before. He couldn't get his breath.

The world slid to the side; Talen's vision narrowed. He was passing out, and the last thing he thought was that he'd better collapse onto this branch squarely because he didn't want to fall from this height.

26.

BAKER'S HERBS

Talen found himself face-first on the branch. He was still straddling it, still panting, but not suffocating like he had been before.

He reached up and felt the wetness on his cheek. He'd bloodied his nose. Bloodied a small circle of the branch for that matter.

The men stood below him. "He's not here," one said. "There's not one leaf that's bent out of place."

"Then he jumped out earlier," said the one who had first commanded Nettle to stop. "Where is he?"

"I told you," said Nettle. "He's headed west. They've got family out there."

"Maybe we'll take you along just to make sure."

"Have they arrested my father?" asked Nettle.

Talen heard one of the men spit.

A beat passed.

"No, they haven't," said Nettle. His voice changed. It rung with confidence. "Perhaps you should know that my family dined with the warlord just last week. Maybe I should pass your names along to him. Put in a good word." This last he almost hurled at them.

They did not immediately respond to Nettle's threat.

One finally spoke up. "We're wasting time here."

"He's not telling us something," said another.

"Interrogate him then. I told you we should have broken up into groups. I'm going back to look for spoor by the gate."

Saddles and harness creaked below as men mounted up. A horse stamped its foot.

"I'm going to be watching you," a man said.

"Good," said Nettle. "Then when it comes to it, we'll know exactly where to find you."

The men urged their horses forward with grunts and clicks. Then the horses thudded away.

Talen dared not say a word. Perhaps it was a ruse, one or two of them staying behind.

He waited, the itch to move began building in his limbs again. Or maybe it had never gone away. His breathing had eased, but he was still light-headed.

"Talen," Nettle called up.

Talen didn't dare move.

"They're gone. Talen," Nettle hissed. "Get your Koramite arse down here. We need to put some distance between us and that pack of turncoats."

Talen looked at the ground so very far below. How in the world had he gotten so high? "I don't know how to get down," he said.

"Jump," said Nettle. "I'll catch you."

Talen smiled. And it was enough to take the edge off his fear. He saw a branch he could let himself down to.

Then another and another until he swung down the trunk and shinnied to the ground.

Nettle held a hand to his ear. Blood stained his fingers. "Did they cut you?"

"You owe me," said Nettle. He pulled his hand away. The ear was bloody from a slice nearly an inch long.

"Goh!" said Talen. "That's going to require sewing."

"Just get into the wagon bed."

Talen put a hand on the sideboard and sprang over. "We're not going to be able to take the normal roads home."

"Brilliant deduction," said Nettle.

"And there's something else." His legs, arms, his whole body itched to move. "I'm not quite right."

"I'd say," said Nettle.

"No," said Talen. "I'm telling you, something inside is very, very wrong."

It made no sense. There was a Koramite boy in the district who had difficulty breathing and was always carrying camphor of peppermint about to clear his lungs. But this didn't feel like he couldn't get air. This felt like he did when he sprinted a great distance, except he hadn't sprinted, hadn't felt any awful exertion.

Talen fetched one of the last ginger cookies. "Taste this."

"I don't want your nasties."

"Taste it. I think our baker put come-backs in here."

Nettle took the cookie, broke it, and examined the pieces. "If anything's in here, then the baker must have ground it into powder." He took a nibble and grimaced. "There could be horse plop in here and it wouldn't taste any worse." He handed the cookie bits back to Talen.

"What do you think he put in here?"

"I don't know," said Nettle. He looked up at the tree Talen had jumped into. "That's quite a jump you made."

"What are you saying?"

"I want to try something. Take the reins. Swing the wagon around and approach the spot like we did before."

"Don't we need to get out of here?"

"Just do it," said Nettle.

Talen took the reins, turned the wagon around, and approached the tree as they had before. Nettle stood on the wagon seat as Talen had when he'd jumped. They rolled under the tree. Despite his injured ear Nettle leaped, tried for the branch, and grabbed nothing but air. He landed with a grunt and rolled.

He stood and put a hand back to his ear. Leaves were clinging to his back. "How close did I come?"

He hadn't come close at all. "Two, maybe three feet away. You're about as lively as a pile of lead."

"I don't think it's lead."

"Inferior breeding then. What are you trying to prove?"

Nettle looked at him, as sober as stone. "Are you sure that girl didn't do something to you?"

Of course he was sure. "This odd exhilaration didn't start until we left the city gates. I'm telling you: it's comebacks. I'll bet your smelly little linens on it."

"Maybe," said Nettle. "But what herb changes a man that much?"

"Maybe I've got stag legs," said Talen.

"You've got the legs of a scarecrow," said Nettle.

"Then you're a piss-poor jumper," said Talen. "Try it again."

"I saw you up there, clinging like a bug. It wasn't natural."

"Try it again," Talen said. He didn't want to hear this. Lords, if this was Sleth work—but it couldn't be. It wasn't.

Nettle shook his head but he got back up on the wagon. Talen wheeled around, and they tried it again.

"Concentrate," said Talen.

Nettle crouched. He breathed deeply. But he didn't come close to anything except spraining his ankle.

When Nettle was back in the wagon, Talen shook his head and made a small sound like he had empathy for Nettle's plight. "All your da's gold and cattle and you can't outjump a runt like me."

Nettle's ear had started bleeding again. He put his hand to it, pressed, and gave Talen the eye.

"Don't look at me like that," said Talen.

"Maybe their magic is like some mushroom that takes a while to work its effects."

"She was on my lap and then off," said Talen. "She didn't have time to do anything."

Nettle raised his eyebrows. "She had time to kiss you."

"And what's a kiss? Nothing."

"You don't know that."

Those words sliced right to his heart. He didn't know. Besides, she could have worked something in the night. She'd almost admitted doing just that.

Rot those hatchlings. Rot them.

Talen looked at the ginger cookie in his hand. "What we need to do is get one of these to River. She can ferret out what the baker used."

"And if it isn't come-backs?"

"Then I'll become a Sleth toy," said Talen. "And my first depradation will be to wring your neck." He handed the reins to Nettle and stepped out of the wagon. "What are you doing?" asked Nettle.

"Getting away from your stink," said Talen.

Now that Talen had said it, he realized that he did smell more than before. Or that what he did smell was stronger. The smell of Iron Boy, the road dust, the woods, Nettle's clothes that had sat in a cedar chest—the scents all lay heavily in the air.

What's more, the itch in his limbs almost compelled him to move. "I'm going to jog a bit," he said. "All we've got to do is work these come-backs through my system. A few hours and I'll be right as rain."

HUNGER STOOD IN a grove of trees smelling the the dead hanging about him, smelling the burning boy on the breeze. He'd been here. Been here recently.

He looked up at the bodies slowly twisting. A trio of magpies stood on the shoulders of one carcass that had a rope punched through its ribs. They jostled one another, flapped about, and pecked at the old flesh on the head.

He knew this place, but the name slipped away.

Hunger walked to the road. The scent lay here like a river. It took him a few moments walking up and back to discover the direction the boy had traveled.

He tried to guess how far he was behind. It was not far. Perhaps no more than an hour.

The smell of horses and men drew his attention. Hunger looked up the road. He couldn't see them, but he could see the haze of dust they kicked up. The riders were coming fast.

He did not want to draw attention, did not want to delay reaching the boy, so he slipped off the trail and squatted behind a thick clump of brush.

The riders soon crested the hill. Six of them wearing Shoka colors, two wearing Fir-Noy. He watched them gallop by, watched them fade in the distance.

Hunger stepped out of his hiding place and suddenly knew where he was: this was Gallow's Grove. A piece of the map in his mind locked into place. He knew where this road led. It led back to the hills where the boy was from.

Hunger checked the road once more in both directions and then began to lope after his prey.

27.

THE GLASS MASTER'S
DAUGHTERS

When they came to the crossroads, Talen decided he'd jogged far enough. His legs didn't feel tired. But Talen's thirst had steadily grown since the run-in with the riders and it felt like the back of his throat was going to cleave to the front.

He dipped the water ladle into the small barrel lashed to the side of the wagon and drank. He'd drawn this fresh from the well this morning. It was warm and clean and tasted of the oak barrel, but it did not quench his thirst. He took another drink, then a third.

This was an unnatural thirst. "That baker should be hung," he said. "These come-backs are killing me."

Nettle's ear had stopped bleeding, but didn't look any less horrible. He gave Talen a look that said they both knew this wasn't come-backs. "I'm worried about the Fir-Noy," said Nettle. "If Shoka were looking for us then you know the Fir-Noy are. They've probably sent riders to search the roads from Whitecliff to your farmstead."

"Fabbis," Talen said with disgust. He pointed at the crossroads. "So which path do we risk?"

The crossroads sat at the juncture of five roads. It was a large oval that often was the place for gatherings or a small market. But no matter what was going on, there was usually a Shoka tinsmith here. His rat dog would lie in the shade under the wagon while he sat with his tin goods and tools under a blue awning that folded out of the side. Today there was nothing here but grasshoppers and the rutted and dry roads stretching out from the place like spidery fingers.

"Why risk any of them?" asked Nettle. "We should leave the wagon and set out on foot through the woods."

"That's reasonable," said Talen. "Except the woods are most likely already full of Sleth hunters who have set a multitude of snares and traps. And I'm not leaving Iron Boy tied to a post, which means we'll have him clomping along with us. I'd dare say the woods are more dangerous than the roads. Besides, it makes us look guilty."

"You," said Nettle.

"Huh?" asked Talen.

"You're the one who will look guilty. I'm just along for the ride."

"Thanks," said Talen, "you're always such a big support."

Nettle sighed with exaggerated humility. "I suppose I am. Especially when I've been promised a throttling."

Talen waved Nettle off. "Look, I've got a better idea— what we need is an escort."

"An escort?" Nettle asked. He looked at Talen as if he'd just sprouted a cabbage out his ear. He motioned at the empty field. "Who are you going to get? Grasshoppers?"

"If we were close to your home, we'd get a number of your father's men to go with us. But we're not. So we get someone who is a friend of your father's."

"And who would that be? I say we go through the woods. If we run into anyone, we tell them we were hunting Sleth. We just don't tell them we've found them already."

"We don't have any black cloth for armbands. And even if we did, we have no tokens. Anybody we came across would spot us in a minute." Talen pointed to the road at the far end of the crossroads. "We're going to the glass master's." He was a powerful man with many men in his employ.

Talen would not have considered this, but Uncle Argoth

had recommended Talen to a number of respectable Mokaddian families, including Bartem the glass master. And the glass master had expressed some interest should Talen get his Shoka clan wrist.

Uncle Argoth had once told Talen that his mother's Shoka blood would eventually overpower the Koramite blood he'd gotten from Da. This, of course, had incited Da, but then that's why Uncle Argoth had said it in the first place. The two of them liked to dig each other as much as he and Nettle did. But lately, Da had come around to Uncle Argoth's arguments that what Koramites needed was some binding to the Clans. Talen was almost too old to apprentice himself out, but there were other ways Uncle Argoth might find a place for him among the Shoka. It wouldn't be a powerful position, but it would be better than being an unconnected Koramite.

Just at that moment, a Shoka boy, holding a throwing stick in one hand and two dead ducks in the other, walked from one of the roads into the clearing.

"Lords," said Talen. All they needed was someone to see them.

"Keep calm," said Nettle and hailed the boy.

When the boy came close, he said, "There's men looking for you. Hunters." The boy was short for his age, but wide.

"Oh?"

The boy looked at Nettle's ear, but did not remark upon it. "A group of about ten Fir-Noy." He pointed up one of the roads. "They accosted me. Asked me what I'd seen."

"What did you tell them?"

"I told them I hadn't seen nothing but ducks."

"You keep telling them that," said Nettle.

"They accused you of Slethery, but I spoke up, told them Captain Argoth was worth all ten of them."

The boy had done no such thing, Talen thought. What's more: he was a risk. What were they going to do with him?

"Fir-Noy rot," said Nettle and spat. "Always blaming their troubles on someone else. This whole Sleth madness started in one of their own villages. Not ours."

"Aye," said the boy. "But we'll catch them. My da and I, we've got ourselves half a dozen traps set in the woods."

"You're a brave one," said Nettle, "walking out here on your own."

The boy puffed up a bit.

"If enough Shoka take the initiative like you and your da," Nettle said, "we'll have the Sleth for sure. And if any other Fir-Noy come by, you've seen nothing but ducks."

"Aye," said the boy and raised the end of his throwing stick to the side of his nose.

Nettle flicked the reins and directed Iron Boy toward the glass master's road.

Talen considered his cousin: he'd handled that situation well. Of course, the boy was still a risk.

When the boy was out of earshot, Nettle said, "I hope your glass master is willing."

"Of course, he'll be willing. He trusts your father. Your father trusts me."

Nettle nodded. "Well, then let's get out of here before some Fir-Noy finds us and prevents us from testing your theory."

THE ROAD TO the glass master's was broad, but it wasn't straight, and they were constantly worrying they'd turn a bend and run into some vigilante patrol, but they never did. When they came to the part of the road that crested a hill and gave them a view of the glass master's vale, Talen heaved a sigh of relief: there were no Fir-Noy to be seen. Just the fields, the main buildings, and the glasshouse belching smoke out of three of its five chimneys.

Talen had walked the whole way. Now he told Nettle to pull up. He drank deeply from the barrel, then dumped the rest over his head. He was more thirsty than ever. And the itch in his legs had grown.

He hadn't worked anything out of his system. In fact, he wondered if there had been anything in his system to begin with.

"You know the stories of peopled bewitched to dance until they starved," Talen asked, "until their very bones turned to dust? Do you think it's possible to curse someone like that?"

"So now our hatchling wasn't just a post when she kissed you?" asked Nettle.

"She was a post," said Talen. "It's just my legs have put me to thinking what could have happened in the night."

"Who knows?" said Nettle. "If you wake up tomorrow and find yourself doing a chicken trot with Prince Conroy, then I'll be leaning towards curse."

Talen shook his head and began down the slope. Partway down the hill, he said, "If Atra comes to the door, I need to have something to say. Otherwise, I'll be staring at her like a great ox."

Atra, the glass master's daughter, had expressed an interest in him at the last harvest dance. Or at least it had seemed she had, and he'd thought about her ever since. He knew it was nothing more than a fancy, but such an arrangement would be good for everyone: Da would get a family member into a clan, Uncle Argoth would keep his promise to his sister, the glass master would be able to tie his interests with a man close to a warlord of the Nine, and Talen, if she accepted him, would be able to serve and ponder one of the most stunning creatures he'd ever beheld.

He remembered that River had told him once the key to conversation is asking helpful questions. Good humor,

302 • JOHN BROWN

a few good stories, and a few helpful questions. Not the stupid lines men came up with after a few pints of ale.

"Helpful?" he'd asked.

"Yes," said River. "A question that makes it easy for the other person to talk."

"Well, how's a question going to do that? Either they have something to say or they don't."

"No," River said. "Everyone has something to say. There are some people that are like an irrigation ditch. You pull the stop up and they'll go on until you shut them off. But others aren't like that. Other people are like a pond or lake. You've first got to make an outlet for them, only then will they flow."

"I've never heard you go on and on about a man's questions," said Talen. "All you talk about is their brilliant parts and all the presents they bring."

River smiled. "Trust me, little brother. The splendor of fine hair fades quickly."

"Yeah, well I'd rather fade than never shine at all."

Except after trying to think up great things to say, Talen was thinking maybe River had the right of it. Let them do the talking. But he'd never asked River for examples. What was a helpful question? How did you make an outlet for them to flow?

Well, it couldn't be that hard. He began to mumble questions to himself.

"What are you doing?" asked Nettle.

"Thinking up something to help Atra flow like a river."

"What?"

"Conversation. I'm thinking about making conversation."

"We've got men bent on doing us harm, and you're worried about conversation?"

"I've had enough of hunts and hatchlings and baker's

come-backs. I want to think about something pleasant for a while. Is it going to tax you?"

"No," Nettle said. Then he grinned. "Tell her she looks beautiful and then ask her if she wants to breed."

"You can rot," said Talen.

"Touchy," said Nettle.

Talen waved him off. Maybe he could ask after Atra's mother's health.

"Who cares what you say?"

"I do," said Talen. "It doesn't matter what you do, you're Captain Argoth's son. Honor and cattle hang on you like apples from a tree. You've got a garlic-eater's wrist. You can do what you want and still be attractive. But I have to make a good impression, especially when I tell them I need an escort and then have to wait around for the glass master to gather one. Besides, we don't want them asking us questions, do we?"

"You have a point," said Nettle.

"So?"

"So we keep it short. You've been threatened, falsely accused by Fir-Noy. I show them my ear. Then we say it would be mighty nice to have some Shoka with us the rest of the way home."

Talen nodded. Short and to the point. And if he got to talk to Atra that would be a small gift in a day that was turning out to be one big stinking cow pile.

They crossed the fields and stopped at the border of the yard proper. It could be dangerous to walk into the grounds of a place where the dogs did not know you. But nothing barked. And so he led Iron Boy in.

The glasshouse sat many yards away from the yard, its chimneys smoking. The doors stood open, and and Talen could see men moving about in the shadows. He could not tell what they were doing. And that's why it had been set apart from the house. The glass master wanted to avoid prying eyes that might discover his secrets.

The dogs lay under a wagon out there, probably to guard the glassworks. Talen knew that sand was a part of glass-making. And a fiery furnace. This land had once been covered with trees, but they'd chopped down at least a square mile of the wood and fed it to the furnace. A glassmaker needed wood to make charcoal to burn in his ovens. And so there was heat involved. He knew they used lime. He'd heard the dark blues were made with cobalt. But how it all was put together and blown into shape, he'd never know. Nor would anyone outside the glass guild. It was a rare art, and the secrets were guarded with oaths and penalties of death.

A grove of willow grew all up and down a creek. The willow branches were used to weave about some of the glass to keep them from breaking. Three women sat at the side of the glasshouse weaving willow sticks around large glass jugs.

Talen heard laughter and looked over at the house. Women busied themselves in a back room. Was Atra among them? He hoped not.

But even if she were, he would simply ask for the master.

His thirst was such that he thought about going straight to the well, but that would be rude. He was still wet from dumping water over his head, and he supposed proper young men did not come begging favors in soggy clothes, but what else could he do?

There was no one outside, so Talen would have to strike their bell.

He smoothed back his hair the best he could. Then wiped his wet hands on his tunic and walked up to the door.

A brass bell hung to the side of the doorpost. The artificer had engraved delightful scenes of bears and deer on the bell. He'd engraved the symbols for health and welcome upon the striker. The bell and striker were beautiful.

Talen's family could never afford such things. When people came visiting his home, they simply said, "Hoy," and waited for someone to respond.

He struck the bell twice.

He heard footsteps as someone came to the door. He hoped it was not Atra. Then the door opened and Talen saw a serving girl of maybe twelve years.

"Good day," said Talen. "I need to talk to the glass master."

"You're Horse's son, aren't you."

Talen nodded. Da had earned a new name a few years back. They did not have Iron Boy then. On a wager, Da had altered his harness, hooked the plow to himself, then told Ke to keep the lines straight. They had plowed their whole field that way. Not as deeply as a horse might, but deep enough. So he had earned the name Horse.

"I'll take your request back to the mistress. You can go on around to the well to water your mule."

As Talen walked back off the step, he got a feeling someone was looking at him. He turned and he saw a curtain slide back into place. Talen could just see the outline of someone through the curtain. Could that be Atra?

Talen smiled, then the person moved the curtain slightly, very slightly and stared at him.

It was Elan. Mad Elan, Atra's older half-wit sister, hiding where she obviously thought Talen could not see her. She had a mole on her face from which long hairs grew and an awful habit of chasing boys and giving them huge slobbery kisses. As a child he'd been terrified of her. She had caught him once, and he'd had to scream bloody murder to escape. She still put him on edge.

Some had suggested the glass master sacrifice her. It

was common for the lame, blind, or maimed to give themselves up to the Divines. When a war is being waged and you cannot see, you can still give Fire to those who can. If you cannot lift a sword, you can give Fire that will allow a man to wield his sword with incredible might. In fact, the glass master had offered her up once for the war weaves a few years back. Or so it was said. But they hadn't needed her or hadn't the time to draw her. And so Elan was still with them.

He hoped Elan had learned to keep her affections to herself. Him being chased around the glass master's yard simply would not do.

He motioned Nettle to take the wagon around to the trough. He could smell the smoke from the glassworks, but he could also smell the cold well water, a whiff of leather, hay, a rose. It was odd. There were suddenly too many smells. And he realized he'd been smelling too many things for some time now.

He glanced to the back of the house where the women were. Their talking had quieted. One woman sat breaking beans, glancing his way. Then he saw Atra. She walked past the other woman, picked up a basket, then walked out of his line of sight.

He heard a sound from behind. He turned slightly. Someone hid halfway behind a tree trunk a few paces behind him, holding a long arching stem of wild, white rose.

"Hoy, Elan," said Talen.

She quickly moved back behind the tree.

He wondered if half-wits had any special feelings for the opposite sex. You couldn't tell for sure because her face defied a precise age, but he guessed Elan was perhaps twenty-five years old: well beyond the age of marriage. He wondered if she dreamed of some handsome man giving her children and if she knew that such a dream would never become reality for her.

"There's a fine scent on the breeze that I cannot identify," he said. "I wish I knew what it was."

He glanced back, but she did not reveal herself.

He wondered how long it would take to get the glass master. Even if he did agree to send some of his men, Talen would probably end up waiting here for an hour or two. An hour or two that could land them in more danger.

He heard footsteps and turned around, only to come face-to-face with Elan. The rose stem in her hand was about three feet long and bent over to the ground. She held it out to him, beaming with delight.

Elan had a yellow ribbon tied in her hair. It did not do anything for her. In fact, it looked as if it had somehow snagged there.

"Muffin," she said.

"Talen," he said. "You must call me Talen."

"Muffin," she said and smiled her huge smile. She was missing a few teeth. And while he could see no long hairs growing from the large mole on her cheek, he could see a distinct shadow of a mustache.

Talen shook his head. She'd called him Muffin Bunny ever since she'd caught him that one time.

Then she straightened and said something.

Talen couldn't understand her. She spoke like she had a severe sore throat. "What?"

"I had a man call. Da made a good bargain."

At least that's what he thought she said. A man called for Elan?

"Really?"

"I a strong worker," she said. "I better than a watchdog with babies. I not some cheap servant."

"I'm sure," said Talen.

"He paid gold."

Who would pay gold for Elan? It didn't make sense. She was not bright, but maybe she was indeed a hard worker. Life had many simple tasks. Maybe the best deal the glass master could get was to sell her as a servant. He wondered: would the purchaser treat her kindly?

"I hope it goes well for you," said Talen.

"Muffin Bunny," she said. "You wet."

Then Atra called Elan.

"He here!" Elan shouted back.

Talen turned and saw Atra walk down a path that led from the back door of the house. She was wearing a sky blue, sleeveless surcoat. The armholes were huge and showed her bright red tunic underneath. The effect with her black hair was stunning.

Talen's heart jumped. He took a breath. His hair was sopping wet, so he released the thong that held his long hair together, smoothed back as much water as he could, and quickly retied it.

By the time he finished, Atra stood next to Elan.

She looked at Talen with a sad smile then said, "Elan, you're not done inside yet."

"I found him," said Elan. "I found him, Atty."

"Elan," said Atra a bit more forcefully.

Elan sniggered then walked back to the house. Before she went inside, she shouted out, "Atra told me a secret!"

Atra only rolled her eyes.

Elan was a half-wit, but she had clearly enough wit to tease her sister. Talen smiled. There was more to Elan than he had suspected.

Atra waved at Nettle.

"A secret?" asked Talen.

Atra shrugged. "Don't listen to her."

"How's the captain's son?" she called out with some tease and walked toward Nettle.

"Loafing," he said.

Atra wore working clothes. The sky blue of the surcoat was from woad, not the expensive mollusk blue. And the red was not the scarlet of the grain, but something else. Beautiful but practical.

Talen looked at Atra's smooth cheeks and nose. He looked for a pimple, and saw none. How was such skin possible?

His father had once told Ke how to look at a beautiful woman and still keep your wits straight. "Look her right between the eyes."

"Oh, that's good," Ke had said. "I'll be staring at her cross-eyed. That's sure to impress her."

"No, you won't," said Da. "Look at me. You can't tell I'm looking at your nose, can you?"

"Cross-eyed," said Ke.

"I am not."

"Are."

"Am not."

They had argued until Da finally chased Ke out into the pasture.

"Atra," Talen said.

She stopped and glanced back at him.

Nothing bespoke confidence more than the eyes. Talen wasn't going to appear to be the shy little boy Nettle talked about, so Talen looked her right in the eye.

He promptly forgot what he was going to say. All that came into his mind was Nettle's line about breeding. The silence stretched on a bit too long.

"The sun burns brightly," he finally said. "And so does your face."

He had known it was stupid before he'd said it, but couldn't help himself.

She looked at him quizzically, then came that sad smile again.

"Yes, very hot," Talen said.

Nettle laughed then tried to cover it with a cough.

"You two dare to travel alone?" she asked.

"Yes," Talen said. "Actually, my Da was summoned to the Council. We're on our way back."

Now was when he could use one of River's helpful questions.

"We heard about the creature coming for that woman," said Atra. "To think she's loose again. My da hopes the Skir Master mounts a hunt the likes of which has never been seen. When he does, Da will volunteer to fetch the crows that will pick her head to a nub."

"Oh?" said Talen.

"Yes, he's been quite affected by this whole thing. You wouldn't know anything about this, would you?"

He could feel that something had shifted between them. When he'd last seen her, it seemed the stars and moon and torchlight had danced in her eyes and smile. All that was gone.

He thought about the two hatchlings.

"What do I know?" he said. "Nothing. Except that this woman should be brought to justice. Tell me what you've heard."

Atra began to talk. He hoped she was an irrigation ditch because that's the only topic he could remember to bring up and because he hoped that her talking would simply fix whatever had happened between them.

Atra went on to repeat many of the same rumors Talen had heard today. He nodded and added a comment here or there, but mostly he just let her talk.

She was definitely an irrigation ditch.

Or maybe she wasn't. Maybe "tell me" was one of those helpful questions. Thank the Creators he'd stumbled on it.

As she talked Talen looked at her eyes. He concentrated on them. He noticed that they were not all of one color. There was a darker ring of brown inside a lighter one. Talen wondered if that's what perhaps made them so beautiful. But he decided against it. It was more their size and the loveliness of her brow.

Then Talen realized she had just said something and he had no idea what it was.

"I'm sorry," he said. "I fear the new baker puts more than flour and honey in his cookies. What did you say?" Da was right. She'd gone from Sleth to something else and he'd missed the whole journey looking into her eyes.

She shook her head. "I said that it seems Koramites are out of favor."

"Well, not all Koramites I hope."

Her mouth was drawn in a line of disappointment. Had she just told him he was unwelcome? His heart began to sink.

"You can't judge a whole people by the actions of a few."

"No," she said. "But some people do."

Then she changed the subject. "Would you like to see my new saddle?"

"I'll gladly view anything you want to show me."

She looked at him oddly.

"Anything having to do with saddles," he said.

The humor he knew her for flashed across her face, but then faded. He needed another helpful question. He couldn't quite believe, didn't want to believe she'd said what she had about Koramites. Maybe she wouldn't lump him in that group because he was going to be part of the Shoka.

"Tell me about your saddle."

Atra turned to Nettle. "Does the loafing captain want to see a saddle?"

"Naw," he said. "One saddle is pretty much like the other."

He gave Talen a look then. Nettle was trying to buoy him up and tell him that he should take his fish elsewhere.

"Suit yourself." She turned to Talen. "This way," she said and led him to the back of the stable. It wasn't proper for a boy and girl of courting age to be alone. But Talen decided they weren't really alone, they were just going to look at a saddle. Nor were they courting. Besides, Nettle was in the yard. They would come right back out.

She laid her hand on one of the finest saddles he had ever seen. It had silver trim worked around the edges. The leather had been dyed black. The many tassels of green and scarlet all ended in a bead of silver. The horse blanket was indigo blue.

Talen felt the smooth surface. "It's perfect." Her horse was black and well-muscled. It was such a magnificent saddle. Atra told him about the quality of the silver, which required frequent polishing, and showed him the fine stitching of the leatherwork.

He wondered if he would ever be able to afford such a saddle. He might. But it wouldn't be enough. That was the way of fine things. You couldn't just purchase one. You had to purchase sets and pairs. A fine blanket to go with a fine bridle to go with a fine saddle for a fine horse. Fine horse combs. And fine servants to take care of the whole lot. He could work all his life to have the wealth contained in only the glass master's stable.

Better to be plain than servant to such a master.

"You're a graceful rider, Atra. You'll look stunning at the races."

She smiled. "You won a number of contests at the dance."

Talen had won nothing. There hadn't been any contests. "I don't remember receiving any prize."

"It wasn't a public contest. Just among us girls."

What was she talking about?

"We rated you all during the King's March."

The King's March was a dance that only the men performed.

"A prize for hair, one for shoulders, for hands, for eyes, one for every significant part."

"That sounds like a lot of prizes," said Talen.

"You took one," she said.

So perhaps she was simply tired. Perhaps that explained her demeanor. This was going far better than he had ever hoped. "So what is my claim?"

He waited and when she didn't speak, he asked, "You're not going to tell me?"

"Talen, things have changed. You should probably not come around anymore."

She said it with kindness, but his discomfort at her rejection left him fumbling for a response. "Because of this," he said and motioned to his clothing. He knew that wasn't the reason why, but what else could he say? He tried a jest. "Next time, I'll dress down for the occasion."

"Talen," she said.

"What's going on here?"

Talen turned. The glass master stood with his hands on his hips. Talen had met the glass master when Uncle Argoth had introduced them last spring. He'd complimented Talen on his aim with the bow. But today the man had a hard look that suggested to Talen there was probably no helpful question that would ease this man into a conversation.

"Zu, your daughter was showing me her fine saddle. We were talking in the courtyard."

"Atra," he said and waved her out.

She turned to Talen and curtsied. "I'm sorry," she said. "I hope your horse was well watered."

When she'd walked out, her father looked at Talen. "I want you off my land."

"I was hoping to get your help," said Talen.

"I don't care what you were hoping."

"Zu," said Talen.

But the glass master turned and walked out.

Talen followed.

"Zu," said Nettle. "We need your help."

"I trust your father, Nettle," said the glass master. He looked at Talen. "And I've never had anything against your da. And so I'll give you a warning. Stay to your own race. Atra's too expensive for you, even if you were to be adopted by your better half. Now, I need you to leave."

Talen turned and looked up at him. He had not said that with malice. But Talen wanted to respond. "You know what's down in Whitecliff has nothing to do with me." Talen pointed at Nettle. "Do you see his ear? I've been falsely accused of Slethery. Him of aiding. We're here to ask for an escort. If you won't do it for me, then do it for Argoth's son."

"I don't have any men to spare."

There was nothing Talen could say to that. Talen looked past the man's shoulder and saw Atra glance at him, then enter the house. Her bride price was probably set at more than his father made in five years. But he couldn't let it lie. "Sleth blood does not run in Koramite veins. It does not run in mine."

"I didn't say it did, boy." The glass master didn't say anything else, just folded his arms across his chest and waited.

Talen knew there was nothing he could say to ease this man, so he tugged on Iron Boy's reins and walked out of the yard. He glanced back at the house and saw someone at the window.

For a moment he thought it was Atra, but it was Elan flapping her hand at him with that simple grin on her face.

Talen waved once. He would never be able to afford a

girl like Atra. He probably couldn't even afford Elan. And it wasn't because of the money. When they pulled out on the main road, Talen climbed onto the wagon and let out a heavy sigh.

"You can't listen to people who make glass," said Nettle. "What do they know?"

"They know who they want their daughters to marry. They know that it was a Koramite in Whitecliff."

"You didn't learn anything back there, did you? The glassmaster was never interested in you. I say good riddance."

Easy for Nettle to say. Talen had learned plenty and it had nothing to do with the glassmaster. He'd learned that Koramites would never rise as long as they protected and hid the bad elements among them. He'd learned that no matter what he did, his blood would drag him down. He'd learned the smith's wife had stolen from him, stolen from them all. Talen flicked the reins and started Iron Boy walking.

First he's beaten by villagers who know him. Next he's attacked by hunters and accused of Slethery. Now this. It would only get worse. There was only one way to turn things around. He had to prove in some way that evil did not run in his blood. That it didn't infect all Koramites.

He'd told the glass master he had nothing to do with Sleth. And yet he himself was falling into the trap, hiding the bad elements.

"I'm going to turn in those hatchlings," said Talen.

"You do," said Nettle, "and you start the wheels of your own doom. They'll pry your name out of that little blind one. What then?"

"Look," said Talen. "We wouldn't hide a thief or murderer, why then should we hide Sleth, which are both? There's got to be some way to deliver them and preserve ourselves."

"There's only one way to do that," said Nettle.

"And that is?"

Nettle gave Talen a sober look. "Dead. You'll have to deliver them dead."

28.

ALLIANCES

Rubaloth stood on the portico, the sun-warmed marble under his naked feet, the warm breeze washing across his legs and bringing the sulfur scent of the hot mineral pools. Behind him in the chamber, the lord of the Fir-Noy, the one they called the Crab, lay on a couch, trying to gather his wits.

"Pour him another cup of the tea," Rubaloth said to Leaf, the dreadman who was his guide. Rubaloth had just performed a seeking and then a minor binding on this man, forming a link between the Crab and an escrum, a weave that would allow them to communicate over distances. Bindings disoriented a man, made him dizzy and stupid. But Rubaloth did not have the time to let this man sleep it off. It would take a few days for the binding to cure completely, but that didn't mean it wouldn't be useful before then.

He heard the clink of the teapot, the sound of a cup being filled with wizard's tea, then Leaf's footfalls over to the couch.

Rubaloth had been cold the whole time on the sea and rummaging through this man's mind made him feel filthy.

He ached to submerse himself in the hot water that lay at the end of the marble path.

"This is a bitter brew," said the Crab.

Rubaloth did not reply. He waited for the clink on the platter that would signal Leaf had returned the empty cup.

"So what is it you want us to do?"

"I want you to find out all you can about this Captain Argoth. Where his family is from, his business dealings, the types of foods he eats. I want to know if he has a regimen of exercise."

"Exercise, Great One?"

"I want to know what he puts in his body and what comes out. You'll dig in his privy. You'll search his pantry and root cellars." Anyone who used the lore needed to eat certain foods to keep the body from wasting. They needed to exercise in a certain way to prepare the body for the moment of quickening.

"Do you suspect him?"

"I suspect everyone, Clansman, including you."

"Argoth's sister married a Koramite," said the Crab. "There are a number of us in the Council who have never trusted him."

"You will provoke nothing," continued Rubaloth. "He must know nothing. His wife must suspect nothing. You will take action only upon my command. And that will come through this minor binding."

"What about questioning the Koramite?"

"Your tower is not secure. You'll move him immediately. Far from Whitecliff."

"Yes," said the Crab.

"Do not touch him." If the Koramite had anything to do with the rebellion here, if he had any secrets, Rubaloth would seek them out himself. He did not want to risk incompetent men killing or damaging the man.

"You do not want us to press him?"

"What did I just say?"

The Crab bowed. "Please forgive my stupidity, Bright One."

"Be faithful over these few things and you shall be made ruler over many. Fail me, and you will be cast aside like rancid meat."

He heard the Crab rise. His voice slurred slightly. "My heart is given to Mokad," he said.

His heart was given to Mokad only because he saw that as his path to glory. Rubaloth felt that clearly during the seeking. He also felt nothing to suggest the Crab was part of the cabal that had murdered Lumen, which meant such ambition could be used.

"Prepare yourself. Wait for my command to use the weaves I've given you."

"Yes, Bright One."

Rubaloth turned the screw one last time. "I expect great things from you. Remember, the Glory is searching to replace Lumen. Which means he is also looking to raise one or two as candidates. It is not"—he paused—"impossible for a man of your experience and talents."

The Crab's voice echoed strongly off the floor, which meant he was bowing deeply. "I will not disappoint you, Bright One."

Rubaloth dismissed him. Leaf walked the Crab out. When he returned, he said, "Do you trust him?"

"I trust his ambition." Rubaloth took a breath, satisfied with this part of his plan. "Where's Uram?"

"He's coming, Bright One."

Moments later the sound of studded sandals echoed down the hallway and stopped in the room. "My Lord?" said Uram in his pleasing voice.

"Argoth must come to the ship willingly. That is your mission. If he tries to escape, subdue him, but avoid killing him at all costs. When we're out to sea, I will be more comfortable pressing him. But not a moment before. Defer to him, treat him as you would a lord."

"May I respectfully suggest that we do not know the enemy's size or strength. Will it not be safer to take him directly to the ship, Bright One?"

"Safer, yes, but also less effective. This enemy is a serpent, Captain. The moment it feels threatened, it will attack or flee. And so we shall give it no cause for alarm. When he's cut off from all help and all prying eyes, I shall crack his mind like a nut. In that moment, surprise will be on our side. We will know his secrets. And if he is Sleth, then I will direct our allies here to quickly and quietly move on them all."

"Yes, Bright One."

"You may go, Uram. I will see you on the morrow."

Rubaloth turned to Leaf. "Now our part. We cannot let a pack of traitors think we are uneasy, can we?" He held out his arm for Leaf to take and turned to the pools. "Have you got the wine?"

"Yes, Bright One. I have arranged for a massage."

They walked out of the chamber and down the path arm in arm. At that moment a clamor arose ahead, punctuated by screams.

Rubaloth felt for Leaf's mind so that he might see. Had they underestimated the enemy?

Through Leaf's eyes, he saw a number of knee-high, red-faced beasts run across the path. A troop of green-and-white-clad servants ran after them with sticks and stones.

"G'alls!" he exclaimed. "Woodikin?"

Leaf drew the sword he kept at his side.

The beasts ran up the hill on his left and disappeared over the top with many screeches. The servants followed, throwing rocks and ringing bells.

Another servant carrying the wine walked along another path as if nothing were happening. Leaf called to her. "Hoy, what is this?"

The servant bowed deeply. "Monkeys, Zu."

"Monkeys?" said Rubaloth.

"Yes, Bright One, we must be ever vigilant to keep them from the baths."

Rubaloth shook his head in disgust. "What Lumen saw in this land I will never know." He released his hold on Leaf's sight. It was not something he wished to do often, for after long periods of that a man could lose himself, leave his body and not return. He and Leaf continued to the pools and their fingers of softly curling steam.

ARGOTH SAT UPON Courage, his tall black warhorse, sandwiched between five dreadmen who rode ahead and five who rode behind. A breeze blew crossways and carried the dust from the horses' hooves out over the half-mown fields of hay on his right.

The bright, brass armor of the dreadmen clinked and clattered and blazed in the sunlight. Beneath it they wore close-fitting scarlet tunics and black pants. But this armor was meant only to dazzle the eye. The metal of their cuirasses was exceedingly thin. Brass was not a metal to stop swords.

If they had wanted protection, they would have worn steel segments or plate on top, a chain mail tunic underneath, and padding beneath that. They would have worn helms with faceplates. All the better to deflect arrows. But they weren't worried about being attacked by cohorts of men. They were worried about him escaping, about facing a smaller group of attackers. That much was transparent.

And why would the Skir Master expect a loyal servant to run? He wouldn't. He would only expect it from someone he didn't trust. These dreadmen would be on their guard, watching his every move.

His plan was simple. He would bind the Skir Master and force him to reveal who knew about his secrets. His plan hinged on getting a great quantity of Fire, which he would use to quicken a weave that had been in his family for generations, a weave that would enthrall the Skir Master.

Argoth had sent a messenger to Matiga with two requests. He knew the Skir Master would have the man followed, but what other choice did he have? Besides, the messages would be coded. The messenger would simply relay the news of the Divine's arrival, then he would ask if she was going to need any help this year preparing her garden for the frost. That was her signal to bear the Grove away.

Next the messenger would say that Captain Argoth wanted a sour apple pie for dinner this evening. Matiga was known for her pies and tarts. In fact, there were some in Whitecliff who sent servants to fetch her pies once a week. What was not known was that this specific request from any of the Grove meant one thing—they needed to tap into the Grove's reserve of Fire, something that could only be done in extreme need. Matiga held the Grove's weaves, two of which were stores of Fire.

When he got the Fire, he would replenish his guttering flame. Then he would quicken the weave that would enthrall the Skir Master.

It would not be an easy task, but it was less risky than declaring open war. Keep small, keep quiet, avoid attention—that was the way the Order had survived all these years. But this time he did not want to run. And if he failed? He would fire the ship, sending all who sailed upon it to the depths.

He didn't relish that idea. But at that point he wouldn't

have the luxury of finding out who had the knowledge of the Order and who didn't.

This raised another issue. If he succeeded and returned, he would have to deal with Shim.

Tucked under his sash was a message forced into his hand back in Whitecliff by an unmarked messenger:

> *To Argoth, an Old Woman's Delight:*
> *I was right; we are now in our extremity. Remember the offer of a practical friend. Do not turn your back on those who love you. We await your reply.*

There was no seal or signature, but Argoth knew the sender. "Old Woman's Delight" made that clear. Shim gave him that name one day long ago when he and Shim found themselves past the Gap in the wilds with the sun going down. They were forced to sleep in hammocks far above the ground to avoid the wurms that hunted below. It took them almost a week to escape that death trap, and during that time he told Shim a story from his distant past.

Of course, he didn't reveal to Shim his true age, but eighty years ago, as a boy of sixteen, prime, and available for marriage, his father began to receive and make marriage offers. One such came from a very ugly, but very rich woman. She tried to seduce Argoth and, failing that, tried to pressure his father into marrying him off to her.

Shim found the story hilarious and made Argoth tell it a number of times. However, he'd never passed the story on. Only Shim had ever called him "Old Woman's Delight."

The practical offer obviously alluded to Shim's offering to ally himself with Sleth. Shim knew what Argoth was, but that wasn't as fearful as the "we" in the final sentence.

Shim had told others; he'd won them to his idea. Who they could be, Argoth did not know. Would it be men of Shim's clan? Or had he talked to other warlords?

The Grove would have three choices when he returned: flee, kill Shim and all those he'd told, or bring them into the Order.

And if he brought them into the Order, as Shim desired, they would want to fight as multiplied men. Knowing Shim, this would not be a handful of men. Shim was thorough. He would have gathered up enough to defend the land.

There was no way to hide that many. Introducing such a force would reveal the Order.

He imagined this people throwing off the blinders put upon them by Divines. Some would live to the age of trees like the ancients had. A man and a woman would have the power to heal their children, but also every living thing in their domain: oxen, goats, chickens, a generous fruit tree succumbing to a blight. It was said that the ancients at times walked with the Creators. If then, why not now?

Of course, they'd tried. Many years ago, Lord Shaydis, the head of the Order, disappeared with many eager members into the deep interior of this land, intent on laying the foundations for a city patterned after the ancients.

A great secret trail led to that city. Groves manned the waypoints, each knowing only the preceding and subsequent waypoint and the places and signals for meets. This ensured the traveling members found help along the way, but it also reduced the risk that any in the standing Groves might be caught and questioned. Hogan's was the last waypoint, but none in this Grove knew the final destination.

Their instructions were to lead whoever was traveling to the city to a certain lake three days' travel through the mountains. Lord Shaydis would send someone to gather them in.

But none from Hope had come for a number of years. Many had struck out to find the city. Most did not return. Those that did spoke of terrible creatures that burrowed vast warrens, small men that lived in the tops of the great trees, a salt sea, mountains that smoked, and other wondrous and perilous things.

Fifteen years ago was the last time any group had been gathered in. The flow along the great trail diminished to a trickle and then dried up altogether.

But the hope of such a city had not died. And Shim had unwittingly pointed out the opportunity to build it.

Argoth saw a land brimming with Divines. It was a bright and overpowering vision.

He had never thought it possible. Not here.

He took a deep breath.

It was possible that Shim was loyal to Mokad, that he was an agent of the Seeker, trying to ferret out information about the Order. But Argoth didn't think so. He trusted Shim with his life. Always had. Still he would have to test him.

As he rode, he thought of how to write the message and get it to Shim anonymously. When he got home he found a new parchment and wrote:

Show me the depth of your love.

He sealed it with a blob of wax, but not with any mark that would give an indication of who had sent it. Then he secretly gave it to a servant and told him to deliver it without being seen by even Lord Shim himself.

There was nothing more to be done. Hogan would be

furious. But he would come around. The vision was breathtaking. The opportunity was right. He could feel it quaking in his bones.

Argoth basked in that bright hope for a moment longer and then brought himself back to the present. Right now he needed to focus on the Skir Master and these dreadmen; otherwise that fine dream would never come to pass.

29.

FRIGHT

Murder, Talen thought. That's what Nettle was proposing.

Except killing those outside the law wasn't murder. It wasn't murder to kill Bone Faces wherever you happened to find them. It wasn't murder to kill someone the law demanded exterminated. The lords would prefer Sleth be brought in alive so they could question them, but dead was perfectly acceptable.

Talen had never killed a person. He'd fought in last year's battles with the Bone Faces as a skirmisher. But who knew if your arrows and stones actually finished a man or merely wounded him? With these two it would be very clear. He'd need to smoke himself with godsweed to prevent the souls of the slain Sleth from trying to attack him.

Just thinking about killing these two turned his gut. It was different from going to battle. It would be a nasty business. If they were simply what they appeared to be—two unlucky children—then an arrow in the back would be enough to bring them down. Another to the heart or through a lung would end it.

A dark, nasty business. But he couldn't understand why he should hesitate, why he didn't feel right about it. None of the old tales of Sleth hunters ever mentioned this. Those men and women had never balked at cutting the abominations down. But who was he kidding? He wasn't a mighty Sleth hunter.

But what if they *were* innocent? What if they were just like him? Caught up in the bad decisions of their parents.

"It's possible they learned nothing from their mother," Talen said.

"Anything's possible," said Nettle. "But that's unlikely. Either way, masters of the dark or snotty-nosed children, I don't think anybody is going to care. After all—" Nettle stopped himself.

Talen knew what he had been about to say. "After all, what?" said Talen.

"Nothing," said Nettle.

"My hairy arse," said Talen. "You were going to say it didn't matter. After all, they're just two Koramites."

"I knew you'd take it that way. But it's not how I feel. It's how the lords feel, and I can't help that. All I'm saying is that nobody is likely to accuse you of a crime."

No, of course not. But that didn't seem to matter. "It would even be less of an issue if you did it, Mokaddian captain's son," said Talen. "If any murdering is to be done, then you'll have a hand in it, you can be sure of that."

The sins of Purity had done nothing but put his family in danger. And the danger and risk would only increase. They'd have to kill the girl and boy. There was no way around it. A sick feeling welled up in Talen, a black numbing.

Talen flicked Iron Boy's reins. They'd wasted precious time going to the glass master's. The only consolation was that nobody would expect them along this route. Of course, nobody should have expected them to pass through Gallow's Gate either, but riders had come after them all the same. Nettle must have felt the black numbing as well, for he said nothing. They traveled for many rods in silence, Talen pondering this bloody medicine and hoping no Fir-Noy had thought to search this road.

If he killed the boy and girl, his father would be furious. But how did he know that Da wasn't threatened? Da hadn't told him a thing. Why? Why couldn't he tell them his big secret on the way to Whitecliff? Why wait?

Because he wasn't going to tell them anything. He just wanted them out of the way.

Da was involved with something. And that something included a Sleth woman and her monster.

As they traveled Talen began to feel tired. The itch in his legs was lessening. They turned down a narrow trail that led into a piney wood, and an overwhelming weariness fell upon him.

The baker had probably used something like thresher's seed. It was the way with such herbs that they left you weaker than when you first took them. And that herb was probably the root of his black thoughts.

No, it was not the herb. It was his heart. It was sometimes said the heart perceived things the head could not. It was said that sometimes the ancestors could speak to a man's heart even when his head was full of stone.

"We're not going to kill them," said Talen. "Not immediately." The road here was thick with pine needles. It muffled Iron Boy's hooves. It seemed to muffle Talen's words. He knew it was not a smart decision, but the moment he said it the dark cloud smothering his heart seemed to lift a bit.

"They're going to tumble mountains of troubles upon your whole family," said Nettle.

"You're probably right," said Talen. "But we can't just kill them. What if that brings the monster? What if this nest does something to Da in retaliation?"

"Is it right to appease evil?"

The answer to that was obvious. As were the risks.

Talen looked at Nettle. It was unfair to ask him to assume these risks. There was trouble down this road and there was no reason he had to travel it. "You're a good friend, cousin. Maybe you should go home and tell your father what's going on."

"Now?"

"Yeah," said Talen. "He might be able to help."

"You just want me to get up and go?"

"I think so."

Nettle gave Talen a frustrated look. "Even you," he said.

"What?" asked Talen.

Nettle set his jaw. "I'll leave and you'll get turned into some wicked minion, and then, no doubt, I'll be the one that will have to kill you. No thanks. I'm coming."

"You'll drag your whole family into this. Even if Da's right and the children are not Sleth, there's a huge chance anybody involved is going to find themselves hanging in Gallow's Grove."

"I'm not running home to Daddy," said Nettle.

Talen heaved a sight of relief. "I was hoping you'd say that," said Talen. "I guess this means when monster comes around, you'll be the man to take it."

"I said I wasn't running home. Not that I was an idiot."

"Oh, you're an idiot," Talen said. "I think that's already been established."

"Right," said Nettle. "And if I'm an idiot, that puts you somewhere on the level of a cabbage."

Talen smiled. With all that had happened and all that was at risk, the clear and easy choice was for Nettle to take his leave. A wave of gratitude washed through Talen. There probably wasn't a finer friend in all the New Lands than the one sitting next to him on the wagon. He reached over and clapped Nettle on the shoulder.

"What?" asked Nettle.

"Nothing," said Talen.

Up ahead there was a break in the tall pines to either side of the road, and the sun cast long shadows across that part of the trail. Talen saw one lone firefly shine and wink out as it ascended to a tree. In a few hours the woods would pulse and sparkle with thousands of them.

Iron Boy's ears suddenly pricked forward.

Talen looked up the road, but didn't see anything.

The mule held its head up, alert, and slowed.

"What is it, boy?"

Talen scanned the woods and caught movement out of the side of his eye. He turned.

Iron Boy had stopped now. He stamped one foot.

"Where are they?" asked Nettle.

"It's not a they," said Talen. "But an it."

"Where?"

Talen pointed at a tree in front of them. Something was standing in the boughs about halfway up. It was not a mountain cat. Not nearly that large. Nor was it one of those troublesome monkeys that were expert in stealing everything from knives to fruit. It was about the size of a small dog, hunched, and long-limbed.

He looked closer. It was a light gray, the color of shadow and bark, and its limbs seemed awkward and long. Or maybe it was just the light. "What is it?"

Nettle followed Talen's gaze and stared. "Well, it's kind of hard to say. I can't be sure, but it looks like a tree to me."

"Goh, *in* the tree. About fifteen feet up that pine. There's something looking at us."

Nettle looked at Talen, he looked back at the tree, squinted, and looked back at Talen.

"Nothing's there."

"It's right in front of your face."

"Hallucinations." Nettle said. "Maybe those stupid ginger abominations did have come-backs."

Talen wasn't seeing things. It was right there.

"I never have this problem with bread pudding," said Nettle.

Whatever it was moved out of the shadows of the trees and into the waning light.

Talen blinked. It was still there.

Iron Boy chuffed.

"See that?" Talen asked. "Iron Boy didn't have any ginger."

He had to admit the coloring of the thing made it difficult to see. It put him in mind of insects that camouflaged themselves to look exactly like bark or leaves.

"There's nothing in the tree," said Nettle. "Nothing on the trail. Let's just get home."

Talen flicked the reins and started Iron Boy into a trot. The mule protested and tried to turn away, but Talen gave the reins a good tug and shake and put Iron Boy in motion.

When they passed by the pine, the creature began to move again.

Iron Boy whinnied and picked up his gait.

The creature swung down the limbs of the tree to the needle-strewn road. Then it began scampering after the wagon in an odd, hunched gait, quickly closing the distance.

"You're right," said Talen, "I'm hallucinating."

Because if he wasn't, that meant they'd attracted the attention of a small nightmare. What else could it be? As the thing drew nearer, Talen could more easily discern the eyes, hands, and feet. But they were misshapen. The nose was flat and crooked. The fingers too long.

There were creatures not wholly of this world. There were the mighty skir that the Divines enthralled and the souls of the dead. But there were also other things, some of which could, under certain circumstances, be seen with the naked eye. This thing matched the descriptions of one of those. Talen had never seen one before, but he'd heard about them. They fed upon the Fire of the weak and dying. Like the creatures that ate carrion of the flesh, they were attracted by death and disease. They shadowed the edges of armies and hid in cellars and the thatch roofs of villages smitten by pestilence. They did not flock in great numbers like crows and ravens. At least, he'd never heard tell of anyone seeing more than a handful together at once. But did numbers matter? When they got a hold of you, they burrowed in like ticks to gorge upon your Fire. And like ticks they were hard to dislodge and sometimes left bits of themselves behind.

Godsweed was supposed to keep them at bay, which is one of the reasons why soldiers smoked themselves with it before battle. Drinking it in a tea was also supposed to help, but such a tea gave men horrible cramps. Talen reached up and felt the godsweed braid on his arm. Even wearing it was supposed to have an effect.

Iron Boy trotted down the road, nervously turning his head to the left then right so he could get a better view of what was behind him. The odd-limbed thing was only a few paces behind them.

"I believe," Talen said, "that we've just attracted ourselves a fright."

At that moment the creature closed the final distance. It grabbed the wagon bed with one long-fingered hand and disappeared underneath.

30.

SECRETS

W ill you shut up?" said Nettle. "You're giving me the willies."

Iron Boy kicked, then jerked into a canter. It would not do to lose control of the wagon. He braced himself, but Talen felt like he did after an exceedingly hard day's worth of work. Then a wave of weariness fell upon him, and he could not keep his eyes open. He sagged into Nettle.

Nettle elbowed him back to his senses. "What are you doing?"

"The come-backs have finally worked their way through," said Talen. "Take the reins. I've got to lie down."

"What about your fright?" asked Nettle.

Talen looked down at the boards beneath his feet. Frights did not have power to steal from a healthy man. He and Nettle had nothing to fear. And panicking might only lead to them crashing the wagon. Besides, they had gods-weed with them.

"It's gone," said Talen. "A vapor of my mind."

"I've never heard of come-backs like this," Nettle said. He cursed. "I'm getting you home."

Talen wasn't going to argue, "Sure," he said. Then he handed the reins to Nettle and half climbed, half fell into the wagon bed.

He rode that way, flat on his back, looking up at the tops of the pines and the darkening sky beyond. Nettle took the reins and drove. He drove too fast. Once, Talen almost bumped completely out of the wagon bed. But he couldn't bring himself to object. Nettle kept turning around to look at him. At one point he reached down to feel Talen's forehead for fever, then turned back and spurred Iron Boy even faster.

Talen said nothing. The moon and the stars shone through the breaks in the tops of the trees. After a time he realized something cold lay on his ankle. Talen looked down. There, squatting in the back corner of the wagon bed was the fright. It was a hideous thing, all twisted and gray like a piece of knotty driftwood. One of its long fingers touched Talen on the bare skin of his ankle.

He kicked, and the thing released him, but it stretched out its finger once again.

"Nettle," he said. Or at least he thought he'd spoken. "Nettle!"

But Nettle did not turn.

Then Talen remembered the godsweed charm about his arm. He could brandish it and chase the thing off. He yanked on the charm, but it would not tear free, and the knot was suddenly too complicated for his fingers.

He was so very tired. The touch of the fright was so very cold. It wasn't supposed to touch him, not with the godsweed. So maybe this wasn't a fright. Or maybe it was and godsweed didn't have the virtue everyone claimed it did. Besides, what if it did take some of his Fire? At least it didn't have the power to eat his soul.

The creature reached out with another finger.

Talen kicked again. But he could not kick a third time—he was exhausted and in a cold sweat. His thirst was beyond anything he'd ever experienced. There was not enough spittle to wet his tongue, much less swallow.

Then Talen recognized the trees and the run of the slope to his left. He twisted around and saw their barn ahead.

Nettle did not slow quickly enough and almost crashed into the well. When he finally got Iron Boy to stop, he turned around and looked down at Talen. "Goh, you look rotted through. This isn't come-backs. This is some plague. Can you stand?"

"I can get up," said Talen.

But he couldn't. He could hardly move. His lower left leg was ice. The fright had elongated its fingers, split and multiplied them, and wrapped them around his calf. It looked as if the spidering root of a young tree had attached itself to him.

Nettle called out for help. Then he jumped into the wagon bed and helped Talen sit up. The fright moved slightly, but it did not disengage.

"The fright," Talen said.

"Yes," said Nettle, then he looped his arms underneath Talen's and around his chest. Nettle dragged Talen to the back of the wagon. He dropped the back gate of the bed. In one fluid movement Nettle jumped out, then pulled Talen over his shoulder like a sack of meal.

Talen's head hung low. He could see his leg. He could see that the fright still clung to him with one of its odd hands. Talen kicked, then Nettle pushed the door open and Talen found himself in the main room. River sat at the table, the candlelight shining off the beads in her hair. She was braiding clippings of Da's hair into an intricate decoration.

Talen looked for the hatchlings and saw the door to the cellar lay flat, shut up tight.

When River looked up, Talen saw her face go from annoyance to concern. "What's happened?" she asked.

"It's an overdose of come-backs," said Nettle. "Or worse. Earlier, he's a picture of liveliness—blinding fast, wrestling Fabbis to the ground, leaping to the tops of the trees. Now look at him. Nothing more than a smelly dishrag. And he's seeing frights."

"I need something to drink," said Talen.

"He's drunk a barrel today. I've never had to stop so many times waiting for a body to relieve himself."

River cleared the table. "Put him here."

"Did the Fir-Noy come here?" asked Talen.

Nettle dumped him on the table.

"I haven't seen any Fir-Noy," said River. She began pulling up the sleeve of Talen's tunic. "Where did Da tie the charm?"

"How did you know he gave me a charm?" asked Talen.

"Where did he tie it?"

"Here," said Talen and lifted the other sleeve. He looked down at his leg. The fright was there, squatting all knobby and hideous, staring at him with one of its raisin eyes.

River fingered the braid and cursed. Her face turned grave. "And *he* talks about risks." She removed the charm and cast it to the floor.

"Who?" asked Talen.

"Nobody," said River. She slid her hand into the collar of his tunic. She had no sooner put her hand to his chest than she gasped and withdrew it.

"He's got the plague," Nettle said. "Doesn't he?"

"Do you have any of the baker's goods left?"

"Three cookies," said Nettle. Then he went back outside.

"Has he poisoned me?" asked Talen.

"No," said River. "And it's not Nettle's plague either." She looked at him, and Talen could tell something had happened. She was deciding if she should share some secret with him.

"Goh," he said. "It *was* the kiss. That girl!" He'd been wrong; they would have to kill her after all. Talen's weariness pressed down upon him even more. "And her familiar has attached itself to my leg."

River said nothing. Of course, River wouldn't kill her. Not if the girl had magicked her. His thoughts strayed for a time. He looked at River and for a moment forgot what she was doing. Then it came back to him in a rush.

"We'll have to be quick," he whispered.

"What?" said River.

"Quick," said Talen more loudly. "Quick. Kill them, the boy and girl, quick."

At that moment he saw movement out of the corner of his eye. He turned and saw the girl standing in the doorway to the back room.

River followed his gaze. "He's out of his mind," she said to her.

"I'll divert her," said Talen. "You clobber her with the pot."

"Be still," River commanded.

Talen looked at the girl for a while, waiting for her to spring. "Playing us like a cat? Is that your pleasure?"

"Sugar," River said. "I need you to fill the mule's watering trough. We're going to need to lay Talen in it. Have Nettle help you drag it in here."

Sugar looked at the two of them, a storm brooding on her face. Talen thought she was going to say something, but she must have decided against it, for she strode across the room and out the door.

"Now's the time," said Talen.

"Will you shut up," said River. "You have no idea what you're talking about. This isn't her doing. It's Da's."

That made no sense, no sense at all. But River wouldn't listen to him. She brought a candle near to get a good look at his eyes and mouth. Then she began peppering him with questions: when did the thirst start, how many cookies did he eat, what did Da do when he tied the charm on his arm, had he been hearing a ringing in his ears? Talen struggled to answer them all. Twice she had to repeat a question.

Finally, he held up his hand. "My leg. It's sucking the life out of my leg."

Then he saw something at the window.

The shutters had not been closed tightly and pale twigs seemed to shoot in over the sill. From his position on the floor, he couldn't make any sense of them, but there they were. Tree roots on the window. Then a twisted head appeared, followed by a long body. Another fright, smaller than the one about his leg. It pulled itself up onto the sill.

"There's another," he said.

"Another what?"

"Nasty little thing," he said and motioned at the window. "It's got cold fingers."

River looked up and followed his gaze. "There's nothing there."

"There is," said Talen. "And there's another wrapped about my leg. Right there by your hand."

The creature about his leg didn't move. It just sat and watched them.

River put her hand on Talen's leg, partially covering the thin fingers of the fright. Her hands felt warm.

"How many are here, Talen?"

"Two," he said.

She cursed, then she calmly picked up Talen's godsweed charm, took it to the hearth, and thrust it into the fire. "And thus a portion of my life goes up in smoke," she said. Which made no sense to Talen. She picked up a bowl and put the smoking weed in it. Then she took a pair of tongs and removed three hot coals from the fire and put them in the bowl as well. The weeds smoked.

"Where are they now?" she asked.

"The little one's at the window. The bigger one is right here." Talen moved his leg.

River approached, blowing on the smoking braid. She blew it on his face. Then she blew it on his leg.

"Don't worry," said Talen. "Nettle says it's just the come-backs."

"Be gone!" said River. She blew again on the smoke. Godsweed was not a sweet herb and Talen did not like the taste of its smoke.

The knobby creature on his leg eyed her.

"It's not afraid of you," said Talen.

River blew again and waved the smoking bowl around him.

The creature turned as if trying to avoid the smoke. But River blew again and the thing released Talen's leg and jumped to the floor.

"There it goes," Talen said. The thing only shuffled a few steps then stopped. But the little one at the window was gone.

River followed Talen's gaze. She waved the smoking bowl around in the air. Blew more smoke. Then the fright that had been attached to his leg scuttled up the wall and out the window. However, River kept moving about as if it were still there.

"You got it," said Talen. "It's off to torment the chickens." Then Talen wondered why it would do that. Was this the reason Da's last batch of hens died off? It seemed reasonable. "They're the ones killing the chickens," he said.

"You're babbling," said River. She went to the window and waved the smoking bowl there. Then she closed up the shutters and brought the bowl back and placed it in the middle of the room on the floor. There was no fire to it anymore. Just coals and smoke.

Nettle and Sugar opened the door and bumped their way through with the empty trough. They set it close to the hearth.

"Stand over that bowl," she said. "Smoke yourselves."

"Goh," Nettle said. "Are you kidding? A real fright?"

"Just do it."

When Nettle and Sugar finished, River said, "Now get the water going."

"With a fright out there?"

"Move!" said River.

Nettle growled, and Talen couldn't tell if it was in frustration at River or to muster up his courage to face the fright. Then he marched out the door, the girl right behind him. River walked over to the wall where their five white ceramic plates hung. She took down one plate, brought it to the table, and broke a cookie upon it. Then she lit four more candles and turned them on their sides about the plate to give the cookie more illumination.

She dug at it with the point of a knife, examining the crumbs. "I see nothing."

She held one up and sniffed it. She took a bite. After savoring it for a while she shook her head and swallowed it. Then she ate the other two cookies and drank a cup of water. "Sometimes certain herbs magnify the effects of the charm. But I can detect nothing of that sort in these," she said. "If there's anything in them, we will shortly know. In the meantime you need to soak. Take off your clothes."

All this time Nettle had been hauling in water, first to fill the large pot Sugar had put over the fire and then to fill the trough. The thought of moving daunted him, and Talen found he couldn't do more than look at that trough.

"Never mind," she said. "I'll do it. Sugar, is that hot yet? We don't want to freeze him."

Talen wanted to protest, but it was no use. River had him out of his tunic and pants in moments. Mercifully, she left his linens on.

The trough was slick with slime and the freezing water just about sent him into shock. But he soon didn't care. The cold meant nothing. He didn't even care when the girl dumped the boiling water in too quickly and scalded his legs. The hatchlings were in control now. It was too late for all of them.

His eyes were heavy. They itched with sleep and he tried to close them, but River kept slapping his face.

"Let me alone," said Talen. Then he drifted off into no thought at all.

"Listen to me," said River. "You will die tonight if we do not change the course of what's happening." She felt his chest again as she had done at first. "This isn't come-backs. Some herbs can heighten the effect. But there was nothing in those cookies. If there had been, I would be feeling the effects by now."

"Effects," repeated Talen. Something about that struck him funny and he giggled.

River stood and addressed Nettle. "You keep him awake. Use whatever it requires—don't let him sleep." She moved to the table and began unraveling her weaving of Da's hair.

Nettle first tried to make Talen talk. When that failed, he began with slapping, pinching, and poking.

But Talen didn't care. He just wanted to close his eyes.

That's when Nettle retrieved a stick from the fire and burned Talen's arm with it.

Talen started and yelled.

"Aha," said Nettle. "It's fire that will keep him awake."

But soon Talen's eyes began to droop, and Nettle had to burn him twice more before River returned.

"Put your tortures away," said Talen. He looked at Sugar. "She can perform her depradations after I've rested."

But River said nothing. She tied what she'd been weaving to his arm where Da had tied his charm.

"I'll give it a few minutes," she said. It sounded as if she were trying to reassure herself.

"There's no virtue in hair," said Talen.

"There isn't?" asked River.

"I've never heard of it," said Talen.

"What about Atra's hair?"

"She's given me up," said Talen.

River made him relate the whole story of what happened at the glass master's until Talen realized all she was doing was trying to keep him talking so he'd stay awake.

"I'm going to sleep," he said. "Burn me if you like. I don't care."

River put her hand to his chest again. She looked desperate. She took him by the head then, her two hands clasping the back of his skull. "You need to help me," she said.

"I can't get up," he said. "You'll have to kill her yourself."

"Talen," said River. "I can't stop the flow. You're bleeding Fire. Your days are rolling off you like smoke. You must help me."

"Fire?" asked Talen.

River glanced at Nettle and Sugar. Then she faced Talen. She'd decided something. He could see that by the set of her brow.

"You've been multiplied," she said. "Da has begun your awakening. But it's all gone wrong. You need to close it off."

That made no sense to Talen. Only dreadmen and Divines could do that. Then through the fog of his mind he began to feel at the edges of a horrible idea.

"You're going to feel an intrusion," said River. "Fight it. Push with all your might. You're leaking through a thousand holes. You've got to close every last one of them."

Suddenly he felt something enter him. It was crushing, and he gasped.

Push! a voice in his mind said.

He'd been caught once in a tumble of earth, and this was what it had felt like. A panic began to rise in him.

He could feel her. He could feel River in him. It terrified him. The weight of her presence began to bear down.

Talen tried to flee, but she was everywhere. A crush of sand.

Fight me, you fool.

He struggled against her.

Fight!

"I don't know how!" he shouted.

All about him the sand of her presence pushed at him, coming in through his ears, his nose, his mouth. She was the very air he breathed.

Talen struggled in panic, and then in one part he felt her recede.

Was it his imagination?

He tried again, but whatever he'd done fell to pieces and River's presence swallowed him. He was trapped, pinned, a man under a ton of grain. He couldn't breathe.

His panic rose to a pitch, then he did something—he couldn't explain it—he pushed, and he found he could breathe again. He pushed again. And she moved farther.

That's it! Fight!

River rushed at him with renewed force, but he held his space and withstood her. He did not know how long he struggled, managing only to keep her far enough away to breathe. Then he closed a small rent in his fabric.

Another, she said.

But there were so many.

Close another!

Talen was so tired, but he fought. He fought and lost track of time. It was only him and the suffocating sand of his sister.

After what seemed like hours he found himself facing

the last hole, one rent in his fabric that separated him from the rest of creation. It was like trying to stop the sea with his hand. Talen fought to no effect.

"I can't do it," he said and did not know if he'd spoken this aloud or just in his mind.

You will, said River. *Mother didn't save you only to have Father kill you with his reckless ways.*

It's just one hole.

Close it!

Talen mustered the last of his strength and tried to close the rent. And to his surprise he felt it narrow and then shut up as tight as boiled leather.

He slumped in the tub. Tired. He was deathly tired. And thirsty. But the ragged edge of his weariness was dulled, if only a little.

Talen opened his eyes. Most of the water had sloshed out of the trough to the floor. River's tunic and pants were soaked all down the front. She slumped alongside the trough, and heaved a sob of relief.

Behind her stood Nettle and the girl, their faces slack with confusion or shock. Which it was he could not tell. Talen started to say something to Nettle, but his exhaustion overwhelmed him, and he closed his eyes.

TALEN WOKE AND found himself in River's bed. Someone had slipped small heated sacks of grain under the covers next to him to keep him warm.

He could see through the shutters that it was still dark outside. On the floor beside the bed stood a jug of water. Talen slowly sat up. His head swam, and he clutched it until the dizziness passed. He grabbed the jug and took a long drink.

When he finished, River stood in the doorway.

"I don't know that I want to hear it," said Talen. They were caught, all of them. In a black web of Slethery.

"It's too late for that," said River. She walked in and sat beside him on the bed. "How do you feel?"

"Awful," said Talen. "But not as bad as before."

Nettle came to the doorway. His ear had been stitched and cleaned. "So he's not dead yet? There goes my wager."

"Ha," said Talen.

Nettle grinned.

"Are you well enough to travel?" asked River.

"I don't know," he said.

"Well, it doesn't matter. We have to leave tonight."

"What do you mean?"

"Ke has come and gone since you slept. They're holding Da in Whitecliff."

"The Council?"

"He's been accused of being Sleth."

Talen recoiled.

"Talen," said River. "I need you to listen to me. I need you to be calm and listen."

He looked at her.

She took a breath then said, "You know how Mother died."

Talen nodded. She'd died in the pox plague year. Died of stress and worry.

"You think you know: laid into the ground, she was, without a blemish upon her. Perfect and whole, broken with grief for her little boy who was covered with the ugly rash, all blisters and pus. This is what you think, but grief did not break her, brother. Grief could not have broken that woman, not in a million years."

She paused.

"It was love that broke her. Your little body was consumed with sores. Da called every healer he knew; we tried every herb known to have any effect. We danced and sacrificed to the ancestors. But the disease only grew.

And so Mother and Da did what any loving parents would do. They gave their Days to make you whole."

Surely, she was talking about a Divine's gift. "They went to the temple?" he said.

River shook her head, and dread came over him.

"You were broken in body and soul. Da could not see how to heal you and steeled himself to losing you. He had given up. After all, many families lose one here or there. But Mother would not give up. She saw possibilities invisible to him.

"You struggled a week, then two. Everyone marveled at your spirit. But then Da discovered one night it was more than your tenacity keeping you alive. He caught Mother pouring her life into you. Her Fire flowed through you and held you together. And when you finally vanquished the disease, she was spent. A whole lifetime spent in two weeks."

River smiled, but her eyes glistened in the dim candlelight.

"She died in the morning the day after your fever broke, holding your hand."

Talen could not speak.

"Do you understand what I'm saying?"

He nodded. But it just couldn't be.

"Your veins, brother, run literally with our mother's Fire."

"But—"

He glanced at Nettle. His expression was unreadable. The girl stood behind him in the doorway. He hadn't noticed her come.

"Shush," said River. "Mother said that parts of you, parts of your weave were . . . twisted. Most of that she was able to heal. But as she delved into the fiber of your being she found other parts that defied her knowledge.

Parts that she said were complex, beautiful, unlike anything she'd ever encountered. There are things about you she could not change. Things she dared not change." River paused. "At the end, she was half mad with the effort and kept telling us you needed a flaw. She thought you were perfect. We've all been waiting to see what you would become, to see what gifts the wisterwives had bestowed."

Talen felt lost. It was all too much. Wisterwives, Sleth, weaves. "Nobody's seen a wisterwife," said Talen.

"They are elusive, but Mother and Da found the charm."

"The charm? You mean that odd necklace she used to make me wear?"

"The very same. Legs has it now. Mother gave it to Purity when he was born, thinking it might still have some virtue."

"It was yours?" the girl asked in confusion.

River nodded. "Mother woke early one morning to find the shutters to her room open and the mosquitoes buzzing about her face. The charm was lying on the chair inside the Creator's wreath. Something had taken the wreath from above the door to the house and brought it inside. Mother looked out the window. A troop of ferrets stood about the yard gazing at her, still as stone. They stood for some time, considering her in silence like wise little men. And then, just before the light broke above the hills, the little creatures turned and disappeared into the forest. Mother conceived Talen with that charm about her neck, and he wore it for the first few years of his life. But when Legs was born, she thought it had a better purpose."

Talen had heard about the ferrets, but not the charm.

"But my da said it was given to us," said the girl.

"It was, but not by a wisterwife," said River. "He probably didn't want to repeat the story. Such encounters are special, and should be treated so."

"Did she see the wisterwife?"

"No, but how else do you explain the curious charm, the ferrets, and the wreath?"

Talen wondered. Wisterwives were said to bestow great blessings upon humans. Some said they served the Divines. Others said they served none but themselves.

It puzzled him that his family hadn't said anything about this. Of course, a wisterwife's charm was a rare and precious thing because it gave fertility and health. He supposed if people knew the source of that necklace, they would have stolen it. Perhaps that was the reason for the silence.

"Regret has servants as well," said Talen. "How do you know it was a blessing? How do you know it even has anything to do with me?"

"I don't," said River. "I am trusting Mother's judgment."

"I might not manifest anything at all," said Talen. "Maybe those changes were already in the bloodline. Traits can sometimes skip generations."

"That's true," said River. "But your differences were exceptional." She shook her head. "And they needed exceptional care. Da was reckless. I have no idea how much of your life you've lost. Nor whether you've burned yourself to the core."

River's description of his "weave" bothered him. "You talk as if I'm some piece of wrought jewelry."

"We all are, Talen."

He didn't know what she meant by that. "So what was different about me?"

"I don't know. Mother died and took her secrets with her. But there's this: Fire can be eaten only very slowly and so it must be given only very slowly. To do otherwise is to risk the life of the person you're giving it to. How she transferred a lifetime of Fire in the space of only a few days is beyond us. It should have killed you. Your exhibition tonight should have killed you. You were pouring forth quantities of Fire that would have killed ten men had they tried to tap into it. The amounts of Fire you're able to handle is astonishing. On the other hand, Da's charm: that should have had only the slightest effect on you."

"You're talking about that godsweed charm, aren't you?"

"Yes," said River.

"That was a weave?"

"Yes."

Talen looked at Nettle and the girl. Both of them were standing aside with grim faces.

Too many thoughts coursed through Talen's mind. But one stood out from the rest. Mother and Da had been using lore for years. These hatchlings hadn't subverted them.

"You're saying we're soul-eaters," he said.

It couldn't be, but a number of things that had puzzled him suddenly made horrible sense. Harboring the hatchlings, for one. Da's dislike of the Divines, for another. His demonstrations of uncanny strength when there was nobody but a son to see them, his odd lack of sickness.

Talen thought of Ke. His brother was as strong as stone and just as unmovable. Yet, at other times he was lively as a cat. Talen remembered once a few years ago spying Ke upon a cliff in the distance. One moment he was standing on a ledge, then next he was moving, leaping and scrabbling up the rock like a mountain goat. Talen knew that cliff. He'd asked Ke how he'd done it, and Ke had said he had a rope. And that Da was pulling him up. It seemed plausible and Talen had dismissed what he'd seen. But now it made sense. Ke hadn't used a rope. He'd jumped, just as Talen had jumped and scrabbled up that elm earlier today.

Dozens of such events came rushing back to him. River

swimming out in impossible seas to help Blue. A deer Da brought home from the hunt with a broken neck and nary an arrow wound. The time Talen went out to chase after Ke, who had just disappeared down the trail, only to find the trail was empty for as far as he could see.

Talen thought about his earlier daydreams of hunting and catching Sleth. There was nothing like this in the old stories.

"Am I not myself then? I'm just bits and pieces of what Mother stole?"

River cleared her throat. "That is the difference between us and them. When you give Fire freely, it flows between two people as clean and easily as the wind. Freely given it is without taint. You haven't a speck of her soul, Talen. What she gave was all Fire—pure and brilliant and sweet. It is only when you forcibly take, as the Divines and soul-eaters do, that you contaminate. Taking tears the soul and brings madness to the thief. The Divines think to avoid the consequences with their filtering rods. But you cannot filter away the darkness such deeds sow into the heart."

"But the people freely sacrifice themselves."

"They offer themselves up. But that is not a free gift. You must know what you're giving. And to do that you have to be able to give it yourself. Why do you think they drug sacrifices with wizardsmeet or opium? No, they do not gift their Fire. What they do in reality, Talen, is promise to struggle less. And if they only take part of a man, they're still killing him, only it's by degrees."

"So you are not Sleth?"

"Do you know where that word comes from?"

Talen did not.

"It comes from Urz. In that country it is the name given to the dry killing wind that comes from the east. The wind that steals all moisture from the crops." River paused. "Brother, I do not steal life."

Talen searched his sister's eyes, those kind, lovely eyes, and he believed her. "But what are you then?"

"In the beginning, the Creators taught all how to use their powers. Some excelled in the lore, but instead of sharing their knowledge, they hoarded it, and in some instances killed to keep their advantage. Over the ages, those people have gained the upper hand. Look at the Divines: they kill any who try to use what was given freely in the beginning."

"There are others then?"

River nodded. "A few. We cannot do the mighty deeds that were done of old. But still we work what we may. We are banded together in an order whose purpose is to break the yoke of the Divines and let every man, woman, and child control their own Fire just as they control their own breath."

Her words astonished him. "How do you know you're not under some spell? How do you know your master, or whatever you call it, hasn't subverted your will?"

"Talen, there are those that practice wickedly. There are indeed nightmares in this world. But I'm not one of them. This is the truth of the matter."

"But why was all this kept from me?"

"Because telling you would endanger many lives."

"Despite what Da thinks, I do not have a butter jaw. I can hold my tongue."

"No, that isn't what I mean. It doesn't matter how much you want something, you need the skill to perform the act. You have a pure and loyal heart, but you don't have the skill to close your mind to a Seeker. And that can't be taught to a child. And so it is better to tell you nothing so that if something happens, and you are taken, you have nothing to share. The Order is not yet powerful enough to reveal itself. One day we will walk in the sun, but for now we must keep to shadows. We are bound by oath to do so."

Nettle, the girl, and the boy stood in the doorway. He was ashamed to look at them.

"Purity, Sugar's mother, and Uncle Argoth are both part of the Order as well."

Talen's world was spinning. "And the creature?" he asked. "That thing that fetched the Sleth woman?" Talen did not want to hear the answer to that question, but he steeled himself.

"Her name is *Purity*," River corrected. "And we have no idea what the creature is, much less who it belongs to."

Talen heaved a sigh. At least there was that. Then something struck him. "If I couldn't keep a secret yesterday, what has changed so I can keep it today?"

"Nothing," said River. "A Seeker would ransack your mind as easily as you would that cupboard. But, as I said, we are leaving. And in time you will learn the skill."

"Leaving? But what about Da?"

River looked down. "We are bound by an oath," she said. "Da." Her voice faltered. She closed her eyes and regained control of her emotions. When she opened them they were wet with tears. "Ke has been set to watch him. Once he's assessed the situation, he will meet us at the refuge where I'm taking you. We'll see what we can do at that time. But you need to prepare yourself because Da might not ever be coming back."

PRUNES WAS ROUSED by a sharp dig into his ribs.

"It seems we have ourselves a situation," said Gid.

Gid had already wakened him twice. Once to tell him that he'd had to tell a pack of Fir-Noy they already had the place under observation. Another time to watch the spectacle of two boys in a wagon pull into the yard. If this was another false alarm, Prunes was going to throw the man off the side of the mountain. And he didn't care about blowing their cover.

Prunes sat up. He was wrapped in his soldier's sleeping sash. "This had better be good."

"Oh, it's the tart's delight. They've been busy as bees down there all night. In and out, lamps burning. And something interesting just went into the barn but she'll be back out."

"Who?"

"The girl who told the bailiff she was from Koramtown. But what do you know? It appears there's also a boy with her that can't find his way unless she leads him about by the arm."

Prunes blinked the sleep out of his eyes. The moon was not large, but it was big enough to see shapes. The door to the house stood wide open, light spilling out into the yard. Someone exited the old sod house and walked toward the wagon in the yard, holding a lamp in front. That had to be the older sister. She made her way around the buildings and entered the house. That's when two figures stepped from behind the barn, walking as boldly as you please.

One was a girl. And the other, the smaller one, she led him by the hand. Even from here he could see the boy was blind.

Prunes was wide awake now.

"Busy as bees," said Gid. "And preparing, in haste it seems, to depart."

Their duty was to watch, but if they left now, it was likely they'd lead a hunt back to a deserted farmstead.

"I say we don't take any chances," said Gid. He held up his knife. "We take them one by one."

"This isn't an extermination. The lords will want someone to question."

"We'll do our best," said Gid. "But if things begin to sour, I'm not going to hesitate. Besides, all we need to do is kill one of them as an example and the rest will comply."

"And who will that be?"

"Who else? The blind one."

Gid was perhaps too eager, but he made sense. These youth might look like babes; however, a callow youth, given the right opportunity, could kill a man just as easily as a veteran of many battles. They might need to kill more than the little one. But that didn't matter. They only needed to keep one alive for the questioners.

Prunes nodded agreement.

"You and I, friend," said Gid, "are going to be rich."

"Not if we don't get you downwind," said Prunes. He motioned for Gid to lead, and the two began to pick their way quietly downhill.

31.

A BROKEN WING

Hunger stood at the edge of the wood. The scent of the burning boy lay in the hollows and ravines here as thick as fog. He looked over a bend in a river. Beyond it lay a farmstead. That's where the boy would be, waiting like a fat chicken in his coop.

He began to descend the bank to the water when a woman came out of the house carrying a lamp. He only saw her face for a moment in the light, but that and the gait of her walk, the angle of her shoulders, it all pulled a memory into his mind.

He knew her. He was sure of it. . . .

Moments passed.

She went to the well, drew water, then returned to the house. Hunger stood in the shadows as still as a heron stalking frogs.

Then the name came as softly as dew: River.

Yes, that was her name. And with that name a number of strong memories rose in his mind. He followed them, and every one of them ended with this: she'd held his hand once and he had been unable to speak. Not because she was his lover, although she was lovely. No, it was not his desire for her that had stolen his words; it was gratitude. He remembered: one spring evening in a bower, blind-folded, waiting for River who had worked so hard to make the match, waiting in the moonlight with the lilacs in bloom, their fine scent perfuming the night. Waiting to hear the feet on the path, the rustling of skirts, and then River taking his hand and putting Rosemary's warm, strong hand in it. River removing the blindfold so he could see Rosemary standing there before him, holding the flowered crown that meant she'd accepted his offer of marriage, looking at him with those laughing, moon-sparkled eyes.

Rosemary, the carpenter's daughter, the face of the woman he'd remembered after eating the man who had been humming as he washed himself. The man who was called Larther. And now Hunger had a name to hang that sorrow upon.

The water ran below him; three deer came to drink and left.

River was the one he needed. Her brother, the burning son, was nothing. He wasn't even part of the Order yet. But River, she was skilled at all sorts of weavings. She would know the workings of the collar. She would fix it. And he would bind the Mother. Bind her and destroy her.

River had been a beauty to him, then friend, and finally

sister. She would not run away; she would see through his rough form. He was sure of it.

He took a step toward the water and something moved downwind of the house.

He peered closer. Two men crept along in the grass, their helmets and knives shining in the moonlight.

Whatever their intent, they would flush River like untrained dogs bark and flush quail from the brush. Except once River ran, you did not catch her.

Those two would have to go. Silently, but they would have to go. Hunger waited to see if there were more of them, and when he saw they came alone, he descended the riverbank and quietly entered the dark waters.

PRUNES STOOD IN the shadow of a tree. Across the yard, Gid peered between the cracks of a shutter on that side of the house just to make sure there were only five of them. Prunes scratched his neck, and when he looked back at Gid something monstrous and dark rose, it seemed, from the very earth.

It was bigger than a man. Shaggy. Then Prunes recognized it from the stories of the creature at Whitecliff.

He shouted a warning.

Gid turned, but it was too late.

The dark shape engulfed him. Only the silhouette of Gid's lower half was visible in the moonlight.

Prunes watched in horror as Gid struggled, cried out, and then was silenced. The thing shook him out like a wife shakes a rug. It cast Gid's body aside in a heap.

The creature raised its head and chuffed like a horse. Then it turned and looked straight at Prunes across the yard.

He'd fought in a number of battles, nearly lost his life a dozen times. But nothing had ever put fear into him like the gaze of that rough beast.

By all that was holy . . .

His bladder released. He dropped his knife and backed up in horror.

SUGAR STOOD IN the barn, filling a barrel with barley and oats for the horse. They had a long ride ahead and the animal would need rich food. Legs stood by her side.

"Did you hear that?" he asked.

Sugar hadn't heard a thing, she was so lost in thought. Zu Hogan's daughter sat at the table back in the house with Talen, making him open and close the doors in his being, whatever that meant, over and over again. For the last hour all River had done was sit there, holding Talen's hand at the table, telling him to open and close, again and again, telling him that she had to be sure he could hold himself to himself.

In her mind, Sugar knew it was a great evil they practiced at the table. But in her heart she could not help but want to learn it as well, for when River had told her what her mother was, it had come, not as a shock, but a loss. Because she didn't believe Mother was wicked.

"The story is never what you first hear," Mother had always said. And she'd practiced that philosophy. When Sugar was a little girl and had been accused of stealing a village boy's carved cherrywood horse, her mother had believed her denials. And later that day, when Sugar finally confessed and showed her mother the horse, her mother had not sent her away. She'd taken her in her arms and stroked her hair and kissed her forehead and said, "It's a brave thing to admit to a lie. Foolish to lie in the first place. But brave to put the lie out in the sun for everyone to see." She'd hugged her tight. "Your bravery is as fine as peas and fatty beef," Mother had said. "Fat peas and fatty beef." From that time forward "fat peas and fatty beef" had been their saying.

How many times had Mother seen through her mistakes to what was praiseworthy? Even when Da was teaching her to fight. She'd believed Sugar would find a young man in Koramtown and raise splendid children. And they'd talked about what they'd do together with Sugar's future children, all the wonderful places she and Mother had visited with Legs in tow which they would visit with Sugar's children. The crabbing bay, their waterfall in the woods, the patch of wild blueberries by the buttes. And Mother would come stay with her in Koramtown and join in the knitting hours and teach Sugar's daughter how to knit just as she'd taught Sugar.

So much lost. For the first time since they left, Sugar could feel the emotion rising in her.

"There's that sound again," said Legs.

"What?" asked Sugar.

"A man," said Legs.

The hairs on the back of Sugar's neck stood up and she doused the lamp. She stood in the dark for a moment listening, then ran to a knothole in the side of the barn that gave a view of the yard. She put her eye to the hole and saw nothing at first. Then something large moved by the house.

She didn't have her night vision yet, and thought, unaccountably, that it was the mule. But then the body of a man fell to the ground and a dark shadow walked out from the side of the house and into the moonlight.

The man was dead and broken, and the creature looked right at her, as if it could see her eye at the knothole. Fear ran up her spine. She drew back, grabbed Leg's hand, and pulled him down. Surely it had seen her light earlier and heard her talking. It would know they were in the barn. Yet, she didn't dare run, for then it *would* mark them.

She heard the sound of steps on hard dirt, someone running away from the beast.

They needed to hide, to burrow in the hay, but the creature was coming too fast. The door stood wide open to the moonlit yard and Sugar could do nothing but watch as a misshapen thing, huge and shaggy, walked into view.

A scream rose inside her. She cried out. She could not help herself, and the beast glanced her way.

But it did not stop. It walked past the door. Then it began to run and its heavy footfalls receded from the barn.

Sugar could not move. Her heart beat in her throat. She could barely breathe.

"Those heavier footsteps, what were they?" asked Legs.

Sugar did not reply.

"It was the thing that carried Mother away, wasn't it?"

Sugar looked at him. How could he have known that? "I don't know." And yet, what else could it be?

"I held the charm today, down in the cellar," said Legs. "Do you think the creature has come to help us?"

"No," said Sugar. Not that thing. The wisterwives created beauty. That was from some other source. Whatever it was, River could offer more protection than this barn ever would. "We need to get to the house."

"I saw Mother. I held the charm in my hand and saw her."

"What?"

"I saw Mother."

"With the charm?"

"Yes," Legs said.

"But I thought you said you didn't trust the charm."

"River said it was a gift."

She *had* said that. "Mother's alive?"

"She was calling. Telling me to watch and be ready."

"This is all too confusing," she said. "River claims the creature is not part of this Order she and Mother belong to. It's a wicked thing."

Legs said nothing, and she could tell he wasn't convinced.

"We don't have time now," Sugar said. "Keep it away. We'll discuss it later with River." She gripped his hand tighter, stood, then inched to the barn door. She peered into the night. Then with all the courage she could muster, she tightened her grip on Legs's hand and dashed across the yard. When they burst into the dimly lit house, both Talen and River looked up at them.

"It's here," said Sugar. "The creature from Whitecliff."

"What?" asked River.

"It killed a man right there," said Sugar and pointed to the wall where she'd seen him fall.

River rose and cautiously looked out the door to the side of the house. She gasped.

"I told you something was there," said Nettle.

Moments later River shut the door up and turned to face them. She made Sugar relate everything she'd seen. Sugar told her everything except Legs's comments about seeing Mother. When she finished, River stood looking at the floor, gathering her thoughts.

After a moment, she looked up at them. "Listen to me. You have one chance, and that is out the back window. Run as quickly and quietly as you can. Under no circumstances will you come back here. None. I will meet you at the Creek Widow's."

The Creek Widow was like an aunt to them. Every year Da hauled them over to help her harvest her apples. Except this year, of course, because of their feud.

"Where are you going?" asked Talen.

"To play a game," she said, "of hide-and-seek."

Talen set himself to argue, but before he could say a word, River slipped out the door and into the yard.

Sugar felt like her one stay had just been taken out from

underneath her. She wanted to cry out, but could find no words.

The four of them stood frozen. Then Talen broke the silence. "You heard her," he hissed. "Out the back!"

Nettle went first, then Legs and Sugar. Talen tossed his bow and a quiver of arrows through to Nettle, then he tumbled out. When he rolled to his feet, he pointed toward the shallows dozens of yards up the river and said, "We'll go to the bank of the river and then up to the crossing." He turned to Nettle. "We'll take the hill road, past your house, then on to the Widow's."

He and Nettle dashed for the river. Sugar held Legs's hand and followed, crouching low, the tall autumn grass brushing the tops of her thighs. At the lip of the bank, she risked one look behind her and stopped.

Beyond the house and barn, past the pigpen, out in the mule's field, she could see River's slender shape in the moonlight and the beast's larger form approaching her.

River changed her course and began to walk away from the creature. It followed her, and Sugar realized River was leading it along, dragging, as it were, a broken wing like a mother bobwhite luring a fox away from her nest.

She turned and ran with her brother to catch Talen. And in that moment Sugar realized she was running again. Running as she had when Mother and Da were cut down. Running from the very creature that knew where Mother was.

Things to act. Things to be acted upon. Now was not the time to flee. She knew what she had to do. It was mad. Wild. But no more so than anything else that had happened in the last few days.

"Talen," she called.

Talen made an angry silencing gesture with his hand, but he did stop.

When Sugar caught him, she held Legs's hand out. "Take him."

"He's *your* brother," said Talen.

"You don't have time for me to explain," she said. "Keep him safe."

She couldn't argue or wait. She bent low to her brother's ear. "I'm going to find Mother."

Legs, ever brave, reached out for her arm and gave it a squeeze.

She squeezed back then turned and ran to the house and around the corner to the moonlit yard. She glanced back at the river. Talen and Nettle ran along the bank, each holding one of Legs's hands. Talen could have balked. He could have left Legs on the bank of the river. He could have done a great many things besides help, and a wave of gratitude welled up in her.

She faced the yard and field beyond. This was the creature that had stolen Mother. It hadn't killed her, but taken her away. And this might be, as crazy as it seemed, the only chance to follow it and find its lair. Or its master's. Perhaps it had fed on Mother and all she would find was a half-rotted carcass. But perhaps it had not. Mother might yet be alive. And who knew: finding the location of the monster's lair might tip this battle.

She had no idea what she would do if she found Mother. But whatever it was, it would be more than she could do hiding in holes.

And if the monster caught her, would that be any worse than being caught by the Fir-Noy or some bounty hunter? What could it do to her that the flaying knives couldn't?

She stole past the house, across the yard, and into the shadow of the barn. When she looked out at the field, she thanked the Creators that River had not yet disappeared into the woods.

Sugar crouched as she ran to the fence bordering the field, then it was up and over and into the field as sly as a cat hunting prey. She moved as quickly and silently as she could, and when both River and the creature finally did disappear into the woods on the other side, Sugar stood and ran.

RIVER CAME WITHIN a half-dozen paces of Hunger, but then she began to walk at an angle away from him. Hunger followed, but she kept just out of his reach, like a reluctant horse that didn't want to be harnessed.

He held his hands wide, then knelt upon the field and prostrated himself in submission. How else would she know he meant her no harm?

When he looked up, she stood still, studying him. He made one of the signs of the Order with his right arm, and stood again.

She backed away.

He motioned for her to halt. Then he made another sign. This time she stood still when he took the next step, and the next. One more and he would be able to reach her.

Of course, she was frightened. Who wouldn't be? But he'd catch her, and when she'd calmed, he'd make her understand.

He lunged for her.

But River danced out of his reach.

He made another sign of the Order and took a step. *It's me, River. Can't you see past this form?*

Another step. She danced farther away.

He would have to do this the hard way then. He picked up a stone, made sure she saw he had it, and hurled it at her head. Not too hard, but enough that she'd have to duck. Enough to distract her.

But instead of ducking, River rolled away and was instantly on her feet again.

Would that he had a voice. Hunger expelled the air in his gullet in frustration.

She took another step back.

Hunger lost patience and charged her. One, two, three steps, her hair flickering through his fingers, and then she was into the wood, running, lively and elusive as a deer.

He crashed along after her, over a fallen stump, around a thick bramble, down a ravine, expecting all the time to lose her, to see her marvelous burst of speed, but she did not widen her lead on him. Perhaps it was the dark or this new form he wore that gave him greater speed; whatever the cause, he could keep pace, and that gave him great satisfaction, for she would tire. He would not. It might take some time, but she would tire, and he would not.

She's leading you along, you fool.

The Mother. But she had been sleeping.

Turn around, and she'll come to us.

Hunger resisted her. *I won't kill her.*

Turn around. Now! Run back in the direction you came.

Hunger could not resist. He turned and ran. Back she pushed him, around a bend, down the trail until the darkness of the ravine lay at his feet.

Here, said the Mother, *this is where you'll take her. Quick now. Hide in the shadows.*

I won't, he said. But he did. He descended into the darkness and stood waiting, the exposed roots of a tree at his shoulder. He prayed River did not return, prayed the Mother was wrong.

I don't want her, said Hunger.

Oh, but you do.

He knew what she wanted River for. *Your ugly children can rot.*

You simple creature. Did you think I would waste her on something like you? No, she will become one of those that govern.

He could not imagine of what she spoke. But he did not have time to ponder it through, for River appeared at the top of the ravine in a shaft of moonlight. She paused, silent and lovely as a moth.

She took a step down into the ravine and paused again, listening, paused like a huntress stalking her prey. Another step, another pause, another step.

The Mother had been right. River was coming back to find him, to lure him, to make sure he didn't find the others.

Another step, pause, another, until she stood only feet away. Down in the depths of the darkness of the ravine, he could only just see her face and the pale whites of her eyes. He smelled her stink. But underneath that, Hunger caught mint and sweat and the smell of fresh-cut barley.

He pushed his fingers into the bank of dirt at his side. He would throw it at her in warning, and she would run away.

Now, said the Mother. *Take her!*

At that very moment, as if River had heard the voice in Hunger's mind, she turned and looked at him.

He could not fight the compulsion.

Forgive me, sister. Lords, forgive me.

He struck and, with his rough hand, snatched her by the face.

32.

SPOOR

Hunger could not contain his rage. He hated the Mother. Hated her.

He quickly changed his grip on River and threw her over his shoulder. With his free hand, he grasped one of the roots exposed by the bank of the ravine. The root was as thick as a man's leg and rough with bark.

Hunger gave the root an angry shove. Other roots popped, the tree shook and listed to one side, then the root he held broke with a loud crack.

This infuriated him even more, and he jumped to the top of the ravine, River still upon his shoulder. He struck the tree squarely in the trunk with all his might. Once. Twice. Each time hating the Mother more. His blows shook the tree, rustling the branches and leaves above and knocking a dead branch loose from the canopy. The branch crashed through the lower branches and fell to the ground a dozen paces away with a heavy thud, only to be followed moments later by numerous other smaller branches.

He gave the trunk one more shove that sent the whole tree crashing down, breaking other trees as it fell, lifting the earth with its root pan under his feet.

He jumped to get out of the way of the lifting root pan and realized that he could have killed River. If that branch had come down upon him, it would have broken her like an anvil upon a gourd.

He sagged with dismay. The Mother made him destroy everything that was most precious to him. And it did not matter that she'd not made him shuck River's soul from her body. This only meant River would have the agony of living in the darkness with the other woman before her end came.

River lay on his shoulder struggling against his grasp like some animal caught in a snare. It could not be comfortable being held there for great distances. So he brought her around front and cradled her like a father might his babe. Her face, he knew, would be bruised from his initial grip.

He tried to stroke her hair to calm her, but River did not stop struggling. She pounded at him and then began to tear at his eyes.

She would hurt herself more than anything else, so he caught both her hands in his ragged mouth and held them there.

I cannot die. I cannot disobey.

He held River close.

I am so sorry, sister. So very, very sorry. He repeated it over and over in his mind, then began to make his way back toward the Mother's caves.

After only a dozen paces, he heard the distinct thock of someone stepping on and breaking a branch behind him.

He stopped and turned toward the sound. It was not an animal, for no beast that size would have remained close after he'd knocked over the tree. And it was not the sound of a branch falling.

Leaves rustled as if someone had tripped.

Someone following him in the dark. The burning son, perhaps. Or the older son. Or maybe even Zu Hogan himself.

She would take them as well, the Mother would. She would command him to kill them, and he would do it.

Horror rose in him at the thought, and he turned and ran away from the stalker. Through the trees, crashing through the brush, trying to cover River from the branches that whipped him. He ran up a slight hill and stopped to listen for his pursuer.

The sound of running footsteps rose from the forest below. A light sound, not a heavy animal. Not a large person.

He turned to run again. He would outdistance him in the dark, but what if he couldn't outrun this pursuer? The family was all part of the Sleth nest, the Order, he corrected himself. What if his pursuer followed him all the way back to the Mother's lair?

They'd find the Mother, that's what. And she'd take them there.

Or would she?

Zu Hogan had fought him in the tower. But what if there had been three or four with his strength? Perhaps it would have been Zu Hogan taking him, instead of the other way around. The Mother had said something once about humans long ago, rising up against their masters. Perhaps Zu Hogan knew such secrets. Perhaps Zu Hogan's failing to stop him in the sea tower had been more a function of surprise than strength.

His terror turned to hope. He could lead whoever was down there to the Mother. And that person in turn would lead Zu Hogan. And if not, Hunger could come back and lead Zu Hogan himself. Hunger looked down the dark, wooded hill.

Nothing moved. They were waiting for him to continue.

He grabbed a branch and broke it smartly to announce his position. Then he turned and walked away. A few paces later he broke another branch, and a few paces after that, yet another.

HUNGER WALKED THROUGH the remaining hours of the morning, keeping only slightly ahead of the person following him. When dawn arrived he stood atop a ridge and looked down at the small valley below. Just beyond the edge of the wood, still in the shadow of the hill, a flock of sheep grazed the grass bordering both sides of the road running toward a village. The sun lit the fields and thatch roofs with a rosy light. Still farther along, a man drove a wain laden with a fifteen-foot pile of hay. Two boys sat atop the pile, stabilizing themselves with one hand on the side pole while sharing what looked to be a red cheese round. They passed by a woman throwing kitchen scraps to her white-and-black-speckled chickens.

This was the village closest to the Mother's lair. He'd smelled these villagers with longing on many an evening. These were the homes he'd stolen about in the darkness, listening to the humans, tempting his appetite, until the Mother had ordered him to stay away.

He had not heard the person shadowing him for some time. But that probably only meant it was light enough for them to see the way better and avoid things that cracked in the dark.

This also meant he could leave visible spoor. Nevertheless, it was quicker to follow sound. So he broke yet another branch and continued along the ridge past the village, past the stand of fat spruce from which the Mother had called him, and to the entrance that stood up on the hill above the swamp.

There were three entrances he knew about. The one in the cliffs by the sea. This one. And another found in the buried ruin of the stone-wights on the other side of the hill.

Hunger stood at the entrance, the small stream running out of the lopsided mouth and down the hill. He looked down at River and released her hands from his mouth. She clutched her shoulders in pain.

He was sorry. He should have thought about the pain

and numbness that would result from holding her arms in one position for so long. He smoothed her hair back from her face with one finger. She did not pull away this time. She looked so fragile in his arms.

For a moment he lost his courage. The Mother was cunning and strong. How could beings with such frail bodies hope to contend with her?

But they had. She had said so herself. Hunger looked back. He hoped whoever followed him had such power. He felt the Mother's compulsion upon him. Hunger stepped into the thin, cold water with River in his arms and disappeared into the dark.

33.

BODY AND SOUL

Hunger laid River down next to Purity in the ink-black chamber. Both River and Purity cried out at first, but then they recognized each other and began to sob. For joy or despair, Hunger did not know. He left to get some of the wood he'd stored in another chamber to make a fire.

He'd left Purity with fire in the beginning, but she'd tried to run away, and the Mother had made him steal hobbles from a smith and put them on her ankles. The hobbles had taken all thoughts of flight out of her. And, in truth, it would have made escape impossible, for there was a steep cliff she'd have to scale to escape, if she could even find it in the dark. He supposed he'd have to get hobbles for River as well.

River and Purity talked in low voices, but they stopped when they heard him enter his chamber. He placed his small nest of tinder and kindling a pace from them on the floor, struck the flint against his fire-steel until three sparks fell into the tinder. Then he blew. A small flame leapt up. He added small bits of kindling. The fire grew. And he finally added a small stick.

He felt the Mother behind him.

Had she discovered his plan? A small panic rose within and he turned.

But it was not the Mother that stood before him. Instead, a woman of strange and exquisite beauty, clothed in brightness, looked upon him. Dark hair tumbled down her naked shoulders. Pale shoulders. Pale skin. He'd seen this woman before: the memory of that face lay just under the surface of his mind. But she was not human. Was this another of the Mother's kind then, come to steal the souls of these women?

He rose in alarm and prepared to defend them.

"You've lost your focus," the beauty said.

Hunger could not tell if she spoke the words with her mouth or directly in his mind, but he knew it was indeed the Mother.

"You are beautiful," he said in both wonder and confusion. But this was some trick. He looked closer to see if he could detect the lie, then reached out and touched her arm, but she was as real as the rocks about him.

What kind of power must one have to change the very form of one's body? Surely, more than anyone in the Order, and that thought filled him with dismay.

He looked at her again and swore her visage shifted. "What are you?" he asked.

She ignored his question and held up the stomach that contained the souls of his family. "You still fight me.

Have I ever given you a reason not to believe I will do what I say?"

What was she going to do with them? His panic began to rise again, but he could not let her know that. She was wicked. Wicked and cruel and the slightest slip would mean the end of his wife or children. He looked at the stomach and said nothing.

"Wicked?" she asked. "Is it wicked for the master to demand obedience from his dog? Is it wicked to break a beast of its rebellious ways? And if it demonstrates quality, is it wicked to administer praise and reward?"

"I am not your dog."

"Oh, but you are. And I will have loyalty from you. It is your decision. Obey me and you will eat from my table. Defy me and you will learn by the things you suffer."

"I can withstand your pain."

"Perhaps I did not state myself clearly before—you can be free one day, and so can your family. I'm not a cruel master. I don't want to be such, even when such methods do have their advantages. No. I govern by giving you choices. You've chosen poorly and shall reap what you've sown. But I will give you this: I will let you decide which one I shall eat."

His panic swelled. "No," said Hunger. "Please."

"Choose."

"I'll do whatever you say," he said. "Spare them."

"It is too late," she said.

"Take me then. Eat *my* soul."

He was close enough to reach out and take his stomach from her, but he could not move. And the horror of his helplessness washed over him.

"Then I shall choose," she said. "I will take the lesser of them to show you I am merciful. I shall take the youngest male."

"No," he said. Not, his son.

Not any of them!

She opened the mouth of the stomach, reached in, and withdrew a shining form. It bucked and sparkled like a hooked fish in the sunshine.

Souls held the same rough form as the bodies they animated, or so the wise ones said. And while Hunger could see part of the form, he could not see it all. It was like glimpsing something in the water, seeing only one distorted facet. But distorted facet or not, he knew this soul. "Russet," he whispered. "Son!"

This was a nightmare.

"I keep my promises," she said. "Remember that." Then she opened her mouth and fell upon the shining like a cat might the neck of a large hare.

"No!" Hunger cried.

The silvery light struggled violently.

Then she wrenched it. The light flexed in one brilliant flash, then hung limp in her hand. She gulped a portion of his son like a swamp snake gulped in part of a piglet, like a man gulped overlarge quantities of blood pudding.

Hunger's mind split. His world turned white.

Rage and horror and grief flooded him. He turned to the women behind him. The Mother wanted them, well, he would deny her that. He might not strike her, but he could strike them and deprive her of their service, whatever hideous form that would take. And by so doing, he'd save them from her awful bondage.

"Halt!" said the Mother.

"Let me go!" he said and fought her binding with all the force he could muster. He succeeded in taking one step toward the women. *Ha!* he crowed in triumph.

"Enough," said the Mother, and Hunger found he could

not move. A smoke of confusion clouded his eyes, and he knew no more.

HUNGER WOKE ON the cave floor. He smelled the women—Purity and River. Smelled the coals of the dead fire. And remembered Russet, his son.

His grief rose like a tide.

"You have a choice," said the Mother.

He wanted to strike her, but could not. "I will not listen to you."

"Quiet."

Hunger fell in on himself.

"Pursue this course and I will eat them all. There are three others here in this stomach. Live to free them. I've given you my promise. I am not cruel. Obey me and reap your reward."

He could not trust this creature. "When will you free them?"

"When your loyalty is thoroughly tested. And then, after a time of service, I will free you."

"You lie."

The Mother shook her head. "Prove to me your loyalty. Stop fighting me. You will see I am just."

He could be freed if he could only fix the collar.

"No," the Mother said. "Do you think I did not know your plans the very moment you removed the collar from the woman? Do you think I was ignorant of the man washing himself or the burning son? Did you think you could hide your thoughts from me?"

"Yes," said Hunger in defeat. And he knew it was hopeless. It had been hopeless from the beginning. He should not have resisted her.

His stupidity had cost him his son.

"Your people will prosper under my hand. Not be left

to fend for themselves as happened with your last, inattentive master. I will make your lands fertile. I will fight your battles and keep you safe. Serve me and all your kindred will flourish."

He could not die. He could not disobey. He could not even hide his thoughts. What was left to him? He was indeed a dog on a chain. A horse corralled for the breaking. The Mother, this creature, whatever it was, held more power than any human. More power than the Divines. She was as far above him as a man was above a beast. Besides, he wasn't even a man anyway. He was something else—a soup of souls and stone. Why then should he not obey?

Perhaps she was just. Perhaps she was doing nothing more than teaching the dog that it was a dog, not a master. And in that thought he saw a clear path, a small glimmering of hope—he would be her best servant. He would meet her every whim. He would be the dog that the master grew to love and called to feed at his lap. And by so doing he would save his wife and daughter and remaining son.

He would serve this creature with all his mind, might, and strength. "Will you forgive me?" he asked.

"Forgive? That word has no meaning. But I shall give you one more chance to prove yourself. And in time you may win my trust."

"Tell me then what you desire."

"We shall continue what we've begun," she said. "Gathering the ones that stink. Yours was a good plan, even if wrought with the wrong intent."

He felt a lightening in his mood. He had chosen the right course.

"The one you led here," she said. "You will take her and see if she is fit to lead or ripe for the harvest. And then you shall find the rest."

"As you command," he said and turned back toward

the mouth of the cave. The last moments of his son's existence played before his mind—all his cursed fault. He should never have fought her.

Never.

And he would never do it again; he was the Mother's now, body and soul, and he would demonstrate that to her.

SUGAR FOUND THE monster to be one of the easiest things she'd ever tracked. A stupid beast that could not navigate well enough in the darkness to avoid the branches. But when there was light enough to see, she realized that the branches being broken were not those that someone would accidentally step on and break, nor were they ones that would break easily as someone brushed past. No, they had been broken on purpose. She concluded River knew someone was following and had done this to leave a trail.

But Sugar now looked down at the spot where an immense rotted log had recently lain and was not so sure. Worms and grubs wriggled in the soil of the impression. This log had obviously been moved aside, but it was too large for River to do such a thing. Sugar attempted to push it, but could not move it an inch. How could River have moved it as she was carried along by that beast?

To Sugar's left rose a steep hill. On her right the ground descended to a cluster of hundred-foot bald cypress, their massive knees rising out of the dark tea water. A muskrat swam through a layer of duckweed out to a clear slip of deeper water.

She wondered if the creature had taken River into that mess.

Lilies, bog bean, and goat willow choked the far side. The place breathed with the croaking of frogs and stank of things rotting in the water. But she knew that it was full of far more than frogs and stink and scum. She'd find snakes, leeches, and snapping turtles there in abundance.

A chip of something small and dark fell from the cypress trees above. Sugar looked up and saw a handful of grayfans, large game fowl that fanned their tail feathers when threatened. They stood in the branches above, pecking for the cypress seeds. More dark chips fell and she realized it wasn't bark, but grayfan droppings.

She stepped aside in disgust and walked toward the swamp to see if perhaps the mud at the edges would show any footprints, but as she did so a crack sounded up the hill.

The creature had gone up the hill, not into the swamp. She turned and followed the noise, glad to leave the stink and the rising mosquitoes.

A few paces later the tree cover gave way and there at her feet a trail of footprints led through the dew-soaked undergrowth, clear as you please up the hill.

Sugar followed the trail back into the trees, always going up, finding scuffled leaves here and there or matted grass, until she came to a small stream. She stopped and looked about, then saw a footprint in the stream itself. She followed the stream uphill to a slight ridge of rock. She crossed the stream and found herself standing in front of the mouth of a cave, a cool breeze blowing out of the darkness and into her face. She immediately crouched and moved to one side so she did not darken the entrance with her silhouette.

She wondered if this was a natural cave or one made by the stone-wights. If it was one of the ancient ruins, did that mean this creature was connected with them? Many had been lost in the stone-wight ruins. All of Sugar's life she had been warned to stay clear of them, for who knew what dark thing waited within? But this is where the creature had taken Mother, and so this is where she would have to go. She looked down the hill. Only someone standing right where she was could see this opening. And now she'd wished the monster had taken River to the swamp. In a swamp you could at least see what you were about. Here the creature might be only a dozen paces away, watching her from the darkness.

The hair on the back of her neck stood up. Sugar listened. She could hear nothing but the trickling water. She waited for a long time, but nothing stirred. The breeze meant this would be a long cave. It was quite possible that the monster's lair was hidden deep within.

She would have to go in, if only a small distance. Whomever she brought back would want to know what lay just inside this entrance so they might avoid a pit or slope. Any information she could give them would be better than leaving them to charge in completely blind.

She edged toward the darkness and then crab-walked in and waited for her vision to adjust.

The walls were narrow and tilted to one side. Water oozed down their face. The ceiling of the cave trailed up and was lost in the darkness.

Sugar moved farther in, away from the sound of the water outside and listened. She thought she heard voices, but then decided it was only the breeze or water. Rocks fell in the distance, the sound echoing along the cave walls. Moments later something splashed through the water. And then she realized it was moving, not away from her, but back toward her and the mouth of the cave.

She could not judge the distance well, but it sounded close.

Fear rose in her. She turned and scrabbled back, trying to keep a low profile. When she reached the mouth of the cave, whatever it was began to run.

34.

SACRIFICE

Argoth held Serenity, his youngest daughter, in a great hug, her legs dangling loose. She growled like a bear, bit him on the neck, and then giggled.

He growled and bit her back. "Little beast, you go help your sisters outside. Your mother and I need to talk." He set her down.

Serenity ran out the back door of the kitchen, and Argoth shut the door behind her. He turned to Serah.

She leaned back on the dry sink, one long dark tress curling across the sweat on her neck, and stretched. Before her on the table lay the carcasses of five pheasants along with the celery, raisins, and cut onions she'd been stuffing them with. The giblets from the birds soaked in a bowl of brine. Serah's eyes brimmed with onion tears.

It could not be easy being pregnant as she was and carrying the workload she did. And he wasn't going to make it any easier.

"The servants are all outside?" he asked.

"You could have sent someone ahead to give me warning. We have so little time to pack. I can't show up in Mokad in rags. And I'm not going to leave my sisters in these lands to face the Bone Face attacks that will surely come."

Argoth shook his head and spoke in a low voice. "I'm not taking you with me on the ship. In fact, from this day forth, Mokad will be your death."

Confusion clouded Serah's expression.

"Listen to me. You and the children must disappear tomorrow before noon. Go into the wilderness, book passage on a ship under another name to another nation—I don't care. In fact, I must not know how you do it."

"Why would we need to—"

"Do not contact your sisters. In three days I will either return whole, or your world will begin to fray like a cheap rope. I am sorry, Serah. I never wanted this. But it has come upon us. Do not wait. You will not be able to flee in the moment of your crisis."

Serah's face turned from confusion to disbelief. "Mokad has made some treaty with those blackheart Bone Faces, haven't they? Giving these lands away like Koram did when they lost the wars with Mokad."

Argoth shook his head. "No. Nothing to do with the Bone Faces. I cannot explain it to you now." He held his hand out to her. "Trust me. As soon as the Lions depart with me, you must go. Pack light. You will have only a short time."

Serah did not take his hand. "This isn't just another battle you're riding off to, is it? You've plunged into some idiot's plot."

"My love," he said and reached out for her again.

She took his hand this time, but did not embrace him.

"You will come back to me," said Serah.

He hoped that would indeed be the case.

He thought of his children, of his girls begging him to take them on his hunting trips. Of Serenity's growls and bites and Grace's affinity for dogs, training his proud coursers to jump through hoops and wear bright ribbons in their collars. He thought of Joy leaving messy clay puppets in his pockets and Nettle who wanted so much to be a man. He thought of Serah's contagious laughter.

But he always knew his joys in this life might suddenly end. Any man of war knew that. If that happened, he was prepared, and he'd wait for them in the world of souls.

"Husband," said Serah, more tears brimming in her eyes. "I am weary of worry."

"I would rather you eat that bitter bread than feast on the bleakness that comes with oppression and slavery."

She looked down, and he stepped toward her, enfolding her in his embrace. Her hair smelled of the lager she used to bring forth its brilliance.

This time she yielded to him. "I know you must go. But sometimes I wonder if you love war more than flesh and blood."

"My capable and sweet wife. I love our life so much I cannot see it ruined or stolen by wicked men."

She sighed. "If you were a little less noble, I think we'd find a little more peace."

He did not respond. How could he?

"Come back to us," she said. "Come back and put down the sword."

"And what would I do?"

"Grow vegetables, race your dogs, and sit in the sun. When our children are grown, you can dote upon your grandchildren with figs and cakes. And when you die, you will be old, shriveled, and happy."

The vision of it tugged at his heart. "Will you be shriveled by my side?"

She looked up at him, her smile full of weariness, pain, and love. "Women do not shrivel."

Argoth laughed. And in that moment he realized he'd made a huge mistake. He should have never kept the Grove from her despite the risk her blabbermouth sisters posed. If he survived, he would never keep another thing from her.

"When I return," he said, "I'm going to tell you a story about a man who held too many secrets and the woman he loved. And then you will tell me what the woman did when she found out she married a monster."

IT WAS WELL past midnight. Argoth stood outside the house in the dark, his chances of ever returning to his wife and children slipping between his fingers like sand.

There had been no word from Matiga. He wondered if perhaps the Skir Master had killed the messenger. Had he killed Matiga?

No, the Skir Master wouldn't be so foolish. He wanted to only give them a scare so they would run and he could follow.

Perhaps the messenger delivered the coded requests, but Matiga felt it too risky to send him the weave he needed so desperately. Or perhaps she had already gone to the Grove's refuge to prepare to bear the Grove off and the messenger found her house empty. Whatever the reason, dinner had come and gone. And now it was late, exceedingly late.

Argoth did not have the Fire to battle a Divine. And even if the weave arrived this very minute, he suspected it was too late. Fire could be poured out in great quantities. But to swallow such a flood would be the death of any man. Fire could only be accepted in a trickle. It took time. And time had slipped away.

Half of the Lions patrolled the border of his yard. One stood just a stone's throw away, his bright helm gleaming in the moonlight.

Argoth thought of Shim. He could send word to him. And what? Have him arrive here only to be slaughtered by this troop of dreadmen?

No. This was his burden. His mind raced for other options. But all of them ended in death. And then he heard the Lion below him call out for someone to identify themselves. Nettle's voice came in reply.

Argoth's hopes soared. Perhaps Matiga was sending the weave with Nettle.

Argoth left the side of the house and went to greet his handsome boy. He found the dreadman holding him at the point of a spear. Nettle's face was anxious. And there was no sign of his horse. Something was wrong.

"He's mine," said Argoth.

"Yes, Zu," said the dreadman, raising his spear out of the way.

Argoth put his arm around Nettle and began walking him back to the house.

Nettle looked up at his father with urgency. "Da," he said.

Argoth shook his head. "When we get in the house."

They walked in silence until the front door of the sleeping house was shut behind them.

"Have you been to the Creek Widow's?" asked Argoth.

"No," said Nettle. "We're on the way there."

Argoth's heart fell. Without a weave he could do nothing. Nothing. "Who's we?" he asked.

Nettle spoke in barely a whisper. "River told me everything."

"What do you mean?"

"I know, Da," he said. "I know what we are. River sent us to the Creek Widow's. The hatchlings were at Uncle Hogan's. Then the creature came, and River led it away. Talen and the boy are waiting in the woods."

"You mean the monster from Whitecliff?" Argoth asked.

"Yes."

Argoth groaned. This confirmed his previous guess—it was the Divine's creature. And that meant the Divine would be watching his family. It meant Serah and the children would be caught when they ran. Caught and questioned and tortured. In the end, they would die horrible deaths. The picture of Serenity being flayed to make Serah speak rose in his mind.

"Da?" asked Nettle.

He couldn't believe the end had come like this. He was caught. His family was caught with him. There was only one way out. He still had the tin of poison he'd given to Purity. He looked down at Nettle. He had enough for all of them.

"Come with me," he said, motioning to his library. He opened the door, the comforting smell of the two well-oiled sets of armor that sat in either corner filling the room. He followed Nettle in, then barred the door behind him.

"Da," said Nettle, his voice full of intensity, "are we Soul-eaters?"

Argoth looked down at his son. He'd never wanted it to happen this way. He looked about the room collecting his thoughts, at the smudged maps he'd used on campaigns in other lands, at the feather-festooned spear he'd broken in the leg of a Black Hill giant and the lock of hair from that giant's head, at the necklaces of teeth. Years of prowess at war, and he still had to hide. Still had to face his son as if he were some ignominious criminal.

Argoth walked to the hearth and grabbed one large flagstone set at the bottom of the face on the right. It was about four feet high and two wide. He caught the hidden ring that would release the catch and pulled. The stone swung inward to a dark compartment.

"In, to your right one step, then take the ladder down."

Nettle looked at Argoth with disbelief.

"Hurry now."

Nettle crouched, then twisted through the opening and disappeared into the darkness. Argoth followed. It was a tight squeeze, but just big enough for him. He stood in the oversized space between the walls and shut the narrow flagstone door. Then he descended the ladder in perfect blackness to the hidden cellar below.

Nobody knew about this place. Not even Hogan. This is where he kept his secret books, his weaves, and the implements of his life before the Order.

"Da," said Nettle in the darkness. "What is this?"

Next to the ladder stood a case with many shelves. He felt for the lamp with a flint striker, then worked the striker until a spark ignited the wick. When the flame burned brightly, he set the lamp down on the small table and motioned for Nettle to take the one chair.

Nettle sat, looking about the room with puzzlement. Argoth noticed his ear had been cut and stitched.

Argoth had used good timbers and brick to build this room. All had been sealed over with a thick layer of white lime render. This kept the room bright. Furthermore, Argoth made sure to lay drainage tiles into the soil all around this part of the house so that all the runoff was taken down the hill and away from this dry room.

There was not much in this close room: a stack of wood next to a small, smoke-blackened hearth; a long, but narrow table; a chair; and two cases for his books and the implements of the lore.

"Son, tell me what River told you."

"It's true, isn't it?" Nettle said, looking at the plates of inscribed tin that lay on one of the shelves.

"That depends on what you've been told."

Nettle turned back to his father and related everything that had happened since Nettle had left for Hogan's, the discovery of Purity's children, the events at Whitecliff, the cutting of his ear. He repeated everything River had said about the Order, about Talen's days pouring forth, and what happened afterward with the creature.

When he finished, Argoth did not immediately respond. River had taken upon her a right that was his. He had looked forward to testing Nettle and bringing him into the Order. He had planned it for so many years. She had taken that anticipated joy from him, but he couldn't be angry with her.

"I am a root in the Order of Hismayas," said Argoth. "And we are not souleaters." Although that's exactly what he once had been. Bless the Six, but the memory of his years before the Order still pained him. "You will never apply that term to us again."

Nettle didn't speak for a moment. When he did his expression and voice were full of desperate relief. "It's true then, what River said? We do not prey on others. We haven't stolen Fire?" He was almost pleading to hear that his father wasn't a monster.

But what struck Argoth was that Nettle used "we." He'd expected his son to fight against this idea. The Order had to be so careful. They had to teach their children the propaganda of the Divines just as any common parent might teach their children so that no one would suspect them. And Argoth had done his job well. But here his son, his loyal boy, had already decided to follow him, come what may.

Argoth would not betray that trust with prevarications. "I was once a nightmare," he said. "But then I was brought into the light."

"I don't understand," said Nettle.

"You won't," said Argoth. "Just know that I found the right path. And that I do not steal and haven't since before you were born. And know too that you have a choice. Not all are brought into the Order. Your mother, for example, does not know." He regretted how he'd misjudged her.

Argoth continued. "I was going to introduce you to everything later. But now that you know the secret, you must make a decision. I'm going to need some help."

"Father," said Nettle. "I would never betray you."

"Hear me first," said Argoth. "If you join, you will be bound by oaths of loyalty. Oaths that cannot be broken."

And when Nettle joined him at his side, they would go and administer the poison.

Argoth thought of the position he'd put his family in. He hoped they would forgive him. "There is so much to say, but we have no time. We believe the creature was sent by this Skir Master and Lumen to destroy us."

"Lumen? He isn't dead?"

"We do not think so."

Shock shone on Nettle's face. "But why wouldn't they muster a massive hunt?"

"A hunt is like beating the bushes in a great ring. If you have enough people to ensure none of the game escapes, then you can close the ring and slaughter the game within the ring at will. But what if most of the game is outside the ring you've formed? What if there are well-concealed bolt-holes?"

"Are we going to attempt to escape?"

"In a manner of speaking," said Argoth. "We were going to attack them. Enthrall the Divine."

Astonishment shone on Nettle's face.

"Bold, eh? Then we would have hunted down those who could threaten us one by one. But I misjudged. I don't have the Fire I need. I have no weapon to take to battle."

"Fire?" Nettle asked. "That's all you need?"

He smiled at his son's statement. Fire was not so easy to obtain. "Yes, that's all," Argoth said. "A man, any man, can learn to speed, slow, give, and receive the Days of his Fire. I am old, Nettle. Far older than you can imagine. I have secretly given my last days out to the dreadmen of this land. My Fire gutters low. So low I dare not multiply myself for great tasks. And I cannot accomplish the task at hand as a normal man."

"There is no difference between you and the Divines?"

"Not when it comes to basic principles," said Argoth.

"Then teach me how to release my Fire to you," said Nettle.

"That won't work. To learn that very elementary skill can take a very long time. Weeks. Sometimes months."

"But Talen sat at the table with River doing just that, opening and closing his doors, Fire pouring off him."

"Talen is not what he seems," said Argoth. "Besides, even if I could teach you in a matter of hours it would be too late. It takes too long to transfer the quantity I need."

Nettle pointed at a pine rod lying in the case. "That's a filtering rod, isn't it?"

"It is," said Argoth. "Something from before." He'd kept all the old implements around to remind him of those former days, to remind him what he was so that he could never forget how the Order had changed him.

"Do you know how to use it?"

"It has been a very long time but yes I know how."

"Then take the Fire from me."

"Son," Argoth said. "You don't know what you're asking."

"Do I have enough Fire to supply your need?"

"Yes, but that's not—"

"Then use it, Da."

He was so brash. He had gotten his clan wrists this year, but he was still a boy. "Nettle, I swore never to take Fire again. Only to receive it from those who freely give. If I take your Fire, you will be changed. When you forcibly take Fire, you cannot avoid also taking portions of the person's soul. You take their memories. You take the force that controls the very nature of their bodies."

He continued, "This is why many who go to the temple to make an offering claim to feel as if they've lost something. But it is not an effect of being touched by holiness as is claimed. It is the effect of having your Fire ripped from you. The Divines are no better than soul-eaters—both are thieves. Do you understand?"

"I understand."

"Do you? Do you know why some die on the altars? When the Divines take a great quantity of Fire, they will simply drain a man until he dies. Because if they were to stop short, we'd all see the effects of someone having so very much of their soul leached away into the rod. You might become a drooling invalid or a wild man to be roped and chained. You might lose all memory of us. No one can predict the full effects of taking the quantity of Fire I need. It cannot be reversed. At least, none know that lore."

"But we can predict the effects if I don't, can't we?"

Argoth said nothing. Such courage and trust—Nettle did not know what he was saying. Argoth had seen that ardent desire so many times in the eyes of youth going off to their first battle. None of them knew the sacrifice that lay ahead.

"Da," he said. He held up his wrists with their tattoos. "Do you, even you, mock me?"

"No."

"But you do. Every time you allow others to stand in my place on the patrols. Every time you assign your men to shelter me."

"I don't want to risk you unnecessarily."

"Life is risk," said Nettle. "I am now a man of our clan, a man of my father's house. And I want to protect my sisters. My mother. I want to protect my friends. Would you prevent me? Would you tell me I am not worthy?"

"Son, you're worthy." He was more than worthy. He was precious. He was a prize that Argoth did not want to part with.

"Then pick me up, Father. Let me be your weapon. Let me be your sword."

Argoth looked at Nettle, the desire burning in his eyes. Such a son!

"And if this takes part of my soul," Nettle continued, "we will count it no less an honor than if I had lost an arm or a leg in battle."

"I can't," said Argoth.

"If you did, would you be able to save Mother? Would you be able to save Serenity and Grace? Little Joy?"

If he took the Fire, he could spring the Skir Master's trap. The odds were long, but there was the smallest of chances. "There's no guarantee."

"There are never any guarantees, Da."

This would put his family at such great risk. But they were already at risk. They were already targets. He could kill them all tonight. Or he could fight and try to save them. If he failed, their deaths would not be easy. But if he succeeded. If he succeeded, he would save not only his family but the lives of many others. The Divines stole so much. They made so many people suffer. And Serah did have a chance to escape. Someone would surely follow her. But it wouldn't be a dreadman.

He looked down at Nettle. He didn't have to draw all his Fire. He didn't have to kill him. He knew of no lore that could return the soul once it had been taken. They'd hoped such things would be contained in the Book of Hismayas. But none had been able to open that book. And Argoth could not make this decision based on a wild hope. If Nettle sacrificed himself, there would be no restoration. Argoth found tears in his eyes. Nettle reminded him so much of Ummon, his son of so long ago. His son who had ridden out and never come back. His son who he had risked unnecessarily. He wished this crisis had come upon them six months later. By then he would have brought Nettle into the Order, and Nettle would have been able to give him his Fire. But he knew that was a lie. He wouldn't have brought Nettle into the Order. He'd pushed the testing off for more than two years now. He would have waited another year. They would have been in the same position they were now.

"Pick me up, Father. Let me stand at your side. Let me be a man and fight for what is ours."

Yes, Argoth thought. Let us fight. Let us not falter in the moment of crisis. The Divines were no better than soul-eaters. And was he not a Root of the Order of Hismayas? An Order established by the Creators themselves to bring humankind back into the light. To restore that which was lost.

He looked at his son with new eyes.

"I will pick you up," said Argoth. "You will stand at my side. And together we shall smite the enemy." And if they died, then they would die with honor.

He reached out and took his boy in his arms and hugged him tightly, hugged him for what would be the very last time because if he did survive, if he came back from this battle, the Nettle he knew would be gone.

ARGOTH LEFT NETTLE in the secret room and went to the kitchen and put a pot of water over the fire to boil. He listened to the sounds of his family sleeping upstairs and a memory of Nettle as a little boy pushed its way into his mind. He and Serah stood to the side of the kitchen window spying on Nettle playing with Grace and Joy. Each child had a number of Nettle's new, brightly painted wooden animals. The animals mustered a defense against raiders in the flower pots. When the waves of Bone Faces had all been tromped, gnashed, and thrown in the privy, Nettle's pig said, "Want to roll in the mud?"

"A triumph celebration," said Grace's horse. Soon all the bright animals and the children were covered with mud. The children had played until dark fell, and Argoth and Serah had been content just to watch.

Tonight that little boy had shown his mettle. And Argoth, for all intents and purposes, was going to have to kill him.

Kill his own son.

But maybe not forever. His heart swelled within him, and then the water began to steam. He swung the pot off the fire. He poured steaming water into a teapot, brought a pitcher for himself, fetched a cheesecloth teabag, and returned to the hidden cellar. He was going to have to make a wizardsmeet tea.

A fire burned in the hearth of the underground room. Nettle stood at the case examining a rough necklace.

"That is your great-great-great-grandfather's weave," said Argoth. "A thrall that we will use upon the Skir Master."

He took a porcelain crock on the shelf and placed it on the table. He unstopped the crock, removed a pinch of the small wizardsmeet leaves, measured a small amount into the cup of his palm, then put the rest back.

"Wizardsmeet has a stench that makes many gag. And not only does it smell but it will leave a taste in your mouth that will take a day to fade. But you need this, for your first response will be to fight me."

Nettle picked up the cup. "How old are you?"

"I am in my ninety-sixth year," said Argoth.

Nettle's mouth hung open in shock.

"Before I joined the Order, I did what the Divines do—consumed Fire harvested from others to renew my body and extend my days. I was eighty when I joined the Order and swore to live by the Fire I possessed or that which was freely given."

"Then I have brothers who could be my father."

"No," said Argoth, and he did not expect it to hurt so much to remember. "They were all murdered. But that's another story." He motioned at the cup. "It doesn't need to steep long. You can drink it now."

Nettle drank it with a grimace. Then he handed the cup back. It would take a few minutes for the herb to work.

Argoth motioned for Nettle to take the other end of the table, and they moved it close to the hearth. "Take off your tunic, then lie here." He went to the case and retrieved the draw collar, tongue, filtering rod, and stomach. "You're going to feel a relaxing comfort come upon you. Next, you'll find you can't move, not without great effort. Do not panic."

Argoth laid the harvesting weaves onto the table beside Nettle. He covered Nettle's lower torso with his tunic, leaving his chest bared. Argoth picked up the draw collar. "Do you know why weaves are so often made of gold?"

"Because it's a noble metal?"

"Yes, but why is it noble?"

Nettle shrugged.

"You can make a fine, powerful weave out of willow. In fact, in some ways it's better than gold, but only if the branches are still green. The moment the wood cures, it leaks, sometimes like a sieve. Gold, on the other hand, holds it tight as a drum. Gold can also be wrought into many shapes. You can pattern a weave with gold wire that's impossible with plant materials or harder metals. Now I want you to look at this." He held up the collar. "Such things are woven by Kains. And they would have you believe only they possess the secrets. But you see here that it is a lie."

He paused. This was the moment where his words became deeds. One last time he considered giving up and killing them all with a quick poison. But he looked at Nettle again. He thought about the girls and their eventual children. He thought upon grandchildren and great-grandchildren. Sometimes the choices of one father or mother affected generations. Nettle's might be the sacrifice that opened the way to thousands throwing off the yokes of the Divines.

And if they failed?

Then they did so in struggle, not by choice.

"You," said Argoth, "are a lodestar shining in our bright heaven." He loved him, loved him with all his heart.

He lifted Nettle's head and placed the collar around his neck. Into a lock on the collar he fitted the end of the rod of pine.

"The collar is woven to draw the Fire forth. The rod will catch your soul. But we shall not burn it as the Divines do. No, we shall keep it as the testament of your sacrifice. We shall keep it in hopes of restoring you one day."

He stroked Nettle's hair. "Can you move your arm?"

Nettle just looked up at him. The wizardsmeet was taking effect.

"In reality any wood might do as a filter. But it was found long ago that pine held on to soul better than any other wood. Leave the bark on, and it holds it all the tighter. But bark can easily be chipped away. That is why this rod has been stripped. I will not suffer one particle of you to be lost."

Argoth picked up the tongue. He inserted one end into the pine rod, the other fitted into the stomach, a weave of gold, shaped like a grip.

Collar, filter, tongue, stomach. All was ready. It was said that those who stole Fire opened themselves up to invisible influences from the unseen world. Evil skir or even Regret himself. Perhaps what he did was an evil, but the cause was just.

"The collar will grow cold," he said. "Very cold. Can you blink?"

Nettle did nothing at first, but then he blinked once very slowly.

"I'm going to begin," said Argoth. "We should have heated blankets, but that cannot be helped. I'll just have to keep the hearth stoked."

He hesitated. Nettle looked up at him with such serenity. He knew it was from the wizardsmeet, but the trust in his gaze was unmistakable. "I'm proud of you, son. I will not disappoint you."

He took a breath, and the whole world seemed to hang on that moment, then he began to sing the ancient forms.

After a time a grayness seeped into the collar like a thin wash of paint. Argoth continued singing, and the grayness slowly darkened and turned black.

Minutes sped by and the blackness entered the filter and slowly rose up toward the stomach.

Without tasting a great quantity of Fire, there was no way to tell if it was polluted with soul. But this unused filter had been cut from a thick, long branch. It was three feet long, more than enough for the souls of a dozen men.

Soon Argoth was sweating with the effort, but he continued to sing and pull. Water condensed on the collar and rod, then the tongue. He stopped to build up the fire, but the water did not evaporate. Despite his efforts, a fine frost began to form along the collar.

He stoked the fire until the hearth could not contain it. An hour passed. He was drenched with sweat, his voice hoarse. He stopped to take a long drink.

Argoth smoothed Nettle's hair back. Tears sprang to his eyes again, tears full of sorrow and pride. "We're halfway there, son. You're doing fine." He raised the pitcher for another drink, then set it down, and continued.

He lost track of time. The Fire flowed up the rod into the stomach. He estimated what he was taking from Nettle—not mere days, but years. The frost spread from collar to the rod, then extended up Nettle's neck and down his chest. He took off his tunic and spread it over Nettle's chest, hoping to warm him. Then began again.

How much would he need? He had to quicken the thrall. He needed great quantities himself. He pulled and felt the stomach fill.

Nettle blinked.

Argoth looked down at his son's face. Nettle's eyes brimmed. Tears ran down the side of his face. Argoth pulled back his tunic and touched the collar. The tip of his finger froze to it.

He winced. So much. Too much. The frosted skin would die and leave a scar. He was sorry, so sorry, but he couldn't stop yet; he didn't have enough. "Just a little more," he said and began to sing again.

A soft moan escaped Nettle's lips. He turned his head, pain wrenching his face. Then he raised his hand, the one with the clan wrist, and grasped the filtering rod.

The wizardsmeet was wearing off.

Argoth felt Nettle's wrist and sought to gauge how much Fire was left in his boy.

Enough to continue, but less than he'd thought. He'd drained so many of Nettle's days away. But if he didn't get enough the weave would never quicken and it would all be for naught. He saw the pleading in his son's eyes.

"Courage," he said. He could not stop now. To do so would be to waste all that Nettle had given. He gently pried Nettle's fingers off the rod, and began again to sing.

Nettle tensed; his back arched.

Argoth chanted, grief welling up inside him. Perhaps they should have just run, the whole family. But he ground that idea into the dirt like he would a spider. He'd made his decision. He would see it through. Second-guessing, questioning, would only poison his resolve.

He continued to pull, watching his son's slow writhe. "Lords," he said. "Forgive me."

Then Nettle spoke one word in a broken voice. "Father."

Argoth closed his eyes. He could not continue. He would have to succeed or fail with what he had.

"It is at an end," he said, his voice faltering with emotion. "Your test is past."

He quickly removed the rod from the collar and began to chant the form of emptiness. It was a more powerful magic, and the blackness in the rod quickly leached up into the stomach. When he could see no blackness in the tongue or rod, he set the rod, tongue, and stomach aside.

Nettle lay upon the table laboring to breathe, then his breathing calmed and he fell asleep.

Sometimes people died during the rite. But if they made it to this point, they would live. Argoth left the collar around Nettle's neck. It was still black, but if he left it there, the body would quickly draw back the essence captured within.

His mouth tasted like a bitter cucumber, a side effect he'd forgotten about. He put his hands to Nettle's chest, trying to warm it, then added more wood to the fire. When he'd finally cleared the frost, he saw the skin underneath was dead and white, blackened in spots.

Argoth pulled his own tunic off and stretched himself along Nettle's side, warming him with the heat of his own body. He held Nettle close until he could no longer feel the cold of his skin.

When he was satisfied, he clothed Nettle, then sat with the stomach and thrall. He pulled Fire into himself. Then he directed it to the thrall. When he began to worry that he would not have enough for the thrall and himself, he felt the weave quicken in his hands and thrum to life. It was metal, nothing more, but it felt like a living thing, like a snake in his hands.

He did not know what time it was and feared dawn had come, so he put the stomach in his pocket and clambered up to the room above. It was still dark, but he did not know how close morning was. He would have to wait to eat the Fire he'd need from the stomach.

Argoth carried Nettle from the cellar back to the study and laid him upon the couch as if he'd fallen asleep there. But he needed to get something to cover that neck.

He stroked Nettle's hair again. Such a fine, strong young man. He wondered: What would he have become?

Argoth would never know, and the pang of that loss stretched as wide as the sea.

He kissed Nettle's brow, then heard a knocking at the door. He crossed the room to the door and unbarred it. Uram stood there in the darkness holding a pry bar.

"Forgive me, Zu, but we thought something had happened. I've been knocking for quite some time. We need to be going; the Skir Master likes an early start."

"It's been a long night, Captain. My son has fallen ill."

Uram looked beyond Argoth into the room. "I'm sorry to hear that, Zu."

"Captain, if you'll step aside, I shall call my family and bid them farewell. Then I will join you outside."

"Yes, Zu," said Uram, "Of course." He stepped aside.

Argoth retrieved a lap blanket to pull up around Nettle's neck. Serah and the children were already roused. He bid them a teary farewell, then joined Uram and the other dreadmen outside and mounted his horse.

As they rode away, he turned to survey his family and lands one last time. But the night still lay thick and all was dark.

RUBALOTH, THE SKIR Master, stood on the deck of the ship watching the sun rise, the stiff morning breeze at his back. On the main deck half a dozen sailors guided the last pallet of barrels that contained seafire down into the main hold. "Report," he said to Uram.

"Argoth and his escort are eating a fine breakfast at the Shark's Tooth."

"Did he give you trouble?"

"None, Great One. But I did find something odd."

"Oh?"

"His son's neck, Great One. In the early morning I caught the Clansman locking the door of a room. His boy was inside, lying on a bed. The Clansman told me the boy had fallen ill. And the pungent odor of a healing salve did fill the hallway, but underneath it all I thought I smelled the faintest trace of wizardsmeet. It was there one moment and then gone. Still, when my men had everyone outside, I went back in and quietly forced the door. They'd wrapped the boy's neck with fresh linen and plastered it as if for a sore throat. But when I pulled the bandaging back, the skin on the boy's neck had all the markings of a hasty and large harvest."

Rubaloth nodded. He'd been right. These cursed Clansmen. Another scion from a vanquished line no doubt wielding old magics. Was he the one who had wrested Lumen from the Glory? If so, this could be tricky. But Rubaloth savored the challenge.

"When we're a few miles from shore," he said, "you will quietly search all his belongings."

Uram bowed. "I shall, Great One."

Yes, he'd have to be careful. But this Captain Argoth would soon find he was not the only one prepared for battle.

35.

PURSUIT

Sugar ran out of the cave into the light. She considered running back downhill to escape whatever it was coming at her in the inky dark of the cave, but because that was her first choice, she rejected it. It would expect her to run downhill; it would expect her to hide somewhere away from the cave, perhaps in the waters of the swamp. There was no way she could get far by trying to steal away quietly. Her very footfalls would make her an easy mark.

No, she wouldn't run. She looked around for a place to hide close by and spotted one above the mouth of the cave behind an outcropping of rock. She didn't know if it was big enough to hide her, but it would have to do.

Quickly, carefully, she moved away from the mouth and climbed up the small ridge that ran along the brow of the cave.

Something splashed through water just inside the mouth of the cave.

She pulled herself up the last few feet and slid behind the rock. But she didn't have time to lie down, for the beast burst into view below her. It took a number of steps then stopped, surveying the slope below.

The creature stood like a man of freakish proportions. Heavy-limbed, wide, maybe seven feet tall, with a small, odd-shaped head. It was immense. She thought she saw an ear on the side of its head, but it was too ragged to tell exactly what it was. Shaggy grass grew unevenly over the whole of its body. Along its shoulder and back clung a large swath of blackened, ashy tufts and blades. Yet below the burned part, about where a man's ribs would end, grew a patch of what appeared to be green grass mixed with the small white flowers of creeping wood sorrel.

If it turned around and looked up, it would see her. But she didn't dare crouch, didn't dare make adjustments for fear of making even the smallest of sounds.

The creature moved slightly and made a hideous sound that froze her spine.

It moved again. Again, the awful sound, and Sugar realized it was the intake of breath. A horrid gasp. Loud, like a man suffering from the black lung.

Was it trying to scent her?

The air about her was still, no morning updrafts or crosswinds. No downdrafts. The breeze in the cave blew outward, and so the thing would not have smelled her in there. But that also meant the breeze might, at this very moment, be carrying the scent that pooled about her.

A crack sounded from the woods below.

The creature turned to it.

Heartbeats pounded in her ears.

Then the thing moved, loping downhill in the direction of the sound, the grass about its body jolting with every stride.

Sugar realized she'd been holding her breath and gasped for air.

The creature leapt into the air, clearing a large tangle, and landed heavily on the other side. Two more strides, and then it was nothing but a flash through the trunks of the trees.

She gauged the distance it had covered in the few breaths since it had first moved. Never in her life could she have outrun it.

The rustling of a tree sounded from below, and she knew when it found nothing below, when it smelled her trail growing stale, it would come back.

Her legs shouted out for her to run, but she fought it. Sugar turned and carefully, oh, so carefully began to ascend the hill. She would find her escape on the other side, or not at all.

HUNGER BACKTRACKED FOR about a quarter of a mile along the trail he'd taken earlier and then stopped under a cluster of tall pines. He had seen nothing. Heard nothing but a bunch of noisy grayfans. He would find nothing along this trail. The scent had been stronger back at the cave. He turned and began to walk back, looking, listening for anything at all.

He came to the tree in which the grayfans sat. He searched the ground and then looked up. It didn't take long before he found it: one rotted branch hanging at a broken angle. Noisy birds cracking branches—that's what he'd chased after. Or maybe some deer. It could have been anything that had made the noise earlier.

He cursed himself, crouched down on all fours, and began to follow the scent more closely. It was a woman; he could smell that.

Back up the slope he went, making sure to check for trails of scent leading away from this one. But he found none. He stood at the mouth of the cave, and could smell her in there. Could he have run by her in his haste? He followed her trail in, but found it ended not far inside.

If he'd run by, then she had come back out, but she hadn't run downhill. No, Hunger examined the area around the mouth of the cave and found her scent clinging to the rock. He followed it up to a ridge and found a pool of her scent. She had stopped here. She could have been squatting right there when he'd run downhill like a fool.

But it didn't matter. He had her scent and her trail. He would catch the wily thing and bring her back. He was the Mother's now; his family depended on it.

He felt good to have such a clear purpose. He felt as if a burden had been lifted. Serving the Mother wasn't such a bad thing after all.

Hunger followed the woman's trail, sometimes loping on two limbs, sometimes staying close to the ground on all fours. He followed it up over the crest of the hill and back down into the valley on the other side and to the banks of a marshy river.

Wily, she was. But there were some parts of a person's scent that did not sink into the depths. Some of it hung in the very air. Oh, water made it harder to track. Sometimes it flowed away at great speeds, erasing all traces of a trail, but not this sluggish river, this half marsh. He got down on all fours and strode out into the water and smelled her on the surface. The scent was faint, but it was thick enough to follow.

Then he lost it. She had fallen or dived under and swam. He searched in widening circles around the area where he last smelled her, and in a short time found her again and followed her to the far bank.

He began to lope, and her scent grew with every step. Fresher, stronger. Through the woods he ran, the dampness there and the cover from the sun keeping her trail together, making her as easy to follow as a slow parade of cattle.

Stronger and stronger it grew until he broke from the woods upon a small farmstead.

Hunger paused and watched. A small herd of brown-and-white milk goats grazed in a pasture beyond the house. The scent was strong here. Exceedingly strong.

He followed the woman's trail to the barn. The doors stood open and he strode inside and stopped. He smelled horse and hay and harness. He smelled her as if she were standing in front of him.

He had her, had her trapped in this barn like a mouse in a box.

Hunger closed the doors to the tidy barn behind him. There was a stall and a loft of hay. He looked in the stall and found it empty. She was in the hay in the loft then.

He leapt to the loft and landed in a crouch, watiting for her to try to run by him. He waited. Nothing. He kicked through the hay, reached in to the deepest parts. But she wasn't there.

Hunger cursed and walked back out and circled the barn. Only then did he realize what had happened. He breathed in deeply to smell it for sure—she'd taken the horse.

He followed the scent a number of paces down to the trail that led from this house.

She'd taken the horse and was at this very moment trotting away. He looked at the hoofprints. She was not galloping. Not that woman. She had shown herself too smart for that.

Hunger almost chased after her, but he stopped himself. He could match the speed of a horse, but not for long. He needed food. He would fail along the way if he didn't replenish his Fire.

He pushed the door to the house open and found only a table and an orange cat hiding under a chair, looking up at him in fear. An old couple must live here. He saw one pair of large, muddy, wooden clogs next to the door. Or maybe it wasn't a couple. Maybe it was just an old man and his cat.

He left the house and cat and went to the pasture. The brown-and-white goats scattered at his coming, but they were no match for his speed. He caught one whose horns had split into four curls and devoured its Fire and soul. It was not enough, and he chased down three others, leaving their bodies lying on the chewed grass.

When he'd drained the last one and felt satisfied, he stood. The power surged in his limbs. The scent of the horse mixed with the female still lay thick along the road. The sun and wind would disperse it. But not before he caught her.

36.

CROSSROAD

Talen squatted with Legs behind a tangle of blackberry brambles that grew at the wood's edge. In front of them a small orchard of pear trees glistened in the moonlight. At the end of one of the rows and across a path stood Uncle Argoth's home. And patrolling the grounds about the house were three Lions of Mokad, dreadmen all.

Talen had his bow and more than twenty arrows. He might be able to pin three regular soldiers down, might even be able to take out one of these Lions if his aim was true and the arrow took the man in a vital part, but the others would not stay put. And once they entered the woods, his arrows would be worth nothing.

So Talen sat and waited, and while he waited he practiced what River had taught him, to open and close himself. To pour out Fire and to stop it up. He could still feel the memory of suffocating, of her pressing into his being. And he wondered if what he did at this very moment was Slethery.

"He's not coming," whispered Legs. "It's past time."

What did this boy do—count the seconds? "Since when do the blind know what time it is?" asked Talen.

"The mosquitoes have begun to rise. The mice and deer are moving. Morning's coming."

Mice and mosquitoes? He realized he had indeed just shooed away a mosquito. He looked to the eastern horizon and saw the faintest lightening of the sky over the peaks of the mountains. The boy was right.

"So you're not blind?" asked Talen.

"I'm blind. I just pay attention."

Talen grunted. What had happened to Nettle? Was he sleeping peacefully, knowing to come out would only reveal them, or was he on some table being put to the question?

"What else have you paid attention to besides deer and mice?" asked Talen.

"Nothing," said Legs. "If the dreadmen know we're here, then they don't care."

"Or they're waiting for daylight to get a good look at us. Give me your hand," said Talen. "It's time for us to go."

"You're just going to leave him?"

"I don't see that we have much choice," said Talen. "Besides, Uncle Argoth's with him."

"Maybe they have him too," whispered Legs.

"Then our only hope is to muster the rest of this . . . Order." "Nest" is what he wanted to say. But he just could not apply that term to Da, River, and Ke. He didn't know what terms to use. Sleth, good soul-eaters, bad Divines—it was all a bewildering mess.

He took Legs's hand and picked his way carefully down the line of brambles. The forest canopy here was thick, and as a result, squelched almost all growth on the forest floor. Still, he had to keep an eye out for branches.

They passed a fat chestnut and Legs pulled on Talen's hand. "There's something dead here."

Talen paused and smelled the air. Some carcass was

indeed rotting nearby. The leaves off to their left suddenly rustled.

Talen froze. The last thing he wanted was to stumble upon some bear's or wildcat's kill. But then, Argoth had dogs, and they would have smelled this out long ago. They would have chased off any cat or bear except he hadn't seen or heard Argoth's dogs.

The leaves rustled again.

Whatever made the noise, it was something smaller than a bear or wildcat, a weasel or badger perhaps. Talen's heart stopped palpitating.

He realized he hadn't seen or heard Blue or Queen last night. Where had his dogs been? They'd often go hunting in the evenings, but they never stayed away. They always came home before it got too late. Had they gone to River's aid?

He thought of River running out to draw that thing and a gloom descended upon him. Da had fought it to no avail. It had eluded the cohorts of the fortress. Surely, one girl, even with River's talents, could not best it. He wanted more than ever to get to the Creek Widow's to see if River had arrived. They needed to move faster.

"This way," he whispered to Legs and pulled on his hand. "We're going to take the roads."

"Won't that be risky?" asked Legs.

"Yes, but I don't know the woods in these parts like I do at home. We'll be stumbling about. If we're going to sneak, I want to do it quickly."

They left the line of bramble and, as carefully as they could, took a direct route to the road that cut like a pale ribbon through the dark woods. When they came to the road's edge, they stood in the darkness of the forest for some time watching and listening. When Talen was satisfied they were alone, he led Legs out into the moonlight. Hand in hand they went, Legs keeping his other hand out in front of him so something didn't smack him in the face. Down the hill they walked, to the first crossroads, a left, over a muddy brook, around the bend where a woodikin had been spotted last year, and along the Misty Falls trail.

Their grip became wet with sweat. "Change hands," said Talen. He released his grip and switched his bow to the other hand.

"We'll go faster if you just give me a stick," said Legs.

"I don't doubt it," said Talen. "But the last thing we need is for someone to hear you rattling along. Change hands."

Talen couldn't quite believe what River had told him earlier. In fact, the whole incident with the beast was unreal. But her comments about him were more disturbing. So he could handle astonishing amounts of Fire, so what? And the whole business about Mother and the wisterwives, her pouring out her life into him and her odd comment about him needing a flaw. What did it all mean? A hundred questions coursed through his mind. But all of them came back to the fact that he was walking a lonely road in the wee hours of the morning, holding hands with this hatchling like a lover.

"So did your mother teach you anything about the black arts?"

"They're not black," said Legs.

"No, of course not. There's just that ragged grassman killing people left and right and chasing down our women. But other than that, I'm sure the whole business is as pure as the morning's dew. So, did she teach you anything?"

"She taught me that some people are idiots," said Legs.

Talen looked down at the boy and his wild hair. "A lot of squeak for a little man. Look, you and I are in the same boat, heading down the same river toward the same rapids. Besides, having been worked on by not only my father and my mother, but now also my loving sister, I suppose I'm more hatchling than you."

And it was true. Lords and lice, what would the bailiff say now?

They took another few steps in silence.

"Do you trust your sister and father?" Legs asked.

"Do you trust yours?"

"I'm blind," he said. "I've had to trust them all my life."

"So it doesn't bother you that your mother is Sleth?"

"'Sleth' isn't the word we use," said Legs. "Weren't you listening?"

Talen looked at Legs again. Squeak indeed. "Whatever they're called. The Order then." And was that just another lie? They'd lied to him all this time. Years of lying. And if they could hide such a huge mountain of stinking cess, then they could lie about anything.

"Your mother lied," said Talen.

"Yes, she did," said Legs. "But everyone lies."

"No, they don't."

"Yes, they do. You're telling me a Mokaddian hasn't ever pushed ahead of you in some line, and you nodded politely, but inside you were all resentment?"

That wasn't a lie. That was avoiding a beating. Of course, it wasn't the truth either. He wondered, was it a lie to swallow your tears when you got hurt so others didn't think you a child? Was it a lie to act bravely when facing an enemy, even when you wanted to run? Maybe everyone did lie. Maybe the kinds of lies you told defined who you were. And what did it say when the lies were as monstrous as the ones his family kept?

"You asked me if I was bothered," Legs said. "Yes. But mostly I just feel a crushing nothing where my da used to be. I feel like I've taken a step where I thought ground was, but there's nothing there. And I'm falling"—His voice grew small, as if he'd curled in on himself—"I'm falling. And I have no idea how I'm going to land, or if I'm going to break my neck."

That was exactly how it felt, Talen thought. "My da says Sparrow was a great man."

"He was," said Legs. "He was everything."

They walked a few dozen yards farther, and when they came to the turnoff that led to the Creek Widow's, Talen stopped.

"What are we doing?" asked Legs.

"I'm getting my bearings," said Talen. "Give me a moment."

If they continued on the current trail, they'd eventually arrive in Whitecliff. And that was the trail he should take. Everyone knew Sleth twisted things. If his family could be redeemed, then only a Divine could do it. But if they couldn't be redeemed, then they would only spread the poison of these arts to others. He should follow the trail to Whitecliff, to the first official he could find and ask for the Skir Master. He should offer his services to inform on the activities of this Order. After all, who better than a trusted family member? And if they tortured and killed him, what of it? He'd done his duty.

Dawn was coming. It was light enough for him to see quite a distance down the path. He could be in Whitecliff before some of the rich there took their breakfast.

But what if River was telling the truth?

What if?

Following a trusted face—that was how one lost his bearings. You hesitated, wanting to show mercy and patience, wanting to give people the benefit of the doubt, and soon enough you've lost all perspective. Soon enough you want justice to prevail only when it is convenient, and then not at all, for by that time your idea of right and wrong is so warped it cannot serve as a standard. Perhaps the only defense against the dark ones was a heart of stone. A heart so hard with righteousness it could carry through the murder of those it loved most.

No wonder the Divines destroyed whole families.

He knew where his duty lay. He should march this blind boy right into the hands of those who sought him.

Still, despite the secrets River had revealed, there wasn't an evil bone in her body. Nor in Da's. Or even Ke's. This he knew. Of course, that didn't mean they couldn't have made an honest mistake joining this Order. It didn't mean they couldn't have been coerced.

But if what River had said was true, if the Divines really were nothing more than a guild that had chased away all competition, then he'd be making the biggest error of his life. Was it possible that the world was as topsy-turvy as she described, with Divines hunting down those who encroached on their monopoly like greedy merchants and the Creators giving vast powers to commoners?

It didn't explain the grassman or all the horrifying stories of soul-eaters. But then, it did explain how some Divines fell from grace.

She could be right, even if the possibility was remote.

Talen looked down the road to Whitecliff again.

He owed it to River to give her a chance. He owed it to Da and Ke and Mother. To Uncle Argoth.

It was wicked, but he couldn't see a better way. Besides, maybe it was his task to walk into the heart of the black forest in which they were lost, find them, and bring them back from shadows and into the light.

He sighed and shook his head. This whole situation was unreal—a tavern story headed for a dark end. He looked down at Legs. "So you don't know any tricks? No bloody rites? It's just me and you out here on our own?"

"I can sing you a ditty about a one-legged slave," said Legs.

"Your mother put half an army to flight and that's all you've got?"

"I can do this," Legs said. He looked up at Talen, the whites of his eyes rolling in their sockets.

He'd seen that before, and it was even more unnerving in the early morning twilight. "Right," said Talen. "When we want to make our enemies lose their breakfast, we'll bring you in."

"And what have you got?"

"I've got my bow," said Talen. "I've got my brains. They'll get us to the Creek Widow's. And maybe there we'll find some clarity."

Legs cocked his head and held his hand up for Talen to be silent.

Talen looked around. The woods about them were dark and deep.

"Somebody's coming," Legs whispered.

Talen listened. At first there was nothing, and then he heard the soft thud of men running on dirt, running down the path that led to the Creek Widow's.

"Off the road," Talen said. He grabbed Legs's hand. "Quick." The road here was bordered by a few tall pines and some beech, which meant there wasn't a whole lot of cover. But if they could get fifty paces in, the trunks of the trees would hide them.

They didn't get fifty paces before three Shoka appeared on the road. They'd barely gotten more than fifteen. There were two bowmen and a spearman. The Shoka stopped, and Talen halted Legs.

"You two take that side," one of bowmen said. "We don't want to proclaim our presence."

None of these three looked to be much older than Talen. One of the bowmen and the young one with a short spear stepped into the woods on the far side of the road. The one who had spoken walked five paces in on Talen's side. Not straight in front of Talen, but at a slight diagonal from where he and Legs stood. He stopped at the trunk of a fallen pine, knocked off the nub of a branch, then sat himself down.

He was close enough that Talen could have pinged him in the head if he were the target of a muskmelon seed-spitting contest.

Talen carefully took one step back and a twig popped underneath him. He froze.

The Shoka on the pine log turned his head slightly as if trying to listen.

By the Goat King's hairy arse, Talen thought. He's going to turn, and I've got my bow in the wrong hand.

37.

SLETH

Talen held still. The seconds stretched into a minute, maybe two. Then the Shoka on the pine turned his attention back to the road.

Talen didn't dare take another step. He didn't even dare switch his bow to the other hand. Movement drew the eye. And even though it was yet dark, if he moved too quickly the two across the way would see him. He knew that because he could see them even now.

But he and Legs had to move. Right now, there was still enough darkness in the woods to obscure them. However, in a half an hour the morning would lighten most of the shadows and they would be standing there as plain as day for anyone who just happened to take a gander in their direction.

Slowly, he couldn't move faster than a snail, Talen reached back with one bare foot to feel the forest floor for a likely spot. He moved a twig aside with his toe and transferred his weight. He turned his head downwards so his voice wouldn't carry. He whispered one word for every few heartbeats. "Slow," he said. "Slow."

Legs turned his head ever so slightly to hear him better.

"Feel. Your. Way. Back," he said. "Slow. Pause. Slow."

Legs reached back with his bare foot, found a spot. They moved in miniscule increments. Stopping, moving an inch, stopping, moving again.

A squirrel chittered off to Talen's right.

Sweat ran down his back.

He moved aside dry leaves with his toes. A mosquito buzzed him. It landed on his cheek, a large smudge at the bottom of his vision. He moved an inch. Stopped. Moved another. He felt the pinprick. He continued to move. Pause. Move. The bug buzzed away with its stolen treasure.

This was taking too long. The morning light was coming too fast. He could see the two Shoka on the other side of the road well enough to make out the colored bands on their arrows. Talen glanced out of the side of his eye. At this pace they weren't going to make it.

The hoofbeats of a galloping horse sounded along the road. The Shoka stood. Moved forward to the edge of the tree line and looked up the road.

"Slowly," Talen said.

In moments, Talen spotted the rider through the trunks of the trees. He rode a tan horse. The three Shoka stepped out onto the road, bows and spears pointed at the horseman. The man brought his horse to halt. It was another Shoka, wearing the green-patterned sash of that clan.

"Hoy," the man said.

The three Shoka must have recognized him, for they lowered their weapons.

"Move," Talen whispered. He took another step, then another.

"Spread the word," the horseman said. "The hatchlings have been spotted. Prunes saw them with his own eyes."

"Where?" one of the Shoka asked.

The tan horse pulled on the reins, trying to get its head. "At the farm of Hogan the Koramite."

Wonderful, Talen thought. Just wonderful. He knew Prunes. The man had been one of those the bailiff had brought with him to search the farm. Which meant the bailiff must have posted a watch.

They should have thought of that. They should have scouted the woods. For those Fir-Noy armsmen, if for nothing else.

There was an enormous beech with a trunk a few feet in diameter only a few paces away. If they could get behind that, it would hide them. "To your left," Talen whispered.

"There's worse," the rider said. "That grass monster from Whitecliff was with them. It killed Gid. Twisted him up like a rag. The bailiff's calling a full muster. Half a family's men to stand their watches, the other half are needed in Stag Home."

"There's another nine men down the trail," one of the Shoka said. "We've got dogs."

"Bring them or keep them with you. We've already sent out for five teams of hounds to follow trails in and out of that place. Now, out of my way. I'm off to Lord Shim."

The rider urged his mount forward. The three Shoka stepped aside to let him through.

Talen and Legs were almost to the beech. One more step.

The rider thundered away.

One of the bowmen turned and sprinted back down the

path he'd first arrived on, probably to spread the word to those nine other men.

Talen took the last step and brought Legs with him.

He put his back flat up against the trunk and held his breath. He shifted just a bit to make sure both of them were completely behind the tree. Legs stood up against him, his hair bushing Talen's chin.

Dogs, Talen thought. Not only did he have to escape with a blind boy in tow, but now he had to deal with dogs.

Before noon today everyone in Talen's family would be famous. And the bailiff wouldn't give them an easy pass this time. They'd done more than make a fool of him. They'd stabbed him in the back. No, there would be no easy pass. The bailiff would come with those ice-cold eyes and there would be no deliverance.

Talen thought of Da in the hands of the Mokaddian Council. This news was not going to help him there.

Resentment began to build in Talen again. If only Legs and that Sugar girl hadn't shown up. Why couldn't they have gone to some other member of this Sleth nest? Why couldn't Da have turned them away?

He couldn't because he wouldn't. That was Da. And even if he had, sooner or later something would have happened. You can't sow deceit and not expect to eventually reap its bitter fruit. But all that didn't matter anyway—assigning blame wouldn't get him out of this mess.

They had to get to the Creek Widow's. They had to get there quickly. Talen counted to six hundred. His heart beat like a drum in his ears. He measured his breaths.

The squirrel they'd heard earlier chittered again in its tree.

Slowly, Talen turned around so he was facing the beech. Then he leaned ever so slowly until he could just peer around the side of the smooth trunk.

Both of the remaining two Shoka were in the woods on

this side of the road. They were crouched over, slowly moving forward, weapons at the ready. The bowman carefully stepped over the fallen pine where the third Shoka had been sitting. They were listening, watching the woods.

Talen pulled back.

By all that was holy! They must have caught something of his and Legs's last quick move to the beech. But they obviously hadn't seen the movement clearly enough, or they would have been focused on the exact tree.

Up ahead was a line of clumped-up shorter pines and growth. If they could get behind that greenery, they'd be hidden. Talen took Legs's hand. "Run," he said.

They ran, but it was clear that running wasn't going to get them very far. Legs stumbled. Then he cried out and stumbled again. Talen gripped Legs's hand tighter and hauled him to his feet.

The Shoka shouted and called for them to stop, but Talen kept moving until he and Legs skirted the end of the clump and were well behind the thick boughs. This small line of pines ran to the dry bed of a brook. And while the undergrowth on the short banks of the brook might be tall enough to give them some cover, there was no way he and Legs could outrun the two Shoka. They'd corner them soon enough.

"Show yourselves," one of the Shoka called.

There was no time to dither. "Come on," Talen said. "Just a little farther."

He had a plan. He doubted it would work. But something at this point was better than nothing. The ground here was slightly rocky. He couldn't imagine running on it blind. But that's what had to happen despite the sharp edges of the rocks and branches.

Legs stumbled once more on the way to the dry brook bed, but he did not cry out. He did not reveal their position.

"I want you to keep low and move down this dry brook bed. I need you to draw their attention."

"You're leaving?"

He couldn't squat here and jabber. "Just keep their attention." Talen rose and dashed back to the line of pines. He needed to get on the other side so he could circle around behind the two Shoka. Of course, this wouldn't work if the Shoka had decided to split up.

Just before he got to the other side, Talen stopped. He looked down the edge of the line of trees. Nobody was there. Maybe they ran back to the road for help. That would give him and Legs time. But that hope was short-lived.

"Stop and show yourself," one of the Shoka called. "We see you there in the brook."

"I'm nobody of any account!" Legs shouted out.

"Then stand and show us who you are."

Good, Talen thought. They didn't know they hadn't cornered two hatchlings. Not yet. He slipped to the far side of the line of trees and carefully made his way down the line.

"Promise you won't hurt me," said Legs.

"We'll promise you nothing."

Talen had his arrow nocked, a second in his bow hand.

"I'm going to stand up," said Legs.

Talen took a few more steps and realized that his way was clear from this side of the pines. He could be across the road and into the woods on the other side before these Shoka realized their mistake. He could leave Legs and save himself. Claim he'd been entranced by the hatchlings, taken prisoner after their monster had attacked his farm.

"There were two of you," said a Shoka. "Where's the other?"

"He won't stand up," said Legs.

"Get up," the Shoka commanded. "Or we'll shoot your friend. And then we'll hunt you down and shoot you."

"Stand up," Legs pleaded. "They're going to shoot me."

The little man was quite the actor. And under the threat of death to boot.

Talen took a breath to brace himself, then he quietly continued down the line and turned the corner.

The Shoka with the bow stood only a few paces away, his back to Talen. His bow was drawn, the arrow pointed at Legs. The boy with the short spear was moving up and to the right, probably trying to flank Legs and his imaginary friend. Legs stood a few yards from where Talen had left him, his whole torso rising above the banks of the brook bed

"Stand up!" Legs said. He flailed his arms as if Talen were hunkered down right next to him.

Talen took a careful step. Then another. He raised his bow. Took another step reaching out with his toes.

"This is your last warning!" said the Shoka. He pulled the arrow back the last few inches to his cheek.

Talen recognized him. He'd competed with him before in the Shoka practice musters. He was young, even if he did have the clan tattoo on his wrist.

"Put the bow down," said Talen.

The Shoka startled and twisted to look at Talen.

Talen took the last step and brought the sharp tip of his iron arrow point to the young man's neck. "No," said Talen. "You're not quick enough. Don't even think about it."

The bowman's eyes went wide with fear. "You," he said. Then the fear was joined by something else. A decision?

The bowman's aim had been altered, and Talen didn't want him to get it back. "Legs, get down."

Legs dropped back into the bed of the brook.

"Nobody needs to get hurt," said Talen. "Just toss your weapons."

Neither Shoka moved.

"You know who I am," said Talen. "I could have drilled both of you with an arrow while you were doing your sneaking. And I will if you don't listen to me."

"You're going to have to kill me, half-breed," said the bowman. He didn't say this in defiance or anger. He said it as if resolved to his fate, and Talen gave him points for bravery.

"No," said Legs. "We've got something else that will do that for us."

The bowman's eyes widened enough to reveal his fear.

"He can squish up both of you like rags," said Legs.

Huh, Talen thought, that was too much squeak. It was one thing to threaten a Mokaddian. It was quite another to claim they had some Sleth monster on a leash. This mire just got deeper and deeper.

The boy tossed his short spear aside. "Don't hurt us."

"Put your bow down," said Talen.

For one brief moment Talen thought he was going to have to kill the Shoka. He didn't want to. He had nothing against him. And it would do their cause no good to add another Mokaddian death to it. Talen could see the calculation in the Shoka's face. Then he relented. He released his draw, then dropped the bow and arrow onto the pine needles at his feet.

"Knives too," said Talen.

Both Shoka unlooped the knives at their waists and cast them aside.

"On your bellies over there," Talen said and pointed to a flat spot of ground.

Legs decided that was the time to step out of the brook bed. When he got to the top of the short bank, he walked, both hands in front of him, one high, one low.

"He's the blind one," the bowman said.

"Indeed, he is," said Talen. "Now move."

They didn't have much time. The third Shoka could be returning this very moment to the road. He might have his dogs with him. Nevertheless, he waited for the two Shoka to move. By the time they were on their bellies, he stood by the Shoka's bow.

"Legs," he called. "Unstring this bow at my feet. We're going to tie them up."

FIFTEEN MINUTES LATER Talen and Legs were making their way toward moving water. There was at least one river and two creeks between them and the Widow's and they'd have to use all three now that dogs might be involved.

The Shoka's bow string hadn't been long enough to bind both Shoka to different trees. So Legs had cut two strips off his tunic to use as rope and two more to use as gags.

"Do you think they will stay put?" asked Legs.

"Oh, I think your little eye show gave them quite a scare." That and the fact that he'd married his freaky eye-rolling with odd gaggings and contortions. It was quite an effective method to cow the two so they didn't try anything stupid while Legs tied them up. It had almost put Talen himself on the run.

And when the one Shoka had asked what was happening, Talen had played it up. And why not? How could the story get any worse? His family had already been caught harboring the hatchlings. They'd already been connected to the monster. And, despite the usefulness of claiming the hatchlings had enchanted them to do their bidding, there was no one else in the family who might be tempted to say such a thing. Truth be told, even he wasn't going to give into that. Besides, they needed time. An hour's head start might not even be enough if the dogs came.

"You know full well what he's doing," Talen had said.

The Shoka had taken it, as intended, for Slethery. And then the bright idea had come to Talen to say he believed Legs was calling the monster to watch them, to make sure they didn't run.

Oh, yes. Talen was in this up to his neck.

Now the question was not if he was going to die. It was only, when? And would it include a lot of torture?

He thought of Da in Whitecliff. Surely, Uncle Argoth would protect him. Surely, Uncle Argoth would be able to convince Lord Shim. Because Talen certainly wasn't helping him any.

Talen stopped before a clump of poison ivy. "We need to move faster." Much faster. They needed to get to the first creek and wash their trail away. Then they needed to get to the river. Maybe float a bit.

"I can't," said Legs.

No, he couldn't. His bare feet were already bloody in three places.

"Too bad you really can't call that monster," Talen said and unstrung his bow. He put the string in an oiled leather pouch that hung from his quiver and told Legs to hold the bow staff. "Raise your arm, brother Sleth. You're going across my shoulders."

Legs raised one arm.

Talen took it by the wrist, bent low, grabbed Legs's ankle with his other hand, and stood up straight.

"Right," he said. It was like lugging a sack of beets. That's all this was. He adjusted Legs to more evenly distribute his weight. Then he plodded forward, around the clump of ivy, over a flat of rock, and then on to a game trail no wider than his foot.

38

TRAPS

Argoth ate at the Shark's Tooth like a starved man. Eggs, sausage, thick cream on cherry biscuits. He stopped a serving maid as she walked by. "A bit of salted lard," he said.

She bowed and hurried away. Lard, suet, butter, or cream—it didn't matter. What Argoth needed was great quantities of bread and fat, for that was what softened the hunger that would come when he multiplied himself.

The sun had not yet risen, but the Skir Master wanted an early start. "Is the Captain easy at sea?" asked Uram.

"I regularly run the dreadman's course, including the two-mile swim," said Argoth. "And these are not tropical waters." He bit into a juicy link of sausage.

"An admirable habit," said Uram.

"Indeed," said Argoth. "One can do worse than modeling the diet and activity of dreadmen like yourself."

"But what about the captain's stomach? Fatty foods on a rolling ship has laid low the strongest of men."

A man spoke from behind in a dry voice. "There's no need to worry, Zu. Lord Iron Guts will not lose his breakfast."

Shim stood holding a mug of ale, a wide grin cracking his leather face.

Argoth considered Shim for a moment, but he saw no sign that the man had come to betray him.

"Some lords prove their stamina by drinking the hardiest of men under the table. Not Lord Porkslop, he buries them with a mountain of food."

"Blighter," said Argoth with a mouthful of eggs. "I didn't see you arrive."

"Of course, not," said Shim. "Not with a plate of sizzling hog-tail sausages calling you like a lover."

Argoth grunted, then patted the stool next to him.

Shim sat with his mug. "Captain," he said to Uram. "Have you ever seen the like?"

"He does have a prodigious appetite."

"Prodigious? I dare say Argoth's stomach is by itself a force of nature. It is wise to keep all fingers outside the range of his fork."

Argoth reached over and grabbed Shim's mug. "If you don't mind?"

"I do."

But Argoth slipped it away, quaffed three gulps, then set it back down in front of Shim. "Nothing like a bit of ale with your eggs, eh?"

Shim looked into his mug. "Or a bit of eggs *in* the ale."

It was like it had been; this was the man he loved, and Argoth laughed. In front of Uram, they discussed the defenses of the land, who would take Argoth's place. But when they stepped out of the Shark's Tooth onto High Street and began to walk down the cobblestone street to the wharves, Shim turned serious.

"I received a love letter," he said.

"Oh?" asked Argoth.

"Yes, they always want some proclamation, some proof. I daresay I don't know whether to write a stinging rebuke or show the sender some of my family history."

Shim reached into his coat. He retrieved an object, and then grasped Argoth's hand and placed it in it. "My great-great-grandfather made that."

Argoth glanced down at it and closed his hand again. It was a weave, an ancient dead thing that looked like it should hang from a necklace, but a weave neverthe-less.

Shim put his arm around Argoth like a friend. "Have I proven my love?"

Shim was not a dreadman. That meant this weave was his or one loaned from another. In either case, it meant he had placed himself in grave danger because possessing such a thing was a crime punishable by death. Unless, of course, he was part of this Skir Master's plot.

Argoth looked into his friend's face, but found no de-ception. It was a risk to trust him. He hadn't been proven properly. But then this wasn't a proper situation either. Besides, Shim had revealed his character through years of friendship.

Argoth sucked his teeth to get the last morsels out; a cart with a load of fish passed them going up the hill. Argoth turned to see the dreadman following them and passed the weave back.

"You don't need it?"

"No," said Argoth. "But you will. What else did Grand-father pass down?"

"Almost nothing."

"Then you and I are going to have a long talk when I get back."

"You're making me nervous," said Shim. "The streets are choking with the Crab's men. I don't think we have that kind of time."

"Such little faith," said Argoth. "You worry about the tactics. I'll worry about the strategy."

Shim rolled his eyes. "I know what you're doing."

"Oh?"

"I appreciate the sentiment, but now's not a time to pro-tect your friends by keeping them in the dark."

"Yes, it is. Especially if I don't return."

"Well, then let's hope our blueberry Divine is as ineffectual as he seems."

"Ineffectual?"

"You haven't heard?"

Argoth shrugged.

Shim pointed at the Skir Master's chaser. "Look."

The chaser stood out from the other merchant ships and galleys like a doe amid a herd of goats. The *Ardent* was a special ship; she stretched twice as long as she was wide, fine-lined, and able to set an amazing amount of sail. Half a dozen sailors scrambled up the rigging of the two masts. And then Argoth saw it. "Why isn't she rigged with square sails?" A Skir Master's ship didn't need fore and aft rigging to sail close to the wind. You didn't tack in a skir ship. You ran on an acre of square canvas, rigged with wide studding sails on booms to both sides of each of the main sails. You ran like a dolphin in the wake of the creature's wind.

"The old skir died on the voyage over."

"Died?"

"That's what's been noising about. Took them two weeks longer than planned to get here."

"Died," said Argoth. That was good news indeed.

"And he couldn't catch another," said Shim. "Mokad has grown weak."

They reached the bottom of the street and proceeded along the docks. Two porters rolled a fat barrel onto a loading pallet next to a merchant ship. Another tried to steady a nervous mule that powered the boom to move that pallet. In front of the next ship, an officer inspected a handcart loaded with wicker cages full of russet chickens. A whistle sounded, and a group of boys, young sailors who had been standing in a cluster on the wharf, strode to the gangplank. One of them lingered, letting a

426 • JOHN BROWN

girl with dark hair tie a bright blue scarf about his neck. A gull standing on a post next to them squawked, then launched itself just over the tops of the crowds and wheeled past the *Ardent*.

Argoth pushed through the crowd and stood before the gangplank, the water slapping at the wood posts and the ship's hull. The hull gleamed. It was said that the Skir Master had his slaves scrape and wax the hull between every voyage to keep her fast.

She was painted in a dull gray. There were no striped sails. A stealthy ship. The only bright colors were the blue, yellow, and red eyes painted on the prow and each of the oar paddles.

Such eyes, it was believed by sailors, helped a ship avoid shoals and sandbars. But they were also a sign of the Glory of Mokad. I can see you, those eyes said, I am with you, via my servants, even upon the waters and in far lands. To some this gave comfort. To others it was a warning.

A large crowd clustered about Argoth. Bosser, the Prime, and others stood among them.

Bosser smoothed his long mustache, watching the last of the fire lances swing aboard. "This is madness."

"Indeed," said Argoth. "I wish the Skir Master had come to stay. But I do what I am bid."

"They are cutting us off," said the Prime.

"But you have the new weaves."

"Gah," said Bosser. "It's like giving a starving man one withered fig."

They talked of business then: what manner of defense they could prepare along the rivers, and how long it would take to cast more fire lances. Then the captain had the mate call all aboard, and he bid the warlords farewell.

Argoth's quarters lay in the stern under the aftercastle, but he did not inspect them. Instead he turned to those on the docks. A number of the men he commanded had joined the crowd. One fellow suggested that now perhaps was the time to strike a deal for one of Argoth's daughters. Argoth shouted out that Serah would drive a much harder bargain than he. The crowd laughed, but Argoth worried, wondering if she'd left yet.

Then it all came to an end. The first mate called for the gangplank to be removed and the moorings untied. Then the oarsmen on the starboard side shoved the ship away from the dock. A twelve-man rowboat pulled them away from the dock. Then the captain called for the oars. The deck held benches for thirty oars, fifteen to a side, each with two men on them. A drummer, seated in the stern, played a short rhythm and the oarsmen in unison dipped their oars. The drummer played a different rhythm and the oarsmen set themselves. Another tap to the light drum, and the men pulled. The taps continued and the oarsmen pulled in time to them, the eyes dipping in and out of the water.

When they cleared the docks and turned the ship, the captain ordered the oars back and a number of the sails unfurled. The men climbed the rigging and dropped the canvas. It snapped in the wind, filled, then the *Ardent* leaned and leapt forward under his feet.

Argoth turned and looked back. The fortress standing upon the hill with the morning sun gleaming off its towers and walls, the temple on the second hill, the rows of buildings and the fine streets, the white cliffs behind—it was all beautiful. A glistening, rich land. He loved it like no other he'd ever lived in. And somewhere in those green hills and vales were his wife and children. All the Lions had left with him. Which meant Serah could slip away unseen.

A midshipman appeared at Argoth's side and relayed that the Divine requested his presence up on the deck of the aftercastle.

Argoth nodded, took one last glance, then joined the Divine and captain on the upper deck.

The Skir Master wore dark blue trousers, a dark shirt, and a gray, close-fitting coat. About his wrist he wore a leather band that glinted with metal. Argoth assumed those metal bits were weaves. Some were probably escrum. The Skir Master did not appear feeble. Perhaps he lost his skir simply because those creatures too were susceptible to age and death.

The Skir Master looked directly at Argoth. "Don't waste your time. Your future lies in front of you, not behind."

"Master?" said Argoth.

"I'm not all blind, nor deaf. I know what my visit has meant to the lords of this land."

Argoth said nothing.

"But in the end there must be priorities."

"Yes, Great One," said Argoth. Then he stood there in an uncomfortable silence watching the sailors move about their tasks below. The ship sailed out of the harbor and into the wide sea. After a time, Argoth spoke. "Great One, I need to check on the seafire below. It needs to breathe. Otherwise, the vapor can build up and crack the barrels."

That was a lie, but none on this ship would know it. Those who had worked with the seafire might wonder, but before they could question him, they'd be dead. He sighed at that thought. They were good men. Good men caught in events beyond their control. Good men who did not deserve to die.

"Be quick," said the Skir Master. "For I shall go fishing very soon. And I will want you here to observe."

Fishing for skir. Argoth had never seen it done before. "Yes, Great One," said Argoth. Then he left the Skir Master. On his way he surveyed the ship's boats. There were three of them. The two larger ones had been turned over and stacked, the medium-sized one inside the larger, forward of the oars. Ropes bound them tightly to the deck. But the third, an eighteen-footer, hung by davits off the stern. If there was to be any escape, it would be in that boat.

Argoth descended the stair to the main deck and entered the doorway to the aft cabins. A narrow stair twisted down. Argoth descended this to the lower deck. He asked the cook where he might find a hatchet. Then, hatchet in hand, he walked past the goats, the water room, and barrels of hard bread.

This ruse was necessary. If he opened one of the foul-smelling things in the middle of the night, it would wake the whole crew, and he could not afford that. His plan required he avoid fighting as much as possible. So if he made regular visits through the day and into the night, closing one barrel and opening another, the crew would pay neither him nor the odor any mind.

He found the seafire stowed a little aft of center, a perfect spot for setting a fire. The twelve large barrels stood two high next to the fire lances. Thick ropes tied them all fast to the struts of the deck. Argoth glanced toward the bow of the ship. Ahead, under the forecastle was where the crew slept. They would probably shut the door to their quarters against this stink. And that would only make it easier for him should it come to this.

Argoth pried the bungs out of three of the barrels, releasing the strong, unhealthy vapors into the hold. He held his breath and wedged both the bungs and hatchet tightly between two crates. Then, with the first part of his plan executed, he returned to the Skir Master and fresh air.

They sailed until the New Lands disappeared behind the horizon, then the ship's captain called for the crew to strike the sails.

The aftercastle swept back out over the water farther

than any ship Argoth had ever seen. But it did so not to accommodate another mast. No, the Skir Master used that deck to work his magic.

Argoth climbed the stairs to that deck. Above him a team of four sailors stood in a row on a balance rope belaying the last of the sails to its yard. Others tied down the coils of rope: something he'd never seen done before. Soon the ship no longer leapt to the wind, but sat in the water, rolling gently with the waves.

In the middle of the aftercastle stood a railing like something you might put around a pulpit. A pace or so aft rose what looked like a huge bowl turned on its side; the mouth of the bowl faced the sea off the stern of the ship. The bowl stood taller than a man and was woven of stiff, bronze wire, but the weave wasn't solid. It looked more like a large, dark lattice with gaps in the weave that would allow a man to slip an arm through. It glinted in the sunlight, and as Argoth approached he saw silver lines threading through the whole of it.

"Come," said the Skir Master, standing next to the bowl. He pointed to a spot along the railing. "There is the best spot for viewing the catch."

Argoth took a spot at the railing next to the captain. The massive Leaf stood close to the bowl to assist the Skir Master. Two of the crew stood by the other stair, holding a young boy between them.

"Captain," said the Skir Master. "The bait."

"Affix him," the captain said to the two crewmen. They brought the boy to the bowl. He looked at Argoth and smiled, his eyes full of pleasure and lassitude.

He was drugged.

He stood in the trap, and when they bound him with hemp cords, he laughed in a high, little boy voice. Argoth thought of Nettle lying on the table in his workroom, his eyes brimming with tears. The sight of that boy pained him.

The Skir Master stood before the boy, poking and prodding him, inspecting him like livestock. Then he checked the bonds.

Argoth spoke aside to the captain. "I thought the practice was to use a goat or ram."

The Skir Master answered. "Some fish fancy flies, others worms, others a bit of stinking gore. It all depends on what you're trying to catch and what the beasts are biting."

"Yes, Great One," said Argoth.

The ship rolled with a large wave, and Argoth held to the rail.

An officer called to the captain from the main deck. "Everything secured, Zu."

"Great One," the captain said and bowed slightly to the Skir Master.

The Skir Master faced Argoth, his coat flapping in the breeze. He withdrew a large spike from his coat pocket and held it up. "Here is the spark. When I set it and quicken the weave, the bait's essence will rise into the sky like a smoke. It will call to them like bloody chum calls to sharks." Then he turned and inserted the spike into a slot. When it was set, he inserted a pin crossways through the end of the spike to secure it.

The boy in the bowl sagged.

In that moment Argoth told himself he was not like the Divines. There was a difference. But then the boy looked up through his drugged eyes and Argoth saw Nettle, drugged and lying on the table.

What had he done to his son?

"Can you hear it?" asked the Skir Master.

"Great One?"

"The singing."

Argoth did not know what he meant.

He patted the great bowl. "The weave. It's calling, singing. They all do, great and small. That is the Kain's art—to weave the songs of power. You can hear this one if you listen carefully."

Argoth knew that weaves thrummed when you quickened them. But singing? He closed his eyes and focused. He heard the waves slapping the hull, the creak of the rigging. Then he heard something else. Something very soft that he immediately lost. He focused, then caught it again—a chorus of winds, rising and falling in a pattern, with a deep rumble running through them. Then one voice rose above the rest. He opened his eyes in wonder.

"All living things sing," said the Skir Master. Then he smiled, and the look in that smile was so malevolent it took Argoth aback. But as soon as it came the look was gone.

"I see," said Argoth.

"No, you don't." The Skir Master gestured out over the sea. "Empty. Nothing but a few thin clouds, right?"

Argoth did not have an answer.

"It's full," said the Skir Master. "Teeming with life. The air, waters, heavens, and earth—teeming. The Creators let nothing go to waste. Humans see, smell, perceive almost nothing."

"And do you see it all, Great One?" asked Argoth.

The Skir Master did not reply. Instead he reached into his coat and retrieved something made of gold. He held it out to Argoth. "Put these on."

Argoth bowed slightly, then walked to where the Skir Master stood inside his pulpit railing.

All this time the bowl and boy had claimed Argoth's attention. Now he saw the pulpit railing circled a large weave of bronze inlaid into the deck of the ship.

Argoth took the object from the Skir Master's hand. It was made of two wafers of milky stone, about the diameter of duck eggs, affixed between two bows of gold. Two long hooks were attached to the points of the bows.

"Spectacles," said the Skir Master. "Place the bow upon your nose and the hooks about your ears."

Argoth hesitated.

"It's wondrous," said the captain. "I've looked through them myself."

Argoth could not fathom how he might see anything through the opaque stones, but he put the spectacles on. He felt a thrumming and knew it was a weave.

"Give it some time," said the Skir Master.

Argoth stared at the milk walls of the stones. He wondered how many other weaves were aboard this ship. For a moment he thought about looking for them. They would be a boon to the Order. But then he discarded the idea. He was going to have enough problems enthralling the Skir Master and finding out who else knew their secrets.

He stood at the railing for half an hour and then he noticed the stones begin to clear. That or he was seeing things.

"Great One?"

"Do you see them, Clansman?"

He saw a flash of something: the palest of lavenders with a yellow streak running through it. Then the milk of the stones was gone, and he saw it was not one thing, but three, no, five.

He took in his breath. There before him was a ghostly image of the ship and bowl. He could see the Skir Master and the sea. But they too were insubstantial. Mere phantoms. And clustered about the boy were creatures as long as one of his arms. They had attached to him like a remora attaches to a great fish.

"What are they?"

"Hoppen. Minor things."

"I thought all skir were fearsome."

"There are indeed skir deep in the earth, beings so frightful none dare call them. But there are also small things, playful things, curious things."

"What are they doing?"

"Feeding on the boy's Fire," said the Skir Master. Then he took what looked like a brush of long horsehair, a fly-swatter, and waved it amid the creatures. They scattered like fish.

Argoth lifted his spectacles. The sunlight made him squint, but he saw it wasn't horsehair at all. Only a thin bone wrapped with leather at one end. A bone from a human forearm maybe. He replaced the spectacles and lifted them again. Only part of what the Skir Master held in his hand was visible.

"Do you see the ignorant pride of humans?" said the Skir Master. "And this is only a part. Every time we extend our ability to perceive, we find a world already there."

A chill ran through Argoth then. All his life he had thought himself wise with lore. Wise with years. And now he realized he knew nothing. When he attacked the Skir Master this night, would it be like a little boy carrying a stick attacking a man in full armor?

Argoth lowered the spectacles back to his nose. Two of the creatures returned like magpies to carrion, hovering in the air just out of the Skir Master's reach, their bodies undulating like sea snakes in the tide.

The wind rose sharply about Argoth, tossing his hair and wetting him with sea spray. The captain let out a slow moan, and suddenly the wind was *in* Argoth, passing over his bones. All about him shone a brightness, a translucent presence like the rounding of a thinly tinted glass.

The presence flowed over him and then to the bowl. Argoth gasped. It was a creature as thick as a horse but far longer, tapering and flattening at each end. It coiled one end about the bowl, the rest of its body stretching along the aftercastle and ending far out over the water. Argoth thought at first it was a giant serpent, but it had no head. No mouth. Not one eye. Along its whole length undulated thousands of bright, fine hairs half as long as he. In those hairs smaller creatures moved like band fish in the tentacles of an immense anemone.

"What is it?" Argoth asked.

"An ayten," said the Skir Master.

The ayten inserted one of its ends into the bowl and began to feel the boy with its bright hairs.

"How they can eat both Fire and soul," said the Skir Master, "we do not know. But when she's finished the sacrifice will be hollow."

The boy cried out. A soft moan that rose into a desperate keening.

Then the ayten bent that end and pressed into the bowl, engulfing the boy in its hairs. The hairs tossed and jerked as if the boy struggled within them. Then they were still.

"Lords," said Argoth in horror.

"An amazing thing," said the captain, "isn't it?"

Amazing was not the word Argoth would have used. When he finally found his voice, he said, "And this creature then powers the ship?"

"No," said the Skir Master, raising his hand and pointing behind Argoth. "She does."

Argoth turned, looked up, and the immensity of what he saw stole his breath.

Off port and high in the air flew a pale blue behemoth; it stretched hundreds of yards across, dozens deep. A mountain of a manta ray, flying toward them over the waves, its wings undulating with slow power. A multitude of other creatures whirled about it like gulls about a ship.

A fear rose in Argoth. He hadn't felt this since he was a boy standing on the banks of a river and seeing something monstrous turning in the murky green waters at his feet.

"That," said the Skir Master, "is Shegom."

Argoth lifted the spectacles. He could discern nothing in the air. He replaced the spectacles, saw the behemoth dive nearer the water. He lifted the spectacles again.

The evidence of her passing was clear: the water fluttered and flattened out as if a white squall passed over it. The strip was darker than the sea about it, reflecting the sun differently. It seemed almost calm in the center, but at its edges the wind kicked up a scud of thick sea spray as it went. Argoth wondered if all dust devils and squalls he had seen were merely the effect of a passing skir.

Suddenly the squall picked up speed.

The captain braced himself. Argoth did the same and lowered his spectacles.

The creature bore down upon them. It covered the distance to the ship in only a few breaths, kicking up a huge wall of sea spray. Just before the wall broke upon the ship, the Skir Master said, "It's a large one, my beauty. Enjoy the feast."

The sea spray soaked Argoth, then the wind slammed into him, almost ripping him from the railing. Again, something passed over and through him, the cold literally sweeping his heart. The ship leaned with the gale.

The noise of the wind grew to a screech. He felt his spectacles almost torn from his face, then the wind lessened, and the ship rocked back.

Argoth caught his breath and turned.

Long hairs covered Shegom's body. But along the edge

of where he imagined her head would be grew a beard of whips or tentacles. She held the struggling ayten with these.

The ayten thrashed, trying to break her hold, but Shegom shook it violently, then wrapped her prey with more of the long whips.

Another thrash, then the ayten sagged. Shegom enfolded it in the hairs along her belly just underneath her front edge. Then with a gust of wind and sea spray, she rose above the ship.

"Where is the hook?"

"Hook?" asked the captain.

"Was that not the bait?"

"She's already mine," said the Skir Master. He gestured at a weave inlaid in the deck at his feet. "She's long been a part of this ship."

"But I thought your skir died on the way."

"Of course, you did," said the Skir Master. "That's why I started that rumor. Tell me, Clansman." He gestured at the bowl and Shegom. "Does your lore even touch this?"

An alarm sounded in his mind. But then the fear drained away and he felt a bit giddy. "No," he said.

"I didn't think so. How many are in your Grove?"

"Almost a dozen," said Argoth.

He knew he shouldn't be saying such things. Not with the captain standing right there. Not to the Skir Master. It was death, but . . . did that matter really?

"And you're their leader?"

Again the warning. Again it drained away. The Skir Master's ghostly shape moved toward him. Why had they ever thought they should fight against such marvelous beings? Then he realized what was happening. The Skir Master was seeking him. But how? Panic rose in him.

The spectacles. That was how he was doing this. But seekings were accompanied by bindings and torture.

Argoth raised his hand to remove the weave.

"Leave them on," said the Skir Master.

Yes, that was wise. It would be nice to have them off, but it didn't seem to matter much either way.

"Are you the leader?" asked the Skir Master.

Argoth tried to remember his training.

"Answer me."

He fought against the compulsion. He needed to remove the weave. "No," he said. "I'm not."

"Who is?"

Argoth succeeded in reaching the weave.

"Leaf," said the Skir Master. "I believe we're going to have to restrain him."

"Great One," said Leaf. He approached Argoth. The tattoos flaring out from the man's eyes made him look wild.

Argoth took one step back. He needed to do something, but couldn't remember what it was.

"Stand still," said the Skir Master.

The weave. He needed to remove it. Argoth gripped it with both hands. It took all his effort. Then he ripped it from his face. The world of sunshine and sea burst upon him. He squinted, cast the spectacles from him, and began to build his Fire.

He'd failed, failed before he'd even begun. Find the barrels. Burn the ship. That was his goal.

Leaf drew a cudgel. The muscles rippled in his tattooed arm.

"We need him whole," said the Skir Master.

"I just thought I'd limit his mobility a bit," said Leaf. Then he swung the club at Argoth's knee.

Argoth dodged aside. He saved his knee, but the blow struck his forearm and snapped the bone.

Pain shot up his arm.

Leaf changed his grip on the cudgel and rammed it into Argoth's gut.

Argoth doubled over.

Leaf shoved him up against the railing and held him there. Argoth tried to struggle, but Leaf held him like iron. Then he shook Argoth's broken arm. Pain screamed through him and Argoth saw white.

"That will do," said the Skir Master.

Something cool wrapped itself about Argoth's neck. He felt fingers clasping it. Then his Fire was gone. He could not reach it. Could not magnify himself.

A collar. A king's collar.

"No!" It couldn't end this way.

"Bind him," said the Skir Master, "and take him to my quarters."

Leaf twisted Argoth's arm behind his back, then grabbed a handful of Argoth's hair and shoved him down onto the deck.

39.

KORAMITE

After consuming the goats, Hunger chased the female. She was keeping to less-used roads. Of course, it wouldn't have mattered if she had ridden on well-used ones: he still would have been able to sniff her out of the mix. Up hill, down dale he went, all the time the scent getting stronger, which meant he was getting closer. And then he found that she had separated from her horse.

Perhaps she'd been brushed off by a branch. Or it had run off on her while she'd gone to get a drink or relieve herself. Or maybe she'd run it too hard. He didn't know.

He didn't care. He was getting closer. He would have her soon.

The road he was on now wasn't so much of a road but a wide wash for the spring rains. Only the smallest trickle of water ran down the bed of the wash now. The last stretch had been rocky. It would slow her down, but it wouldn't slow him.

Trees grew thickly along the banks of the wash. Hunger raced around a bend and saw a trail split off the wash and rise up and over one of the banks. He saw one of her muddy footprints at the base of the trail. He splashed through the tiny brooklet and prepared to charge up the bank. But before he could start up the trail, he caught the stink of magic on the wind.

He ran a few more paces and then stopped. The female had left the wash. He could smell that. He followed her trail up. The trees along the banks immediately gave way to mown oat fields. He could not see her, but he could see that the trail ran straight for some distance through the middle of the fields.

However, the stink was weaker at the top of the bank. He descended back to the bottom of the wash. Yes, it was here. He had found that the human's magic all had a slightly different taste to it. River's had carried a slightly different odor from Argoth's down in the cellar. And the scent of the burning boy had carried, yet again, a tinge of something else. He thought he recognized this one.

He took his time, opened his mouth wide, and followed the scent a few paces up the wash. Hogan, the Koramite, had been here. And his scent had been kept in the shade from the sun. Hunger crossed the wash.

It didn't take him long to puzzle out what had happened. Many men on horses had come this way, traveling from the fields where the female had gone, down into the wash, and then on to a trail that led up the opposite bank.

He'd smelled no magic on the female. He'd hoped she'd lead him to Sleth. And she had. He had a sure trail now. He would follow it. Besides, the female was on foot, which meant she'd leave a stronger trail. She wasn't that far ahead. Maybe a mile or two. He could come back here and resume his chase later.

He breathed in the Koramite's scent. Yes. He would take the sure thing first.

40.

THE THRALL OF MOKAD

Argoth lay bound on the surgeon's table, his arm throbbing with pain. Old blood stained the wooden floor in blotchy patterns and spattered up the wall on his right. Above the blood spots hung a bone saw, pincers, a long, wicked implement he could not imagine a healthy use for, and flesh needles. To the side of the surgeon's tools sat blue and yellow bottles of nostrums neatly arranged in a three-shelf rack.

The Skir Master held Argoth's thrall in one hand, the stomach holding Nettle's Fire in the other. "Clansman?" he demanded.

Argoth said nothing. It was treason to possess such things. If you found one, it was treason not to immediately report it. He could say nothing. He simply looked the Skir Master in his inhuman, black eyes.

The Skir Master examined the thrall. "If I'm not mistaken, this is a pattern of the Trolumbay masters, isn't it?" He nodded to himself. "Of course, they were destroyed centuries ago. So that means you either stole it or are the heir of a vanished glorydom."

The door opened and Leaf entered, moving with his deadly grace.

The Skir Master looked over at him.

"Great One, nothing was found among his effects or the cargo he brought on board."

The Skir Master shook his head. "I'm disappointed." He looked down at the stomach. "I'd hoped there would be more like these." He turned to Argoth. "I tasted the Fire in this stomach, Clansman. Clean, sharp—delicious. I must compliment you."

Argoth could not speak.

The Skir Master turned to Leaf. "The link with the Fir-Noy has not yet matured. So send a pigeon back to him. Tell him we'll return in a week with two full cohorts. Tell him there's going to be a cleansing."

Fir-Noy?

It was the Crab. Argoth was sure of it. But the news of the cohorts is what shocked him. It would require three or four ships to carry so many men. And even with the Skir wind, going to and from Mokad would take almost a month. The only answer was that the ships were waiting off one of the outer islands or along the coast a few days south of the settlements.

The Skir Master seated himself close to Argoth's head and spoke to him like a friend. "You see, the spectacles are useful, not only for partially extending sight, but also for questioning all manner of lord and lady. Yet the spectacles, while they influence, do not enthrall. They're a tool used best with subtlety. But this rudimentary thing." He held Argoth's thrall up. "This will bind you quite nicely."

He smiled at Argoth. "You, Clansman, are going to die. As will your family." He held up his hand. "I know you think they fled, but we foresaw that."

Despair welled in Argoth.

"Disheartening, isn't it?"

"You are a blind fool," said Argoth. Blind about life. Blind about everything that was important. Argoth thought of the Crab. If he were in league with the Skir Master, he could have easily hidden in the woods and moved in on Serah and the children soon after Argoth left. Argoth was going to kill that one himself.

"I will seek every one of you and know every last one of your secrets. But it doesn't need to be too painful. Cooperate, and I'll make your wife comfortable. We'll need a little agony, but I'm sure this arm," the Skir Master prodded just below the break, sending pain shooting through Argoth's body, "would feel better set and splinted. Tell me who killed Lumen, and I'll help you."

Lumen? "I know nothing of Lumen's death."

"Oh, come."

"We know only what his servants claimed: that he lost himself to the call of the warrens."

"You're talking about the stone-wights, aren't you? What's in those caves?"

Argoth hesitated. He realized there was leverage here, something he could do with this information.

The Skir Master sighed. "I suppose you must fight. But it doesn't matter." He held up the thrall. "The Trolumbay patterns were crude and slow, yet for all their clumsiness they were still effective. I estimate this one will take two or three days. Two or three days and you will beg to tell me all."

He placed the thrall about Argoth's neck, lifting his head and clasping it at the back.

"I'm going to remove the king's collar. It interferes with the working of the thrall. But do not think of escape. Your bonds are woven with wire. You will not be able to break them. Not even one as powerful as Leaf can do so."

Then he released the collar. Immediately Argoth felt a change and began to build his Fire.

The Skir Master smiled. "Multiplying yourself will only multiply the effect of the thrall, Clansman. Of course, it would please me if you'd do so."

Argoth paused. Was he lying? He didn't know. And that realization struck him like a hammer: the Order didn't know.

"Do you know how to quicken a thrall, Clansman?"

Argoth said nothing.

"Come, come," said the Skir Master. "Do not be modest."

Argoth ignored the Skir Master. All he could think of was the fact that Nettle had given most of his life for nothing, to support a hero who had no skill.

The Skir Master grabbed his face with two fingers and turned it so Argoth was looking at him. "Speak to me. How do you quicken a thrall?"

"You can't feel it thrumming?" asked Argoth.

"Thrumming?" said the Skir Master. "You soul-eaters are so sloppy with your terminology. Weaves do not 'thrum'; I told you before, they sing. 'Sing' is the right word. But that's not quite all there is to it." The Skir Master paused. "You haven't ever used this, have you?"

Argoth looked the Skir Master in the eye. He'd read the old texts. He'd quickened a variety of other weaves. This couldn't be so very different.

The Skir Master shook his head. He reached back and took Argoth by the nape of the neck. "It's appalling, such ignorance."

Then a giddiness washed through Argoth and a door opened in his mind. Behind it stood the Skir Master. Beyond him another door opened, and Argoth perceived the Glory of Mokad. But yet another door opened behind the Glory, and Argoth perceived . . . something luminous, something so beautiful it took his breath away. A woman who consumed all thought. Then she turned and noticed him, and fear mingled with his adoration. He wanted to join her, but didn't dare. She regarded him for one more delicious and terrible moment, then all the doors between her and him slammed shut and the force of it made him gasp.

"And so it wakens," said the Skir Master. He released his hold upon the thrall. "Two days to work its way into the fiber of your being." He stood and grabbed the pincers from the wall. "We've found that a bit of pain in the very beginning speeds the process. Is that because it distracts the mind or stresses and weakens the body? We don't know. All we know is that it works." Then he wedged the large pincers under the break in Argoth's arm and turned them so they pressed upwards.

White flashed in Argoth's mind. He arched his back and gritted his teeth against the pain until he could no longer contain his cries. But by that time the Skir Master had walked out and shut the door.

FOR SOME TIME Argoth fought just to control himself. He moaned, panted, lost consciousness twice. And in the pain one thought rose and kept him from losing all hope: the barrels still sat below. Somehow he had to get to them. He had to get to them and then give the liquid inside one sweet kiss of fire.

Argoth multiplied himself, but found he could not break the bonds, could not wriggle out of them. He couldn't rock the table for it was nailed to the floor. And so he lay there in his sweat and pain, praying to his ancestors to help him get just one more chance.

THE SKIR MASTER returned around midmorning. "Do you want us to splint that arm?"

He could barely control his voice. "Yes," he said.

"A reasonable choice," said the Skir Master, and he removed the pincers. He picked up a cloth from a cabinet and wiped the snot and tears from Argoth's face. "It would be petty and pointless for anyone to expect you to choose otherwise since nothing but your comfort is lost."

"I don't know who or what killed Lumen," said Argoth.

"We always need subjects for our experiments. In a few days I will know if you're lying. If you are, we can put you to a great many uses. Of course, that's after we've used up your wife and children."

"I have talents," said Argoth. "I have connections."

"Your paltry talents I already possess. Your connections I will take from your mind."

"I'll prove myself," said Argoth.

"Please," said the Skir Master. "Your fate is set." He felt along Argoth's arm, then jerked the two ends out and reset the bone.

Argoth closed his eyes against the pain. He took three deep breaths. "The seafire," he said. "That was mine. You'll need more than facts, more than a simple recipe to make that."

The Skir Master retrieved two thin slats to use in Argoth's splint. He looked down at Argoth and said nothing.

"I could show you how," said Argoth. "You could let my wife and children go free."

"Stop it," said the Skir Master. "I detest sniveling."

Argoth looked away from the Skir Master's face. "Yes, Great One."

And in that moment he saw an opening, a slim one but an opening nevertheless. If he could only convince the Skir Master he was one easily turned.

"Why did you bring this thrall aboard?"

"To bind you, Great One. To take what we could from your mind, then destroy you to preserve our secret."

"Ambitious. And who is your master?"

"Hogan, the Koramite."

"The one the Fir-Noy so desperately wanted a seeking for?"

"The same."

"And this man of grass and earth? Who does it belong to?"

Argoth paused. "We thought it was yours, Great One."

The Skir Master stood silently looking into Argoth's eyes. "Are you telling me there is more than one murder of soul-eaters in the New Lands?"

"I don't know," said Argoth.

The Skir Master laid his hand on the break he'd just set. "A broken arm is a small thing, Clansman."

"I'm not lying," said Argoth. "When you seek me you will see I tell the truth. Perhaps it is the Bone Faces. Perhaps someone else has begun to move their wizards. Perhaps that is what took Lumen in the caves."

The Skir Master's gaze bored into Argoth, his tongue feeling the edge of his lips as if he were in thought. "If you are lying to me—"

"No," said Argoth. "No, I'm telling the truth. Why else would we risk something so stupid and foolhardy as attacking a Divine himself? Please, believe me."

The Skir Master gazed at him a few moments more, then he shook his head in frustration, laid the splints on Argoth's chest, and walked out.

He returned some time later with Leaf and two dreadmen.

"How long would it take to mount a fire lance on this ship?" asked the Skir Master.

Argoth thought. "A day, Great One, with a good carpenter."

"And the seafire below, how many lances will it support?"

"That depends on the length of the battle and how hard the pump gang works. The distance too, for you have to force a large quantity to build the pressure that will send the fire even sixty yards."

"How many?" the Skir Master snapped.

"Three," said Argoth. "Three if they're careful and do not waste."

"Three?" said the Skir Master in amazement. "I saw lances on six galleys. Are you telling me that you left the seafire for those galleys behind?"

"No. We only supply the galleys on patrol. I dared not make great quantities. The Bone Faces sent many spies seeking to steal the seafire so that they might unlock its secrets."

The Skir Master's face turned to thunder. "So you had them load the few barrels of finished product and left the component materials on the land?"

"No," said Argoth. "No, we have them aboard."

Argoth could not read the Skir Master's face. Could the man already know his thoughts? It was impossible.

"Splint his arm," said the Skir Master to Leaf. "Then bring him below."

Leaf took Argoth's arm matter-of-factly as if Argoth's arm were nothing more than a spade that had come loose from its handle. Then he splinted Argoth's arm using strips of the surgeon's cloths. Argoth studied the flaring eye tattoos as he worked. Each eye's tattoo was different, one sharp-edged and jagged, the other smooth, but Argoth could not read their meaning. Leaf finished, then led Argoth out to the area of the lower deck where the barrels were stored.

The Skir Master stood, holding a covered lamp. "You're going to teach me how to make this seafire. And then you're going to teach my men how to use it."

"Yes, Great One," said Argoth. "Thank you."

THE SKIR MASTER wanted four lances: two just off the prow on both sides, and two at either side of the ship's waist.

Three triangular sails, jibs, were rigged to lines running from the foremast to the bowsprit that stuck out over the prow. Those jibs might prove troublesome if a crew on one of the fore lances were spewing fire and the wind changed. So Argoth convinced the Skir Master to move the lances back.

Argoth directed the carpenter and his boy for most of the day as they installed the fittings for the four lances. Three times during the day he felt an intrusion upon his mind, a constricting. He dismissed the first two as the effects of fatigue. But when the third came, he realized what it was: the thrall had begun working into him.

When they finished the last fitting and mounted the lance, it was early evening. The sun was an hour or so from setting. Argoth leaned against the railing and stared at the sails in the orange and yellow light. The ship had two masts that were three sails high, and, with the studding sail booms rigged on both ends of each yard, three sails wide—it was such an amazing press of sail.

He couldn't see her, but somewhere above the sails in the clear evening sky, Shegom moved, the wake of her passing creating the wind that filled the canvas.

They moved south, at an angle to the normal winds. Argoth knew this because at the edges of Shegom's wind, in an oval perhaps a league across, the winds clashed, kicking up a scud that blew westward.

He imagined the clan galleys in a battle against this ship now fitted with fire lances. With Shegom above, moving hither and thither to the Skir Master's commands, the sails of the clan galleys would be of no use. They would have to furl them and move under the power of the oarsmen. And all the while the *Ardent* would race about them, blown by Shegom, throwing her deadly fire at will. She'd be a wolf roving among lambs.

Argoth knew if he followed Shim's advice and ursurped power in the New Lands, he'd face the *Ardent* at sea, and she would sink anything he sent against her. She'd shut down all trade. She'd land cohorts of men on any beach she liked. And she wouldn't be the only one. Others would be built like her. He suspected the only way to fight her would be to harness a skir and blow the fire back in her face.

There were no Skir Masters in the Order. And he saw that the Skir Master was right: such ignorance posed an immense danger to them all.

Are you finished?

Argoth turned, expecting to see the Skir Master standing right behind him. But the Skir Master stood almost a ship's length away at the rear of the after-castle. It had not been a shout, but a voice right behind him.

Clansman?

It was the Skir Master, a whisper almost. He could have counted it as a trick of the wind, but the Skir Master's lips had not moved. He stood gazing at Argoth across the length of the ship.

"We are finished," whispered Argoth.

Meet me in the officer's mess, said the Skir Master in his mind.

ARGOTH STOOD WITH the Skir Master at the table. Leaf sat with quill and vellum. Bowls of firewater, sulfur, and pitch lay between them.

"You will teach me how to make the seafire," said the Skir Master. "I must be able to replicate it before morning."

Argoth felt a light wave of desire wash over him. "Of course, Great One," he said. And for the first time he meant it. The Skir Master *was* great. A fine man. No, not just a man. A master.

Moments later the desire ebbed and left him standing in shock. He'd always imagined it would be more like a battle, a contest of wills. But this thrall did not batter him down; it simply turned his will traitor.

"Well?" said the Skir Master.

Argoth brought himself back to the task at hand. "Let us begin with the firewater, but may we open the windows first? The vapors are not good to breathe."

The Skir Master opened the windows, letting in a small but ineffective breeze. Then Argoth began. He told them how one gathered the firewater from black springs and distilled it. When Leaf had captured every detail on the vellum, Argoth poured a small measure into an empty bowl and lit it on fire.

"Such is good for firepots, but you want something that will burn on water and cleave together like tar. For that we must add pitch from pines and terebinth trees and a fine sulfur powder. Such a mixture can be extinguished only with great quantities of vinegar, urine, or earth."

He told them how to make the pitch, how to find sulfur of the right color and grind it to powder. Leaf wrote everything up, and was as graceful with the pen as he was fighting or walking. But he did not write quickly and made Argoth repeat his instructions numerous times.

An hour passed, maybe more. They moved to the process of mixing. He showed the Skir Master how he had to mix the firewater and sulfur first and wait. He showed him how he could tell this preliminary mixture was correct by the color of the flame, and the quantity of smoke. Then the Skir Master demanded to do it himself.

Argoth walked the Skir Master through each step and admired his quick mind, the way he said aloud what he was doing as he did it.

At one point, the Skir Master stretched as if to relieve his back, and Argoth found himself standing next to him holding a chair.

"Perhaps you'd like to sit, Great One."

"No," the Skir Master said and waved him off.

Argoth was crestfallen. "Forgive me," he said and replaced the chair. How could he have been so stupid as to offer a chair? Who needed chairs? Certainly not someone as strong and capable as the Skir Master.

Argoth resolved to be silent until spoken to. He stood aside, watching the Skir Master continue with the preparations.

A thought came to him: how many had the opportunity to stand in the presence of such a man? How many people had the opportunity to share their talent with him?

Argoth was among a fortunate few, and he beamed at his fortune.

In the back of his mind a resentment, an anger, twisted upon itself. How dare this man take on such honors with lies? But Argoth began to admire the fine lines of the Skir Master's hands and the thought passed.

The Skir Master arrived at the step where he needed to measure in the pitch. He had too much. Suddenly the Skir Master stopped.

"No, I don't," said the Skir Master. "One measure. That is what you said."

Argoth was disoriented for a moment, had he actually spoken those words unbidden? But Leaf looked as confused as he. Then he realized the Skir Master had heard his thoughts.

And in that moment he knew he did not have two days. He didn't have one. The thrall was changing him, bending his desires and forming a link between their minds. It might take two days for his admiration to bloom into full worship, for his thoughts to roll open like a scroll before his master. But long before that the Skir Master—

He cut himself off. He needed to move them down to the lower deck next; he needed to get to the barrels of seafire.

The Skir Master looked up. "What did you say?"

"A semiliquid is what we want," Argoth said. "Too thick and you'll plug the pumps and lances."

Argoth felt light-headed. He needed to think and not think. He walked to the window to breathe in fresh air. The sun had sunk low in the west. Over the horizon lay the New Lands and his wife. Nettle. Shim. Thinking of them brought clarity. "Great One," he said. "We've been using bowls. If we want to produce a great quantity, I fear we must move to a larger, more ventilated place."

"There are too many eyes and ears on the main deck," said Leaf.

"Then, Great One, let us work on the lower deck, where the materials are."

The Skir Master looked at the bowls and nodded. He turned to Leaf. "Have this moved to the lower deck. And I want something to eat."

HALF AN HOUR later Argoth stood on the lower deck, the barrels of seafire half a dozen paces aft of where they were set to work. The cook's boy brought three bowls of food to them. Both the Skir Master and Leaf were given beef, pickled radishes, and rice. Argoth was given a foul-looking stew full of knuckles, the hard cartilage between bones. He dipped his spoon in and saw a white hair poking out. He plucked it up. It wasn't a hair, but a whisker still attached to the severed muzzle of a rat. Argoth dropped it back. He turned the stew with his spoon. There was an ear and a foot, and who knew what else.

He set the stew aside.

"Eat," said Leaf with a grin.

"I'm fasting," said Argoth.

"Eat," said the Skir Master. "We have a long night ahead of us."

The Master was right. Of course, he should eat. The food may be filthy, but he needed his strength to teach. Argoth dipped his spoon into the stew, filled it with a hearty helping, and brought it to his mouth. It stank, and when he put it in his mouth, he convulsed, but the Master needed him, so he crunched the knuckles and other bits and swallowed the mess down.

The Skir Master scooped the last clumps of rice from his bowl and set it aside. "It is too quiet. We need more privacy. Order pipes and dancing."

Leaf nodded. He took the stairs above. Soon the sound of pipes and pounding feet came from above. Leaf rejoined them, this time with grog. Argoth was sure someone had pissed in his cup, but the Master had said he'd need his strength.

He brought it to his lips and thought of Nettle. The boy had pissed in his cup once as a child when they'd weaned him from diapers. He'd cleverly, if mistakenly, used it as a chamber pot.

Argoth put the mug down.

Upon the table two open-flame lamps burned. They were there for light, but also to test the mixtures. They were too large to fit through a bunghole.

The Skir Master looked at Argoth with puzzlement on his face.

Argoth cursed himself and quickly shifted his focus. It was good the bungholes were so small, he thought. Very safe. Very much like keeping the lamps away from the bed when he and Serah made love. However, the crew should be banned from this area. No telling what careless men might do. "Let us compare your mixture, Great One, with the finished product."

"Leaf," said the Skir Master and gestured at the barrels with his chin.

Leaf walked over to one of the barrels, easily worked its lid off and set it aside. Then he dipped a cup and brought it back to the table.

The open flame of the lamps on the table, the bowl of dark seafire, the barrels just paces behind—this was his opportunity.

"Now the consistency," said Argoth.

The Skir Master reached out and grasped both lamps and pulled them back slightly.

Argoth dipped the thumb and two fingers of his good arm into the bowl of seafire and rubbed them against each other. He held them out for the Skir Master to see. "That is what you want, Great One. Mark it."

"What are you hiding?" asked the Skir Master.

He should not hide things from the Master. He should tell him all.

"This," said Argoth. Then he stuck his fingers in the flame of one of the lamps. They flashed blue, then spat into flame. Argoth brought them up.

The Skir Master raised an eyebrow in alarm.

Then Argoth mustered all his will, turned, and dashed for the open barrel.

"Stop him!" shouted the Skir Master.

Argoth raced to the barrel, his fingers aflame.

One pace from the open barrel, Leaf grabbed his splinted arm and jerked back.

The pain screamed up his arm. But he'd fought through worse. He turned and shoved his flaming fingers into Leaf's eye, wiping seafire along the socket and nose and up the tattoo.

Leaf cried out, raising one hand to his face. But he did not fully release Argoth.

Argoth twisted and chopped down with his good hand. Then he was free. He turned, lunged for the barrel.

"Stop!" the Skir Master commanded.

Argoth froze, the sea fire inches away, his fingers blackening and blistering in the flame. The pain was immense.

The Skir Master strode toward Argoth, and horror overtook him: what had he done? How could he have betrayed his master? He almost fell to his knees. But there was one small part of him that wanted something else.

"Nettle," he said.

"Down!" ordered the Skir Master.

Argoth faltered. Then he mustered all his strength. "Nettle," he said. His son's sacrifice would not be wasted. And suddenly the Skir Master's command seemed less important than it had before.

"For Nettle," he said more forcefully. This was for him and for Grace, Serenity, and Joy. For Serah. A battle cry rose within him, and he shouted his son's name. "Nettle! For Nettle and light!"

His mind cleared momentarily and he thrust his burning fingers into the black liquid.

A blue-green fire raced over the surface.

Argoth almost faltered from the pain, but he snatched his hand back and wrapped it in his tunic, wiping off both flame and skin.

The seafire in the barrel spit, flashed, then, with a cracking thunder, flames exploded upward. Thick smoke poured forth and rolled along the ceiling.

The Skir Master took a step back.

Argoth retrieved the hatchet he'd stowed between the barrels earlier. He brought it up and swung it against the rope binding the barrel. It split cleanly.

Leaf had fallen to his knees, violently trying to wipe the seafire from his face with his tunic. The Skir Master leapt over Leaf.

Argoth grabbed the lip of the burning barrel with the head of the hatchet and pulled with all his weight.

The barrel tipped, fell over, and spilled the burning seafire over the deck, over the Master's boots. It circled the man.

The blue flame raced over the surface of the widening pool.

Argoth backed away.

The Skir Master looked down at the spreading fire. Then the pool of seafire burst into flame and choked the passageway with smoke. And Argoth felt the Skir Master recede from his mind.

Clasping the hatchet, Argoth turned and ran. Men shouted from the stern. The cook stepped out holding a long knife and looked up the passageway. Argoth swung the flat of the hatchet and struck him in the face.

Argoth raced up the stairs to the main deck. Thick brown and yellow smoke billowed out of the hatches, the skir wind carrying it forward over the deck into the sailors who had recently been dancing. An officer shouted for a team to descend with barrels of sand.

Argoth leapt up the stairs to the aftercastle and raced to the stern. A dreadman stood by the helmsman. "The Skir Master!" Argoth shouted. "Help me get the ship's boat in the water!"

The dreadman hesitated, then joined Argoth. He ran to the rope and pulleys of one of the davits, Argoth to the other. But Argoth had no time for an easy lowering. He hacked through the ropes and his end of the boat swung down and out.

The unexpected weight caught the dreadman off guard.

The rope raced through his hands, burning them. He stumbled forward, cursed, and looked at Argoth with anger.

The boat had fallen, but not all the way. It dragged behind the ship, half of it still out of the water.

Argoth raced to the dreadman's side. He acted as if he were going to hack through the tangle. Instead, he buried his hatchet in the man's leg.

The dreadman yelled out.

Argoth pulled the hatchet out and kicked him overboard.

Men raced up the stairs to the aftercastle.

Then an explosion rocked the ship and the men racing up the stairs fell from the stairs or sprawled forward.

Argoth brought the hatchet down with all his might, cutting the rope, and the boat fell to rest of the distance to the water.

A man shouted blood-curdling intent behind him.

Argoth turned and saw a dreadman charging him, sword held high. A large eye had been tattooed on his bare chest.

Argoth brought up his hatchet and parried the blow, but the force of it knocked the hatchet out of Argoth's hand.

The dreadman brought his sword back.

Argoth was no match for him, so he scuttled backward and over the edge of the stern. Then he was falling, watching the *Ardent* pull away and the dreadman looking on.

Argoth pulled his broken arm to his chest to protect it, bracing himself, thinking he was going to land on the boat.

But he did not land on the boat. He crashed heels over head into a shock of cold water and pain. He gasped in a lungful of water, rolled, then came to the surface choking.

Argoth turned, looking for the boat. A wave lifted him. He spotted it, and began to sidestroke with all his might, holding his useless arm at his chest.

The dreadman flashed down in the corner of his eye and splashed into the water.

At the crest of the next swell, he looked back. The dreadman was swimming after him, gaining on him.

Argoth swam with all his might. Two, four, eight strokes.

He looked back. The dreadman was only a few yards behind.

Another stroke and he touched the boat. Argoth reached up with his good hand, grasped the top wale, and swung his leg up.

Then it was over the wale and onto one of the thwarts.

He looked frantically about for a weapon. There was nothing but the length of rope that had attached the boat to the davit.

The dreadman's hand grasped the wale behind him.

Argoth lunged for the rope where it lay under one of the thwarts.

The dreadman pulled himself up.

Argoth spun around, lunged at the man, and slipped a makeshift noose over his neck. He looped the rope about his body and heaved back.

The rope tightened about the dreadman's neck and pulled him into the boat.

But Argoth knew that wouldn't be enough. He turned, and before the dreadman could gain leverage to pull Argoth to him, Argoth took one bounding step and jumped off the side of the boat opposite the dreadman and into the water.

He attempted to swim under the boat, but he came to the end of the rope.

It wasn't going to work. The dreadman would pull him

back in. But no tug came, and Argoth burst to the surface. He tread water, fearing what would come, but nothing moved on the boat.

The dreadman could be waiting in the boat, waiting for him to swing over.

Men cried over the waves. They would see this boat and those that knew how to swim would soon reach it.

Argoth steeled himself, then he reached up and pulled himself in.

The dreadman lay across the thwarts, his neck broken, the water from his clothing dripping into the bilge.

A good soldier, thought Argoth. A good soldier gone to waste.

He unlooped the rope, pushed the body aside, then began to tie the tiller. He would not have enough time to erect the ship's small mast and rig the sail. If he tied the tiller, he might, with one oar, row in a straight line away from the burning *Ardent* and her men.

With the tiller tied, he looked back at the ship. The sails had caught fire—yards and yards of fire billowing in the evening sky.

Then an enormous explosion cracked like thunder, shuddering the ship, throwing men, wood, and great gouts of fire up into the rigging and out to sea. One of the thrown men, his entire body aflame, snagged in the rigging and writhed there.

Moments later a rain of fire began to fall to the sea, great infernos and small drops, all of it streaking through the sky to burn atop the darkening sea.

Another explosion tore the air. The force of the blast, even from this distance, almost knocked Argoth into the thwarts. It rent the ship, and she began to list.

Argoth retrieved an oar, fitted it, and sat on the thwart. He was about to turn the boat to row directly away from the *Ardent* when a fierce wind kicked up about him. Sea spray stung his eyes.

The skir wind.

He crouched low in the boat, the wind whipping about him. Moments later a violent gust kicked the boat, knocking him into the wale. And then, as quickly as it had come, it departed with one final line, a spray that receded away toward the *Ardent*.

Argoth's fingers throbbed with pain. They were black, and where the outer charred skin had sloughed off, a bright pink. They didn't hurt as much as he would have suspected, but that only meant the fire had burned all of his nerves. He might never feel in those fingers again.

The splint about his broken arm hung loosely. He tightened it up as best he could with his burned hand. Then he set one oar in a lock, sat upon a thwart, and began to row, the red and green eye of the paddle dipping in and out of the water.

He hadn't gone very far when he heard the Master's command in his mind. *Come to me.*

"Nettle," he said. "Serah. Serenity. Grace. Joy." He began to repeat the names of his family members again like some murmured prayer, and the Skir Master's compulsion eased.

The Skir Master shouted in the back of his mind.

But Argoth rowed on, the names covering that voice like a blanket.

The ship burned brightly. Any ship within miles would be able to see it. His only hope was that they were nowhere near the other ships the Master had brought. His only hope was that the Master would die before they came.

When he did, Argoth would feel it. For the thrall only had power when the Master was alive. When he died, so would the bond. Of course, he had read that the bond worked through a man like roots in the soil. So although the bond might die, the roots would remain, and it would take some time before all traces of the thrall were gone.

Argoth wondered how many thralls the Master had. Dozens? A hundred? Surely, the inlay by the pulpit was some thrall. And how many of his slaves were skir? Certainly Shegom was one of them.

He looked up and found that the sky was clear. The first evening stars shone in the heavens. He took a moment to get his bearings by them and considered trying to rig the sail.

A wind buffeted him, then another.

At first he thought it a normal gust, but it did not abate.

The sound of sea spray hasted toward the boat. Argoth turned and saw the skir wind racing to him.

Shegom.

He had heard of Skir Masters summoning whirlwinds to the field of battle, of men being picked up and carried away.

Argoth released the oar and immediately wriggled underneath the thwarts, wedging himself as best he could.

The wind knocked the boat, lifting it to one side and pushing it sideways. Then the pitch of the wind rose, screeching over the wales.

The oar jerked violently in its lock, then it broke free with a wrench and flew away into the air.

The pitch of the wind screaming over the wales rose until it howled.

The boat tipped precariously on its side and scudded over a wave. The dreadman tumbled out and disappeared beneath the water.

Sea spray kicked up, driving into Argoth's face like needles. He shut his eyes against it and turned his face into the side of the boat.

The boat lurched, twisted, was tossed about like a leaf.

And then it was airborne. He felt as if he were going to slide out and braced himself. But it wasn't enough, he *was* slipping.

Moments later, through the water and spray he smelled the foul smoke of the seafire and felt the heat. Then the boat slapped down into the water. It bobbed then rocked.

Argoth opened his eyes. The sky was full of smoke.

When nothing happened, he wriggled halfway out from under the thwarts and looked around. All about him pieces of flotsam burned, smoke piling into the sky.

Someone shouted.

A hand grasped the wale.

Argoth kicked at the man's head as he came over. He bent over to untie another oar so that he might use it as a weapon. But the boat rocked again.

Argoth turned, oar in hand.

Leaf stood before him, water running from his clothes into the boat. The skin about his eye was blackened and cracked from the burn. Raw pink and red flesh shone where much of his eye tattoo had been.

Argoth drew back to strike, but Leaf simply snatched the oar out of his hand and kicked him into the prow. Argoth's head smacked against the side of the boat.

He tried to get up, but couldn't seem to get his balance.

Another dreadman entered the boat.

Then Leaf reached over the side and pulled the Master up. Clutched to his breast was the weave that had been inlaid into the deck of the ship by the bowl.

Shegom's thrall.

The Master wore no boots. The legs of his pants were scorched. The flesh underneath blistered.

A normal sailor tried to climb into the boat.

"What are you doing?" said the Master and kicked the man in the face.

Then he stepped over the thwarts to where Argoth lay and looked down upon him.

"You should have drowned yourself, Clansman. You should have tied a stone to your neck and jumped into the sea. For now you will taste the fury of the Glory of Mokad."

"Dreadmen!" he shouted over the waves. "To me!"

41.

MUSTER

Talen lugged Legs until his collarbone felt like it was going to break. He rested. Picked him up again. Rested. He carried him across the two creeks, hid him in a canoe they'd found on the side of the river, and lugged him through the woods downstream and on the other side.

He'd scuttled their trail as best he knew how from any dogs that might be following. But that didn't keep them from having to skirt around two more groups of men on the watch, nor did it help them avoid the farms and wooden shacks that stood in their path. In the end, they'd used a whole day to do what should have taken, at most, two hours.

At last, they crested a hill that led down to the Widow's valley. They were both bloody-footed, but they'd made it.

Talen didn't dare climb a tree to get a look below. The branches would shake too much as he ascended. But he knew a spot on the hill that opened to a good view. He and Legs sat there for some time watching. He saw nothing but vultures circling in the updrafts, the horse the Creek Widow called the Tailor eating away at the grass in the apple orchard, and the Creek Widow digging herself a new cesspit for the privy.

He was satisfied nobody waited for them there, but nevertheless, he waited until the sun set to descend the hill and enter the Creek Widow's yard. He wasn't more than a dozen paces from the front door, when someone spoke from behind. "That will be far enough."

Talen froze.

"State who you are and what business you have sneaking about my yard at night."

It was the Creek Widow herself. But where had she come from?

Talen turned. She held a pitchfork out in front of her with a fair amount of menace. Warrior, her ancient dog, stood at her side. He mustered one woof and fell silent.

"I told you before," said Talen, "one old woman out here on her own—you've got to have a dog that will chase more than biscuits."

"Talen," she said. "Lights, you're lucky you haven't got the tines of my pitchfork in your back." She turned to Legs. "It's good to see you, Purity's son."

She looked out into the yard, across the pasture. "Now, both of you, get in the house."

"I hope you've got something to eat," said Talen, "because we're starving."

"Food?" She stabbed the pitchfork at him. "I think I promised a beating the last time you were here. Now get." She eyed the woods behind them. Perhaps the valley wasn't as peaceful as it had appeared from the top of the hill. Talen turned with Legs and hurried into the house. A Creator's wreath hung above the widow's door. The Festival of Gifts was coming, and everyone wanted to thank the Creators and invite their blessings. The wreaths would soon be everywhere—above the gates of each city, on the bows of ships, over the windows of barns.

The Creek Widow came hard on their heels and shut the door behind them. Then she turned on Talen. The fire from the hearth was the only light in the house. Something delicious cooked on the stove and filled the room with the smell of beef and onions.

"What are you two doing?" she said.

"Is River here?"

"River?"

Talen's heart sank.

"You tell me what's happened," she said.

Talen did. He told her about going into Whitecliff, the weave, and the little creature at the window. He told her about packing up to leave, about the monster, River and Sugar going after it, and his encounters with Fabbis and the hunt.

His tale elicited a running commentary of grunts from her. When he finished, she put her hands on her hips. "Men," she said in disgust. "I told them it was time when Purity was first caught. I told them, but they wouldn't listen. Men," she said again. "Always leaving the woman to clean up." She looked at Talen and Legs. "And you can be sure I will clean up. We must leave; this house isn't safe."

"Where are we going?"

"The refuge, my boy. The refuge." she sighed. "I knew it was fraying apart when your da sent his letter. I told him. I told your da. I told him, I told him, I told him. But no. That man won't listen. Now if I were his wife, I would have made him listen. River, bless her heart, I know she tries. But a daughter can't hold her own like a wife can. Men get stupid when they run on their own, Talen. That's just how it is. And your father's gotten stupider than most. Your mother kept the beef out of his brain. But she's too long gone. Too long without a good woman. And that's the truth." She grunted again and looked to the rafters for answers. "May the Six bless him. He's going to need it." She directed her attention to Talen. "Fetch the Tailor from the field."

"Will the others be there?" asked Talen.

"Others?"

"Aren't there a number of other people in the Order?" asked Talen. "Won't we need them to attempt a rescue?"

"Son," said the Creek Widow, "your uncle's on a ship headed for Mokad, your da's who knows where in the custody of Lord Shim and the Fir-Noy, we've got some creature from the tales taking us down one by one. I don't know where your brother is. We weren't many to begin with. You want others?" She spread her arms wide. "I'm afraid you're looking at them."

"But—"

"If anybody has survived, we will find them at the refuge. I was waiting for the final word. I cannot wait anymore. We must leave immediately."

TALEN SADDLED THE Tailor and brought him around the front of the house, worrying the whole time that someone was spying on them. The Tailor was named after a man the Creek Widow had loved once. Talen had never gotten the full story and didn't know if the man died or simply jilted her.

He helped Legs up and then held the horse as the Creek Widow filled the saddlebags with a few necessities and what she said were her three most prized possessions—a fat codex of lore she'd been hiding in a stone box under the floor, two yards of bright yellow silk she had not yet been able to bring herself to wear and probably never would, and an ancient cooking pot her great-grandmother had given her.

When she finished tying everything off, the Creek Widow walked to the well, drew a bucket of water, then carried it to the south side of her home where her almond tree starts stood in a single straight line of pots on a narrow table. She watered them, gently brushed each with her hand, then stood back and addressed the group. "I cannot promise I'll return, lovelies. And there's no time to put you where you belong." She grunted over that fact and shook her head.

"No, I just can't," she said. She turned to Talen. "Bring me a spade."

"But—"

"Cha!" she said.

Talen fetched a spade from the barn and brought it to her. "I thought we had to leave immediately."

"Hush," she said. "Gather an armful and follow me. Those pots will dry out in a day."

They carried the nine starts to the garden and hastily planted them between two rows of cabbage.

"I know you'll be a bit crowded," she said to them. "But it will have to do." Then she stood and said good-bye to her apple trees and the two walnuts she prized the most. She walked to the chicken coop, opened the door, and bid her birds farewell. Then she walked to Warrior lying on the porch.

"My lovely old man," she said, giving him an affectionate rub about the neck. "Keep a good watch on the ladies. I'm counting on you."

A branch cracked in the woods that started just on the other side of the road running by the house. All three of them froze. The crack was followed by the sound of someone pushing through brush.

The Creek Widow pointed at the barn. "Hide," she whispered.

Talen took Legs by the hand and walked as quickly as

he dared to the barn door. It squeaked, even though he only opened it wide enough for the two of them to slip inside.

There was more cracking and sweeping of limbs, then a "Hoy. Anyone?"

"Sugar!" Legs called. He let go of Talen's grip and darted out of the barn, almost running toward the sound, one hand high, one low in front of him. "Sugar!"

"Hush," said the Creek Widow.

Sugar ran to her brother and wrapped him in a hug. "Thank the Creators," she said.

"Thank Talen," said Legs.

Sugar looked over at him.

"Oh, we've become bosom buddies," said Talen.

"Have you been followed?" asked the Creek Widow.

"No," said Sugar. "Well, I don't know."

"There was no way you were coming back from chasing that monster," said Talen.

"Well," she whispered. "I guess you underestimated me."

"Quickly," said the Creek Widow, "give me the facts."

Sugar related her tale of following River. She ended by saying, "I trailed the monster to its lair. But I did not go far. It returned. I was close enough to almost reach out and touch it. It chased me for a time, but I haven't seen sign of it since this afternoon."

"You're a brave one," said the Creek Widow. She looked at Talen. "That's something to mark."

He couldn't tell if that meant Sugar was to be lauded, or that he was cowardly in comparison and should learn from his betters. Or was she suggesting he should consider Sugar as a potential quality mate.

"Are we going to help my mother?" asked Sugar.

"What happened to River?" Talen asked.

"Everything in its time," said the Creek Widow. "And

now is not a time to chat in the yard. You three will follow me. And not a word until I say so."

Talen looked at Sugar for his answer.

"It took her," she whispered. "I saw it, in the morning
light, carrying her like a baby."

"Sst," said the Creek Widow to silence them. She pointed
at Legs. "Get him up on the horse."

Then she walked out into the road.

"Was she alive?" Talen asked.

Sugar hesitated. "I couldn't tell."

Talen nodded, then he lifted Legs onto the Tailor's
back. At least River wasn't twisted in a broken heap like
the Shoka they called Gid. He took the reins and followed the Creek Widow into the night.

At their departure, Warrior hauled himself up, padded
over to the chicken coop, and dropped his bones squarely
in front of the door. Talen considered the dog. Perhaps
liveliness wasn't the only asset a hound might possess.

Sugar walked alongside the Tailor, holding her brother's
ankle. She *had* been brave to follow that creature. Braver
than he. The thought had never occurred to him to follow
River. It was true that she'd ordered him away. But he
hadn't given it a second thought.

They walked in silence, the Creek Widow in the lead,
Talen coming behind, leading the Tailor and Legs. Talen
whispered a prayer to the ancestors to protect River.

The moon rose and moved across the starry heaven.
Talen's weariness threatened to overwhelm him. He tried
walking with his eyes closed, but stumbled over a rock
and upset the Tailor.

The old stallion jerked his head back and lurched to
the side. Legs, who *had* drifted asleep, fell to the ground,
and only cried out when he landed with a thump. Obviously, Sugar herself had been too tired to react swiftly
enough to catch him. Talen steadied the horse and moved

him away from Legs. Sugar moved to her brother's side, feeling for breaks and cuts.

"I'm fine," he said and got to his feet.

"Tie him in the saddle this time," said the Creek Widow.

Talen moved to the saddlebags to find the rope the Creek Widow had put there.

"Look at the three of you," the Creek Widow said. "Bone-tired." She produced three sticks of horehound from a pocket and gave one to each of them. "A bit of sweet should help." Then she cupped each of them in turn about the neck just as Da had cupped him about the neck when he'd tied the godsweed charm about his arm before they'd gone to Whitecliff. Just like Da's, the Creek Widow's hand was icy cold.

She smiled at him. "We cannot afford to be caught sleeping."

In moments, his fatigue lessened, and he knew she'd just worked some Sleth business on him.

Talen sucked on his horehound. "What else have you got in those pockets?" he asked her.

She smiled. "That's my secret."

They continued on around hills, through black ravines, always traveling the smaller roads. Twice they took disused trails that had surrendered to weeds and thin saplings. Sucking the horehound did help keep him awake, but it disappeared too quickly. Even the effects of the Creek Widow's magic eventually faded. The fatigue returned, and he plodded, wanting nothing more than to lie down in the dirt. He looked back at Sugar walking alongside the Tailor. The effect didn't seem to be wearing off on her. She smiled at Talen and he turned back around. When they finally branched off onto what could be no more than an animal trail, the Creek Widow spoke. "I think we're safe. The refuge is only a mile or so away."

"This is by Boar's Point, isn't it?" asked Sugar.

On the south end of the settled lands, at the edge of a vast, fertile valley, a line of hills ran like a great crooked finger down toward the sea. At the tip of that finger two rivers converged. Sometimes, in the heat of the summer, you could see hundreds of boar there. They came to wallow in the mud on the banks of the shallow, wide river, not only to cool themselves, but also to protect their hides from insects.

"It is," said the Creek Widow.

"Does this refuge have a bed?" asked Talen.

"Beds, baths, and dancing girls," said the Creek Widow.

"You can watch the girls," said Talen. "I'm going to sleep."

"That's a good boy."

They walked a few more paces, then Talen asked, "And how will River know to come here?"

"Because it is the refuge."

"And if she doesn't come?"

The Creek Widow looked over at him. "What do you want me to say, Talen?"

He wanted her to say that everything would be all right, that this awful storm would blow over and they could go back to mowing hay in the autumn sun. But he knew that would never be. Everything was all wrong, and it would only get worse. "I don't know," he said. And suddenly the whole mess overwhelmed him. Da, River, the beast. It was too much, and his eyes began to sting.

A few paces more and the Creek Widow reached over and felt the tears on his cheek with the back of one finger.

When she pulled her hand away, she grunted. Then she turned and stopped them. "I want you three to listen to me."

"I wasn't weeping," said Talen.

"Cha," she said, cutting him off. "There is no shame in

tears, especially when they're motivated by love. But the strong do not wallow in bleakness. Until the very end, they look for leverage, for a way to make the best of the situation. They generate options and plans and act. Hope, we must never lose hope."

"It's not that easy," said Talen.

"Of course not. That's why it's so powerful." She pointed her finger at him. "Even death can be turned to victory."

Talen did not see how that could be.

"Your mother did that," she said.

"What was her victory?"

"You don't believe me."

"My mother was a soul-eater," said Talen. He didn't mean it that way, but that's how it came out.

"Such words," she said. "I should slap you down. Your mother was no soul-eater."

"My mother doesn't matter," he said. "The question is what do we do about Da? What do we do about the creature and River?"

"We stop the creature," she said. "As for your da, Ke will let us know the situation. We will slay him only as a last resort. Despite your da's ardent wish for us to escape, I'm in command now. And I'm loath to leave that man behind."

"That's not a plan," said Talen.

"Interrupting is not helpful," she said.

"You're right," he said. "Let me begin again. What manner of creature is this?"

"That is a more fruitful question. We shall talk as we go." They began walking the animal trail again.

She held a thin branch out of the way. Talen took it, made sure it didn't smack the Tailor or Sugar, then joined her again.

"When Argoth told me about the fight in the tower

with the beast, I began searching my memory. I remembered a small note on one of the sheets in a codex about a beast made from the thin branches of a willow, a wickerman, if you will. But it was only mentioned in passing. I think it was a copy of a fragment long forgotten."

"But this thing was covered in grass."

"Not quite wicker, is it? But I wonder."

"So we don't know what it is."

"We have no name for the thing," she said, "but that doesn't mean we don't know anything about it."

"Do you think there are more? That this is some male claiming his territory? Or a female preparing to breed?"

"No. Not even the ancients knew the patterns that allow a creature to bring forth after its own kind. This thing was quickened by a lore master possessing breathtaking secrets. But the magic to breed was not one of them."

"But every living thing breeds in some fashion."

"No," said the Creek Widow. "That's not true. The armband your ridiculous father almost killed you with, that was a living thing. The weaves given to dreadmen—they live, after their fashion. You'd be surprised how many weaves of one kind and complexity or another there are in the world. But there's a sharp dividing line between those that can bring a soul into the world and those that cannot."

Those that can bring a soul into the world . . .

"People are weaves?" Sugar asked.

"Mark it," she said. "A manifestation of the perceptive nature of females. I told your mother, may, the Six keep her, you should have been brought inside the Grove last year."

How could people be woven? It didn't seem right. People, animals, even insects weren't things to be fashioned. Of course, they could be bred, and wasn't that a type of weaving? "So I'm a weave?" asked Talen.

"A bit shabby here and there, but yes, and with enough brilliant parts to capture the eye of those who can see it for what it is."

But Talen wasn't thinking about the compliment. He was thinking about the power to weave living things. And if this lore master could weave a wickerman, what other living things could he make?

"So," continued the Creek Widow, "*if* this thing is akin to the creature I read about, *then* we have at least three options. We can kill it, bind it, or kill its master."

"I don't think the first is an option," said Talen.

"Then it's a good thing you're not the one doing all the thinking."

"How can you do what Da and Uncle Argoth and a whole cohort at the fortress could not?"

"What are you going to do?" she asked. "Talk or listen?"

"Listen," he said. Of course, that was if she could get to the point.

"That's better," she said. "I'm telling you this because you're now part of the Grove, do you understand? Whether you like it or not, you're one of us. You're in an inch, you're in a mile."

Indeed, Talen thought.

"We are not without hope. There is lore, very old lore. The Divines have their dreadmen: we have something else. I'm not saying their weaves are evil. They can be used for much good. But what I am saying is that there yet exists lore that is older than dreadmen, older than the Divines themselves." She reached into one of the Tailor's saddlebags and withdrew something wrapped in dark cloth.

"We need some light," she said and stepped into a patch of ground fully lit by the moon. She motioned to him and Sugar. "Come here, both of you."

Talen and Sugar stepped to the Widow's side. Sugar stood so close their arms touched. He found it amazing that one day earlier he had been prepared to kill her.

The Creek Widow unwrapped the cloth. In it lay a square of gold half the size of his palm. "Look at it closely," she said. "This is Victor's crown."

Talen leaned in close, but not so close that he obscured the moonlight. The face of the square was covered in an exceedingly intricate design. A leather strap dangled from each of two opposite sides. It looked like something you might tie around your arm. Even so, it was nothing impressive. He'd seen gold medallions and brooches far more intricate and weighty on the hats of fat town wives.

"We only know of five of these that survived the ancient wars. Three were destroyed. One taken by the Witch of Cathay. The final was lost." She took the object over to Legs on the Tailor and let him feel it.

Legs picked it up. His head was turned as if he were looking off in the distance. Suddenly, he held the crown out, a look of surprise on his face. "Take it," he said.

"What is it?" the Creek Widow asked.

"It's," he said, "nothing."

"That doesn't sound like nothing."

"It doesn't feel like normal metal," he said.

She considered him for a moment, then took the crown back.

Talen recounted the numbers she'd just recited. "You said only five survived?"

"Only five."

"So how did you get this one?" he asked.

"Something lost can be found, can't it? Especially if a thief is the one who caused it to be lost in the first place."

"*You* stole this from a Divine?"

The Creek Widow cocked an eyebrow, but did not answer him. Goh, he thought. Nobody, not even the Widow, was what they seemed.

Talen looked at the object again. He picked it up as Legs had, but couldn't feel anything special in it. It was crude—too simple to be a crown. "I've never seen a lord tie anything like this to his head."

"Perhaps there's a message in its simplicity," she said. "But it's a weave nonetheless. An immensely powerful one."

Talen put it back.

"What does it do?" asked Sugar.

"There are three great powers in the world—Fire, Earth, and soul. This harnesses Earth and soul in a way that gives its wearer the power to cut through illusion and keep a clear heart. Of course, it also bestows incredible might."

Talen had never heard of such a thing.

"Can anyone wear it?" Sugar asked.

Talen nodded. "Like a dreadman's weave?"

"No, I told you. This isn't the work of Divines. This is the work of the old gods. When the Divines stamped out the old ways, they targeted the victors first. With them out of the way, their battles with the old gods went much easier."

"But if they were so easily overcome, doesn't that mean the Divines had a better way?"

"Were they overcome because the Divines overpowered them? Or did they fall because of the treachery of those who were close to them?"

Talen couldn't guess. He'd never heard of the victors.

The Creek Widow smiled. "I can't relate the whole history of the world in one night. Neither can I explain this. I—none of us—totally understand the old lore. Much has been lost. But you can be assured that we will deal with the creature and its master."

Talen examined the square again. It was gold, not black. "But it's empty. How can you use it?"

"I told you this wasn't the work of Kains and dreadmen. This isn't a weave just anybody can wear. This is not a weave you pick up lightly. It must be used with great care—and not until it's absolutely necessary. Not all can survive such a thing—it will kill the wearer if there isn't enough strength to draw upon."

She folded the crown back up in its cloth. "There are few men I know with the might to wear this. Maybe only one in our Grove."

Talen thought of all those he knew were in this Order. "Uncle Argoth is an incredible warrior."

"He is," she said. "But I'm not talking about him. I'm talking about your father, Talen."

Da?

"Physical strength and skill are important. But the strength I speak of is something else. You have to be bred to it. For the most part, the ability runs in family lines. Ke is close in strength. In fact, he might be able to wield the crown as well. But he hasn't been tested. River is not able. That's why we were so interested in you."

"I don't understand."

The Creek Widow paused. She took a deep breath through her nose. "Everyone has some gift. Part of the joy of the lore is watching what gifts are made manifest in each person. Sugar and Legs will have theirs. Ke has his. Your mother discovered things about you."

Talen thought about the revelations of the previous night. "Yes, I'm some accident, some freak of nature. River already told me."

"No. You are not an accident of nature. You grew under the influence of a design. A pattern, if you will. Born a grub, like the rest of us, but blessed, from the moment of conception, in your growth. And what you'll be when you've fully matured is anyone's guess. You're not some common worm."

"I don't know that I want to be a worm at all."

"Oh, worm, flower, seedling. You've been pruned and grafted for a great purpose—that is the truth of it. We all are."

"Pruned by whom?" asked Talen.

"Well, think: who would want that? There are stories, very old stories, of cultivated lords, but there's no agreement on the source. Most say this cultivating was one of the lost arts of the old gods. A few texts talk of dark foes, of creatures with a bloody thirst, which the cultivated lords battled. The old records are not clear. But the point is, your mother discovered, worked into your very being, strange and intricate patterns of power."

"But to what purpose?"

"So impatient. Think! A child born to one of those in the Order. My dear boy, could it be the Creators have seen it's time for a new crop to be planted? A special generation that will bear forth a new kingdom? We've all been waiting expectantly to see the blessing you'd become. Who knows, Talen: you yourself might one day be *more* than a victor."

More? He could not deny that a thrill ran along his skin, even if it was foolish. He wondered: if he could handle the quantities of Fire River said he could, did that mean he might be able to multiply himself more than other men? A supreme dreadman.

"I think you are overly expectant," Talen said. "Whatever these patterns are, they are flawed in me." That had to be what Mother meant. Not that he needed a flaw, but that he was broken by them.

"Who is ever without blemish?" she asked.

"It wasn't a blemish," said Talen. "River used the word 'twisted.'"

"Indeed," said the Creek Widow. "When talking about a weave, twists are very specific patterns of power." She grasped him gently by the chin and forced him to look at her. "Besides, all of us, lad, are broken. Don't worry about your limits. Worry about what you choose to do or not do despite those limits. You are Hogan's and Rose's boy. You have been bred to power and packaged with a few surprises. And if you turn out to be a crooked arrow"— she grinned—"well, they have their uses as well."

Yeah, he thought. Crooked arrows were chopped up for kindling.

"Talen," she said and gently stroked his cheek. "Trust your mother. Trust her. If she had thought your abilities posed some great danger, would she have died to save you?"

That gave him reason to pause. Would his mother have killed him? Or would she have saved him, unwilling to see his flaws? He had so many questions. So many he wished he could ask Mother. He glanced at Sugar. He wondered if her mother had worked magic on her as well.

The Creek Widow placed the wrapped crown back in the saddlebag. "We'll find the others at the refuge. It requires a trio to awaken this crown. And when it awakens and covers your da in its mantle, then we shall go hunting."

"And if we cannot rescue him?"

"Then we shall work around our limitations."

42

LIKE A SPIDER

Hunger had been right: the female's trail was easy enough to pick up again. She'd gained a few hours on him, but he'd made most of that up. More important, the Mother was pleased with him.

Hunger had found the Koramite in the buttery of an old Fir-Noy hunting lodge. The Koramite had been burning his magic, but the king's collar about his neck only shunted it off like a fat stovepipe.

It had been easy to take him. Almost all the Fir-Noy guarding him had run. One guard in the cellar had tried to kill the Koramite, but Hunger had wrenched the guard's arm loose and left him screaming.

Unlike the guards, the Koramite had not run. He had risen and stood before Hunger, the king's collar about his neck glinting in the light. The collar had not tempted him. It only brought to his mind the pain of losing his son. But the Koramite was now safely stowed in the Mother's cave. And Hunger was on the trail of the female. He'd find the others and the remaining members of his family would be released.

Hunger tracked her up one hill and around another. He tracked her past a farm he recognized as belonging to a woman called Matiga, yet another member of the Order. He'd searched the place. Pockets of stink hung here and there, but he found nothing but a dog and a few chickens. So Hunger continued on.

The female had joined up with others, one of which had to be Matiga, for he'd smelled her all over the farm. The whole lot were moving south. In the back of his mind he knew that was significant, but not until he entered a small kidney-shaped vale did he know why. He recognized this vale from the memories he'd obtained by eating Larther, and the memory made Hunger tremble with delight.

He was in the finger of hills that ended at Boar's Point. And not far from that point, in a small, narrow valley hidden in the finger, lay the Order's refuge. It was a cave located at the foot of a large, steep hillside. He could see it in his mind's eye: less than a mile away, through this small vale, up over the saddle between the two hills, and then down into the next valley.

That is where the female and Matiga were going. There the Order would have chambers and rooms, barrels of beans and grainy honey, water from the mountain, and an immense stone to cover the mouth of the cave. It had a place for horses. The Order could live there for weeks on end. Why hadn't he thought of this before? Of course this is where they'd go.

He would find them there. He would find *all* of them there.

Up ahead he heard sounds. Voices. The female and her group were only a few hundred yards away.

Hunger thanked the Creators—his opportunity to free his family had come.

There was a trail that wound through the vale, an animal trail that broke off of the one that ran along by the creek. It would take him to the refuge, but he knew another way. A faster way along the cliff. He would hasten to the refuge. And when they arrived, he would be waiting for them.

THE REFUGE HAD two ways in and out. The mouth, at the base of the hill, and a bolt-hole dozens of yards above on the slope. The Order covered both entrances with large stones. Doing so kept it tight and hidden from man and beast.

Hunger approached the upper exit from above, carrying an enormous log. This he carefully placed on top of the stone already covering the bolt-hole. It would take two or three of them, multiplied, to push that off.

Then he quietly descended the slope. When he reached the base, he caught the faint scent of wood smoke.

The best place to catch one of the Order was in the cave, all bottled up like flies. He stood for a long time looking for the watch they'd surely posted. But he saw nobody on watch.

Hunger approached, picking his way around the brush and trees, avoiding the spots where Zu Hogan had pointed out the cleverly concealed trip lines, and soon stood before the mouth of the cave. A man was burning a small fire inside, Hunger could smell it.

Something moved in the brush behind him. He turned, expecting the watch, but instead saw a small herd of deer moving through the trees off to the right.

Hunger looked about once more, then silently slipped into the cave.

The first chamber was where they kept livestock. It was wide, large enough to hold a dozen horses, but there were no horses, no goats, nothing but a large pile of hay by the stalls. He looked up the corridor that led to the second and third chambers. The far chamber was dark, but the flickering orange light of a fire spilled out of the door to the second chamber and played on the rock wall of the corridor.

Hunger went back to the entrance, took hold of the large squarish covering stone, and pushed it back into place, closing off any escape.

"Who's there?" A voice from the second chamber.

Hunger walked through the first chamber and to the entrance of the second.

Ke, Zu Hogan's son, stood above a small fire over which he roasted three rabbits. He held a knife in one hand, staff in the other. Hunger, as Larther, had been clouted by that staff more than once in weapon's practice. Ke was powerful and fast. Deadly.

"Who are you?"

Hunger could not answer. He simply stepped into the small light.

Surprise flashed across Ke's features, but he just as quickly recovered and with blinding speed threw his knife.

It buried itself in Hunger's eye. He did not expect the pain that shot through him. He thought he was beyond pain. Yet this did not debilitate him. It was strong, but dull, and he shrugged it off.

Ke took advantage of his hesitation and darted past him toward the mouth of the cave.

Ke was fast, but not as fast as River. Hunger ran after him. He caught him at the entrance by the shoulder and whipped him around.

Hunger expected Ke to try to free himself, but Ke grabbed Hunger by the neck and crotch instead. He lifted Hunger and cast him against the wall of the cave.

Ke was always the one to try something surprising. And it had always worked. But not this time.

Ke pushed the stone covering the entrance.

Hunger lunged forward and latched on to Ke with both hands. Then he swept Ke's feet out from under him, dropping Ke like a stone.

Hunger landed atop Ke and knocked out his breath.

There is no escape, thought Hunger. Not for you, brother. Not for me.

Ke struggled mightily, but Hunger bound him as he had his sister, then he tied him up with a rope. He laid Ke in the third chamber where they kept the beans and water, then went back to the mouth of the cave and shoved the rock aside to open it for the others.

He looked about, considering the best place to hide. Then he looked up. Hunger climbed up the wall to the high, sloped ceiling above the mouth of the cave, up into the inky dark. And there he clung, waiting like a spider for the others to enter his trap.

TALEN FOLLOWED THE Creek Widow to the bottom of a narrow valley between two steep and stony hills. Dawn had not yet broken, but the sky had lightened, and he could see the valley well enough. He'd been up now for twenty-four hours and was exhausted. The woods broke on a clearing that began by the brook and ran halfway up one of the hills.

"Here it is," she said.

"Here?" asked Talen. Such a clearing couldn't provide much protection. He thought she'd said it was a cave. But he could see none. "What do we do, hide under the bushes?"

"Yes, Talen," she said. "That's what the great minds of our Order came up with. Hide under the bushes." She shook her head and led him through the waist-high brush to the steep and stony base of the hill.

Talen thought that maybe they'd dug some cellar in the valley floor, then the Creek Widow turned a corner around a tall seam of stone running dozens of yards up the hill and disappeared.

"Goh," he said. He arrived at the place where she vanished and found a jagged cleft in the seam of stone. Before him stood the mouth to a cave, a wan light glowing inside.

"Bring the Tailor in here," said the Creek Widow from inside.

The mouth was barely wide enough for the horse, but it

was not tall enough to allow a mounted man to pass through. Sugar untied Legs and helped him down. Then the three of them entered.

This first chamber stretched perhaps two dozen feet wide. He looked up into the blackness but could not see the ceiling. A light came from a chamber down a short corridor.

"Can you see this in full daylight?" he asked.

"Not unless you're right upon it," she said. She pointed at a large stone behind him. "And that's only when the stone is removed. Replace the stone and this cave doesn't exist."

Something popped. It sounded like green wood in a fire. "Hello?" he said, hoping to hear Ke's voice. But there was no reply.

"You'll find this a comfortable place," said the Creek Widow. "There's no vermin that gets in here. No rats. And there's a spot where the water drips clear and cold."

Around the corner from the mouth lay some horse stalls and a crib of hay. The Creek Widow held an armful of hay and put it at the head of one stall. "Bring him over here. I'll rub him down. You three go see who's here. And get a place to rest while you can."

"Where do you keep the food stores?" asked Sugar.

"I'll worry about that," said the Creek Widow.

Talen was more than happy to oblige. He walked to the lit chamber, but found no one, just a fire burning low in a hearth. Sugar and Legs joined him. He wondered where the smoke from this fire went. There must be a hole somewhere up above. But if no vermin could get in, that meant they had to have a cap for it. If not, this refuge wasn't bottled up as tight as the Creek Widow would like to think. Three rabbits stretched out on forks above the fire. The meat wasn't burned, but it was getting close. To the side he saw Ke's pack.

"It's Ke," Talen called out for the Creek Widow. Then he squatted by the rabbits. "Looks like we've got us a snack."

Knowing that Ke was here sent a surge of relief though him. He did not know until then how helpless he had felt. He put down his bow and removed the quiver of arrows he'd strapped to his waist. Then he squatted close to the fire, and with his knife, skewered one of the carcasses and removed it from the cooking fork. He peeled off a tender piece of loin and stuck it in his mouth. "Not too dry yet." He turned to Sugar and and held the roasted carcass to her.

Legs sniffed. "That had better not be rat."

The Creek Widow cursed. At least, that's what he thought it sounded like. The Tailor had probably pooped on her feet. He smiled to himself thinking of that. Old Lady Brown Toe. He'd give her a ribbing about that.

"Oh, it's rat," said Talen. "Nice and plump. You get the tail."

"Don't believe him," said Sugar and twisted off a piece of meat for her brother.

Talen fed the fire and ate his share of the meat. Nobody said anything while they ate. But when he'd finished, he said, "Where do you think the Widow's gone? It doesn't take that long to put away a horse."

"Maybe she went to the privy," said Legs.

"Probably," said Talen. "And while she's away, I'm going to see what else they have here to eat." He could barely muster enough strength to fight his fatigue, but he stood. At one end of this chamber stood a table and some shelves. He grabbed an oil lamp from the shelf and lit it. Then he walked out into the corridor.

"Aunt?" he said.

The flame guttered in a breeze that he hadn't noticed before. The Creek Widow did not reply, so he headed farther into the cave. The corridor sloped upwards. The flickering lamp cast odd shadows on the wall. Maybe two dozen yards farther he came to what had to be the third chamber. He held the lamp high and saw barrels of food. But it was all grains and dry stuffs, including rope, arrows, and cord.

He exited the room. He was too tired to cook grains, but at least he could get a drink. The dripping rock must be farther up the corridor. He climbed, found the dripping rock, and satisfied his thirst. The corridor took a sharp turn upwards at this point and someone had carved steps into it. The Creek Widow had told him there was an escape route out the back. This must be it.

Despite his weariness, his curiosity took him up the stairs. It wasn't too long and he found the exit. Another large stone sealed it, but it too had been moved aside. He left the lamp burning below and climbed through the exit and out into a cluster of rocks to stand on the side of the hill some distance above and to the right of where he estimated the mouth of this refuge to be. He wondered why the exit was open. Maybe the air in the cave had been stale. It certainly created a nice breeze through the corridor.

Except he was sure there had been no breeze before. "Ke," he called out into the night. There was no response, nothing but the sound of night insects.

Talen turned round, picked up his lamp, and went back down the stairs. He took another drink at the dripping rock and noticed this time that the water from the rock ran into a fissure that ran a dozen feet along the side of the path.

He passed Sugar and Legs by the fire. When he reached the first chamber, he found the Tailor standing in his stall, saddle still on his back. That was bad form. The Creek Widow could have held her business until she'd unsaddled him. He wondered where the privy was. It certainly couldn't be a formal thing. She'd probably just taken a spade with her out the exit.

Talen walked over to take care of the Tailor, but when he got close he kicked something in the dirt. He bent over and picked it up. It was her codex of lore.

Then he saw other things scattered about.

"Aunt?" he called.

Nothing.

He walked over to the mouth of the cave and stood listening. He scanned the clearing, stepped farther out and looked up the hill. Nothing but the insects, the stars, and the moon shining down from the west.

The Tailor might have simply knocked over one of the bags. Or perhaps Ke had returned with something urgent. It was possible. But not likely. She wouldn't just run off.

"Aunt?" he called out again.

When she did not reply, he took his lamp, held it low, and searched the ground.

He found Ke's knife, which was odd. He identified all their footprints. There were five of them. Then he saw a sixth. Talen bent low and measured it with the span between his thumb and pinky finger. It was mishappen and large. Larger than any human's could possibly be.

He knew immediately what it belonged to.

He raced back to the corridor. That thing had been here. A worse idea shivered him. It might be feeding on the Creek Widow at this very moment somewhere outside. Or had it returned?

Talen stood at the entrance of the second chamber looking at the impenetrable depths of the corridor.

Did it see him? Was it watching him even now?

"Aunt?" he called into the dark passage. He lingered a moment more, listening, but there was no reply. He turned to Sugar and Legs. "Get up."

"What are you doing?" asked Sugar.

"The monster," he said, "it's here. I think it's taken them."

And he did not want to be bottled up in this cave waiting for it to return. They had to get out. Sugar tried to wake Legs, but he would not rouse. So Talen rushed in and lifted him over his aching shoulders as he done the previous day.

He carried him out, and put him in the saddle that was still on the Tailor. Sugar was about to tie him on, when Legs blearily asked, "What are we doing?"

Sugar shushed him.

"Leaving," Talen whispered. He untied the horse and led it out of the stall.

He didn't know where he would go or what they could do. They just had to get out. Maybe they could go to the far hill and watch this entrance and hope that this was nothing more than his fatigue and imagination running away with him.

Something scuffled outside the mouth of the cave.

Talen and Sugar froze.

They were trapped.

43.

HAG'S TEETH

Talen pulled out his knife, knowing it was useless.

A group of armsmen rushed in. They held torches in one hand, swords in the other. As soon as they appeared, they split, the larger portion moving farther into the cave, silent, blinding fast, gone in the blink of an eye.

The last two suddenly stood before Talen and Sugar. The one in front of Talen held his sword tip inches from Talen's chest.

Such speed—it took Talen's breath away. These weren't mere armsmen, but dreadmen. In a glance, Talen saw the markings of the Lions of Mokad upon the dreadman's clothing, the tattoos about the lips, the man's deadly gaze. These were the Skir Master's personal guard. And the one holding his sword in front of Talen looked like he would kill at the slightest provocation. A tattoo flared away from one of his eyes. The other eye was puffed, the skin horribly burned.

"On your bellies," whispered the dreadman.

Talen offered no resistance. He dropped to his knees, then prostrated himself. He turned his head so that one cheek was flat against the earth. Sugar lay with her face in the dirt of the floor. Legs hesitated, then slid off the side of the horse and dropped to the ground. If the Tailor stepped to the side, he'd tread on the boy.

Talen looked up at the dreadman. The torch in the dreadman's hand spit. One small burning droplet of pitch struck Talen's neck, but he dared not brush it away. The Tailor was not comfortable with the fire or the men. He protested and backed up, banging into the stall.

Two more men walked into the chamber, a smaller one followed by a larger. The smaller man had short white hair and bushy eyebrows. He stood proudly erect. His clothes were made of sumptuous cloth. But it was the eyes that drew Talen's attention: as black and shiny as polished jet.

Talen had never before seen a Skir Master. And this one filled him with dread. Talen couldn't see the face of the larger man, but it was clear he was the Skir Master's servant.

"Master," the large one said. "Do you see? I'll make up for my sins."

Talen recognized that voice, and he looked on in disbelief: it was Uncle Argoth.

The dreadmen who had moved deeper into the refuge returned to the first chamber. Talen counted six of them besides the two watching him, Sugar, and Legs.

Another man joined the Skir Master—the Crab.

Talen should have known the Fir-Noy would be behind this.

The Crab looked about the chamber. "Well, well. Even I wouldn't have believed it if I hadn't seen it."

"There's nobody here," a dreadman reported.

"No one?" demanded the Skir Master. He turned to Uncle Argoth. "Clansman? Is there another place you haven't told me about?"

"No, no. The stone was pushed aside. Either they've come and gone or they've gone and will return."

Uncle Argoth groveled before the Skir Master. He was so obsequious that if Talen hadn't seen his face he would have never believed it was Uncle Argoth.

"There was a fire in the first chamber," the lead dreadman said. "The coals were still warm."

"Then they're here," said Uncle Argoth.

The Skir Master turned and looked at Talen. "Who are you?"

"Nobody," said Talen.

The dreadman kicked him in the side so hard it took his breath away.

"I am the son of Hogan the Koramite, Horse of Blood Hill. Those are the children of Sparrow, smith of the village of Plum."

The Skir Master made a small noise to himself and walked over to look down upon Talen.

"He speaks the truth," said Uncle Argoth.

The Skir Master considered Talen as if he were judging a poorly fired pot. "Was your father here?"

"No," said Talen. "Not that I know of."

"Do not seek to deceive me," said the Skir Master. "I already know that he, like this girl's witch mother, was snatched from those set to guard him. Tell me where the others are."

The Skir Master's pants were scorched. His feet bare. And there stood Uncle Argoth. A traitor. It didn't matter. They were all dead. Their running had led them straight to those they most wished to avoid. "I do not know, Great One."

"Cut out his eye," said the Crab.

The dreadman with the burned eye looked to the Skir Master.

"Please," said Talen. "We came and the cave was empty. Our guide disappeared while we were in the other chamber. I think the monster took her as well."

"It's as I told you, Great One," Uncle Argoth said. "The creature is not ours. Something else is afoot."

"Maybe not yours personally," said the Skir Master. "But you're only one man. How do you know the two Koramites, whom you trust so much, are not part of another murder of Sleth?"

The Skir Master motioned at Talen, and the dreadman guarding him wrenched Talen up by his hair. He grasped Talen's head in a one-armed lock and held it firmly against his abdomen.

"I swear," said Talen. "I'm telling the truth."

The dreadman drew his knife. "Hold still," he said and gave Talen a shake. The tang of his body odor encircled Talen.

"I can show you the footprint!" cried Talen. "The monster was here."

The dreadman changed his grip on his knife and readied it to plunge into Talen's eye.

"Stop," said the Skir Master.

Talen stared up at the thin point of the blade.

"Tell me everything you know."

Everything? Talen wondered. Where would he start? With his mother? With the fact that he was some soul-eater's artifact? Or should he simply blurt out that his family were all soul-eaters? And then there was Uncle Argoth—was he playing some ruse or had he been subverted? Tell the truth or fabricate a story, either might conflict with what Uncle Argoth had already told the Divine. He decided it would be best to interpret "everything" to mean only what he knew about the monster. He needed to resist them.

"He's going to lie," said the dreadman. His face with its burned eye was terrible to behold.

"Then give him a bit of motivation," said the Skir Master.

"No," said Talen.

But the dreadman brought the knife down. Talen tried to squirm away, but the man's grip was like stone. Talen closed his eyes at the last moment and felt the burn as the blade sliced open the skin on his cheek below his eye.

"I saw it first at our farm," said Talen.

But the dreadman kept cutting. Blood ran down the side of Talen's face and to his ear.

"Please. I only learned about the Grove just two days ago. I'll tell you everything." He was ashamed at how easily he broke. But that disappointment was quickly put aside as he rattled off everything he knew about the creature. His only triumph was that he did not talk about anything else.

The dreadman lifted the knife away from Talen's face.

Talen continued with every detail he'd seen and all those he'd heard from Da about the battle in the tower. He ended by saying, "Its footprints are here. I can only suspect it's taken my brother and the Creek Widow, who led us here. I'll show you."

The Skir Master regarded him, then nodded, and the dreadman let him up. Talen immediately put his hand to the cut on his face. He pressed his fingers to the cut to hold it closed and stop the bleeding, then walked to the clearest set of prints.

"Here," he said and pointed at a footprint. "And here."

The Skir Master squatted down and examined the prints. After some time, he said, "If it's lore masters this creature wants, then a lore master is what it will get. I think I know what's been let loose upon your lands." He stood and turned to the Crab. "We're going to need at least five sturdy ropes, no shorter than forty feet. Go."

"Yes, Great One," the Crab said, then exited the chamber.

The Skir Master turned to the lead dreadman. "This creature cannot be beat by force of arms alone. It was bred by lore, and lore alone can defeat it. If it's rescuing the soul-eaters, then it will come for the clansman. If it's merely collecting them, eliminating them, then it will still come because I will raise a bait it can't resist. We need nooses and snares. You must hold the thing, if only for a moment. I want five of you here. Set the other four to watch. You will distract it. And I shall take it with the ravelers."

"What about Shegom?"

"The skir will conceal herself elsewhere. I must catch the creature off guard. Shegom will only make it wary."

The lead dreadman bowed and led his men out of the cave.

Talen looked over at Sugar. The expression on her face told him she was at as great a loss as he was. Legs had not moved, but still lay upon his belly.

The Skir Master turned to Uncle Argoth. "You didn't tell me about your nephew."

"He knows nothing," said Argoth. "His father only recently tried to waken him. He is of no consequence."

The Skir Master looked down at Talen. "Remember, Clansman, one day more and I will have all of your secrets. Tell Leaf to bring me the sack."

"Yes, Great One. Thank you," said Uncle Argoth.

Moments later Uncle Argoth returned with the large dreadman that had cut Talen's face. The man carefully placed a worn leather sack at the Skir Master's feet. "Where do you want the Crab's men?"

"I want them hidden as much as possible. And where they can't hide, they need to appear to be no threat." Then the Skir Master opened the mouth of the sack and withdrew three items. The first was a thin silver case etched in a marvelous design. It was about a span long and half as wide. The remaining items were two gauntlets worked in silver and gold. They were not steel-plated gloves used for protection in battle. These were made of whitened leather. The sleeve of the glove extended past the wrist partway up the forearm. An unfamiliar looping design was painted there in red and blue. The hand of the glove was studded with gold. Sewn into the palm was a gold disk the size of a small coin. But Talen knew that wasn't a coin. It had to be a weave of some type.

The Skir Master put the gauntlets on and tied the sleeves tight to his forearms. Then he opened the case. Inside, secured by silken threads on a bed of blue velvet lay three gleaming spikes. Their lengths too had been etched with an unfamiliar design. He showed the spikes to Uncle Argoth.

"Are they wild?" asked Uncle Argoth.

"Indeed," said the Skir Master.

There were weaves that only a lore master could use.

There were others, wild ones, like those worn by dreadmen, that operated of their own accord.

"Hag's teeth," said Uncle Argoth.

"Not the proper name," said the Skir Master, "but yes. Does the Order know how to fashion these?"

Argoth looked at the spikes as if he were a boy looking at an unclaimed walnut pie. "No, Great One."

"It will unravel the seams of soul and body and Fire of any living thing. It takes months to complete the very first step, requires the Fire from scores of lives. One of these is worth any number of fiefs. There are only three Glories with the knowledge of how to make them."

"We would not be able to stand against such," said Argoth.

"Of course not. That is why you run and hide."

"We are fools," said Uncle Argoth.

"Yes, but capable enough to attract the attention of someone with power. And since you've been targeted, I think it's best we use you as part of the bait."

TALEN SAT WITH Uncle Argoth, Sugar, and Legs a dozen paces away from the mouth of the cave in the clearing. Before them burned a fire to make it look like they were doing nothing more than preparing a breakfast. A number of hours had passed since the Skir Master had found them. The sun had risen. Because of the steep slopes of this valley, the sunshine had not yet reached every corner of the valley floor. But morning had begun. A meadowlark sang in the scrub a few dozen yards away. The stream that cut through this vale burbled. Beyond the meadow a huge flock of sparrows squabbled in a single tree. And yet, as late as it was, there had been no sign of the monster.

The Crab stood watch a few paces away, while the Skir Master waited by the mouth of the cave. The Crab had brought fifty men with him. They loitered in groups in various positions around the cave. To the casual observer, it might look like they stood in random places. But the Skir Master had ordered them so that only one approach to the cave lay wide open. He expected the monster to come that way. And when it reached them, the five dread-men who stayed with the Skir Master would spring.

He'd overhead some of the Fir-Noy talking. Twenty dreadmen had been in the Skir Master's guard. The big one that was his guide made it twenty-one. But twelve of those had been lost at sea in a fire. And Uncle Argoth had come back, sniveling and cringing. He hadn't been able to hear what had happened. He doubted even the Fir-Noy knew.

The breeze shifted and blew the smoke toward Talen. He picked up the rock he was sitting on and moved out of its way, closer to Uncle Argoth. So much for the Creek Widow's theory of him being bred to greatness. He'd cracked like an egg.

And so much for the Creek Widow. He wondered what had happened to her.

He wondered about Da. The Skir Master had said the monster had taken him. Talen tried to talk to Uncle Argoth. But the man totally ignored him. He ignored everyone and sat to the side, rocking on his haunches and muttered something unintelligible under his breath.

"What do you think will become of us if the Skir Master kills it?" Talen asked.

"I don't think we have to worry about that," said Legs. "Usually the bait is the first thing to go."

"True enough," Talen said.

They were silent for a time. Talen wondered where Nettle was at this moment. He hoped he was safe but wished, nevertheless, that he was here. Then Sugar spoke up. "Once he faces off with that creature, I say we slip away.

Because if he takes it, he doesn't know where the monster's cave is, which means we can walk straight into that lair and retrieve whoever is still alive. And if he doesn't destroy it, then I certainly don't want to be anywhere close."

"The only clear path is up that hill," Talen said. The outer dreadmen and Fir-Noy had positioned themselves everywhere else. Talen didn't think running would work since the Fir-Noy had horses, but thinking about escape was better than thinking of being devoured by a monster or questioned by a Divine whose ship had burned underneath him.

Uncle Argoth reached out and gripped Talen's arm much too tightly.

"Uncle?" Talen asked.

"He knows," said Uncle Argoth, his grip tightening even further. "He knows everything."

"What's he talking about?" Sugar asked.

Talen shrugged. He tried to pull away but his uncle would not let go.

A dreadman broke the tree line on the other side of the meadow on the valley's floor. He was tall and thin and fast, as fast as a horse at full gallop. He ran across the field and in moments he stood before the Skir Master. "Cos and Heel are dead, their backs broken."

"Shegom reports nothing," said the Skir Master.

"They've been dead for at least an hour."

The Skir Master studied the hills about the valley. To this moment, he hadn't yet withdrawn any of the hag's teeth. He did so now, removing one of the silver spikes from its blue velvet bed and grasping it in his white, gold-studded glove. "Where are you?" he said under his breath.

As if in answer Talen saw a stone above the mouth of the cave move. He looked closer.

"Goh," he said. It was as if a part of the hill had come alive.

The Crab followed Talen's gaze.

Then the creature jumped, dropping down with a thud only paces behind the Skir Master. In the morning light its features were clearer than they had been that night in the yard. It was a grotesque giant. And while clumps of grass still clung to it here and there, he saw the underlying color was of dirt and blue stone. One shoulder was burned. Along the other, a patch of small white flowers grew.

The Skir Master turned, but he was too late and the creature slapped the hand holding the tooth. The hand flew backward violently.

The Crab cried out. He clutched at his throat, at the spike that stood out of his neck. Then the end of the spike curled like a worm. In a flash of silver it wriggled into the Crab's neck.

The Crab gasped and stumbled. He tripped toward Talen and the others. Talen tried to scramble back, but Uncle Argoth would not release him. Then the Crab twitched and toppled into the fire. Ash puffed up in a billow.

Talen tried to pry Argoth's fingers away, but could not. He choked on the ash that blew into his face.

The Skir Master danced back with blinding speed, trying to pull another spike from his case, but the monster moved more quickly and swatted the case out of his hand. The case flew wide, disappearing into the brush a number of paces away.

"The teeth," said Uncle Argoth. He released Talen's arm and scrambled to the bushes where the case had fallen.

Leaf cried out, drew a black-bladed sword, and charged the monster. The speed of the dreadman was frightening.

"Shegom!" the Skir Master yelled and dodged away from the monster.

Another dreadman, who had been hiding only paces

away from where the monster had first appeared, stood and flung his wide noose around the creature's head. The dreadman yanked his noose tight about the monster's neck. Another dreadman sprung from his hiding place in front of the cave and threw his noose. A third dreadman joined him, and the two of them pulled the creature back. It lurched into a small trap that had been dug for it.

Yards away, a dozen Fir-Noy heaved on the rope that lined the trap and caught one of the monster's legs. A Fir-Noy slapped the hind of one of the two horses harnessed to that line, and the animals surged forward.

The monster spun. The power of the horses and soldiers would have pulled a normal man to the ground, but the monster was too quick, too strong. Instead of falling to the ground, it took a giant sideways step and then braced itself in a wide stance, the grass still clinging to its body shuddering at the impact.

It reached down and grabbed the line around its foot.

Another noose flew, but missed the monster.

Leaf, the big dreadman with the scorched eye, rushed forward. The blade of his sword was as black as a crow—a spirit sword. In a blinding move he hacked into the creature's side. Talen thought he'd cleaved the monster in two. But the monster did not seem to be affected by the blow.

It ignored Leaf and yanked on the line holding its foot. The group of Fir-Noy on the other end stumbled backward into a heap. The two horses were also forced back and trod upon the men in the rear. Men cried out. The horses whinnied in confusion. One leapt forward again. The other skittered sideways. Then, as if the monster had pinched the thin stem of a weed, the line snapped.

"The teeth!" the Skir Master roared. "The teeth!"

"Here!" Uncle Argoth cried out and held the case up. "Master!"

The Skir Master turned and dashed toward him.

Leaf snatched his sword out of the creature's side. He swung the flashing black blade again in the early light, but the creature ripped it out of Leaf's hand and flung it away. It grabbed one of the lines connected to a noose about its neck. It twisted around violently, and the dreadman who had tied the other end of the rope about his waist cried out. He was yanked from his position and into the air.

The monster twisted and yanked again. In midair, the dreadman lurched horribly in a new direction. This time there was no cry of pain. The monster swung him like a man swinging a stone at the end of a rope.

The Skir Master snatched up the case from Uncle Argoth's outstretched arm and held it above his head. "Here, son of Lamash!" he yelled, his face full of fury. "Here is your doom!"

But the monster swung the dreadman around, the thick rope making a deep swoosh and hiss as it sped in its circle.

The Skir Master saw it, but he was not fast enough, and the dreadman swinging from the end of the rope slammed into both the Skir Master and Uncle Argoth, sending the two men flying.

The monster ignored the third line about its neck and charged after the Skir Master, dragging the dreadman attached to the line like a toy attached to a child's string.

A Fir-Noy standing just beyond Uncle Argoth shouted. He leveled his spear and charged in for a death blow. He struck deep, but the monster simply ran him over, then plucked out the spear.

The Skir Master rose and began to search the ground about him frantically.

There was a movement at Talen's feet. He looked down at the Crab. The man's tunic had begun to smolder; but that wasn't what had caught Talen's attention. Something moved at the man's ear. A glint of silver, and the long hag's tooth came wriggling through the skin at the man's temple.

Talen backed away.

The tooth curled an end as if sniffing the air. Then it wriggled the rest of the way out of his head and dropped to the ash.

Sugar pulled on Talen. "Lords!" she said. "Run!"

He scrambled to his feet, stumbled backward. He turned, only to find a dozen Fir-Noy, weapons drawn, charging straight toward him. Sugar and Legs ran one way. Talen was not quick enough and had to dive the other way to avoid them.

The men sped past and attacked the monster, but with one, two, three backhand swings the creature slew that many men. The remaining Fir-Noy hesitated.

The monster took a step and closed the gap between itself and the Skir Master.

The Skir Master turned and looked up at the beast.

At that moment, Leaf, who had retrieved his sword, screamed his battle cry and charged the monster again. His sword cut into the monster's neck.

The creature grasped Leaf by the throat and lifted him up. Leaf yanked the sword out of the monster's neck, then drove the blade deep into its chest. But it had no effect on the creature.

What kind of nightmare was it that could withstand a black sword of the Kains?

Then the monster twisted its grip and snapped Leaf's massive neck like a twig. The big dreadman sagged in its hand.

The Skir Master rose in fury. In a flash, he charged the monster's back. But instead of striking it with a weapon, he punched into it with his fist, going in up to his elbow.

The monster cast Leaf aside, the black sword still sticking out of its chest.

"Where is it?" the Skir Master cried. "Where is your quickening!"

The creature wrenched around, trying to get at the Skir Master, but the Divine was too quick.

"Clansman!" shouted the Skir Master, feeling inside the monster.

Uncle Argoth lay upon the ground, unmoving.

No, thought Talen. He can't be dead. Lords, no!

Two more dreadmen closed on the creature. They carried spears and harried it, thrusting repeatedly at its head. Their movements were blinding fast. But it was useless, couldn't they see that?

The creature grabbed one of the spears and jabbed it into one of the dreadman's faces. The other dreadman struck, but the monster swung the spear and and gave the dreadman such a blow to the side that Talen was sure half his ribs had been staved in. The dreadman fell over backward.

The Skir Master withdrew his arm and punched into the back of the monster a bit higher. His arm sunk almost up to the shoulder. "Yes!" he said.

The monster reached behind its back. The Skir Master moved to one side, but then in a blinding flash the monster's other elbow slammed into the Skir Master and sent him flying.

The Skir Master landed with a grunt many yards away on a clump of scrub.

The monster made a sound. A loud, horrible sigh. And turned toward the Skir Master.

Men littered this small battlefield. Talen looked around and saw a number of the Fir-Noy running. Those that did remain hesitated. The only dreadman still alive of those that had stayed by the cave was the one the monster had been dragging behind him. He stood, holding his side.

He'd cut the rope connecting him to the monster, but had left the portion of the rope he'd knotted about his waist.

The Skir Master shook himself and rose, distaste and anger twisting his face. He held up something dark. Something he'd taken from deep within the monster. "You will not prevail," he said.

But the monster seemed not to be affected.

The Skir Master stood his ground.

A sudden gust of wind kicked up dirt and debris. A huge crack sounded from the far side of the meadow. Talen looked and saw tree limbs as thick as a man's body tossed into the air, swirling in a violent wind. The wind sped across the meadow, flattening the scrub of the clearing as it came.

The monster charged. One, two, three paces. It was almost upon the Divine.

But the wind was faster. It sped past the monster. The Skir Master stretched his tattooed arms out wide. The wind whipped about him. Then, before the monster could take another step, the wind picked him up and carried him into the air like a leaf in a storm.

The monster took two steps and sprang after him, leaping a dozen or more feet into the air.

Talen thought he saw it catch the Skir Master's leg, but the wind thrashed the bushes, casting debris into his eyes. Then a huge gust slammed into Talen, knocking him onto his back. Something struck his face, nearly blinding him, and Talen covered his eyes.

The wind howled about him, then as quickly as it had come, it was gone.

Talen rolled over and brushed dirt from his eyes, careful of the knife cut. Debris that had been cast into the air still fluttered about the whole meadow. He looked up. At first he saw nothing, and then, hundreds of yards above him, he saw the Skir Master and monster. He watched them sail upward into the morning sky until they were nothing more than black dots.

Talen's hand stung. He found a thin twig sticking straight out of it, which he plucked out and cast aside.

Uncle Argoth shouted in pain.

Talen ran to him. He found Uncle Argoth huddling on his knees, the case of hag's teeth lying in the grass beside him.

"Uncle," Talen said. "Uncle."

"No," he said. "No, no, no." Then he winced as if someone had struck him. He cried out in extreme agony.

Talen stepped back, expecting a hag's tooth to wriggle its way out of him.

Argoth jerked. And then the terror fled his face and he sagged.

Talen put a hand gently on his back. "Uncle?"

Uncle Argoth turned, looked up at him. And then he heaved a great sob. He began to weep like a child.

"Talen," said Sugar from behind. "Get the horse."

"You're going to be all right," Talen said to Uncle Argoth. But it was a lie. "We're all going to be all right."

"By all . . ." said Sugar.

The fear in her voice made him turn. He followed her gaze into the sky and saw the Skir Master plummeting from the sky. Down he fell in a slow turn, one leg in front of the other as if he were taking one long lazy step.

He landed with a large, sickening thud at the edge of the clearing.

"Men!" the dreadman who had been dragged behind the monster shouted. He ran toward the Skir Master. One dreadman, the last that had manned the outer perimeter, followed. All the other dreadmen lay upon the ground. A group of the remaining Fir-Noy soldiers moved to join the dreadmen, but then exclaimed and shouted and pointed toward the sky.

Talen looked up. Another figure, larger and darker than the Skir Master fell from the heavens. It slammed to the earth only a few dozen paces from the Skir Master.

The Skir Master did not rise. But the monster did. It rose up, towering and fearsome.

It was impossible. This is the end, Talen thought. The very end.

The dreadmen halted, then turned and ran. The Fir-Noy shouted. Those on horse galloped for the other end of the valley. Those on foot followed, casting their weapons and what armor they could from them.

"Run!" he shouted to Sugar. "Run!"

He turned to Uncle Argoth on the ground. "Get up, Uncle! Get up!"

He pulled and tugged. Uncle Argoth looked up at him. "My boy," he said and touched Talen's face.

"Get up," said Talen. "We need to leave."

"He's gone," he said. "He's gone."

Talen glanced back. The monster raced toward them with giant strides.

There was no way Talen could outrun it, no way he could get to the Tailor in time. The creature crashed through the brush behind him.

Talen turned.

It stood not more than two paces away. Great hunks of dirt were missing here and there from its body, exposing bones of rock and some other substance. And yet the skin, if that's what you could call it, moved like hundreds of worms to cover the rents.

The thing snorted and shook its head. It reached out and took a step forward.

44.

THE MONSTER'S LAIR

Hunger's desire to chase the Fir-Noy and consume them was immense. The battle with the enemy's Skir Master had required huge amounts of Fire. The Skir Master had been very hard to break, but he'd killed him, just as the Mother had commanded. Killed him and reached through the doors of his binding to ravage the enemy whom the Skir Master served. But the Mother of the Skir Master broke the binding before he had a chance to do any damage to her.

He needed to eat. While he felt no physical pain, his body had sustained a large amount of damage. It would require Fire and soul to repair itself completely. He needed to eat. Except he dared not. If he distracted himself, he might lose this opportunity while it was in his grasp.

The Mother had commanded him to gather in all of this Grove of Sleth, all those who stunk. She'd commanded him to find the young male. He hadn't recognized him at first. He'd recognized his scent, but couldn't place it. But as he was carrying Ke and Matiga back to the Mother, he remembered smelling him in the yard of Sparrow, smith of Plum.

Hunger had found the male, Purity's son. And he'd found the last member of the Grove. The last member that mattered. From Larther, he knew there were two others, but one had been lost for a very long time. The other, the rumored half-beast named Harnock, was elusive and unstable. In all the years Larther had been part of the Grove, he'd never once seen him. He suspected none even knew where he abode. But all those that lived on this side of the mountains had been accounted for. All except Argoth.

He could feel the Mother's anticipation. And his own anticipation joined with hers. When he delivered these two, his task would be fulfilled. And she would be bound to let his family go. In the back of his mind he feared she would not keep that promise. But he pushed those fears aside. She kept her word; hadn't she already proven that?

SUGAR RAN WITH legs toward an outcropping of rock on the hill. Partway up she turned and watched the monster swat Talen aside as if he were nothing more than a grass doll.

Zu Argoth knelt in the grass, rocking back and forth, back and forth. He didn't even look up to see the creature standing behind him.

Sugar watched as the thing bent over and picked up Zu Argoth, cradling him in one of its massive arms, and then it turned and looked directly at her.

"Down," she said to Legs, pushing him behind the rock. "Down!"

There was no way she and Legs could outrun it. She could only hope it hadn't seen her.

But it had. It had.

She waited there, listening.

Legs clutched at her hand.

She heard it coming, a pounding thump, thump, thump. Closer and closer. And then it was upon them. They couldn't hide, couldn't run. She glanced back, and the creature, in midstride, plucked Legs up and stole him from her grasp.

"Sugar!" he cried, panic on his face.

She bolted after him.

"Sugar!" he yelled.

The creature's strides were immense.

Soon she was panting, her lungs burning, but she ran after him, laboring up the slope. The creature drew away from her, Zu Argoth in one arm, Legs in the other. One, five, ten strides, then it disappeared over the crown of the hill.

"Brother!" she yelled.

She could not go on.

"Brother!"

She doubled over, resting her hands on her knees. He was gone. Gone!

"Lords," she cried. "No. Please, no."

She slumped to her knees, panting, her mind racing. There was no way she could defeat it.

But she did know where its lair lay. She could lead an army there.

No. That would do nothing. It couldn't be killed. Not by dreadmen, not by Skir Masters, not by whirlwinds. And then she thought of the remaining hag's teeth. The Skir Master hadn't been able to use them. Did they still lie below?

She turned and looked back downhill. The bodies of men lay scattered in the grass and scrub. The Crab smoldered in the coals of the fire, sending up a smoke that thinned in the breeze. Across the meadow the morning winds stirred the treetops. She spotted the Skir Master lying at the edge by a cluster of massive elms.

Something moved below. Talen was on his knees in the scrub.

"Hoy!" she called out.

Talen grabbed something then stood. He held his ribs on one side as if he'd injured them. Then he spotted her, and raised something high into the air, something silver that flashed in the morning light.

It was the case that contained the hag's teeth. Maybe,

she thought, they could stab the monster with one of those.

"I'm coming, brother," she said. "I'm coming."

At that moment, one Fir-Noy who had not fled with the others slowly rose from his hiding place. He gave Talen a glance, but turned away. As Sugar raced back down the hill, the Fir-Noy ran to a horse that still stood in the meadow. It was saddled, its reins tied to a bush. The Fir-Noy untied it, mounted, and then kicked it into a gallop heading away from her.

When Sugar reached Talen, he said, "I see you put the fear of Regret into at least one Fir-Noy."

It was a hollow jest, but she responded in kind. "It's a start," she said.

He held the case up to her, showing its contents. Originally, there had been three spikes. Two remained. The spikes were almost the length of a span, their tips sharp as needles. She quickly scanned the ground around her, fearful of where the third one might be. The sight of it working its way out of the Crab's temple still sickened her.

"We're going after the others," Sugar said.

"Of course we are," said Talen.

She pointed, but didn't dare let her finger get close. "What do you think the etching on the sides indicates?"

"Who knows?" asked Talen. "But I'm sure some of that makes them easier to hold." He shook his head. "After seeing the Crab, I wouldn't want one of these to accidentally slip out of my grasp." He closed the case. "We'll finish the job. But I suspect we need the gauntlets to handle them."

Sugar laughed. She wondered how that was possible.

"What?" asked Talen.

"It sounds so preposterous, the two of us finishing what a Skir Master and a host of men could not."

He smiled a tired smile. "Perhaps it is. I doubt the

Creek Widow thought we'd face these kinds of 'limita-tions,' but we will do the best we can."

"You were holding your side; are you okay?"

Talen tried to move his arm and winced. "It's nothing, probably only a minor shoulder break from the monster's love tap. It will heal wrong, and I'll be deformed for the rest of my life, but such is the life of a fearsome Sleth like myself."

"Not if we rescue your sister. The lore can heal as well, remember?"

"Sure," he said.

"Hand the teeth to me," she said. "You're in no condi-tion to slash and throw. It looks like I'm going to be the one who will have to tangle with the monster. Do you think it will scare at my presence as easily as that last Fir-Noy did?"

"Not quite," he said and handed her the case. "You may be the one to deliver the blow, but you'll not tangle with it alone. Nor will we make it back to the cave looking like two Koramite youths, especially not with the Fir-Noy who fled the field alerting the whole countryside. I'm bigger than you are. Not as big as the dreadman, but big enough to wear one's armor and fool people from a distance."

She nodded. Two horses stood at the edge of the meadow. She might be able to catch one, but they had no saddles. They would have to ride doubled up. "You go see if the Tailor is still in the cave." She motioned at the big dreadman. "I'll strip him."

The big man was hard to roll, but she finally got him on his side and out of his shining cuirass. She gathered up his helm, his black sword, and its scabbard.

Talen walked out of the cave leading the Tailor and holding the leather sack from which the Skir Master had withdrawn the hag's teeth and gauntlets. He held the horse's reins as Sugar buckled the dreadman's armor on

Talen and then attached the bright yellow cloak of the Lions of Mokad. When it was time to mount the Tailor, Talen tried to use his left hand to grasp the saddle, but he obviously wasn't used to using that hand.

"Come on," she said. "I'll give you a leg up."

"I don't think that will work," he said. "Because once I'm on, how am I going to pull you up? We need a rock to stand on."

They found a rock. When Talen was firmly mounted in the saddle and she behind him on the horse blanket, she asked, "Where do you want me to hold on?"

"The hips," he said. "I don't think anything is broken there."

They rode over to the Skir Master. He lay on his side as if asleep. She dismounted and knelt next to him and noticed that his limbs lay in odd positions. A few flies already buzzed about his face. Sugar picked up his hand to untie the sleeves of the white, gold-studded gauntlet and found the arm bent like a reed. It was shattered. Gelatinous. She removed the first gauntlet then began to work on the other. When both were tucked firmly in her belt, Talen urged the horse to another rock and she mounted up again. She tried to be careful, but Talen grunted slightly from the pain when she grabbed his shoulder to balance herself.

"We'll need torches," she said.

"I know a place not too far out of the way."

He covered her hand that held his right hip. He patted it. "We'll get him back," Talen said. "We'll get them all back. We have more weapons than just the teeth and the gauntlets."

It was a brave sentiment. She just wished that it were true.

"We have the victor's crown. That, the Widow's codex, and a few other things that were in the Skir Master's sack."

"Then let's hope," she said, "that we find the others before we find the monster."

SUGAR KNEW THERE was no sense trying to gallop the whole way. No horse, not even one that was multiplied, could do it. So they trotted, but that gait proved too painful for Talen. In the end, they stole a small wagon and Sugar drove it while Talen held his side and grunted at every jolt.

They had to cross through three villages, clusters of less than a dozen homes. It was at these times that Sugar gave the Tailor a flick of the reins and urged him into a gallop. They fooled nobody, but she could see from their faces that she and Talen perplexed them. And it was enough to keep them from raising a hue and cry.

When they rode up to the old Koramite chandler and Sugar saw toddlers digging in the dirt in the yard, she had second thoughts. But Talen called out before she could say anything.

"We've heard news," the chandler said.

Talen waited.

"I trust your da," the chandler finally said. He had only three torches, but he agreed to make more and set his daughter to warming the resin and his skinny wife to cutting lengths of rope while the grandchildren looked on in silence.

When they'd finished another three, Sugar said, "We need to go."

"These won't last long," said the chandler. "It takes a good day or two for the resin or tallow to properly saturate the rope. These will burn too quickly."

"We can't wait for more," said Sugar.

"But what if the cave is a mile long?" asked Talen.

"Then a few more torches won't matter, will they?" said Sugar.

Talen paused for a long time. "You're right," he said. Then he turned and fed the Tailor the last bit of oats. When he finished, they climbed in the wagon and bid the chandler farewell.

They drove on for some time. When they passed the last village, Sugar turned into the woods and followed the trail she'd taken the day before until the way narrowed and would not allow the wagon farther. From there they rode doubled up to the spot where she'd seen the grayfans, then it was up the the hill. A few dozen yards from the cave, she stopped and dismounted. Talen slid off with a grunt. He was breathing hard and clutched his shoulder. "Get this thing off of me," he said.

She unclasped the buckles of the cuirass and let it drop to the ground.

Talen untied one of the saddlebags. He pulled out a small square of red cloth and unwrapped the crown. "It doesn't look like much, does it?"

It didn't look like anything at all. A square disk woven of golden wires. She touched the metal square with one finger. "It doesn't feel like much either."

"And yet the Creek Widow practically knelt on the ground and prayed to it."

"Let us hope it is everything she said it was."

Talen nodded, then wrapped it back up and stuffed it in his pants pocket.

Sugar took the Tailor's reins and tied him to a tree. Then she unbundled the torches and gave them to Talen to carry in his good arm.

"Shouldn't we just let him go?" asked Talen.

What kind of an attitude was that? "I'm coming back," she said. "We might need him to carry the others."

"Of course," said Talen, but he was looking at the mouth of the cave and she could tell he wasn't quite sure.

The chandler had given them a flint striker to light the

torches. She took it and worked it to shoot a thin spray of sparks onto the torch. A number landed on the wet rope and glowed. She blew on them. They glowed brighter, then a small flame spurted up. Soon the whole torch head was burning. She handed it to Talen. "I'm going to need both hands for the teeth."

"Give them to me," said Talen. He took the burning torch in one hand and held the others in the crook of his arm.

She pulled the white gauntlets on and fastened them. They were too big for her, but would have to do. Then she withdrew one of the gleaming teeth from the case.

They stepped around the cold stream and entered the cave with Sugar in the lead. Talen walked behind, holding the torch out to the side to minimize the shadows he cast before her.

The breeze fanned the flames on the torch. "It's going to make them burn fast," said Talen.

"Then we'll have to walk quickly," said Sugar.

She passed the spot where she'd crouched earlier. The torchlight revealed walls wet with water and slime. She tried her best to keep from stepping barefoot in the water; the cave was cool and the last thing she needed was to chill herself to the point where she could barely move.

Sidestepping the stream worked for a while, but the dry earth soon ended.

From wall to wall was water. Black, icy water.

Talen held the torch out. There was no way around it.

So be it. Sugar stepped into it. At first it only came to her ankles, but then it deepened and she found herself wading in spots up to her thighs, hoping with each step that the ground didn't completely drop out from under her.

Her feet quickly began to ache from the cold. She had calluses built up from walking barefoot all summer, but they were not proof against the water and sharp points of the rocks.

She stumbled, caught herself, then stumbled again. She did not want to lose her grip on the tooth, and so let her knees take the brunt of the fall.

She landed on the edge of a stone underneath the surface of the water and cursed at the pain.

"Lords," said Talen.

"I'm fine," she said.

"No," he said, "not that. Look." He held the torch higher.

She pushed herself up and looked ahead. The pathway ended in a wall.

"Are you sure this is the right cave?"

"I'm sure," she said. But then her courage faltered: maybe the thing climbed the walls. Furthermore, in many places the torchlight did not reveal this wall's total height. Maybe the creature's lair was up, not forward, and they'd already walked past it.

She took the torch from Talen and splashed forward. When she got to the wall, she held the torch up. The jagged wall stood perhaps twelve or fifteen feet high. Water dripped down from the ceiling. She could hear water splashing from above like a brook cascading over a small fall. She reached out and felt the slippery rock of the wall. There was no way they could scale it.

"There," said Talen and motioned to the right. "We can get up that way."

On her right the rock face was broken and free of slime. It looked like a narrow ledge joined up with the area above the wall.

"How are you going to get up that?" she asked.

"You go first, then pull me up with the rope."

She looked at him. "I don't know if your lame carcass is worth it."

"Oh, it's worth it," said Talen.

She looked back up into the blackness. "It's going to be up there waiting for me."

"Maybe," said Talen.

"And I can't climb that holding the tooth in my hand."

"No, you can't. But I'll hold the light for you."

"Oh, that's a big help."

He shrugged.

"I'll carry the torch in my teeth," she said. At least then she'd have light when she got to the top. She put the hag's tooth back into its case. Then she tied the case to her body. She didn't take off the gauntlets. If something was up there she wouldn't have time to retrieve the case and put them on. When she finished tying the case to her, she put the stem of the torch between her teeth, then began to climb.

If the creature caught them now they were lost.

There were plenty of foot- and handholds, but they were not as dry as they seemed. And her dripping clothes only added to the problem. But even if it had been dry, her feet and legs were still stiff and hurting from the icy water. Nevertheless, she rose. It was slick and slow going and she expected the monster to appear at any moment.

But then she reached the ledge. It was perhaps two feet wide and more than enough for her to sit on. She clambered over the edge, and then took the torch from her mouth and held it to see farther down the passage.

The ceiling seeped. Long stalactites and stalagmites had formed, looking like huge caramel teeth. Farther down, water poured out of a rent in the side of the corridor, then slid over the wall. Beyond that was blackness.

The ledge did indeed join that passage.

She untied the case, placed it on the ledge beside her, then threw down one end of the rope.

Talen tied the remaining torches into a bundle, and she

hauled them up. When the torches were resting next to her, she held the light out for Talen.

"I can do it without a rope," he said.

"It's slicker than it appears," she said.

"I can feel that," he said. "Especially where you dripped."

He climbed, gingerly at first, then began to proceed at a good pace. Soon he was almost to the top

"Ha," he said. "Lame indeed." But at that moment his footing slipped and he lurched to the side, then backward. He tried to grab the ledge with his bad arm, and winced. She reached out for him, but instead of grabbing her hand, he grabbed a thick handful of her hair.

His grasp caught her off guard and she was yanked toward him.

Talen shouted his dismay, his eyes wide.

They were both going to pitch over the ledge.

Then Sugar caught a seam in the rock on the ledge with both hands and pushed back. It was like a man trying to tug a donkey, except in this instance Talen was the man, holding on to a fistful of her hair, and she was the donkey.

He twisted, and for a moment she thought his weight would pull them over, or pull her hair out, but then he got a secure foothold. The change in balance was enough for her to reach up and grab his arm, and then with a mighty tug, pull him over the brink and onto the ledge.

Talen finally let go of her hair and pulled himself to sit with his back against the wall. He held his shoulder and grimaced.

Sugar felt her stinging scalp. "You couldn't have grabbed my outstretched hand? Lords, I don't know who's going to kill me first—you or the monster."

"I'm doing my best."

The way he said it made it sound as if he were doing his best to kill her. She looked over at him and laughed. It was unexpected. Probably nothing but nerves. Yet it felt good.

Talen finally understood what he'd said and laughed with her.

"I guess we could look on the bright side," she said. "If it wasn't already aware, your yelling has certainly alerted the monster to our presence. So that will save us some walking."

"There you go," he said. "Now give me the torch. If I'm going to meet my death, it's going to be with thawed toes."

That was a good idea. They both turned and sat cross-legged facing each other with her holding the torch between their bare feet. Talen's back faced the main corridor beyond.

The warmth was wonderful.

"That's going to be a bugger climbing back down," he said.

"No. Next time, seeing how poor a climber you are, we'll just be sure to use the rope. I think I'll tie it around your neck."

He smiled.

Something sounded in the corridor behind Talen's back.

Talen slowly reached for the torch and took it from her hand.

Sugar opened the case and withdrew the hag's tooth. There was not enough room to stand up, and she doubted whether the monster could fit on this ledge, but that didn't mean it couldn't climb up just as they had.

They waited until the torch had burned through the rope and now was little more than a fire stick.

"I don't think anything's there," said Talen.

"If something were," she said, "then at least we could get this over with."

"Well, we won't get over anything squatting here," he said.

She looked at him. He was not some strapping armsman. Not a formidable warrior. But she was happy he was with her.

"What?" he said.

"We're going to have to light another torch."

Talen nodded. He took one from the bundle tied with rope and lit it.

"Let me go first," she said. "The last thing I want is for the monster to snatch you and leave me trying to strike it in the dark."

"What are you going to do? Crawl over me?"

"Exactly," she said.

When he saw she was serious, he lay on his belly. She crawled over him, careful to not to touch his ribs or shoulder, and then moved along the ledge until it joined the main passage and they could stand up.

Talen held the torch up and scanned the ground. "There," he said and pointed to a spot on the tunnel floor. "And there."

Sugar looked at the ground. There were a brief series of regular markings on the floor. They were partial footprints. Not a human's. But something two-legged that was large and twisted its right foot slightly as it walked. "We're in the right place," she said. "That's a comfort."

Talen held the torch higher, illuminating the path beyond the stalactites.

The cavern walls here were much different from the ones below. They rose up to the ceiling in smooth lines with patterns carved into them.

"This is stone-wight work," Talen said.

"Do you think this monster is one of them?"

"I don't know."

At her feet, covered in thick dust, were different-colored stones set in a geometric pattern. She wondered where the bat dung was. A cave such as this should be heaped high, beetles crawling about in it. But there was no dung. No bats. No cave vermin.

"You keep your ears perked," said Sugar. Then they proceeded down the corridor, always just a stride or two from the swallowing dark.

They passed many carvings. One was of a great tree with all manner of beasts in it. Another of a bear carved with such fine detail she could see individual locks of its fur. Yet another contained a panel of ancient writing carved from top to bottom.

At one point she thought she'd heard something again. They froze, her waiting for the creature to come running out of the shadows, Talen stepping forward and to the side so the torch would illuminate more of the corridor.

She decided the sound was some trick of the cave, and proceeded forward, still tracking the creature by the occasional marks the creature made as it walked. She held the hag's tooth ready in one hand, the case in the other. The silver glimmered in the torchlight. The tooth was long and felt well-balanced for throwing. But she couldn't risk a long throw. After seeing the battle with the Skir Master, she knew she'd only have one chance.

With every step she became more certain that their names were going to be added to the list of those fools who had been swallowed by the ancient stone-wight ruins. Soon the second torch burned low. Talen lit the third. They now had only three left. Not long after that they arrived at a fork. Talen held the torch at a low angle to create better shadows that might reveal footprints. They walked down to the right a few paces and found nothing. A few paces down the left passage Sugar found another half print.

Talen froze and sniffed.

Sugar sniffed as well. Sulfur.

"The monster's up there," she said. "In that stink."

"Aye," said Talen.

Sugar gripped the tooth in her gauntlet, the gold studs gleaming in the torch-light, and took a step forward.

45.

THE GROVE

Argoth could not stop shaking. The tremors came in waves, starting deep within and building until his whole body spasmed. When each wave began, the monster carrying him would hold him tighter to keep him from shaking loose. He thought at first the tremors were signs of his terror at this beast. But the fear of the creature had quickly subsided, and he realized he had begun shaking as soon as it killed the Skir Master.

It was an effect of the breaking of the bond, he was sure of it. What it meant for his survival, he did not know. It might build until, like a case of lockjaw, he died in a horrible contraction. Or it might eventually pass.

Between tremors he examined the creature, the dark pits of its eyes, the rough edges of its hideous mouth protruding like the spines of a cod, the exposed skeleton of stone. A smattering of tiny, pale, white flowers grew across its neck and shoulder. He wondered why they had not wilted and supposed the earth from which they grew was living, part of its skin. At one point in the journey, when the monster stopped to kick a tumbled tree out of its way, a fat bumblebee droned about the monster's head and landed on its shoulder. It had time to probe one of the pale flowers before the monster began running again and the bouncing shook it off.

Argoth could not understand why the creature had taken Legs. Perhaps he would deliver Argoth to the master and then reward itself with Legs as a meal. Whatever the reason, in between spasms, Argoth talked to Purity's blind boy, soothing him, thinking all the while of Nettle, and the sacrifice he'd made—the sacrifice that had been wasted on his cursed, foolhardy scheme.

The creature kept, for the most part, to the woods. Argoth knew there was no use calling for help. He'd tried, and the monster had clamped a rough hand over his mouth. Besides, this was not a weave of flesh and blood. How it lived, he could not guess. What he did know was that it could only be undone by special lore. Lore of which he had no knowledge. He could only hope that the Creek Widow had mustered the strength of the Grove. He was spent, but there still was a chance the Grove could defeat this thing.

The tremors continued for the many miles, but he noticed they were coming farther and farther apart. Perhaps he would survive the breaking of his bond to the Skir Master.

The monster carried them along a ridge of hills. It came to a small bluff, covered in trees, and jumped down to the ground a few yards below. They landed with a thump, and when the creature turned, Argoth saw why they'd come here.

Before them a cave opened into the rock. The monster repositioned them in its arms and strode into the darkness. It splashed through water, icy spray wetting Argoth's exposed feet and face.

"We're in a cave," Argoth said to Legs.

"I know, Zu," said Legs. "Please, unless you see something, it is important that I listen and smell."

Argoth startled at the mild rebuke, but thought perhaps this is how the blind dealt with the unknowns in their world.

The monster climbed hill and valley, taking them ever deeper into the bowels of the rock. His tremors lessened. After some time, Argoth saw a bluish light up ahead. He mentioned this to Legs, who said, "I don't know that I can keep the orientation points all in my head."

Orientation points? Then he realized that the boy was keeping a map of sounds and smells in his mind. Argoth looked at him with new admiration.

As the monster jogged, the light grew stronger. Soon Argoth could make out the walls of the passage they were in. The monster took them past a chamber containing a large pool of black water, past pillars, past openings to other dark passageways. The light grew, they turned a corner, and Argoth found himself in the room that was the source of the light.

The light came from the dead body of a large, pallid beast with an eyeless head. There was no odor of rotten flesh, which meant it must have been recently killed. It lay on the far side of the chamber. It looked like a monstrous salamander, as long as a man, but with a stubby tail and the tusks of a boar. Two vertical cuts ran along its belly. The creature's juices oozed out of the cuts, and when the separate juices ran together, the mixture shone with a white and bluish light. A bowl had been set on the floor beside the creature to capture the fluorescing liquid as it dripped from the creature's side.

Argoth had seen creatures similar to this before. They were called night maws. But those were never longer than a man's hand. And they were rare. That same light shone from two other bowls set in the room. It was not the blinding light of the sun, but an odd light that still left much of the room in shadow.

The monster released Argoth and Legs to stand.

"No," a woman said.

The voice surprised him.

Argoth turned and saw figures chained at even intervals along the walls to his right: Hogan, the Creek Widow, Ke, River, Purity.

"No," said the woman again. It was the Creek Widow, full of despair.

His heart sank. He'd hoped, at the very least, that Ke had escaped to call in the last two members of the Grove. But that would not be. There would be no muster.

Purity looked like the walking dead. Hogan did not look much better.

"Legs!" Purity said.

Argoth stepped toward Hogan, but the monster grabbed him by his injured arm and wrenched him to an open set of manacles. The pain shot up Argoth's arm. He took in a sharp breath.

Legs carefully walked to his mother, hands out front.

The monster stood Argoth a few paces from River, manacled his ankles, then his wrists. It passed a chain through both to a stout ring in the wall. Then it bent two links of the iron with its bare hands to secure Argoth to the ring in the rock. It yanked on the chain to test its strength.

Then the creature gaped open its mouth and coughed. It coughed again and plucked something dark and wet off its tongue. The object writhed like a worm between the monster's two rough fingers. It was as thick as a man's thumb and maybe a foot long.

Argoth backed up against the rock wall.

The monster reached out, steadied Argoth's head with its free hand, then held the wet worm close to Argoth's throat.

Argoth felt a cold touch at the hollow of his throat. Then the creature slithered up and around and circled his neck.

The monster stepped back.

Argoth braced himself, but nothing happened.

The monster ran a finger along the creature, then turned and walked over to Legs. He plucked him up from his mother and exited out of an opening in the far side of the chamber by the pallid beast.

"Mother," he heard Legs call from the corridor.

Argoth stood frozen, still expecting the creature about his neck to bite or burn. He reached up carefully and touched it. It was cold and smooth as silk.

"It's a king's collar of sorts," said the Creek Widow. "At least, none of us can work any power that it doesn't immediately consume."

Argoth looked at each of them in turn—all wore a similar creature.

The Creek Widow shook her head in the pale light. "You were our last hope. We are not going to be able to resist her for long."

Her?

Argoth tested the chains. They were heavy and strong. The weight of them made his injuries throb.

Another tremor built in him. "Who is this enemy?" he asked.

The shaking increased. He braced himself, but it faded as quickly as it had come.

Argoth rubbed his arms despite the fact that this room was warm. "Is this Mokad? Or some rogue soul-eater?"

"Neither," said Hogan. "She is nothing like you have ever seen." Hogan sounded weak. He was covered with bruises and lacerations. The Fir-Noy had obviously tortured him.

"She is looking," the Creek Widow cut in, "for a young male."

"What? Who is this woman?"

"They see a woman," said River. "I see a man."

"She's right," said the Creek Widow. "It's no woman. No human. We are dealing with something else entirely."

And it was searching for a male. They were talking about Talen. They had to be. Except the creature had cast Talen aside and taken Legs. "But how could she know about him?"

"Brother," Hogan said. "We were stewards of a great gift. But we were fools." Hogan coughed wetly. "Rose warned us he was special. We should have known that dark powers would seek to destroy him before he came into his powers and could threaten them."

"We did know that," said the Creek Widow. "But who could have suspected this?"

"At least he's not here," said River.

"No, but who will train him?" Hogan asked. "Who will hide him? Harnock refused to come. And so he is alone." Hogan pulled at the creature about his neck. "It will only be a matter of time before she cracks his identity out of us."

And then Argoth realized what Hogan had just said—it wasn't just a king's collar they wore. Argoth looked at the others. They were all wearing some kind of thrall.

"No!" he said. He reached up and tore at the creature, but it only constricted tighter. He could not bear wearing another thrall. He pulled again, but it was as strong as iron. "No," he said, defeated. He shuddered and his heart sank even lower. "We cannot end this way."

River pointed toward the side of the chamber where the pallid beast lay. "It is not just us that will be broken."

Something lay on the floor beyond the pallid beast. He'd missed it in the surprise of seeing the Grove. It was a body, crude-featured and dark. It looked to be made of earth.

He saw another figure beyond it, and then another, and another.

"Lords," he said and counted them. There were nine. Nine more horrors like the one that had brought him and Legs to this chamber. They had slightly different shapes—one's head twisted into a point like an onion, another had no discernible head at all, yet another seemed to be made more of withies than stone and grass, a fourth had exceedingly long arms. But they were all of the same make.

He'd seen what the monster could withstand. He'd seen what it could do to the mightiest of men. A chill ran through him. All this time they'd worried about Bone Faces and Divines while this was happening under their noses. He felt sick.

He looked at the earthen figures. What rough magic would quicken them? Despair welled up in him like a heaving dark sea. "The Grove," he said, "is undone."

46.

MANTLE AND CROWN

The torch in Talen's hand spit and hissed. He and Sugar proceeded farther down the passage.

Sugar held the tooth in front of her in her white-gloved hand as if she were holding a blade.

The passageway bent and curved. The walls were not as well preserved here. Stalactites had grown. And here and there parts of the wall had crumbled to the floor. Only a few paces farther and they came to a gaping rent in the wall. It was big enough to belly through. Big enough for the monster.

He looked at Sugar. He did not want to go into that dark space.

She pointed ahead at a scuffle in the dust of the floor that indicated the monster had followed the main passageway. However, even as they moved past the rent, he kept his eye upon it. He was convinced something was there, waiting for the right moment to strike.

"Hide the torch," Sugar said.

Talen turned to her. "What?"

"I think I see a light," she said. "But the torch is ruining my vision. Muffle the light."

The hairs on the back of Talen's neck stood up. He peered down the passageway, but saw nothing. The rent was still close. Nevertheless, he found an outcropping of rock and held the torch behind it. The angle was such that it lit the passage behind them, but cast a shadow ahead.

They stood until their vision began to adjust. What he saw surprised him. "There's a faint bluish sheen reflecting from the rocks," he said.

Bluish lights had been seen in the caves of the stonewights before. Of course, very few who went to investigate the lights ever returned. And the reports of those who did seemed to conflict. Some said the lights dashed about like will-o'-the-wisps. Night maws, small lizardlike creatures, made a light if they were cut the right way. But those who had seen the blue light said the light always retreated farther into the cave as if it were leading the explorers to a trap.

But the lights had always been there. Did that mean this monster had been there all along and had only recently come out to forage for its food?

Talen wondered if the monster was like a lion that killed its prey immediately or if it were like a spider that stunned its meals to let them ripen. Or was it like a leech, draining the life out in small portions? What if this monster had a brood to feed? He imagined a number of rough children wrapping their limbs about Argoth and Legs, the Creek Widow, draining them until they were nothing more than husks.

The very thought of being eaten sent fear down his legs to the soles of his bare feet. But it didn't matter. They needed to move more quickly. Every minute they hesitated gave whatever was up there more time to devour those it had taken.

They both stood there a moment longer. He could hear the drip of water. They could turn back and still perhaps avoid the creature. They might deliver the teeth to one of the authorities. But it would be far too late for any rescue.

"We need to pick up the pace," he said. Yet he did not move.

"Right," she said.

Talen mustered his courage and retrieved the torch.

"We have surprise on our side," Sugar said.

But Talen wondered if that was indeed the case.

They stepped forward. All they needed to do was get one of the teeth into the monster. Or deliver the crude crown to someone who could use it. When it came to it, Talen knew his job would be to throw himself into harm's way to distract the monster. Perhaps into the arms of the monster itself. He did not relish that idea.

The torch burned low. He retrieved the fourth. Even if they hurried, he doubted the two remaining torches would be enough for the trip back. But then there would be no trip back if they fell into some gaping hole in the floor.

He lit the fourth torch and dropped the burned one to the floor.

A little farther and the passage opened into a chamber that contained a large pool of black water. They followed the trail that skirted the edge of the water. At one point, he saw something glowing palely at the edge of the water up ahead. When they got close, he saw it was from many small, thin crablike insects feasting on the remains of a spiny, translucent fish.

They soon exited the chamber and passed what looked to be a number of pillars. They came upon openings to other passageways, but the tracks never varied from the path.

The bluish light grew stronger, as did the odd sulfur smell. It was so strong he could taste it on the edges of the back of his tongue. One thing he had noticed was that the light wasn't moving away from them. In fact, he suspected that around the next turn they'd see its source. He signaled to Sugar to stop.

He whispered, "I'm going to douse the torch." The last thing he wanted was for the monster to know they were coming, but the torch would announce them along the walls ahead with its flickering yellow light. Of course, it might already know of their presence and simply be waiting around that bend. And that's why he was going first. Sugar needed to be able to wield the tooth.

"Follow me," he whispered and quietly stepped forward.

He heard something—human voices. Had he heard River's voice? His heart soared. They were yet alive!

He glanced at Sugar, who shared his hope.

Two more steps and he stood at the corner of the chamber ahead. He peered around the edge and saw it opened onto another chamber. This was definitely the source of the light.

He glanced at Sugar one more time. The tooth's sharp point and the intricate pattern on its side shone in the bluish light. In her other hand she carried the silver case that contained the remaining tooth.

He would distract the monster, draw it to them, and she would stab it anywhere she could.

Talen nodded and stepped out into the full light.

He expected an immediate attack. At the very least he expected the creature to see him and charge. But no such thing happened.

Da's voice sounded from around a bend in the room where Talen couldn't see him.

Talen took another step forward, then another, until he saw first Uncle Argoth, then River, the Creek Widow, Da, Ke, and another woman, all manacled at even distances with chains that had been fastened into the semicircular rock wall. Ke stood. The rest of them sat with their backs against the wall.

The monster was nowhere to be seen.

"Mother!" Sugar cried and rushed forward.

The conversation ceased. All of them looked up.

Sugar ran to the woman Talen had not been able to identify. Her hair had been shaved off. She was covered with cuts and bruises.

"No," the woman said. "Not here!" But she held up her arms anyway and received her girl in an awkward embrace, Sugar holding the hag's tooth well away from her.

"Talen," Da said. "What have you done? You must flee."

Talen withdrew the red cloth from his pocket, unfolded it, then held the odd crown up by one of the leather straps. "I thought you might need this."

"Hogan," said the Creek Widow with some hope.

"We can't use it," said Da. He motioned at his neck. "Not with these things devouring our power the moment it springs forth." Da glanced at an exit from the chamber Talen had not seen when he first came in. "I don't know how you found us, but you must leave before it comes back. Go!"

"Wait," said Uncle Argoth. He pointed at Sugar. "She

carries the teeth." He turned to Da. "The Skir Master's ravelers."

All eyes focused on what Sugar held in her outstretched arm.

Uncle Argoth waved to Sugar. "Here," he said. "Quickly!"

Sugar rose from her mother and hurried to Uncle Argoth.

He stretched his neck to one side and motioned to a patterened object encircling it. "Careful now. I want you to prick the surface. Let it get a taste."

"Stop," said the Creek Widow. "What are you doing?"

Uncle Argoth turned to her. "I've been enthralled once. I will not be enthralled again. Let's see if the tooth can unravel this collar."

"It will unravel you," said the Creek Widow.

"Then so be it," said Uncle Argoth. He turned to Sugar. "Quickly, we don't have time."

Sugar glanced at Talen. Then she turned back to Argoth and brought the tooth close to the collar.

The collar moved. Then the worm head of the thing about Uncle Argoth's neck rose as if it were sniffing the tooth.

Sugar paused, fear on her face.

"Go on, girl," said Uncle Argoth.

She moved the point of the tooth closer and the collar struck, curling an end around the tooth.

Sugar cried out.

The tooth seemed to shudder, then it leapt out of her fingers.

Uncle Argoth gasped.

The tooth was wriggling, entwining with the collar.

"Grab it," said Uncle Argoth.

The tooth and collar were now one, struggling, twisting about his neck.

Uncle Argoth fell back against the wall.

Sugar tried to grab the tooth, but it resisted. She tried again. This time she was able to catch it and tug.

She grunted. "It's stuck," she said.

"Yes," said Uncle Argoth. He winced. "I can feel it weakening. Get a good grip. Be ready to yank it back when I tell you."

The collar writhed.

"It's slipping," said Sugar.

Suddenly the collar jerked, spasmed.

"Now!" said Uncle Argoth.

Sugar yanked. The tooth did not budge.

Uncle Argoth cried out, clutched at his neck.

Lords, it was going to burrow into him.

Then Sugar pulled a second time and the tooth came free. It twisted once, twice, and then stilled.

Uncle Argoth grasped the dead worm thing about his throat and ripped it free. He held it up before him then cast it to the floor.

A bright spot of red glistened on his neck.

Uncle Argoth stroked the spot. Then he pulled his hand away and looked at the blood there.

"That was a nasty bite," he said to Sugar. "But well done. Now free Ke and the Creek Widow. Then Hogan, River, and Purity. In that order."

"Bring the crown here," he said. "She'll feel the breach. We don't have much time."

Talen hurried over to Uncle Argoth, who was still in chains, and held the crown out to him.

Uncle Argoth took it by the strap and lay the square medallion in the palm of his hand. He stroked its surface with his finger.

Sugar moved to Ke, who stretched his thick neck to the side.

"Wait," said Talen. "Give me the other gauntlet and tooth. We'll do two at a time."

Sugar nodded and removed the second gauntlet from her belt. She tossed it to Talen.

He caught it midstride. It was as light as silk and thin. Even the weave in its palm was thin. He expected to feel some surge of power when he pulled it on to his left hand, but he felt no such thing. It felt simply like an exceedingly fine glove. The gold studs were small enough that it wouldn't affect the grip of the glove too much. He had no time to tie the sleeve, so he let the straps dangle.

Sugar lay the silver case containing the last tooth on the floor and turned to Ke. He gasped when she put the tooth to his collar. But this time she kept a firm grip and the tooth did not jump from her hand.

Talen bent down, opened the case, and removed the last tooth. He approached the Creek Widow. Her eyes danced with delight. "Did I not say you were the one to watch?"

She turned her head and put her arms behind her back. Her chains clinked and clattered. How they were going to break those he did not know.

He now saw that the collars weren't all one color. Instead, they were dark and muddy, shot through with browns and greens and a heavy blue. There was a pattern to it, but it was all too dark to distinguish it well. They reminded him of hideous, too-short eels.

Talen did not hesitate, but quickly pricked it with the sharp point of the tooth.

He was not ready for the power and slipperiness of the tooth. It jumped like a fish from his hand to twine and wrestle with the dark collar. Then it began to wriggle in.

Frantically, Talen grasped for the tooth. He caught the end barely before it completely disappeared into the body of the collar.

He glanced at the Creek Widow's face. She was grimacing in pain, gritting her teeth.

The collar about the Creek Widow's neck jerked and rolled. The tooth strained against his grasp. And then it stopped and the collar hung limp about the Creek Widow's neck.

Talen yanked back on the tooth and it came out, trailing some substance that was dark and sticky.

Behind him, he heard Ke grunt. Talen turned and saw Ke straining, pulling at the chain where it was bolted to the rock wall. He gave another heave and, with a crack, pulled the iron loop from the rock.

Talen shook his head. Admiration bloomed in him: his brother was as strong as any dreadman. Stronger.

The Creek Widow tugged at the collar. When it came loose, she flung it to the floor and then felt her throat. "You can be sure I won't be asking for one of those during the Festival of Gifts."

The skin where the collar had coiled about her neck was red and raised in a long welt.

Ke strode over to the Creek Widow, rolling his shoulders and shaking his arms to loosen them. He looked at Talen and grinned. "Step aside, little man."

He picked up the chain binding the Creek Widow to the wall, grimaced, and gave it a mighty yank. The chain ripped completely out of the wall.

Ke grunted.

"Handy," said the Creek Widow, "isn't he? Now get your sister."

The Creek Widow joined Ke and Uncle Argoth off to one side in an odd circle. They began chanting—one would speak, then the other two would repeat it in unison. Talen couldn't understand the words and realized they were in some odd tongue. Each one of them had turned sideways and placed their left hand on the neck of the person in front of them. With their right, they each supported the crown.

Talen rushed to River. The left side of her face was purpled with bruises.

Sugar had already set her tooth to work on the collar about Da's neck. He could see his father was in pain.

When he approached River, she turned her head to expose her long neck. This time when he brought the tooth close, it did not escape his grasp.

However, it had only begun to work on the collar when River cried out. "Remove it!" she said.

Talen yanked the tooth back. "What is it?"

She gasped. "It was in me."

To Talen's left, Da fell to his knees, Sugar's tooth still struggling with the collar about his neck.

"What's happening?" asked Talen.

"Grab it," Da said to Sugar, gritting the words out.

Sugar knelt and grasped for the tooth.

Da groaned in pain.

Sugar yanked the tooth back.

Da heaved great breaths. When he caught his breath, he turned his head to look at River. "You and I have worn the collars longer. The binding must be tighter. Be pre-pared: it's going to take a part of you."

"I felt that," said River.

Da turned to Sugar. "Finish it."

He winced when she pricked the collar again.

Talen looked at his sister.

She held her hand up. "Give me a second," she said.

They didn't have a second. Talen was sure the monster was going to walk into the chamber at any moment.

The Creek Widow cried out in delight. "It's quickened," she said and held the crown aloft.

Da gritted his teeth. His face was red with strain. "Now," he commanded, and Sugar withdrew the tooth.

Still kneeling, Da ripped the collar from his neck. His

face was sweating with strain. Blood shone in a thin line around his neck.

"Quickly," he said and motioned to the Creek Widow.

She, Uncle Argoth, and Ke encircled him.

"But it's gold," Talen said. Not the black of powerful magic. "Are you sure it's going to work?"

"I told you," the Creek Widow said. "It operates on different principles, and it's very much alive. Long ago, perhaps in a different age, three years of life were poured into it. The power of three years of life—you can feel it pulsating. It requires three now to waken it."

Da stood and struggled with his chains, but could not remove them from the wall as Ke had done.

"Put it on me," said Da.

The Creek Widow strapped the crown to Da's head.

"It looks so flimsy," said Talen. "What if it comes off?"

"Once the crown and your father are joined," said the Creek Widow, "no power can separate them."

Ke, the Creek Widow, and Uncle Argoth formed their odd circle again, turning sideways to the center of the circle, placing their left hands on the neck of the person in front of them, stretching their right arms out to the center of the circle to rest on Da's head and touch the medallion. This time, Da spoke the strange words, followed in unison by the other three.

Sugar, her tooth in hand, stood in the center of the chamber like a guard dog.

"We need to get this off me," River said. "The three of them will be useless once the bond fully forms."

Talen returned his attention to his sister. "Are you ready?"

She nodded. Her eyes shone with determination.

He held her chin still with one hand and pricked the collar again. It immediately twisted and writhed.

River's face screwed up in pain. She breathed in measured pants.

Talen pulled the tooth back so that the sharp head was barely in the collar.

But tears still formed in the corners of River's eyes.

"Do you want me to take it out?" he asked.

She panted, shook her head. But moments later she sagged to one side, and Talen had to quickly remove the tooth or risk stabbing her.

In spots the coloring of the collar had turned ash gray. Yet he could see other parts were still very much alive, undulating as if it were taking long, slow breaths.

Talen saw specks of light. He blinked and looked down at the hag's tooth. Had it affected his vision? He rubbed his eyes with his free hand and looked again.

A handful of shining flecks were floating in the chamber. They looked like dust motes, except they shone with their own light. What's more, they seemed to be floating lazily toward Da.

"My eyes," he said.

"Not your eyes," said River. "The crown."

There were more sparks now. Talen couldn't tell where they were coming from.

The Creek Widow, Uncle Argoth, and Ke stepped back.

"The crown bestows its wearer great strength," said the Creek Widow, "but it also calls forth a mantle of incredible might. It is said that the Creators seeded the world with power to be given to those of their choosing. And to those who respond to their call, the powers distill upon them as freely as the dews of heaven. Until then, the powers remain locked up within the earth and sea. It is almost finished. A few minutes more."

This didn't make complete sense to Talen. Didn't the Divines wield great powers as well? And this monster was not something to be ignored. Obviously, all the power wasn't locked up.

The sparks floated in through both entrances, but more seemed to simply spring forth from the rock about them. Talen caught a twinkle in the dust at his feet, and then the fleck of light floated free to join the rest.

The sparks coalesced into thin, whirling streams that were drawn to Da like water is drawn to the center of a lazy whirlpool. Da knelt in his chains as the bits of light flowed and clung to him. The shining flecks began to accumulate thinly in his hair and eyebrows, upon his nose and arms, between the very fibers of his clothing. Specks of light tinged ever so faintly with blue and yellow.

River put her hand to the collar about her neck. "She's coming," she said. "I can feel it."

SUGAR COULDN'T HELP but marvel at the tiny sparks that suddenly glimmered and glittered in the stone ceiling, walls, and floor. Each would build in intensity only to break free and float purposefully toward Zu Hogan.

He was drawing the very might of the earth to him. Zu Hogan still knelt on the floor. She wanted him to get up, to take the tooth from her. She wanted any one of them to take it.

But she looked at the others, stooped with weariness, and realized they would not be taking the tooth from her. She would have to defend them.

Now was the moment. Her heart pounded in her chest. She was the only thing standing between the others and their approaching doom.

Things to act, and things to be acted upon. She was not going to quail. She had the tooth. She had seen its power work on man and weave. She was going to face this enemy head-on, just as Mother had faced that mob only a few days ago. Whatever came out of those entrances was going to feel the bite of Purity's daughter.

She glanced at the entrance to the chamber that she and Talen had used. Nothing was there. But then it was so black she wouldn't see anything until it was in the chamber anyway.

There was a slight breeze running to that entrance from the other one. The breeze brought her a strong whiff of sulfur and pine. And then another even stronger.

She turned. The monster would come from that direction, from the second entrance. She wouldn't have much time once it entered the chamber.

"Talen," she said. "Bring me the other tooth!"

Something flickered in the corner of her eye. And then the monster burst from the blackness.

She should have been more used to the sight of it, but the creature was even more horrible to behold than it had been in the vale. Its enormous ragged mouth. Its dark pit eyes. Her knees quivered.

The monster gave her one look and, in an enormous stride, flashed past. It swatted the Creek Widow aside and grabbed Zu Hogan by the throat.

Ke and Zu Argoth did not attack, but stood aside, slumped, the crown obviously having its effects on them.

The monster grasped the crown and began to tug. Zu Hogan clutched at the creature's rough arm. The thin streams of sparks in the room had grown thicker, but now slowed their movement. Zu Hogan was shining with the flecks of light, but the monster grabbed the crown and began to pull. It was going to rip it off. And then it would kill Zu Hogan just as it had the Skir Master.

She thought of Legs and Mother and the tooth in her hand.

The tooth in her hand!

Her courage returned even if the fear remained. She cried out and charged.

The monster turned and caught her by the waist in its enormous grip. It felt as if she'd run herself onto a post. Its fingers, hard as stone, wrapped round and squeezed so hard she could not breathe.

She gasped for breath, tightened her grip on the hag's tooth, then brought it down, stabbing deep into the monster's ragged forearm.

The monster looked down at the tooth.

The tooth bucked like a fish and disappeared into the stoney flesh.

The monster released Sugar. It reeled back, let go of the crown, and clutched its forearm.

Sugar turned, looking for Talen and the second tooth.

Zu Hogan spoke a word under his breath, and the sparks around him grew thicker. A low thrumming began to reverberate through the room. It built in intensity.

The volume and pitch rose, vibrating through her and the very rock about them. The sparks in the room multiplied. The air was thick with them now. The thrumming turned into the rushing of waters or a mighty wind.

Zu Hogan stood, his chains still binding him to the wall, and stretched out his arms. His face shone with fierce knowledge.

The whirling streams of blue and yellow sparks picked up speed, converging on him. The volume built to a roar. Sugar covered her ears.

Then came a concussion, an enormous slap of air that forced Sugar to stagger back. It was followed by a blinding flash as all the remaining sparks in the room rushed to Zu Hogan.

The thrumming and roar cut off, vanished, and Sugar's ears rang in the silence.

Zu Hogan stood. From head to toe, he shone with a

thin skin of blue and yellow light. Joy suffused his face. And when he moved the very air about him seemed to bend and blur.

Zu Hogan took hold of his chains and pulled them apart like a child might break a thin braid of grass.

The monster had fallen on its back, frantically clutching at its arm.

Out of the corner of her eye, Sugar saw the passageway beyond the second entrance flicker and then illuminate.

A ribbon of blazing violet flame flew through the opening. It was followed by another and another. Each stretched a yard or more. Each undulated like an eel swimming through water. The three ribbons of light sped about the room, hissing like the wind through dry weeds. One circled her with blinding speed. It paused momentarily as if looking her in the face, the hot white of its core fading to tongues of violet flame. It seemed to be whispering something.

Fear gripped her. These weren't ribbons of some strange fire—they were alive!

The light in the passageway grew brighter. And as it did a thick knot of the creatures, blazing their oddly tinged light, swam through the opening to the chamber. Some of these were shorter than the first three, but most were as long as a man's leg. Some longer. They moved like a school of shining eels, hither and thither, wrapping themselves around something at their center.

The school of light shimmered to one side, parting ever so briefly, and Sugar saw a glimpse of what it contained—a woman wrapped in undulating, living segments of light.

The first three ribbons swirled about Zu Hogan. In his right hand he held a long length of the thick chain that had bound him.

"Whatever you are," Zu Hogan said to the woman,

"your time is at an end." He stepped toward the knot of light. But as he did so an arm shot out of the knot of shining serpents and pointed at Zu Hogan.

The school of light, paused, shimmered, and then a mass of the creatures sped toward him. The undulating segments struck. She saw one open its mouth, full of thin sharp teeth, and bite him on the throat. Another attacked his cheek, and then the great mass swallowed him like a storm, the ribbons jerking and biting.

Zu Hogan stumbled back, the creatures covering him in a thick knot. He flailed his arms, tried to pull and swat them away, but the creatures attacked as if in a feeding frenzy.

Zu Hogan yelled a word in some tongue she didn't understand. Immediately, there was a flash of light at the center of the seething mass.

A number of the creatures flew back. She could see much of Zu Hogan now. Yet many of the creatures still clung to him, biting in fury.

Zu Hogan reached up and grasped the one clinging to his eye.

Sugar fully expected to see some grotesque remnant of his eye pull away with the eel, but when he yanked it off and flung it to the ground, she saw that both of his eyes were exactly where they should be—perfect, whole, and gleaming with purpose.

The creature had not penetrated the mantle.

He pulled another knot of the creatures from his neck and took a step toward the shining woman.

She was beautiful. Far more beautiful than anything Sugar had ever imagined.

She was singing furiously, holding her arms out. Whatever she was doing, she didn't have time to finish.

Zu Hogan ran at her, weapon in hand. The light that covered Zu Hogan had extended down most of the chain.

He brought the shining chain around in a side stroke like a massive whip and struck her full force in the head.

The woman stumbled back.

Sugar expected the woman to fall dead. The blow would have killed a bull. But the woman steadied herself.

She was dazed, it seemed. That was all.

Zu Hogan swung the chain again, but the woman dodged back. With a roar, he dropped the chain and charged. Midstride he reached down and picked up a stone and then he had her by the throat. Zu Hogan reared back with the stone. He was going to brain her.

"The monster!" Talen yelled.

Sugar glanced at the creature. It held the arm she'd stabbed high in the air. With its other hand, it appeared to have caught something deep in the flesh of its shoulder.

She turned to Talen. He was standing with his back up against the rock wall, tooth in his good hand. His injured arm hung useless at his side. Two of the shining creatures undulated before him. One coiled and struck, but Talen jabbed and slashed with the tooth, sending it back.

"Ready yourself," he said. "I'm going to toss it."

She glanced at the monster. It was tugging the tooth out. "Quickly!" she said.

Talen feinted left, leaned right, and tossed the tooth to her. She caught it in her gauntleted hand, immediately flipped it to get a better grip, then turned.

The monster stood with all the concentration of a surgeon, its fingers deep in its arm.

Perhaps it can contend with one tooth, she thought. Let it try a second.

Sugar hurled the second tooth like a knife. It spiraled, end over end, its sharp point flashing in the unearthly light of the chamber, and buried itself deep in the monster's belly.

The tooth gleamed once, then wriggled and disappeared into the monster's gut.

The creature looked down, gasped horribly, and stumbled back.

47.

MASTER OF THE HARVEST

Hunger felt the second worm burrow in. His panic rose. His arm was breaking apart like dried-out dirt. At one time he'd wanted dissolution. But not now. He saw his daughter, wife, and remaining son before him, caught in a stomach. The Mother would not spare them if he failed.

He was their only chance.

The second worm burrowed deeper, burning, burning, burning as it went.

He resisted the urge to clutch at it. If he released the one in his arm, he knew he'd never get it back again. They were as slippery as a fish, these worms. And strong.

The Mother ordered him to attack the shining Koramite. But he dared not move, dared not let go.

How do I stop the worms? he cried to her.

There was no answer.

His mind raced. Why could he not pry the worm open? It was intricate and oddly familiar, but he couldn't place it. It was like no beast he'd encountered before.

The worm in his arm curled and another piece of him tattered. A clump of soil fell to the cave floor.

No! He had to stop it. He could not bear to think of his little girl being eaten.

The worm in his belly quickly slithered up toward one of his stomachs.

Creators, he prayed in his mind, if you have any mercy at all—

And then he realized where he'd seen the weave before: it was him. It was woven with some of the same patterns as he was.

Yes, he listened to the song of the worm in his arm, its trilling and thrum. He knew this weave. And with that knowledge came the knowledge of how to break it.

And break it he did. With a great tug he yanked the first worm out of his arm.

He punched a hole into his gut with the tips of his free fingers. The second worm was not hard to find. It had paused by one of his stomachs.

Hunger pushed his fingers in deeper and grabbed the second worm. It fought him, wriggling with violence, but he knew its secrets now and withdrew it from his body. In moments he held both teeth in front of him.

The weaves were beautiful, curling in the light. Beautiful and deadly. He grasped them tightly, found their weak points, and attacked. It was only a moment and they were unraveling like a spool of thread. Their curling slowed, their song wavered. And then they stopped altogether.

The Mother commanded him to her.

I'm coming, he said. But he was talking to his wife and daughter, deep in the Mother's cave, still caught in his stomach. *I'm coming!*

ARGOTH WATCHED THE woman catch Hogan's arm midstrike, preventing his blow.

Hogan pushed her back against the wall, throttling her. The lines of his body blurred at the edges, blurred even her form. She was choking. Her ribbon familiars seemed to shudder with a sympathetic pain.

For a brief moment her visage flickered. One moment she was a woman whose face shone with such beauty it almost took Argoth's breath. The next, the woman was gone, and in her place was something horrible with a round sucker mouth full of teeth that looked like it belonged on a leech or lamprey. Her undulating creatures seemed to swim with less vigor for a moment. And then the goddess was back.

She held a pointed weapon in her hand. With a quick jab she thrust it at Hogan's gut. There was a flash, but it didn't look as if it had penetrated the mantle.

Argoth began to believe they might win this fight.

But then the monster flickered in the corner of his eye and Argoth turned. It held up the two hag's teeth in its rough hands.

Argoth watched in dismay as the teeth stilled their movements. Then the monster crushed the teeth and threw the lifeless twists of metal to the dust.

"Hogan!" Argoth yelled in warning.

But it did no good. Hogan was too focused on the woman.

The monster charged. With three enormous strides it covered the distance between it and Hogan. Then it dropped its shoulder and crashed into Hogan, its large bulk hurling him away from the woman.

Argoth wanted desperately to join in the battle. But the crown yet drew from him. He would be surprised if he had enough energy to walk.

Hogan turned on the monster. With deadly violence, he struck it in the head with his stone.

The monster reeled to one side.

Argoth marveled at the power of Hogan's blow. He'd seen the dreadmen attack this thing. He'd seen the Skir Master. None had come close to this.

Hogan followed with another blow, the very air seeming to bend before him.

The monster fell back to the floor.

There was more in those blows than the simple force of stone. The mantle was at work. He could see the stone glistening with the power of it.

The ribbons of light swirled about the room. A number still clung to Hogan, and Argoth could see they'd eaten partway through the mantle.

Hogan raised the stone once more and suddenly jerked back.

The woman had penetrated the mantle with her weapon. It stuck deep in Hogan's back.

He twisted around and caught her with an elbow.

She flew backward, but Hogan dropped to one knee. He tried to rise, but the monster scuttled over and fell upon him. It ripped the stone away from his grasp.

Hogan struggled. He delivered two more mighty blows to the monster, but they were not what they had once been. Argoth could feel a weakening in the binding between him and the crown. The monster caught the second blow in its rough hand, and wrapped Hogan in its long arms. Then it took him down to the floor in a full body hold. Hogan thrashed, but he did not break free.

The woman walked up to Hogan, a number of her shining school of light still writhing, hissing, and whispering about her. She reached down and clutched at the golden square of the crown.

Hogan twisted in the monster's grip.

Argoth felt the woman through the bond of the crown. It felt like something gnawing on his bones. She was breaking the crown.

How was this possible? This was a victor's crown. It was supposed to be impenetrable. And then he realized the crown was, but the bond was another matter entirely.

The bond suddenly changed. The harmony that sang through him departed, replaced by something painfully off-key. Then the bond snapped altogether.

The Creek Widow cried out.

Argoth felt a great gust of his essence whirl up and away. The break had rent him. In panic, he tried to close up the leak.

Hogan grunted and struggled once more against the monster's grip.

Argoth stemmed the break. A portion of his strength returned, but it felt as if a sword had just sliced through him.

The woman ripped the crown from Hogan's head and tossed it aside. It landed only a pace or two from Talen.

The monster squeezed Hogan tighter, then shook him. And as it did, sparks of light fell from Hogan like pieces of ash to the floor.

"Unruly beast," the woman said to Hogan. Her shimmering school drew around her, but not so tightly as before, for she was visible in their midst. She felt the side of her face where Hogan struck her with the chain.

She turned to the monster. "Hunger. Take him there." She motioned to a place next to the rough figures on the floor.

The monster changed its hold on Hogan to clasp him firmly in one arm and got to its feet. Hogan struggled, but to no avail. The monster dragged him to the earthen bodies lying in their horrible rows on the other side of the chamber.

"That one will do," said the woman.

The monster stopped and lay Hogan next to a rock and

clay figure with a vicious muzzle. Splotches of dead grass sprouted from the side of the figure's head and chest.

The woman moved close to the monster. She hovered over it. "This," she said, "will be your first child. He'll be more aware than you were, have more human memories from the start, be more intelligent, more powerful. You were a mishmash of many things; I couldn't recover you whole. Not with the binding your original master had put upon you. But he is unfettered and pure."

What was she talking about? Fear rose in Argoth's mind.

"Separate the man," she said. "Put his soul and Fire into the body of earth."

At first Argoth could not believe his ears. Then the shock rolled over him. She was transferring Hogan's essence—Fire and soul—to one of the still creatures on the floor.

"No!" he cried. "Stop!"

The woman turned to them. "You all will serve me," she said, "with a lesser binding or with one of rock and stone. In your current bodies or that of another. I am now your master."

Hogan struggled in the monster's grasp. "Ke!" he called out. "River!"

Ke was already charging. But how could he? The breaking of the bond had nearly crippled Argoth. Argoth marveled at the strength in the boy.

Ke held Hogan's chain in his hand. In a blinding motion, he drew back and struck at the monster with terrible ferocity. The chain wrapped around the monster's neck.

Ke grabbed the chain with both hands and yanked it backward. Such a move would have ripped the head off a normal man. The monster jerked back, but it did not loosen its grip on Hogan. Instead, it reached up with one hand and tore the chain out of Ke's grasp. Then it struck him with it full in the face. Ke fell to the floor.

"No!" shouted Talen. He held a knife aloft and charged.

The monster turned slightly when Talen got close and struck out in an almost lazy fashion. The blow made a sickening sound and sent Talen flying backward to land sharply on his side.

Talen gasped, rolled over, and tried to catch his breath.

The monster turned back to Hogan.

"Please," said River, her collar still circling her neck. "We can come to an agreement." But the woman paid her no mind.

"Nothing!" Hogan shouted. "Give her nothing!"

The monster covered half of Hogan's face and head with one hand. It put its other hand on the face of the earthen figure.

The woman turned to the rest of them and spoke. Her voice carried like soothing music into his mind. "You cannot hide the one that was conceived and developed by my power."

She held something up. It was the wisterwife charm Argoth's sister had found on the chair in her bedroom. "Where is the one I planted? Where is the one that wore my might?"

Her words confused him. The one *she* planted?

Legs suddenly came shuffling in through the entrance to the chamber, feeling the wall as he went. "Sugar?" he called.

"You are such wild creatures," said the woman. "Such difficult things to manage." She motioned at Legs. "You fooled my servant with your ploy, but you cannot fool me."

The ribbons of light obscured her face for a moment. "A new order is arising here," said the woman. "One that hasn't been seen in ages. The master that leads this harvest will rule empires. You will bring him to me."

Argoth looked at Talen, who was holding his side in pain. Argoth's mind raced. His sister, Hogan's wife, had conceived wearing that weave. She had worn it through the whole pregnancy as the boy ripened in her belly. She had placed it upon Talen from the day of his birth.

They had all suspected he would be a prodigy: a restorer of lost knowledge, a champion. A gift from the Creators to help them fight their enemies.

He looked at the weave. Dear gods, what had they done? His mind snagged on something: "this harvest," she had said.

A great foreboding rose up in him. Snippets of ancient tales and lore flashed in his mind. Tales of devouring. He'd thought they were figurative. But he now realized they were literal.

"I have been calling," the woman said. "I know he's alive. I can feel him. He should have heard me. He should have come. But instead you hide him."

"Lies!" shouted the Creek Widow.

"We shall see," said the woman.

The monster turned back to Hogan and the earthen figure on the floor. Then the creature covered Hogan's face with its massive hand.

Hogan twisted, trying to wriggle away, but he could not. He cried out and grasped the monster's forearm.

"Be careful," said the woman.

Hogan arched his back; he struck violently at the monster's arm. The schools of light moved furiously, shining, shimmering, swirling around the woman, around the monster, around Hogan and the figure on the floor. Hogan jerked once, twice.

Argoth was paralyzed.

How could he fight this being? How could anyone when

they didn't even know what she was? The only thing he did know was that she was full of malice and that she wanted Talen. For what purpose, he could not guess. But she wanted him. And so she must not have him.

Argoth could not save Hogan, but he could rescue Talen from her.

He turned to River, who had almost worked the collar off her neck. "There is no way out," he said. Even if they could find their path in the dark, they could not run fast enough to escape the monster. They could not fight it or its master with lore. "I used to think we could fight the thralls, but we cannot. Better to die free than live a slave to some horrible purpose in which we deliver our kind up on platters."

River paused. He could see the anxiety in her bruised face.

"I do not have the strength, so you must deny her the one thing she desires. Put Talen beyond her reach. And then eliminate the rest of us."

River's eyes grew wide in dismay.

"I beg you," he said. "Tell me another way."

Death was their only escape. He wasn't prepared to go through that doorway, but who ever really was? He thought of his wife, his daughters, and wondered if they still lived. He could not protect them now. He thought of Nettle lying on that table and the sacrifice that Argoth had recklessly wasted. Grief welled up in him.

He could see River felt that same grief. Her mouth was a line of grim determination. Her eyes brimmed with angry tears.

River nodded. Then she slipped the collar ever so slightly to the left, gave it a smart tug, and broke it free.

THE WOMAN'S WORDS reverberated through Talen. They stroked and caressed him. Every time she spoke he was filled with a small elation. He wondered if she were one of the old gods. And yet, there was Da, lying in the dust.

Da jerked. Beneath the monster's hand, he screamed. And then the screaming stopped. Da's body relaxed, and his arm dropped to the floor.

"No!" Talen cried out. "No." His ribs were on fire. They cut like knives every time he took a breath. Talen tried to stand and gasped from the pain.

The woman was cooing, her shining escort swimming about the monster kneeling between Da and the clay figure on the floor.

He needed to stop this. The crown lay in the dust within his reach. It still glittered as it had upon Da's brow. He clutched at his side, crawled forward, and picked it up.

A vast power stirred within. It *was* alive as the Creek Widow had said. He could feel its music. A small thread of peace welled up in him. He could feel the power, but he was blocked from it as if a heavy iron door stood fast in his way. What was more, Talen had no idea what to do with this weave. He knew no lore, only the bestowing of Fire River had taught him. The crown was useless to him.

He looked up at the Creek Widow for help, but she was on her hands and knees as if recovering from a mighty blow. He turned to Uncle Argoth. "Help me," he mouthed.

"I'm sorry," Uncle Argoth said, his face full of despair.

Talen clutched the crown. There had to be a way, but he could not think.

Through the ribbons of light, he watched a thick blackness pass from Da into the monster's arm.

Da's leg shuddered.

The blackness rose into the monster's forearm. It reached its elbow.

Talen could not speak. Was that the essence of Da's soul?

A moment passed. Another. The blackness rose almost to the monster's shoulder.

"Well done," the woman said. "Well done."

Talen felt the praise in those words and craved it.

The monster removed its now black hand from Da's face, and Da's head flopped to one side.

"Da," Talen said, horror slithering itself about him.

The monster held its ink-black arm aloft, then it punched it into the belly of the figure lying on the floor. It knelt there until Talen realized the blackness was leaching out of the monster's arm and into the clay belly of the second monster.

Talen could barely whisper. "No," he said in a small voice. "No."

An eternity passed, and then the monster withdrew its fist. The blackness was gone.

The earthen body upon the floor stirred. Its hideous mouth opened as if taking a breath. Then it turned its awful head to look Talen in the face.

Talen recoiled.

He could not breathe. Could not speak.

They had killed Da, used him to animate that creature.

The woman turned to them. She reached up, her escort shimmering about her.

Talen's attention was drawn to her hands. They were smoky, flickering. Almost like that of a wraith. He had not noticed this before.

"Your former masters were lax and allowed untamed elements into the populace. So I shall educate you. There is a great order of beings. This is the nature of creation. Humans have mastered many things, but not all. There are greater powers still. I will protect you from all takers. Serve me, and I will give you knowledge and power beyond what you can imagine. I shall raise you and crown you as Divines to your people. Think of all you could do with such power. Just bring me the master of the harvest."

Her words were as smooth as silver. She was so beautiful, so convincing. A scrap of a memory came to him. And he realized that when he was a child, he'd dreamt of this woman, of the bands of living light. He remembered the joy of those dreams. So long ago. Before Mother had died.

Part of him wanted to bask in her radiance. But there was a part of Talen that resisted her, part of him roiling with revulsion. If he could only don the crown, perhaps he could do something. But the power of the crown was beyond him.

"So I shall ask again," the woman said. She held up the wisterwife charm. "Where are you hiding the one that bore my might?" Her words caressed Talen like silk. If he had known the truth, he would have told her.

But perhaps . . .

The charm, the dreams, the words River and the Creek Widow had spoken to him—they all roiled in his mind. His mother had discovered, working in the fiber of his body, strange and intricate patterns of power. "Twisted," River had said. "Pruned and grafted for a great purpose," the Creek Widow had said.

They had all suspected it was for some greater good. But none of them could have imagined this.

It's *me*, he thought. I am the one she seeks. With a clarity that rang like a bell, Talen felt the truth of it. It sounded in his very bones.

But what was he? Was he even human? He felt the panic of standing next to a high precipice and knowing he was going to tumble over the edge. He felt the fear of being dragged by a treacherous current far out to the deep and rough waters of a cold sea.

The woman motioned at Da's body. "He's cooling even as we speak, but it's not too late. I can reverse the quickening. Tell me where the master is and you shall save your friend."

He could save Da. Talen's world was gone, replaced by this nightmare. But he could save Da.

His mind told him this was true. But in his heart was a warning.

He looked over at River. Her face was wracked with grief and fear. She shook her head, indicating he should say nothing. He noticed she'd freed herself of the collar, which meant she was probably working her lore, multiplying her powers. Even so, what could she do that Da as a victor could not? Her attack would be as futile as Ke's had been.

"Don't listen," said Uncle Argoth. "She means to put us up like so much smoked meat."

"That is true," the woman said. "But this is the order of things. You love and cherish your cattle, your sheep, your beasts. But in the end you feed off of them. Why should it be any different with us? Besides, you will fare better under my management than you ever could on your own. Your people will grow old in peace. You yourself will live to the age of a tree, doing, if you decide, much good. You will protect those most dear to you. You will put down injustice and grind your enemies beneath your feet. You will heal sickness in children, cattle, and herb. Peace and fatness will reign in these valleys and hills, these shores and mountains, until the end of your days. This is what I give you—the power to bless."

The joy of her vision overwhelmed Talen. Indeed, he thought, why should they fight her? Is this not what every man and woman desired? The good he could do was unimaginable. And how could he be so ungrateful when she was offering him the means to save Da?

Again, revulsion roiled in him. The vision faltered. Was she lying?

He looked at Da lying in the dust. He could save Da. He could do good. And if they didn't pick up the reins she offered, surely someone else would. Someone like Fabbis who would rule with cruelty.

Her words filled him with hope, and he made his decision.

"I am the one," he said. "It is me you seek."

"No, Talen!" Uncle Argoth shouted. "She twists life. She will steal your will."

"On the contrary," the woman said.

Her countenance shined upon Talen and it made him glad.

"An overseer must take the position freely or not at all," said the woman. "It must be so. Thralls do not endure. They are creatures destined for madness and wrath. And when a creature's wrath is full, there is nothing left to do but cut it down for the devouring. Thralls are used for those who fight, but not for those who rule. And it's best that humans rule other humans. It's a matter of trust."

"She lies," said Uncle Argoth. "You can fight her."

"Does not a dog glory in the praise of its master? Has it not been bred to do so? The world of men was domesticated ages ago. Your very nature makes you dependent on us. The only difference between you and your dogs is the genius with which you were bred." She turned to Talen. "You were woven to work with me without impediment. Your only taskmaster will be my approbation."

The woman came to him in her beauty and shining light.

"Save him," Talen said and pointed at Da.

"All in good time," said the woman. "All in good time. First, we shall see if you are what you claim to be."

Yes, he thought. That was right. But underneath it all

he knew it was not. Da was dying. Every second would count.

"You have been bred to wield power impossible to others. We will raise an army from the very earth," said the woman. "And you will command it."

She approached him, reaching out with her smoky hands. Her shining escort enveloped him.

He should have felt fear, but all he felt was the ease of the woman and her smiling eyes. The music in the crown built. He could feel it vibrating in his feet and across his shoulders. But why was he even holding it? He let it drop to the floor. An odd thought came to him: Atra was nothing compared to this woman, yet this woman looked like Atra.

Something probed him. Talen held his doors closed, but he could feel her gnawing all along his essence with something as small and sharp as the teeth of rats.

The probing became stronger.

Reflexively, he shut himself tight as River had taught him.

The woman pulled away and appraised him. He felt her pleasure and it almost sent him to his knees. "You are indeed mine. Mine from the moment you were conceived. The weave has been changed. But it's nothing that, with time, cannot be undone."

She spoke in Atra's voice. Looked at him with Atra's eyes. Except they weren't Atra's. They were at once more alien and more captivating than Atra's could ever be.

Another wave of pleasure washed over him. He looked at Da's body. It was not right to have such wondrous feelings. It was wicked. It was an abomination. And yet he could not deny the power of them.

"In time you will become as great as the Goat King himself."

Suddenly a music inside him swelled. It sang in his

blood and bones. He thought it was the crown, but then he remembered he'd dropped that. For a brief moment the fog in his mind cleared away. The woman's voice fell flat.

Talen looked at her. Gone were the luminous eyes, the elegant neck and brow. Gone the alluring lips. In their place were black pits for eyes and a sucker mouth full of sharp teeth.

He recoiled.

An illusion—she was *not* one of the old gods. Not a benefactor. It was as if a huge blast of cold wind had just awakened him. His mind had been foggy, but now was crystal sharp.

And yet the desire to serve her seeped back through him.

"Yes," said the woman. "He too was a master of the harvest that served my mother ages ago. For a time, the populace under his care yielded marvelous results. You will be his heir."

The Goat King's heir . . .

The title felt marvelous, and yet, underneath it ran a filth with a sickening taint.

The glorious woman was back. His heart longed to serve her. But in his blood and bones he knew the truth— that longing was her doing.

He *had* been twisted—to crave her.

That knowledge momentarily lessened her power, and he wondered: Was this what his mother had seen in him and given her life to fix? Surely even the pox wouldn't take a whole life to heal. No, more likely she'd recognized the enemy's tool and given her life to engineer one small flaw so that his adoration wouldn't be totally complete.

But if that were the case, it wasn't much of a flaw because the woman's joy rushed back to suffuse him.

"River!" roared Uncle Argoth. "Now!"

River rushed toward him. She moved with frightening speed. In an eyeblink she sped from across the chamber and leapt into a flying kick.

He'd fought with River. He knew, at this speed, her kick would carry the force to break bones.

The woman stepped back, and as she did, Talen realized River was not directing the attack at the woman. She was directing it at him. At his head. Her blow would crack his skull. At the very least it would snap his neck bones.

River's face was twisted with fury and grief.

Talen had no time to react.

But the blow did not land.

The monster rushed forward and, in a lightning strike, caught her ankle. River's foot stopped a breath away from his face.

The monster twisted her leg, and River fell to the ground.

"Another one," the hideous woman said. "It looks like we shall raise our army a bit faster than expected. Put her next to the male."

The monster moved to carry River next to Da.

"Wait!" Talen said. "Wait."

The woman turned. "Will you serve me?"

"Boy," said Uncle Argoth. He made a small movement with his hand indicating Talen should come close. In his hand, close to his leg, he held a stone.

Why did they want to kill him?

The answer came: they believed they couldn't fight this creature. They didn't have the power.

But he was something else. "A body," River had said, "can only accept so much Fire at once." He had poured forth Fire that would easily kill ten men. He could pour forth a flood. He had been bred to it. And he'd been given one tiny flaw.

No, they couldn't fight the woman. But perhaps he could.

Yes, he *could*. He didn't have much of a chance. But something was better than nothing at all.

Argoth beckoned. Talen looked again at the stone in his Uncle's hand. Even if he could get close to Argoth, the monster would be watching. It would foil Uncle Argoth as it had River.

He knew what they wanted—they wanted the woman's tool destroyed. But his plan could do that. He might not be a victor. But he could fight despite his limitations. And he would do it in a way that would put the woman on her heels.

The monster still held River's ankle as if she were some child's toy.

Talen stepped around them, toward the woman. "I choose to serve you."

Her pleasure rushed through him; it washed him from heel to crown, an ecstasy like he'd never experienced. His resolve faltered. He wanted so desperately to serve.

"You will have your heart's desires," the woman said. But he knew she lied. She wasn't going to save Da. She wasn't going to spare River. He'd seen her for what she was. Of course, part of him didn't care what she was. Most of him didn't care.

"No!" shouted Argoth. "No good can come from this. You cannot lie with sheep and sire men."

"Hunger," the woman commanded.

"Trust me," Talen said again. But he didn't know if he could trust himself.

He turned to his sister and saw her dismay. He looked into her lovely, grief-stricken eyes. "I love you, sister," he said. "I will see you in brightness."

Her face fell.

"No," said Uncle Argoth, but the heat was gone from his voice.

The living light about the woman reached out to him. "In the end," she said, "they will see your wisdom and thank you. Now we must hollow you so that we may repair what was done. Hunger, come."

The monster took River back to the wall and chained her with double the chains. It left her there and strode over to Talen.

Talen flexed his essence. River had told him to practice closing himself every moment he could. He had done this. He knew how to open and close himself. He only needed to fling himself wide at the right moment.

THE MOTHER SPOKE into Hunger's mind. *As soon as we have the master in our control, you will take the others and quicken your brethren.*

Yes, he said, and his heart fell. Hunger had done all she had commanded. He had kept his part of the bargain. But she had just lied to the boy. And if she lied to her overseer, why would she ever keep her word to him, a thing destined for the devouring?

But what could he do? He could not fight her.

In anger, he reached forward and took the boy by the throat.

TALEN TENSED. THE monster's hands were rough with stone. But more unsettling still was the feeling of something probing along the seams of his being.

The monster readjusted its grip.

Talen prepared to fling himself wide.

Then he was lost, floating, in his body, but out of it.

Panic rose in him. He'd missed his chance.

"River," he called.

With a roar like rushing water, a door burst open within him and another one behind it. He could perceive the chaos of the monster outside that first door, and beyond it, behind the second door stood the woman.

Beauty. Power. Like nothing he could imagine. A being worthy of his every devotion. He longed to make her happy. But the truth sang in his bones. He knew she was an illusion. Knew her promises would turn to dust. However, it didn't matter now as much as it had only moments before. He just didn't care.

No, he said to himself. The link between them must be magnifying her effect. He focused on Da and River, on the monster.

"You please me," said the woman.

He basked in her gratitude and knew he was hanging by a finger. He was slipping, sliding, falling into a powerful river from which he knew he would never return.

He had to act quickly. He could not withstand this longing.

"Come!" he shouted into the roar of noise. "Come and take me!" He threw open the fabric of his being and poured himself forth.

The Fire coursed from him through the monster's arm.

Talen ripped himself wider, a massive rent. The Fire crashed around him like turgid rapids.

But the monster simply swallowed it up.

"Yes," the woman said. "That is good."

How much Fire did it take to break a man? How much did it take to break a monster? Talen had no idea, but what he was doing didn't seem to have any effect.

Talen opened himself as wide as he could.

Black spidery lines ran up the creature's arm, spreading down its side and along its chest. But the creature showed no sign of breaking.

Fear rose in him. This wasn't going to work. He'd been a fool! He should have run to Uncle Argoth.

He tried to pull away but could not.

But he didn't really want to anyway.

No, Talen thought. No! He searched for more to give, to release all that was in him. And then he felt something slip. He had been standing in the rush, watching it flow by. Now he knew he simply needed to let go, to flow with the Fire.

"What is he doing?" the woman asked in warning. "Stop it. Close him up."

Talen ripped the remnants of the wall that stood between him and the monster and let go. Pain shot through him, and instead of standing in the Fire and watching it flow away, the Fire picked him up, engulfed him, carried him like a piece of flotsam.

So much Fire.

The tips of the fingers of the monster lightened like ash. A wave of white passed up the creature's arm.

"It's too much," said the woman. "Close him!"

THE BOY'S POWER was immense. His pool of Fire vast. Hunger had never felt such power in anything he'd ever eaten.

He hadn't felt it in the Mother.

Power rolled off the boy and filled the room. He was a storm, and Hunger was desperately trying to devour it all.

The amount of Fire roaring through Hunger to his stomachs was astounding. But what shocked him was that, Lords, he felt pain.

But no, it was the Mother's pain. How could that be?

The link, he realized. She used Hunger to wield powers she could not. And the link was exposing her to the heat of the raging Fire of the boy.

"It's too much!" she said.

An idea shot through Hunger. Hope sprang forth.

"No!" she said and tried to break her bond to him, but Hunger held her fast.

"Release me!" she commanded.

"Never!" Hunger cried, and instead of funneling the boy's raging might into his stomachs, he directed it all through his bond to the Mother.

TALEN FLOWED FORTH. The Fire engulfed everything. His vision blurred. His body screamed.

The woman yelled but her voice was drowned out by the rushing of the Fire.

He felt her trying to close herself against him.

The monster's arm and chest were now as white as ash.

Talen no longer watched the Fire. He was the Fire. He was a furnace, an inferno, a roaring, molten sea.

The woman yelled, commanded the monster to let go.

The creature ignored her.

"Here," Talen said, "is my heart's desire." And he gave himself, every whit.

A patch on the monster's face turned ash gray. Then all flashed a blinding white.

There was a deafening roar.

The woman screamed.

A huge blast cracked Talen's world.

The shock tore the monster into pieces, flung Talen like a leaf, hurled the others in the room into the rock. The Creek Widow tumbled away and crashed into the pallid beast. The bowls of liquid light smashed into the walls.

Talen reeled and saw a body below him.

He expected to slam into the ground, but did not. He was floating above the scene.

He looked closer at the body on the floor, and realized it was his.

River coughed. She lay on the floor, tangled in her chains. She got to her hands and knees. "Talen," she said.

"River!" he yelled.

But she did not respond.

"Sister!"

She did not hear him.

The fact of the body on the floor finally registered with him and Talen grew very silent.

He'd expected pain would vanish at the moment of death, but he hurt all over. He felt as if he'd lost something essential, a leg or an arm.

He looked about to see if the others were moving. Ke lay on his side, face to the wall.

Something caught him and tugged him around.

It was a hideous thing, all mottled blue with many twisting limbs and too many eyes.

"Save them," it said in a voice of gravel. "My pretty girl. My wife. Unravel the mother's binding."

Talen tried to pull away, but couldn't.

"Quickly," it said.

A piece of the creature before him struggled, then broke away and flitted off over its shoulder. Talen knew this abomination was the monster. It looked nothing like it had in that body of grass and stone, but he knew that was because this was the many souls of the thing.

It pulled on him with violence and carried him to his body.

Another part of the monster wriggled free.

"Quickly," it repeated. "She keeps them in the room where she sleeps." Then it stuffed him back into his body.

Pain slapped him, left, and came back in earnest. Talen gasped for air.

Another part of the monster began to writhe.

A loud buzzing filled Talen's ears.

The monster turned as if alarmed.

Something black darted past it.

"Find my stomachs," it said. "The ones she already took. Unravel them."

Something struck the monster, seemed to bite or bore into its back. The monster winced in agony, but continued to close Talen in.

"Loose them," it said. "Set them free."

Talen's vision of this new world diminished like someone had drawn closed the mouth of a sack, leaving nothing but three horrid eyes. Then they too winked out and the monster, the wicked buzz, the motion and light—all of it vanished.

Talen gasped and choked in a mouthful of dust.

He couldn't see. Couldn't breathe. Lords, he hurt. Something was broken inside his chest, cutting his innards like a knife.

He rolled over and cried out at a searing pain in his ribs, a pain that stole his vision and turned it into a flash of light. "Merciful Creators," he prayed, imploring, begging for help. "Da."

But the pain was too great and his whole world went white.

48.

SHIM

Talen awoke with his eyes closed, wailing in pain.

"Talen," a voice so soft he almost didn't hear it. "Brother."

It was River. But Talen couldn't contain his wails.

River stroked his forehead. "Shush," she said gently. "Shush."

He gritted his teeth, tried to stop. He panted and then the wailing turned to sobs, great wracking sobs, and tears streaming down his face.

He opened his eyes.

Blood had run out of one of River's nostrils and dried in the dust on her face. The odd beast light still lit the room behind her, but it had diminished greatly.

"Where's Da? Ke?"

A weary grief rose in River's eyes. "Ke is fading fast."

"And your father," said the Creek Widow, "let us hope that he has been gathered by the ancestors." Talen turned and looked at her. She'd tried to wipe it away, but he could see her mouth had been smashed. Dried blood caked the edges of her lips. It caked her gums. She was missing three teeth.

A sob rose in him. But he swallowed it. He could not fathom Da being gone.

Talen closed his eyes and composed himself.

"It wanted me to unravel its stomachs," he said.

The Creek Widow narrowed her eyes.

"The monster," said Talen. "Before it put me back."

"Talen," Uncle Argoth said, "how did you do it?"

"River had said you could kill a man by giving him too much Fire," said Talen. "I gave the monster everything."

"Incredible," said Uncle Argoth.

The Creek Widow shook her head. "My boy," she said and took his hand. "My bright, shining boy. You have snatched victory from the jaws of death."

"But I didn't," he said. "The monster put me back."

"What are you talking about?"

"The monster," said Talen. "It put me back into my body."

"But the monster lies in pieces," said Argoth.

"It was there, on the other side. I don't know how else to explain it."

"This place," said the Creek Widow, surveying the chamber. "It will take a great many days to understand what went on here."

"Is the woman gone?" asked Talen.

"Can you feel her inside you?" asked Uncle Argoth.

Talen turned inward. He could not feel her. "I heard her scream," he said.

"Yes," said Uncle Argoth. "We heard it also."

"There were doors between us," said Talen. He felt inward and could find no trace of that link between him and the woman. "They are gone."

"Let us hope. But even if she is gone, I do not think her sisters that rule the glorydoms will sit long. To them we are mad bulls broken from the pens and goring the good villagers."

"Talen," said River. "Do you think you can stand? We need to make our way out while this odd light lasts."

"I can stand," he said. He rolled over and pushed himself to his hands and knees. Every joint of him protested in pain. His head swam. But he forced himself up. "I can stand."

A multitude of what looked to be pale sea kelp littered the chamber floor. "What is that?" he asked.

"The woman's creatures," said River.

"Or were they her children?" asked the Creek Widow. "There are simply too many questions."

SUGAR KNELT AT her mother's side. She wondered how they would remove her collar.

"Mother," she said. "They're gone. We can get you out of here."

Mother licked her dry and peeling lips. She smiled and

reached out to cup Sugar's face. "You take care of Legs," she said and winced.

The way she said that carried a finality that frightened Sugar.

"You're coming with us," Sugar insisted.

Mother smiled again. "You are a strong girl. I will find your father, and we shall prepare a place for you."

"No," said Sugar.

At her side, Legs held Mother's hand to his face. Tears were streaming down his cheeks.

"You beautiful boy," said Mother. She took both Sugar and Legs in her gaze. "I am so proud of you both."

She winced again in great pain.

"Zu Argoth," Sugar called. "The collar is killing her!"

"Listen," Mother said. "I have something for you. I was waiting. Under the hearth—" But her words cut off.

The others rushed to her side. The Creek Widow knelt and felt Mother's face. She felt along the collar. "She's worn it longer than any of us. I suspect its weave destroys its wearer when the bond with the master is broken."

"Purity," said the Creek Widow. "Can you walk? We need to get out of here."

Mother's gaze seemed to be focused on something behind them. She smiled. Her features relaxed. "Sparrow," she said.

And then Sugar felt her go. Mother's hand fell limp. Her breathing stopped.

"Mother," Sugar said.

With that word, the tears and grief that had deserted Sugar since the mob attacked sprang forth. She wept. And as the fountains of her tears rose so did a resolute determination: come what may, the daughter of Sparrow and Purity, the smith's wife, would learn her mother's lore. She would finish whatever it was her mother had began.

TALEN PICKED UP the remaining torches from the passageway to the chamber. They would have to return and recover Da's and Purity's bodies. They lit the torches and began the journey back, but they could not move quickly with River carrying Ke and Argoth and Sugar supporting the Creek Widow. Nor could Talen do much more than shuffle with his injuries.

The torches burned out long before they'd reached the entrance to the caves. However, Legs had kept his wits about him on the way in and had marked orientation points—a dead spot where there was no breeze, the place where you could hear the pouring of distant water, the corridor with the double echo. They walked for what seemed hours, in a line. Each person keeping one hand in front of themselves to feel the blackness. With the other they held the tunic of the next person in line. This is how they worked their way back. And with only a few wrong turns and retracing of steps, Legs led them out of the cave and into the light.

Talen blinked in the sunlight. The warm air of early evening wrapped about him like a blanket. He took in a great breath of free air.

Then the woods about the cave boiled to life with armed men wearing Shoka blue and green. A hundred bows drawn and aiming at the group. Teams of hunting dogs barked, straining at their masters' leashes.

Talen didn't care. He'd already died once today. Take him, string him up, and pull off bits and pieces until there was nothing left. He simply didn't care.

ARGOTH LOOKED AT the faces of the men surrounding him. He looked at their dogs. They stood thirty paces away, the proper distance for confronting Sleth. He knew all of them. Then Shim, the warlord of the Shoka, pushed his way through and stood at the front of their line.

"Captain Argoth," the warlord boomed. "Whom do you serve?"

For a moment Argoth faltered. Had he misjudged Shim? Were all of his pleadings and talks of alliances just a ruse? After all, it was Shim who had told him the lie that the Skir Master had lost his beast. It was Shim who had wanted him to expose the Order just before the Skir Master arrived.

"I serve you, Lord."

"Oh, but I have a bailiff here that says the monster is yours." Shim motioned at the bailiff of Stag Home. Next to him stood the man they called Prunes, a warrior of many battles, a man that was frightened by neither death nor torture. His face, oddly enough, shone with fear. And Argoth realized these men were preparing to slaughter them.

Argoth shook his head at the futility of their fight. They'd just dealt a blow to an unimaginable enemy, and these fools were going to kill them.

"What did you say?" asked Shim.

"The monster," said Argoth, "is destroyed."

"And its master?"

"Fled. But you can search the cave and verify what we say. You will find a room with the bodies of those who fell and of those that would have overrun the land."

The warlord turned to the bailiff. "Since you bring the accusations, I'm going to let you lead the search. Pick fifty men."

The bailiff turned and looked at Prunes, who appeared to quail at the prospect of entering the cave. But he did not refuse and soon the two of them had selected the men to go with them. They decided to use Purity's daughter as their guide, bound her hands, and disappeared into the hole.

Argoth and the others waited outside with Shim's army ready to fill them with arrows.

The search party returned as the sun was setting and confirmed what Argoth had told them. They brought with them the bodies of Hogan and Purity and part of the monster's leg.

"There were eight others like this," said the bailiff.

Eight? But there had been nine. Hogan, Argoth thought, my dear friend—where have you gone?

Argoth turned to Shim. "They need to be collected and destroyed. Their master must not return and find them."

"We also found a passage beyond the chamber where the battle took place. It is deep and broad and leads into the belly of the mountain."

Shim nodded. "For years we've lived with the caves of this land, ignoring them, ignoring those who disappear. Perhaps it is time we find out what lives in their depths."

He walked the distance between his men and Argoth's group to stand before Argoth. Shim searched his face. "You've done well, Captain," he said. "Very well. And you'll have your celebration feast, but not just yet."

Argoth looked into the eyes of his old friend and found . . . honesty.

What a fool he'd been to doubt him.

"What's wrong?" asked Shim.

"Nothing," said Argoth.

"You don't trust me yet?" asked Shim. "Lords, I should take offense."

"I—"

"I nothing," said Shim.

"Do they trust this?" asked Argoth.

"You are so full of doubts and fears. Perhaps that's what comes of excessive hiding. But it doesn't matter. I trust it," said Shim. "I trust you. And they trust me."

"You're taking a great risk," said Argoth in a low voice.

"Such little faith," said Shim.

He put one of his arms around Argoth's shoulders and turned to his men. "My lords," he called.

Lords?

Two men separated themselves from the other soliders. As they approached, Argoth saw it was Bosser, a captain of the Vargon Clan, and the Prime, the head of the Clan Council.

"Do you see?" asked Shim. "You are not alone."

Both Bosser and the Prime came forward to stand before Argoth.

Bosser stroked the mustache that grew down to his chin.

"Welcome back, Captain," said the Prime.

In a quiet voice, Shim said, "It is time, my friend, for us to receive a little instruction."

Argoth should have felt hope or worry, but after all that had happened, he only felt a weariness descend upon him.

"A new order will arise in this land," whispered the Prime.

The words struck Argoth. Weren't those exactly the words the woman had used? Argoth looked to Bosser. "You don't know what you're doing."

"Not all Glories inherited their rule," said Shim. "Some of them had to take it by force."

"There are more powers at work here than just those of men," said Argoth.

Shim shook his head. "Then we adjust the strategy."

He turned to the men circling them. "Men of Shoka,"

he said. "It is time to celebrate, for one of ours has saved the land."

THEY DID CELEBRATE that night at the Shoka fortress Lord Shim himself commanded. Shim made sure to ease his men with plenty of ale. They ate and drank and danced and then Argoth told them about how the monster had come after him and Hogan, the two who had first attacked it in the tower. He described the giant night maw and its bluish light. He described the power of the monster and its beautiful master. He told of Sugar and Talen having the courage and sense to deliver the Skir Master's ravelers. Of the battle, he spoke little. Then he told of how Legs had led them out.

He left huge gaps in the story. He had to. Over the next few days the men would begin to wonder—what of Purity, why did the beast rescue her, what was Matiga's connection? He suspected the Crab, before he died, would have revealed that the Skir Master enthralled Argoth. He was sure that report was running, even now, through the clans. There were knots upon knots left to untangle, and he would cut them all with the truth. But not just yet.

After the tale, someone called out for a song. "That blind one's a singer," one of the men said. Argoth remembered Purity saying something about that.

Legs sat up, chewing on a mouthful of frog's leg.

"Come on, boy," someone called. "A song."

Legs swallowed, put down his frog leg, and wiped his mouth. He rose. "Only if you promise not to pelt me with vegetables, bones, or knives."

A few men chuckled.

"I don't want to be *blind*sided," Legs said.

More laughed at that jest.

Argoth considered Legs again. The boy was resourceful. He kept his wits. He was a puzzle. Had he been changed by the woman's weave as well?

Legs took a big breath, made a flourish, then began a song about the Mighty One Hundred—Sleth hunters in old Cathay. Again Argoth was surprised. Legs sang with strength. It wasn't the full-bodied voice of a mature man. It was simple and clear and Argoth couldn't help but feel the emotion of the story. When Legs finished the song there was silence for half a beat. Then the men cheered and called for another. But not all the men were as pleased. Some of them still looked at Legs with wariness.

Legs next led a group song about a one-legged slave who saved the village onions. Then someone called out for "The Hogwife." It was a humorous song about a beautiful Sleth who had consumed the soul of a boar. Usually the singer sang each verse alone, then the group came in on the choruses. Argoth wondered if this song was right for this moment.

He saw Legs had the same thought, for Legs paused, then he made a decision and started the men by clapping the rhythm.

Legs began.

> Her face fired devotion,
> Her body fired blood,
> If only she'd cease
> Her rooting in the mud.

Argoth watched the faces of the men. This was not the best song to sing at this moment. It would only raise questions about Purity. He wondered if the men would sing the chorus or if they'd feel the jarring as well. Most of the men joined in.

> Oh, I've got me two wives
> All mixed up in one,

A woman and a sow,
But begets have I none.

Legs continued.

I married her sweetly
We labored to breed
But, blister me, monsters
Can't quicken men's seed.

Legs belted out the last bit like some depressed lout and it was perfect. He sang like one of the entertainers at the gaming fields. More of the men joined in this time.

Oh, I've got me two wives
All mixed up in one,
A woman and a sow,
But I want a son.

When they sang the last line, the men raised their fists and shook them in demand.

Ere long came my pretty,
Blackened weave in her hand,
To bed, and I'll make you
A proper hogman.

Someone made a lovesick call. Legs changed his tone and sang on in a secretive voice.

To bed, in darkness
Irresistible she
Fed me the boar
Enhanced my breed.

Now dirt's my mustache,
And worms muddy my eyes

Legs paused then came back full of gusto.

But, oh, honeyed heaven
There's nothing so fine
As Hogwife and I
Rooting side by side.

The men joined in again, some swinging their mugs of ale.

Oh, I've got me two wives
All mixed up in one.
She bore me a litter—
Five smart piglet sons.

The men clapped, whistled, hooted. Someone called out for another, but Legs waved them off, took a bow, and sat down. The men around him clapped him on the back. The ale had loosened them. But tomorrow when they were sober, they would begin thinking. Argoth knew this because one or two were thinking right now, watching their brethren clap and holler.

Argoth looked at Shim who, it appeared, had been watching him. Shim pointed at the door with his chin, indicating he wanted to talk with Argoth outside. Argoth walked out of the room into the night. Behind him a group of men began another song.

The stars hung bright in the heavens. Below those stars, in the middle of the fortress inner court, lay the bodies of the monster's brethren found in the cave. There was so much the Order didn't know.

A few moments later, Shim exited the building. "That blind one's full of surprises," he said.

"I'm sure we don't know the half," said Argoth.

Shim nodded. "Come with me." He led Argoth to his command room across the bailey. Shim lit a lamp. The shutters were closed, but Shim pulled a small, thick blanket across each. In the winter such would keep the cold out. But they also muffled sound.

They sat in chairs, the lamp burning on the table to the side of them. "My friend," said Shim. "I have shown you my love. I have shown you my trust. You need to honor that now and tell me your tale."

Argoth hesitated. Such secrets were so dangerous. But he had hidden all his life. And it had led to nothing but loss. How could bringing the truth into the light of the sun be any worse? "Give me your hand, Lord."

Shim stretched out his rough and callused hand. Upon the wrist was the tattoo of the Shoka clan. Surrounding that and running up Shim's arm were the tattoos of Shoka manhood and his military orders.

Each clan had their own designs for manhood, military orders, and other markings, but each was built around the same simple clan pattern. Each child was required to have that pattern dyed into their flesh by a Divine. The pattern of Mokad.

By all that was holy. He looked at Shim's clan tattoo again, and the true nature of the marking shot through him.

Those who followed other Glories had a different base pattern. And if they should be conquered, the tattoo of the conquerer was added. He thought of Hogan with the simple Koramite tattoo and the Mokaddian added to it. He thought of all those he'd seen—the men of other nations, Bone Faces, Cathay. All wore tattoos. All of them inked by Divines . . .

How could he have not seen it before? So simple. De-

spite all the flourishes added by the clans, the heart of the ·
tattoo, the clan marking, was nothing more than an elaborate livestock brand. The woman was right: they were
indeed cattle, marked by their various masters.

Argoth shook his head and took Shim's hand. Nettle's
sacrifice had not all been a waste. He still had great portions of his son's Fire in him. Shim's hand was rough,
strong, full of experience. Argoth looked Shim in the eyes,
then poured a small amount of Fire into him.

Shim took in a breath, his eyes widened, but he did not
let go.

Argoth spoke into Shim's mind, *In the beginning, all
men were gods.*

ARGOTH TOLD SHIM the fragments of the history of the
humankind as he knew it. He told of the wars between
the Divines and the old gods, knowing now it was not a
war between men, but one between men and the race of
the creature in the cave. He told of Hismayas, one of the
last remaining gods, who sent his followers into the wilderness to hide, to preserve the truth until the time would
come that they might throw off their masters. Then he
told Shim about his tale, of his days of darkness, and stepping into the light. He told everything important up to and
including the recent events with the Skir Master and the
battle in the cave.

Shim said nothing for a long time. Then he pointed at
small chest on the table next to Shim. "Open that," he said.

Argoth did. In it lay folded a cloth. Argoth picked it up
by two corners and let it unfurl. It was a device in the
shape of a shield that Argoth had never seen before: a field
half blue, half white, and upon that field lay a sun, the
thread of which was made of brass. The sun glistened in
the lamplight.

"What is this?"

"White for purity," said Shim, "blue for courage and loyalty. The sun for knowledge and power."

"Where did you get it?"

"It's old, my friend. Very old, passed down for generations. This is going to be our standard."

"Ours?" asked Argoth.

"All those," Shim said, "who fight those that would be our masters."

"I've watched the faces of the men," said Argoth. "They are going to have a difficult time accepting this. We cannot simply dump the whole truth upon them."

"No," said Shim. "First we will demonstrate our power. And when we have the confidence of those who matter, we shall tell them by what means we work."

"We will not have long. A few days at the most before they begin to question the fine points of our story."

"What I need from you is living weaves," said Shim. "A hundred in three days."

"Three days?" It was impossible.

Shim nodded. "We have some dry weaves. Two dozen maybe. You can fill those."

That would leave about seventy-five weaves to create. Nobody in this Grove knew how to make anything but crude weaves in metal. River could weave them of other things. But the amount Shim asked for was out of the question. Besides, they didn't have the Fire. Only the current members of the Grove could give Fire. And Argoth would never take it again. "I can deliver another ten."

"Twenty," said Argoth. "We must come to them in power."

"You can't train up a dreadman in a few hours."

"We don't need full dreadmen. We just need to show them the power available. Can you train the men and women you give the weaves to perform some feat?"

"Yes," said Argoth. "But even if we're able to convince

the lords of the Shoka, the Fir-Noy will not go along. And if they turn against us, three of the other clans will follow."

"In the beginning," said Shim, "they will resist us. But it will not last. The Prime is with us. Bosser as well. Furthermore, I have reports. The death of the Skir Master will shake Mokad. The lords of Nilliam will press this advantage. Mokad, more than ever, has no resources to spare. The Fir-Noy will receive no help."

"The Skir Master gave them weaves," said Argoth.

"How many? A dozen? And every day we will add to our numbers. In a few weeks we shall have hundreds. And then we shall raise dreadmen who need no weaves. Men like yourself. When the Bone Faces come and these Mokaddian loyalists have to contend with them on their own, they will find their objections are small things."

"Yes," said Argoth, "but we do not fight against the men of Mokad or Cathay or even the Bone Face ships. We fight against their masters. We have attacked, maybe killed, one of their kind."

"You think the glorydoms will join forces against us?"

"Look at how Seekers work. They hunt soul-eaters across the glorydoms of the earth, and none bar their way. Why? Because they hunt a mutual threat."

"Perhaps you are right," Shim said. "But perhaps they are not so different from us. Who is to say that some of these creatures might not find it in their interest to stand aside, to delay, in order to weaken an enemy? From what you told me of the creature in the cave, they are not unified."

"We should prepare for the worst," said Argoth.

"If they come at us with all their might, can we withstand them?"

Argoth had witnessed the power of the Skir Master firsthand. He'd felt the might of the being in the cave. She'd raised living things from stone. She'd smitten him so powerfully with the illusion of her beauty that it echoed in his heart still. "The old gods once fought them and kept them at bay for years. But we have lost too much."

"Then we shall find a way to open the seal on this book of yours and learn the things we forgot. We shall raise an army of dreadmen. And we will find someone who can bear the weight of the victor's crown. We cannot hesitate, my friend. Mankind's hour is in our grasp."

Argoth looked at Shim and wondered. The man had a weave his family had passed down, he had an ancient device—what was his history? Not all humans could wield the powers of life with equal effect. Not all could quicken themselves to the same degree. Bloodlines mattered. Was he simply a man with a powerful family heirloom? Or was Shim part of a line that stretched back to the old ones?

Argoth felt as if he'd had this conversation once before. Indeed, had not both Nettle and Ummon, his son of long ago, been asking him to fight? To step fully out of the shadows? Perhaps Hismayas had never intended his Order to hide itself so deeply.

He realized it *was* time, whether he wanted it or not. The wheels were in motion. The Order was going to stand forth in the sun.

"We will fight," said Argoth. "We will raise an army from Koramite and Shoka, from Vargon and Burund." He thought of the Groves scattered through the many glory-doms. He thought of the dark days before he joined the Order. Of the men and women who yet walked those forbidden paths. "There are many in every nation who will anwer our call."

THE VERY NEXT morning Argoth told Serah everything. Serah did not weep. Instead, she turned as hard as stone. Later in the day Matiga, without invitation, showed up with a pot of spicy sausage and potatoes and her famous currant rolls. The girls ate it all with relish, but neither he nor Serah touched their food. They both knew he had stolen her son. She had every right to hate him.

When the cleaning was done, Matiga sent everyone but Argoth and Serah outside. Then she turned to them both.

"I assume he's told you all?"

"Yes," said Serah.

Matiga might not be able to see it, but it was clear to Argoth. She was a pot of simmering fury.

"At least he got that right," said Matiga. "And I assume you know what will happen if you tell your sisters before Lord Shim brings this before the Council."

"I do."

"We will bind you with an oath," she said. "And you will keep it."

"I need no binding," said Serah. "But I will take it anyway."

"Good," said Matiga. "He was stupid not to bring you in. Women provide ballast. And that's something this one desperately needs."

"Indeed he does," said Serah.

Argoth tried to take her hand, but she moved it away. "The woman talked about restoring Hogan to his body," said Argoth.

Matiga and Serah waited for him to go on, but he could not. He could not tell them that he almost wished Talen had not overcome the monster. He could not tell them about the dreams he had of that woman guiding his hands as she had guided the monster's, except instead of him kneeling between two bodies, he stood with one hand on Nettle's scarred neck and the other holding the filtering rod.

Argoth looked down. "I am not myself. The roots of the thrall still work in me."

"That will pass," said Matiga.

So said the books, but he still felt a compulsion and

prying. A door somewhere was still open. A door to another being like the one they'd faced in the cave.

They'd discussed what had happened in the cave, and they'd realized that every Glory in every land was ruled by such a creature. Every Glory was cultivating a field and delivering its harvest.

"We don't have the knowledge to fix this open door in me," he said. "We don't know their powers. It is better to just eliminate the threat."

"No," said Matiga. "We don't have the knowledge. But we will. We have the gifts of Hismayas: the victor's crown and the Book."

"The Book has always resisted us. And the crown—well, we obviously don't know all we should about it."

"No," she said, "we don't. But I think I understand a few things I did not before. I think we should try to open the Book again."

"And if we fail?" asked Serah.

"We have the seafire," said Matiga. "We have our lore. We might know less than we'd like, but we know enough. If we cannot unlock the secrets of the Book, then we shall prepare with the knowledge we do have."

All this talk of the enemy didn't seem to matter at the moment. Argoth thought of Nettle again. Of the trust and pain that had shone in his eyes as Argoth drew forth his Fire.

He looked up at Serah. "Nettle was a man. He made the choice of a man."

"I'm not angry with Nettle," she said, pain and frustration and anger flashing in her eyes.

Argoth waited.

"You said you'd tell me a story about a woman who married a monster. You've told me that story. And it was all true. Now you need to wait for me to tell you the end."

Argoth nodded. He would wait. He'd wait, if he had to, until the Creators raveled the earth.

49.

FAREWELL

In the days following the battle in the caves, Uncle Argoth and Lord Shim began raising dreadmen. The Creek Widow and River began teaching Talen the first things about using Fire and soul and the history of the earth. But Talen found he couldn't focus. The monster had saved them all. Talen needed to honor its last wishes.

Talen was able to convince River and the Creek Widow to join him. He went back and stood on the hill above the refuge and looked down at the valley where the Divine had battled. The damage was clear to see—great erratic swathes and loops of dead grass and trees. Off to one side of the meadow a boar staggered and sounded out its pain.

Talen suspected he knew why. By the time he descended the hill, the boar was on its side kicking weakly. There was a wound on its side—that was probably the spot where the raveler had wriggled in. The boar might have been sleeping or eating. It could have been doing any number of things when the weave had found it. But Talen was sure it was the cause of the boar's throes. Then the boar ceased its struggling.

Talen waited, and not long after his suspicions were confirmed: the raveler worked its way out from underneath the animal and snaked into the grass.

Wearing the white, gold-studded gauntlets, Talen quickly plucked it up. The raveler immediately stilled, and he placed it in the case.

After obtaining the raveler, he searched for the monster's stomachs.

Uncle Argoth and the Creek Widow had taken the

remains of the original monster and opened it up to discover its lore. They'd also search their books for any record of the sons of Lamash.

They did not unlock its mysteries. In fact, the mysteries seemed only to multiply. But Talen *was* able to identify what he might be looking for. Inside the creature's chest had been a row of identical organs, black as coal, woven of willow withies, and merged into the flesh of stone. One, Uncle Argoth said, contained soul.

The monster had spoken of the stomachs the woman had already taken. And so Talen went back into the cave with Sugar and two loyal dreadmen.

They searched the chamber of battle. They searched the passageways leading in and out. They found many rooms, but they never saw a nest.

They were about to descend the broad path that led to the belly of the mountain, when Sugar asked if they'd been looking in the wrong place. Perhaps, she suggested, they should look up.

It took less than an hour to find the woman's roost. In one room with a sulfur pool there were a scattering of her dead eel creatures lying on the floor. When the group held their torches aloft, they saw an opening to a small chamber above. It contained silk clothing that Lumen, the former Divine of the clans, wore, an ancient, cankered sword, and a handful of abominable weaves, including two of the monster's stomachs.

And so it happened that on the morning of a cool autumn day, Talen placed the monster's stomachs on a large slab of granite on their farmstead. The survivors of the battle in the cave gathered around.

Talen donned the fine, white, gold-studded gauntlets and removed the last hag's tooth from its silver case. He held it up.

"This," he said, "is to honor the bravery of Barg,

Larther, and all the many other things that composed the servant of our enemy. May they find the safe path in the world of souls."

Then he lowered the tooth to the stomachs. When its sharp tip touched the first stomach, it came to life and wriggled out of his hand.

All stood around the stone, watching the tooth weave its way in, around, and through the stomachs that lay on the rock. The blackness of the withies leached away, leaving behind simple wood.

A small breeze gusted through, and then, for the briefest moment, Talen thought he heard singing.

The tooth wriggled out of the pile of spent stomachs and rolled off the rock into the dust.

Talen picked it up. It had yet one more task to perform.

THAT EVENING TALEN stood on the hill above the farmstead. At his feet lay three graves: one for Mother, a new one for Da's body, and another for that of Sugar's mother.

When Sugar had said she had no home, River and Talen had insisted she did. It was too risky for her to go back to her village and gather up any of her father's bones that might remain. But that didn't mean they couldn't make a small monument for the time when they could retrieve the bones. Nor did it mean they couldn't bury Sugar's mother here.

Talen had expected someone to desecrate the graves, for the Fir-Noy were causing more troubles than ever. But that had not happened yet. Instead, they'd found gifts left on the graves in respect. Some were gifts of apples, others were bunches of late summer flowers. There weren't many. But it surprised Talen. Once they even found a bowl of blood from a small sacrifice. It was believed by some that the ancestors could drink the Fire of a newly killed animal as it poured forth.

But there were no gifts this evening. Instead, Nettle crawled in circles below the graves as if searching for something in the grass. Uncle Argoth had told them all what he'd done, and it pained Talen to see Nettle so. Half mad, the other half lost. Legs, River, and Sugar were with Talen on the hill.

There were reports of something in the woods, something killing the deer and sheep. Legs said he'd heard it one night in the yard. They had found footprints the next morning, and the evening after that Talen had seen its face in the shadows staring at him. They'd tried to track it, but lost the trail, and the dead bodies of animals began to mount.

"Let us hope it isn't the woman seeking revenge," said River.

"If it were, wouldn't it be killing humans?" asked Legs.

"It's Da," said Talen. "Who else could it be?"

"I don't know," said River. "We hardly know anything."

"Well, I know this," said Talen. "During that last battle, it was Da that was looking at me from the eyes of the earthen figure. It was Da in that awful body, and he wants release."

They built a fire when the sun set, Legs sang a few mournful songs, and then they waited, watching the bats flit over their heads and an owl occasionally swoop silently across the field below.

Talen wore the gauntlets. In his hand he held the last raveler. The case now lay on the ground at his side.

The air was cold with the first breath of autumn. The leaves had begun to turn color and fall, and he could smell the fine scent of leaf mold. It had not yet frozen hard enough to kill all the insects, so the mosquitoes rose as the sun set, but an evening wind kicked up to blow them away. River fed the fire, and they waited, the stars

shining above them in the night sky, a hard-edged sliver
of a moon giving them light.

One by one each of the others fell asleep in their bed-
rolls, but Talen did not. He waited and watched, and when
he began closing just one eye to rest it, he roused himself
and stood.

A light burned in the window of their house across the
field below. Ke was there, being nursed back to health by
the Creek Widow.

Talen walked to a stone on the far side of the hill.
When he came back, he found River awake, making them
both a cup of tea, the Creek Widow sitting next to her.
Talen took his cup gratefully, then sat with the two of
them, sipping the red liquid and letting the cup warm his
fingers.

He looked at his sister. She had tried to kill him. He
did not hold it against her. However, she was not quite the
sister he knew from before.

He'd just poured himself a second cup when a branch
cracked at the edge of the wood behind them.

Talen turned.

He could make nothing out at first; the shadows along
the forest edge were too deep.

"Just to the left of that great pine," said River.

It was the earthen figure, the one with the vicious
muzzle, the one the monster had awakened.

"Slowly," the Creek Widow said.

They rose and faced the creature.

"Da?" Talen called out.

The thing did not move. It was covered in grass as the
first monster had been. Talen hesitated. The other creature had been so powerful.

Behind them the fire popped, and Nettle snuggled up
closer to Legs.

"Father," said River, taking a step forward.

"Careful," said Talen.

But the creature stepped out of the deep shadows of the wood into the remaining vestiges of the moonlight. In one hand, it held a doe by the leg, dragging it along behind like a child might an overlarge doll.

"We've brought help," said Talen and held up the raveler.

The creature opened its ragged mouth.

It reminded Talen of the first creature, and he began to fear. What if the woman *had* returned?

He forced himself to take another step forward. Then another.

Soon he stood an arm's length away.

This body was shorter than the first one. It was made of more than dirt and stone, for he saw many growths of withy wood rising from its skin.

"The ancestors are waiting," said Talen. "It is time for your release." He held the last raveler up.

The creature dropped the doe into the tall autumn grass. It stood for a moment, and then it reached out for Talen. At first Talen thought it was going to grasp him by the throat as the first had, and he stiffened. But it simply ran its rough fingertips down the side of his face.

River touched its arm. "You watched over us here. Watch over us now from the other side."

The Creek Widow said nothing, but Talen could see she was trying to hold back tears.

The monster that was Da grasped the raveler. Talen could feel the horrid strength in that stony hand. Now was the moment. Talen wondered if it would destroy this tooth as the other monster had done.

"We will see you in brightness," Talen said, and he released the raveler.

The monster held it up in the moonlight as if examining

it. Then the spike flashed to life and burrowed into the rough hand.

The creature opened its ragged mouth and took a terrible breath.

River stepped back.

The creature stood for quite some time, its arm outstretched, as if noting the progression of the raveler. Suddenly, it looked down and felt its chest. Then it looked back up at Talen and River and staggered back a step.

"Da," River said.

The monster threw its head back and opened wide its mouth. No sound escaped. But three shining ribbons of lavender light shot out and streaked up into the night sky. Moments later, the monster leaned to one side, sagged, and fell heavily to the earth.

Talen waited for it to move again, to continue the throes of its death, but it did not move. Something silver flashed in the moonlight and the raveler wriggled its way out of the creature's side, dropping into the dry autumn grass.

Talen picked up the raveler and it immediately stilled. He looked around. He hoped the ancestors had been there and gathered Da into safety. "Do you think they came?"

"Why wouldn't they?" asked River.

"Those ribbons," said the Creek Widow and trailed off. "So many questions."

Earlier they had discussed the glorious visions of the woman or man, or whatever it was in the cave. He told the Creek Widow he'd seen its true form, but the Widow had questioned that—how did he know it hadn't shown that awful visage to him on purpose? Indeed, the Creek Widow was right. There were so many questions for which they had no answers.

Talen looked into his sister's eyes, then he took her hand and they walked back to the campfire to sit and drink tea.

The Creek Widow stayed back with the body for some time, talking to it, talking to Da. When she returned, he gave her another cup of tea. He motioned at the gauntlets and raveler case. "A little bit of knowledge," said Talen. "That's all that separated Da from the Divines."

"In a way that's true," said River. "But in another it's not. The Divines serve their own masters. But Da served the Creators."

"At least what we know of them."

"That is right," said River. "He was more like one of the old gods than anything else."

That set Talen back. The old gods were the stuff of stories and legend.

"Imagine what he could have done," said River, "if he had been able to practice in the open."

"He would have blessed the hens," said Talen. "He would have multiplied their eggs."

River looked sidelong at him. "How do you know he didn't?"

"Goh," said Talen. And he realized Da probably had. Their farm had prospered. Not always. The hens had died, after all, but even the peach trees seemed to bear more fruit than those of the neighbors.

"Da would be so pleased to know that the vision he worked for is now beginning to come to pass," said River. "Not in the way he hoped, but coming to pass nevertheless."

"Perhaps," said the Creek Widow.

"We'll be attacked on all sides," said Talen.

"We will," said River. "But we should have a season to prepare. And if we ultimately fail, we will go out like Da, fighting."

Talen nodded. He wrapped the white gauntlets and raveler case in a cloth and placed them in a sack and put it aside. "If Da was like one of the old gods, does that also mean I have to worship you? Because I'm just not going to do it."

River laughed then she hit him on the forehead with the heel of her palm. "You will always worship me."

"I will," said Talen. And he meant it.

They began to reminisce about Da and Mother. The Creek Widow added stories Talen had never heard before. Every remembrance seemed to call forth three more, and soon the bittersweet memories came as a flood.

So many memories.

Sugar and Legs woke to the Creek Widow's laughter, and after being led to view the creature's body, they joined Talen and River at the fire, drinking tea and adding the stories of their family. Nettle slept on. But the rest of them talked through the night, the fire crackling at their feet, the stars shining brightly above.

When the eastern sky began to lighten, Blue and Queen joined them, Blue hobbling up hill on three legs. His hind leg was still worthless, but the injury was healing clean. Eventually he found Nettle and licked his face until he woke.

"Blue," said Nettle in recognition. He turned and looked at the others by the fire. "What have I got to do to get something to eat?"

"He's not all gone, is he?" said River.

"You only wish," said Nettle.

Talen and River looked at each other. Could the old Nettle have come back?

But then Blue licked his face again and Nettle began to roll around like a toddler, playing with the dog.

Down at the farmstead Prince Conroy began to crow, and as the sun rose it turned the ripple of thin clouds a breathtaking gold and pink.

"We'll need to lever that body onto a cart," said Talen, "and take it home to Uncle Argoth."

"No," said River. "I think in this case we shall leave it where it is and build over it a monument of stones."

Talen nodded. "After that we've got a field of barley to mow."

"I will help," said Sugar.

"And I," said Legs, "will dance and sing."

TERMS AND PEOPLE

POLITICAL HIERARCHY
While there are many variations, the basic power hierarchy in the realms of the western glorydoms flows from the Glory down:

Glory
|
Lesser Divines
|
Territory Lords and Warlords
|
District Lords and Village bailiffs

There are still some small areas of the known world ruled by barbarian kings or chieftains, but almost all of these pay tribute to one Glory or another in the form of treasure, slaves, or Fire. The major western glorydoms include Mokad, Koram, Nilliam, Kish, Urz and Cathay.

THE SIX ORDERS OF THE DIVINE
- Fire Wizards
- Kains
- Skir Masters
- Guardians
- Green Ones
- Glories

Infamous Divines include the Goat King, the Witch of Cathay, and Hismayas, the ancient lord of the Sleth.

MAJOR MOKADDIAN CLANS WITH HOLDINGS IN THE NEW LANDS

- Birak
- Burund
- Fir-Noy
- Harkon
- Jarund
- Mithrosh
- Seema
- Shoka
- Vargon

KORAMITES

Hogan
   River
   Ke
   Talen
Sparrow and Purity
   Sugar
   Legs
The Creek Widow/Matiga

MOKADDIANS

Argoth and Serah
   Nettle
The bailiff of Stag Home
Bosser (captain of the Vargon Clan)
The Crab (territory lord with the most holdings of the Fir-Noy clan)
Fabbis (son of a wealthy Fir-Noy lord)
Leaf (the Eye of Rubaloth)
Lumen (the missing Divine of the New Lands)

Rose (sister to Argoth, wife of Hogan the Koramite)
Rubaloth (Skir Master of Mokad)
Shim (warlord of the Shoka clan)

ARMSMEN
Every clan has various martial orders within it. The ranks of the vast majority of these orders are filled with those who are not full-time soldiers, but farmers, laborers, and craftsmen. However, there are orders in some clans of elite and sometimes professional soldiers. The members of such orders are called armsmen.

BONE FACES
Barbarian raiders from the south who have begun striking Mokaddian holdings by sea.

DREADMEN
Those without lore who are endowed by Divines with weaves of might. When such weaves are worn, they multiply the wearer's natural mental and physical abilities. However, the weaves carry a cost: worn too frequently, the body wastes, consuming itself to fuel the magic.

ESCRUM
A weave that binds the wearer to a master, allowing communication over long distances.

FRIGHTS
Not completely of the world of flesh, frights feed on Fire. They most often prey on the sick and dying, attaching themselves like great leeches.

GODSWEED
An herb with properties said to repel some creatures such as frights and the souls of the dead. The smoke from one

thin braid can rid a house of an infestation for many weeks. But its effect does not discriminate between frights, ancestors, or even the servants of the Creators. Hence the saying: Take care to appease those you've chased with smoke.

KING'S COLLAR

A weave wrought by a special order of Divines called Kains. Such collars not only prevent a person from working magic, but also weaken the wearer to make them easy to handle.

THE SIX

Seven creators fashioned the earth and all life therein. However, upon seeing that the finished work was flawed, the seventh, called Regret, wanted to destroy the work and begin again. The remaining Six, whose names are sacred, refused, but they were not able to overcome Regret. And so it is that the powers of both creation and dissolution still struggle on the earth.

SKIR

Orders of beings that inhabit the heavens as well as the deep places of the earth and sea. While invisible to the naked eye, many do exert power in the visible world and can be harnessed by those knowing the secrets. But not all are useful to man. Many orders of smaller skir are deemed insignificant, while other powers are so dreadful none dare summon them.

SLETH

Another term for "soul-eaters." In the Urzarian tongue it literally means "the east wind," which dries and kills life. Applied to those who, in rebellion of the Glories, use an unsactioned form of the lore of the Divines. They are beings and orders of beings supposedly twisted by their polluted draws. Said to have gotten their lore from Regret, one of the seven Creators who, having once seen the creation, realized its flaws and wanted to destroy it.

STONE-WIGHTS
A vanished race whose ruins are found in the New Lands. Some claim plague or war took them. Others find evidence they were destroyed by the Six themselves.

THE THREE VITALITIES
All life is made up of one or more of the three vital powers. There are many names for these life forces. The most common terms in the western glorydoms are Fire (sometimes called Spirit), Body, and soul. There are rumors, among those who know the lore, of lost vitalities: powers that have passed out of human ken.

WEAVES
Objects of power. Some can only be quickened and handled by lore masters. Others, wildweaves, are independent of a master and can be used by those who do not possess any lore. Weaves may be made of almost any material; however, gold is used most often for the wildweaves given to dreadmen.

WOODIKIN
Creatures that live in great families beyond the gap in the wilds of the New Lands. About half the size of a man, they are still ferocious and spilled much blood in the battles fought with the early settlers. Although rare, single woodikin are still sometimes seen in human lands.

ACKNOWLEDGMENTS

For me, writing is about going out to find that which is cool, thrilling, or moving and bringing it back for others to enjoy. The hope of sharing the pleasure I find in the characters, setting, and story is an important part of what keeps me writing, and what kept me going with this project. And so, I want to start by thanking every reader who picks up this book and gives it a go. I hope you are rewarded with an experience full of wonder, suspense, delight, and some poignancy. I'd love to hear from you. Please visit me at JohnDBrown.com.

Next, I must give thanks to my parents: I grew up with a father and grandfather who were florists and pugilists and a mother and grandmother who were literary nuts. The men taught me to prize both the beauty of a Japanese lily arrangement and a blow that could lay a man's nose to the side of his face. My mother, may she rest in peace, made sure our annual family vacations were spent at the Shakespearean Festival in Cedar City, Utah. Despite the many things there that forever dangled above my comprehension, I was caught up in the spectacle, considered myself a bard's man, and enjoyed the ubiquitous tarts (pastries, my friends, not painted women). With such an upbringing, I think it was impossible for some literary production not to bubble forth from my brain, even if there was no guarantee that emanation would ever be anything as grand as, say, a limerick. Luckily, you hold in your hands something that is, if not more grand, at least a bit longer.

For that longer production I am indebted to the wonderful Stacy Hague-Hill and David Hartwell, both for thinking the manuscript was shiny enough to buy and then for putting in the editing work to help me make it better. (Yes, despite the rumors, editors who actually edit have not vanished from the earth.) That same thanks goes to Caitlin Blasdell who saw, edited, and represented (and continues to represent) most excellently. I also appreciate Tor's production department for their attention to detail.

Many helpful souls read early versions of the manuscript. The accurate reporting of their reader experience changed the story. These folks include Christine Mehring, David Walton, Dean Wesley Smith and the May 2006 novel workshop group, Diana Chamberlain, Elaine Isaak, Eric Allen, Gary Eifert, Isaac Stewart, James Maxey, Jared Smith, Mette Ivie Harrison, Miles Pinter, and Trisha Eifert. A monster thank-you goes to Jason Smith, a writing buddy whose friendship helped keep my creative flame alive through a number of difficult years.

The following provided expert input. Chad Floyd gave me an invaluable view into the world of the blind. The ranchers of Rich County, Utah, unknowingly gave me the main seed of this story. Special recognition goes to Robert, LaRue, and Lenn Johnson for letting a city boy play rancher, vet, and manure man, and to Kent Johnson, Stuart Wamsley, and Burdette Weston for fascinating insights.

Two authors have helped me in significant ways. Orson Scott Card conducted a literary boot camp that saved my literary bucket. David Farland started me on the path to writing for publication and offered inspiration, advice, coconut kurma, and encouragement along the way.

I must thank my four girls, Alexandria, Kassandra, Lilia, and Ellianna, for clamoring after bedtime stories (some of which found their way here) and providing abundant, delicious hugs.

Finally, and most importantly, a lion's share of the credit goes to my wife, Nellie, who read every word, listened to every hope and fear, and didn't go mad. She's a rock, and, I am sure, has already earned a plot of ground in that part of heaven reserved for the spouses of those who write.